1983

An Accidental Grace

An Accidental Grace

A novel by

Sister Irene Mahoney, O.S.U.

ST. MARTIN'S PRESS NEW YORK

Design by Laura Hammond

Library of Congress cataloging in Publication Data

Mahoney, Irene.
    An accidental grace.

    I. Title.
PS3563.A366A65   813'.54   82–5648
ISBN: 0–312–00223–8   AACR2

10 9 8 7 6 5 4 3 2

FOR MY MOTHER

I have desired to go
Where springs not fail,
To fields where flies no sharp and sided hail
And a few lilies blow.
And I have asked to be
Where no storms come,
Where the green swell is in the havens dumb,
And out of the swing of the sea.

G. M. Hopkins, "Heaven-Haven"

DIANE GANNON
Born 1956
Entered 1975
On leave of absence
1980–1981

KATHLEEN MARY BOYLAN
Born 1954
Entered 1976

ANGELA FERRATO
Born 1952
Entered 1969

MARGARET (PEG) DARCY
Born 1949
Entered 1971

DARYL PETERS
Born 1945
Entered 1967

JOANNE BERMAN
Born 1941
Entered 1960

ROSALIA DUNNE
Born 1940
Entered 1959

AGNES DEVITT
Born 1938
Entered 1956

ANNE ELIZABETH (NANCY)
LENIHAN
Born 1935
Entered 1957

RUTH ARENDT
Born 1936
Entered 1959
Left 1969
Re-entered 1980

MAGDALEN RICHARDS
Born 1932
Entered 1949

NOREEN MORIARTY
Born 1924
Entered 1943

RITA MCCLELLAN
Born 1923
Entered 1942

TEREZIA SZABO
Born 1919
Entered 1964

EDWARDA RUFF
Born 1911
Entered 1928

SUSANNAH MOLLOY
Born 1906
Entered 1923

ANNA SHAUGHNESSEY
Born 1909
Entered 1928

AIDAN FITZGERALD
Born 1901
Entered 1923

GREGORY O'DONNELL
Born 1910
Entered 1928

RETIRED AND INFIRM SISTERS

TIMOTHY HIGGINS
Born 1902
Entered 1921

MICHAEL NOLAN
Born 1895
Entered 1912

BRIDGET MCGUIRE
Born 1902
Entered 1917

Superiors of the Community of St. Aidan's

1885–1922	MOTHER IMELDA FINNEY
1923–1931	MOTHER KIERAN DOUGHERTY
1932–1938	MOTHER MARY DAVID SWEENEY
1938–1944	MOTHER GERARD REGAN
1944–1950	MOTHER JOSEPHINE RYAN
1950–1956	MOTHER MARY DAVID SWEENEY
1957–1963	MOTHER JOSEPHINE RYAN
1963–1969	MOTHER EDWARDA RUFF
1969–1972	MOTHER JOSEPHINE RYAN
1972–1979	MOTHER MARIAN CONNELL
1979–	MOTHER ROSALIA DUNNE

Novice Mistresses

1890–1904	MOTHER AUSTIN REIDY
1904–1922	MOTHER EAMMON CALLAGHAN
1922–1938	MOTHER BRENDAN WILLIAMS
1938–1950	MOTHER MARY DAVID SWEENEY
1950–1970	MOTHER COLUMBAN O'HARA
1970	SISTER ANNE ELIZABETH LENIHAN

An
Accidental
Grace

Rawlins and Swenson, Realtors
108 East 68th St.
New York, N.Y.
March 15, 1980

Mr. Alec Stafford
Stafford, Connor, Lipsky, Architects
18 Ballantyne Avenue
Glen Cove, New York

Dear Alec,

Julie and I both thank you for a wonderful evening. I think she's grieving that she married a realtor instead of an architect. I can hardly blame her; your house is magnificent. Are you any good at redesigning four-room apartments? That's about as far as I can see these days!

Seriously, I am certainly interested in the project you outlined. I checked through our files and at the moment we have no listing on any property that would be suitable. I will be more than happy to investigate further if you wish.

Let me recap to make sure I understand what you're after: you would like to begin a training center that would teach techniques of preservation and restoration of architecture and decoration especially in the area of Gothic Revival. So what you want is a nineteenth-century Gothic mansion. And since your idea is to run this according to an apprentice program, it would be a bonus if there were sufficient space so that your staff and apprentices could be housed there.

As you know, the Hudson Valley area has some marvelous Gothic homes. May I remind you, too, that taxes there would not run so high as in Westchester or southern Connecticut. Why don't I get in touch with some people I know up there and see if we can turn anything up.

Remember us to Merrilee, please, and thank her for a wonderful dinner. I'll be in touch.

Yours,

Steve Rawlins

1

She had forgotten how cold New York could be in March. Although the nights were still freezing in New Mexico, the days had already slipped into spring. The flowering shrubs around the house had begun to sprout, and the day she had left she had noticed the first tiny shoots on the apricot tree. But although it was almost April, New York was still encased in winter. People passed her in boots and heavy coats, their heads, protected by scarves and hoods, lowered against the cold. In her light coat and open sandals she felt like an alien in the city that had been her home for close to ten years.

She stood for a moment inside the door to catch her breath but also, she knew, to give herself time to deal with the embarrassing fear that she might not recognize Rosalia. It was not until she was getting dressed that morning, pulling a sweater over her head in her hotel room, that it had occurred to her that Rosalia might not be wearing a religious habit. The thought had been disconcerting, for she realized that she had never seen Rosalia in what as novices they had called "real clothes." Rosalia had already been clothed in postulant dress when Ruth first met her—the long, black serge dress covering her legs, her hair pulled back uncompromisingly and held tight beneath the black net of the postulant's cap. Although Ruth herself had entered St. Aidan's only hours later, it had seemed to her that Rosalia must always have looked as she did then, tall and black, scrubbed and unadorned.

What might she expect now? Most nuns, she knew, no longer wore religious garb, certainly not the full encompassing garb they had been used to. What would Rosalia have found to replace that dark, uncompromising witness to their life? But her first survey of the dining room allayed her apprehension. Rosalia was plain for all the world to see—as clearly a nun in her dark blue suit and white blouse as though she were swathed in yards of serge and veiling. She was sitting in a booth near the back entrance, her eyes on the tablecloth, her finger playing with a soup spoon.

Ruth was at her side before she looked up, and Rosalia made an inept motion to get to her feet to greet her.

"Stay there, I'll slip in on the other side." And Ruth eased herself into the seat facing Rosalia. For a moment their hands held across the table.

"Did you have trouble recognizing me?" Rosalia asked.

"Not for a second."

"Well I thought maybe without all the . . ." Rosalia waved her hand awkwardly toward her head.

"It doesn't matter that much. You're still Rosalia. You look wonderful."

"Oh"—she shrugged apologetically—"I think I'm one of the ones who looked better in the habit. You could just put it on and there you were. No decisions about what goes with what. I don't have much style, you know."

For a while they were silent, appraising each other and the changes ten years had made.

"How's St. Aidan's?" Ruth asked as she cut two wedges of bread from the loaf their waitress had brought.

"Coming along. The same—and different. The Community

has gone from eighty-five to less than thirty. I suppose in a way that that's the principal change that's triggered a lot of other things."

"Did that many people leave?" Somehow Ruth had not expected St. Aidan's to be so dramatically touched.

"A lot left. I guess it was the same everywhere. And we've had a good number of deaths among the elderly. The school is smaller too. We've been thinking of giving up the boarding school. There's very little need for a boarding school in that area. It's a hard decision, but we're going to have to face it soon. Joanne Berman is the principal now. She's wonderful. I don't know what I'd do without her."

Joanne: orderly, even-tempered, industrious, born to take charge. Ruth laughed. "Well, that's one of our postulant prophecies come true. What was mine? I don't remember."

"I do. You were going to write the history of St. Aidan's and it was going to be so successful that it would put St. Aidan's on the map and pretty soon we would have the largest and most famous boarding school on the East Coast. Even Mother Josephine would congratulate you."

"That would be a miracle," said Ruth grimly, remembering the years of humiliation she had suffered under Mother Josephine.

"I think she was afraid of you," suggested Rosalia. "That's why she was so hard on you."

"Afraid of me? Whatever for?"

"Well, you were older than the rest of us for one thing and you had been to college and your father was a professor at a university. All of that was an unknown world to Josephine. And then, of course, you used to ask questions."

"Did I? I don't remember opening my mouth."

"Oh, yes, you did and that made poor Josephine nervous. She didn't bother with me at all. I guess she didn't think it was worth her time."

"And now look at you."

"Yes, now look at me," said Rosalia, stabbing her salad

fiercely. "They've elected me superior. Would you ever have thought such a thing could happen?"

"Not in the old days." Ruth laughed. "You're not quite 'in the mold,' as Mother Columban used to say."

"The fact is there's no mold any more. That's how much things have changed. I suspect I'm a kind of token democratic leader. I don't like telling people what to do—and they don't like being told. So we bumble along." She paused and Ruth thought for a moment that she was going to cry. "I don't mean to sound flippant. I do my best. Although God knows it's hard to know what's best these days. I do care very much what happens to St. Aidan's, you know," she finished with the shy, self-conscious smile that Ruth remembered.

"You haven't changed so much." Ruth smiled, feeling for the first time that she was in touch with the old Rosalia. "You still get blotches when you get nervous."

She sighed. "I know. And it's worse now. I used to be able to hide them under all those white starchy things, but they're all in the open now." She stretched her neck upward, feeling the red patches on either side. "I get them on my forehead, too." She grimaced. "Well, here I am, a walking barometer. Anyone can tell how things are going just by looking at me. I would never have made one of those old-time superiors: Hear all, reveal nothing."

Their waitress had taken their plates and poured their coffee. The prologue's over, thought Ruth. This is my cue. She watched while Rosalia put two heaping spoons of sugar in her coffee and stirred it resolutely.

"Did my letter shock you?" Ruth asked The opening sounded blunt and aggressive, but she could find no way to cushion it.

Rosalia hesitated, as though it would be unkind to admit being shocked, but then her native honesty won out. "Yes, it did. I had presumed your life was settled."

"I thought so, too, until after my father's death. It wasn't until I was down in New Mexico, alone, trying to sort things out that I began to wonder. First I thought I was simply indulging in a security dream, that my father's death had left me rootless and that I was trying to re-establish ties with the protective life I had known at St. Aidan's. But after a while I realized it was more than that. That was when I decided to write to you, at least to ask you if it were possible. If you said no, then that would have put an end to it. I had never heard of anyone asking to re-enter the same community they had left—especially after ten years away."

"It's not usual, but some people have. Not many, of course. In your case there's no canonical barrier to your returning to St. Aidan's. It might be different if the circumstances had been different—if you had left because you had been dissatisfied with the life or the Community had been dissatisfied with you. As it was, you left to take care of a sick parent. The pity was that you had to ask for a dispensation from your vows at all, that there was no other way to handle it. I have always—"

Ruth interrupted her. "I know. But that's the way the Rule read. You could obtain a leave to take care of a sick parent, but the Council's decision was that my father wasn't really sick. He could manage physically. It was his loneliness he couldn't sustain, and the Rule had no provision to deal with that. Mother Josephine made the distinction very clear." She paused, remembering her superior's coldly rational interpretation. "My mother's death was so sudden. I don't think Father had ever thought of a life without her. When she died he went to pieces."

"But his loneliness was as real as sickness would have been. It seemed so unfair to force you to make a choice instead of giving you a leave of absence the way we would today."

Ruth shrugged. "I suppose you couldn't really call it unfair. There was simply no provision for it in the Rule."

"All right then: not unfair but certainly narrow and legalistic."

"That I grant you. But Mother Josephine could never have

seen beyond the Rule. She did her duty in the only way she knew. Don't hold it against her, Rosie."

Rosalia sighed. "I know. I suppose I'm working out an old grievance. I hated the way we acted when sisters left. Suddenly someone you had lived with was gone and it was all cloaked in secrecy: the prayer books disappeared from chapel, the cloak disappeared from the hook, the seating arrangement changed in the refectory—and no one said anything. I knew that day when I came out of Vespers that you had left. And then, sure enough, no place was set for you at supper. I knew it had to be something about your father's health, but we were never told."

Something stiff and sharp like a whalebone from the old-fashioned corset her mother had worn pierced Ruth just below the heart.

"I missed you so. It was as though you had died," Rosalia continued. "No, worse than death. Death we would have faced as God's will. It was as though you had done something shameful. I hated you for leaving without telling me, even though I knew it wasn't your fault." The blotches on Rosalia's neck had deepened to scarlet.

Ruth felt as though she had been plunged violently under water—murky water where unknown shapes slid next to her body, nudging her, then slipping away before she could identify them. She had forgotten all those dark memories, and now Rosalia had evoked them for her.

"I'm sorry." Rosalia put out an awkward hand. "That was stupid of me to have brought back all that. It must have been awful for you."

Ruth met Rosalia's hand. "Don't apologize. It was just that I'd forgotten. It all seems so long ago. Anyway, it's nice to know I was missed. I certainly didn't have any evidence of it. I knew none of you could have written personal letters, but the first year I was out I kept hoping that there'd be at least a Christmas card from St. Aidan's, even if it only said 'Season's Greetings.' But there wasn't anything."

Rosalia's lips were pressed grimly together. "That's what I'll never be able to understand. How we could do things like that and think we were living the Gospel. If ever you needed the support of St. Aidan's it must have been during those first months."

"It wasn't all sacrifice," Ruth corrected. "I didn't pine for St. Aidan's forever. I found a life that had many rewards. I loved my work and I loved being with my father."

"And he loved you. I remember how his face would light up when he saw you at the door of the parlor. I thought he had the gentlest face I'd ever seen on a man. My father always looked as though he'd been brought up on roast beef and pork chops."

Rosalia rambled on, recounting her memories of those superficial encounters when the senior novice, dressed in her Sunday habit, her white veil clean and pressed, opened the door to Sunday visitors, showing them into the novices' stiff, crowded parlors.

"I used to love seeing him with your mother. He looked as though he'd do anything for her without thinking twice. Her death must have been a terrible shock."

Ruth nodded, her throat aching. Ellen Farrell, small and quick. Quick in everything—to laugh, to cry, to comfort, to chide. Quick to prod her quiet, reflective husband, who continued to turn issues over in his mind long after his wife had made the decision. She had loved music, not great music but the comfortable music that she could sing or play. She had no inhibitions but banged away at their upright piano until she got the tune to her satisfaction.

Ruth had wondered as she moved through the moody years of adolescence how her mother always seemed so happy. But it was not a trick, not even a discipline. It was her gift, and in her generosity she showered it everywhere. She was not a profoundly religious person, she was not prone to analysis of any sort. Her faith in God was a given; she took it for granted along with the motion of her blood. She knew, of course, that there were people

without faith (she always used the phrase as though it were in
italics), but they were as foreign to her as some tribe of aborig-
ines. They spoke another language, and the only language she
knew was that of Catholicism.

"Mother had always been in perfect health. No one could
have predicted a cerebral hemorrhage. My father seemed to take
it very well at first. Then a few weeks after the funeral he had
a mild heart attack. Even though his recovery was good, he
couldn't get back on his feet. That was when I decided I had to
go home. Once I was back with him he picked up remarkably.
His heart was never strong, but he continued to teach. It was only
two years ago that he retired, and that was a question of university regulation rather than ill-health. He was only really sick the
last three months before his death. He died the week before
Thanksgiving—just five months ago."

"And you were still teaching at the University?"

"Yes, I finished out the term and then took a sabbatical for
the spring semester. I went to New Mexico early in January. I
needed to get away and I thought the climate would be good.
They were very understanding at the University, both about the
sabbatical and in giving me time off before Father's death. He was
very well thought of there, of course. A good friend of his, David
Abramoff, was chairman of the department. He had been like a
son to Father. I don't know how we would have managed
without him."

David. Shall I see David? she wondered. She was ashamed
at the thought of not seeing him, but something pulled her back.
Was she embarrassed about the choice she was making? Afraid
to tell David that she was thinking of returning to St. Aidan's,
lest his clear rationalism erode her dream? But David had no
claim on her. He would be the first to assure her that her life was
her own. Why, then, Ruth thought, do I feel so awkward? Surely
after seven years of friendship, strengthened by the weeks of her
father's illness, the most normal thing in the world would be to
share her plans with David.

"I would like to ask a young man in my department to come over some evening, perhaps for coffee," her father had suggested the first year she was teaching at the University.

"Why not for dinner?"

"It's not too much trouble?" His eyes were mild and apologetic. He had the look of an under-clerk in an old-fashioned department store. His ploys were transparent.

She had laughed. "You *know* it's not too much trouble."

"And Ruth"—his courage brightening—"you will have a very nice dinner? I'm afraid David doesn't eat well."

She had cooked with a vision of a young graduate assistant, recently emigrated from Russia, shy, inarticulate, undernourished. But David Abramoff was none of those. He had filled their living room. His skin was tanned and ruddy, his eyes hazel, his hair a thatch of red. Nothing seemed quite large enough for him. The sleeves of his shirt came above his wrists; his jacket was tight across the back. Her father looked frail and old as they sat, David's legs stretched awkwardly in front of him. But unlike most big people he was marvelously unself-conscious. Nor was he shy. His silences were periods of listening and thinking, not of withdrawal. He made no apology for his accent but spoke slowly, carefully, giving the sounds their full value.

Was there anything, she had wondered as she listened to the conversation, that he had not read?

"This William Faulkner"—he had turned to her—"how about this fellow?" And as she hesitated, he added apologetically, "I have not had yet time to read this in English. I have read only in German."

The thought of following Faulkner's convoluted sentences in labored German prose left her agog. Yet there was no arrogance in his manner, only a single-minded pursuit of his interests.

For the next seven years David Abramoff had been a sustaining force in her father's life and in her own. He had his friends, but he had little patience for the merely social. Even when he had become successful both as a teacher and an authority on Russian social history his life did not change. He continued living in his small two-room apartment, eating most of his meals out, jealous of any time taken away from his Russian studies.

When Joseph Arendt retired and David replaced him as chairman of the history department, her father was radiant. "He is the son of my mind," he had said with the pride and affection of a father.

Yet close as she and David had become, she was reluctant to see him now. She had written occasionally from New Mexico, casual letters describing the drift of her days, her reading, the landscape, and asking him about the University; and he had answered in the same vein. In all the time they had known each other they had always maintained a level of emotional reserve. Their most enthusiastic conversations were often about their intellectual interests. They had been like musicians tuning their instruments to each other's, exhilarated by the harmony of their minds.

David also loved the ocean. He had joined a club on City Island where they could sail on weekends and Ruth discovered to her surprise that he was a remarkably competent sailor. One Sunday evening when Ruth had come home tanned and happy after a day on the water, she noticed her father smiling at her quizzically.

"You had a happy day?"

"Wonderful. The wind was just right. I think David would have headed straight for Block Island if I hadn't urged a little caution."

Her father nodded, saying nothing, his lips puckered as though in doubt.

"I never thought I'd feel at home on a sailboat, but somehow David is so sure of himself that it rubs off on me."

She had bent over to get something out of the fridge when her father spoke again.

"Ruth."

She straightened and turned toward him. "Ruth . . . you and David . . . you are . . ."

For a second his meaning escaped her, but when she caught it her answer was quick and unequivocal.

"In love?" She shook her head. "No, we're not in love. It's perfect just the way it is."

But having started the conversation, he would not be stopped. "Please, not so quick. Perhaps you have not let yourself think in this way because of me. I am already responsible for one great change in your life. I certainly would not want to keep you from happiness again."

She shook her head impatiently, confused by this alien train of thought. "It's not a question of keeping me from happiness. You should know that."

He waved his hand to stop her. "Yes. Well, I know you are not unhappy here, but you are still young. And sometimes when you come home with David it is clear you are very happy together."

"I am. Of course I am. But that doesn't mean I want to marry him. Good heavens, Father, you're turning into an old matchmaker."

"No, please, not a matchmaker; but I had to make sure that you were not sacrificing yourself again for me. That I could not bear. Sometimes at the University, people ask me . . ."

"It's none of their business." Her voice was curt.

"Of course. They know that. It's only, well, you are still young and attractive."

The conversation stirred something in her she hardly knew existed. She put down the salad bowl and faced her father. "Father, listen to me. If I do not get married, it is not that I am sacrificing myself for you. Something happened to me at St. Aidan's. For ten years I lived a vow of chastity. I thought I would live it for the rest of my life. For ten years I lived vowed to Jesus Christ. 'I will admit no lover but him,' we sang on our vow day.

I know that for some people, once the obligation is removed, their lives, psychologically, take another turn. I think for me that will never be so. It seems to me that, at first, religious consecration is largely a matter of the will. Then, little by little, the consecration reaches the heart. For me, it reached the marrow of my bones. I think I will always have a virgin's consecration to God. It's more than a matter of choice. It's the way the tree has been bent."

She could say no more; and her father, too, sat silent and motionless, his chin cupped in his hand.

That night she could not sleep. She lay awed at her own words. What she had said surprised her. Yet she could feel the truth of it. St. Aidan's had changed the direction of her life. Chastity had shaped her beyond anything she had understood or intended. It was not that she wanted to be a nun in the world —one of those caricatures of religion that one occasionally saw in church clutching their rosaries, lighting their candles. Such an image repulsed her. It was not the rituals and discipline of religious life that she clung to but something far more profound.

Perhaps this was why she had never told David about the years at St. Aidan's, knowing that they had shaped her in a way she could not explain. Sometimes she wondered if this was responsible for a certain constraint between them; but then she had defended herself with the thought that he would not be able to understand that period in her life. He was, after all, not a believer. She had explained once briefly that she had spent some time teaching in a Catholic school in upstate New York. At the time there seemed no need for further explanations. Yet now that she was thinking of returning to St. Aidan's she felt awkward in never having told David about those ten years spent at the convent.

She had drifted into daydreams, and when she came to, Rosalia was looking at her inquiringly. "Well, wasn't it awfully hard at the beginning?" she pursued. "After you left I used to think about what you would be doing, how you would be dressed, how you would look without a veil, whether you would still make your meditation and go to Mass every day. Sometimes I'd try to imagine how I'd feel, if I'd have the courage to leave. St. Aidan's was a security. We were together and everything was always planned for us. I know it wasn't a healthy way for adult women to live, but it had its comforts."

Ruth nodded. Yes, St. Aidan's had been a security. The unchanging order, the established pattern of prayer and work, the silence that protected their privacy and, above all, the implicit understanding that in everything God was their goal—these had formed and channeled her; and in her first months out she could not free herself from them. Ten years of discipline had shaped her and she brought the air of the cloister into their small apartment. Her body roused her like a rising bell and she obeyed it: praying in her room, making coffee for her father, slipping off to the early Mass in the parish church, sparsely attended by a few ancient ladies in black hats or bandannas. When she got home her father would be sitting in the breakfast alcove drinking his coffee and reading the paper. His smile was tentative, waiting upon hers. And sometimes in the first months she smiled without saying anything, so inured was she to the sacred quality of morning silence at St. Aidan's.

One morning, in the third month of her return, she had gone to put her prayer book back in her room. When she came out to the kitchen, her father was bent over the sink washing his dishes. She reached for the towel and turned toward him to take the cup from his hands, but he turned away from her, groping for his glasses, which lay on the draining board. She thought at first that he was sick, but when she reached out to help him, he pushed her away.

"Go back," he whispered, his shoulders shaking. "Go back to St. Aidan's. You are still a nun here."

He raised his hands to brush his tears away, and the cup he was holding crashed to the floor. His accusation shattered all her secure rituals. The darkness of her selfishness dropped away and she saw what she had been doing. She had petitioned to leave St. Aidan's, but in fact she had not done so. She had brought St. Aidan's with her, brought it with its patterns and rituals into her father's life. She had not given him back the daughter he needed; she had given him only a nun, one of the sisterhood who would continue to lead her inviolable religious life while ministering in some distant way to her father's need.

For a moment the truth paralyzed her, and they stood before each other defenseless and fearful of what the next revelation might bring. She would never know who made the first tentative movement, but suddenly they were in each other's arms. She was surprised at how slight and frail he felt as her arms reached around his shoulders. His beard was stubbly against her face, as it had been when she was a child. Finally he released her and put his glasses on. She picked up the broken cup, putting her finger to her lips as they used to do when they had broken something and wanted to hide it from her mother. They were laughing when they sat down to a second breakfast. It was noon by the time they finished.

That afternoon she filed her application for graduate study in the department of English at her father's university, and two months later she began work for her doctorate. Her master's had been done in bits and pieces in the customary way of St. Aidan's. Now for the first time she had the exhilaration of sustained study. When she suggested to her father that she find a part-time job to help defray her expenses, he shook his head. "Later," he said. "Later. For now, study. These are golden years."

And they were that. In addition to her courses were the hours of conversation with her father and his friends, with whom she was often more at home than with her fellow students. She was, after all, ten years older than most of them, with a discipline and purposefulness that they had not yet approached. It was her father who encouraged her to do her major work in fourteenth-century literature, even though she pointed out that a later period might be more "practical" in terms of teaching. Again he negated her pragmatism: "Go where your mind is at ease," he counseled, and she had never regretted it. She had graduated with honors, and despite her fear that some might cry "nepotism," she accepted a post in his university when it was offered.

She was surprised at the enjoyment she found in her teaching. Teaching at St. Aidan's had been demanding rather than satisfying. At the time she had made no judgment on it: It was the work of the Congregation and so was included in that unquestioning pattern of God's will for her. That there was never time or encouragement to pursue a subject deeply or even to read beyond the confines of classroom preparation she had learned to accept as her asceticism. Now, however, teaching opened up her own mind. She was fortunate, as her colleagues frequently reminded her, in teaching a subject that did not draw dilettantes. Her classes were small but earnest; and although some of her students slipped away with no more contact than their registration card and their term paper, others became friends—with that unique friendship that the young sometimes form with an understanding mentor.

"It won't last. You'll burn out like the rest of us," a cynical colleague had replied to Ruth's enthusiasm. Perhaps she would have in time, but her time had been cut short; and during those seven years of teaching she had been, she knew, at her best in every way. Those years had deepened her. Her study of the English mystics had affected her own spirituality. They satisfied not only her mind but also her need for prayer. In the process, St. Aidan's was left far behind. She had found her place in the world, she thought.

"I had never thought of returning, you know," she said at last to Rosalia, compelled to correct the image. "I thought I had put St. Aidan's behind me for good. When my father died I expected to continue life as before. I never anticipated any dramatic changes. It wasn't until I was out in New Mexico that I

began to think of other possibilities. I think it must have been
the land that did it. I had never seen expanses of land like that."

"New Mexico?" Professor Allan had expostulated when she
had discussed her sabbatical with him. "You'll hate it. There isn't
anything there. Do you have relatives out there?"

No. She had no relatives, no friends, nothing. Just the
irrational need to move out of her universe, to find something
simple and open and flat.

"What will you do for books?" he had asked. "I can't
imagine you without a library."

She couldn't either, yet that was precisely her need: to cut
herself off from the world she and her father had shared so
closely, so securely. She had never thought of being bound to
him; but now in her grief at his leaving her, she felt a willful need
to leave him, to find a world the antithesis of the one they had
built together.

"Have you ever been to the Southwest?" she asked Rosalia.
"Something happens to your vision. There's nothing blocking
you from the horizon. It's a kind of city dweller's euphoria, I
guess. Everything seems possible. All the neat little boxes are
gone and you start dreaming beyond categories."

"And you dreamed of St. Aidan's?"

"Oh, I had a lot of dreams—St. Aidan's wasn't the wildest.
Suddenly I was free to say, 'What if . . . ?' At first it seemed crazy
to think of going back, but the thought kept returning, and each
time I found myself settling in with it more comfortably. After
all, I had left to take care of my father, so it seemed logical to
think of returning once he was gone.

"One evening I was sitting on the steps watching the afterglow. It was the first evening it had been warm enough to stay
outdoors after the sun had gone down. And I realized I was
singing the hymn at the end of Compline. For a moment I could
hear Daryl singing next to me, her voice soaring the way it used
to, and Noreen behind me, plodding through the notes as though

she was drying dishes—pick one up, put it down. That was the night I wrote to you. The next morning when I read the letter over, I almost tore it up. It sounded like moon-madness. 'Middle-aged woman bereaved at the loss of her parent makes decision to enter convent as she contemplates the desert sunset.' "

Rosalia shook her head impatiently. "But you're not a romantic, Ruth."

"No, I never have been. I've always been able to give a reasonable account of myself. But this time . . ." Her voice trailed off. "I can hardly explain what's motivating me, but the pull is very strong. That's why I had to talk with you, to see how you would react."

Rosalia said nothing. She was tracing a design on the table-cloth with the prongs of her fork.

"Rosalia, don't be afraid to tell me it won't work. Don't think I haven't faced that possibility. After all, that's why we're meeting, isn't it, to get some practical sense of all this?"

Rosalia scowled. "I've already said that there is no canonical reason why you can't return. And as far as the Community goes, I can guarantee that the votes will be all in your favor. You left a lot of friends behind you, Ruth."

"But you're hesitant just the same, aren't you?"

For the first time Rosalia looked up. "I'm not sure what we have to offer you."

"You have St. Aidan's to offer me."

"St. Aidan's has changed."

"Of course, I know that. Nothing is the same as it was ten years ago."

But Rosalia was not satisfied. "I don't know if you can imagine how much it's changed. It isn't simply that the school is no longer so important or that the Community is smaller and older. It's something more than size or age or work. The quality of life is different."

"But the essentials are the same. They must be."

Rosalia nodded. "I suppose they are, but they're lived out in very different ways." She sighed. "It's just that I don't want you to be disappointed."

"I think I could go along with a few changes. I was never wedded to Mother Josephine's vision of religious life."

"None of us were. It's hard to believe we buckled under to all that military discipline." She paused. "It's not that I was thinking of. It's just, well, just that it's *different.*" She shook her head in frustration at her inability to make things clear. "I'm no good at explaining. I just felt that you should know. It has nothing to do with you. I mean it's not that we don't want you at St. Aidan's. I just wouldn't want you to be unhappy."

"I'm grateful for that, Rosie. And I understand why you can't explain. I don't think that if you asked me why I wanted to return to St. Aidan's I could give you a very lucid explanation either. It's just something that keeps teasing inside of me. Not loneliness, not a need for security, not even a vision of the good I might accomplish. Just a sense that my place is at St. Aidan's. That hardly explains religious vocation, does it?"

"Can you?"

"I suppose not, although I did my best in that letter of petition we had to write when we were postulants. I'd like to see it now. I probably sound like a pretentious little ass."

"I'll get it out of the archives for you someday."

"Spare me!" Ruth shuddered. "Rosie, do you remember our clothing ceremony?"

"How can you ask! My sister Kate had lent me her wedding dress, and I'd gained so much weight from all those potatoes we ate that I couldn't button it. I thought Mother Columban wouldn't let me walk up the aisle until I'd lost ten pounds. All that's gone now," Rosalia reflected, "the bridal dresses and the white veils. Now that there's no religious habit, there's not much point in a 'clothing' ceremony."

"It probably should have gone sooner. It was a romantic relic even in our day."

"I liked it." Rosalia smiled self-consciously. "It made me feel like a nun."

Ruth laughed. "I could do without the dramatics, but there was something in the ceremony that I loved. Do you remember old Bishop Farragut, all bushy in his red robes—Sister Susannah always wanted to whisk them away and press them before he came into the sanctuary—wheezing away and asking in that truck driver's voice, 'My daughters, what do you ask?' And we answered, 'The mercy of God and the grace to be received into the Community of St. Aidan's.' "

Rosalia nodded, remembering those portentous moments when, fearful and exhilarated, they had publicly acknowledged their desire to be consecrated to the Lord.

"I loved those words. I used them to steady myself when Mother Josephine and her martial law got too much for me."

For the first time since Ruth had begun to discuss the possibility of her return to St. Aidan's, Rosalia met her eyes and smiled.

"Please forgive me for being such a worrier. Of course it will be all right if it's what you want. I'm with you all the way."

She has changed, Ruth thought, moved by Rosalia's simple act of confidence. She's still awkward and shy and her suit looks secondhand, just the way her habit used to, but the root of integrity has flowered. She may not be self-confident, but she has confidence in others, and she's not afraid to risk.

"It just occurred to me," Rosalia said, "you might like to come up to St. Aidan's for a few days before you go back to New Mexico."

But Ruth shook her head. "I thought about it, but somehow I wouldn't feel comfortable."

"You know it would make them very happy to see you, no matter what decision you make about returning."

"Thank you, but I don't think I'm quite ready for that. I need some more time in my desert. Until I talked to you, it was

all a fantasy world. Now that I know it's a possibility, I have to
deal with a little more reality."

"Ruth"—the worried tone was back in Rosalia's voice—
"you'll give yourself time, won't you? You won't push . . . or
feel constrained. After all, talking to me hasn't committed you
to anything."

"I know that." She covered Rosalia's hand with her own.
"I think I can assure you that whenever I make my decision it
will be made in freedom. No guilt. I don't feel any recrimination
for having left St. Aidan's. If I come back it won't be because
I'm trying to make up for lost years. I wouldn't want anyone to
think that."

Yet even as she said it, she knew that some would and that
nothing she said could stop them. It was part of their triumphal
theology that assured them that they had chosen the better part.

"I suppose you don't have any idea when . . . I mean, how
long . . ." Rosalia stumbled, realizing that, despite her caution
for Ruth to take her time, she was now pushing her toward a
timetable.

"Not long, I imagine. I'd like to get my life in order by
midsummer. In any case, I have a leave of absence from the
University for next year. I knew that no matter how things went
I'd need more time away."

"And what about your house?"

"Father and I had an apartment. He and mother had sold
the house on Long Island the year before she died. The commut-
ing was getting more difficult and they found the house too much
to keep up. I was very lucky. I was able to sublet the apartment
to a couple on the faculty who were dying to move into Manhat-
tan."

Rosalia frowned. "But where are you staying now while
you're in New York?"

"At the Berwick."

"Isn't that expensive?" Rosalia sounded shocked.

"I suppose it is, but I felt the need of a little luxury."

"But surely you have friends who would be glad to have you stay—"

But Ruth cut her off. "I needed to be alone. The greatest luxury, I've learned, is privacy."

"Well, you know you're welcome at St. Aidan's."

"I do know and I thank you, but I'm flying back tomorrow."

"Ruth, there's one more thing. I hope you won't think me presumptuous, but I did go to the Bishop to discuss this. I wasn't sure what the regulations were; and in any case he would have to be consulted. He wanted you to know that although there must be some period of novitiate, the length of time is determined by the Community. I didn't want you to think that you would have to go through a two-year probation again."

Ruth smiled gratefully. "I'm glad you're the lady I have to deal with in all this, Rosalia."

Rosalia sighed. "I'm not always glad. Sometimes I wonder why anyone ever voted for me." She was staring hard at her hands, which covered the saltshaker like a tent, and when she raised her eyes to meet Ruth's they were full of tears. "Today I was very glad. Seeing you and knowing you might come back to us has been like an Easter for me."

There were only two other couples still in the restaurant as they walked toward the door. Rosalia looked at her watch in amazement.

"Do you have a train to catch?" Ruth asked.

"No, I'm driving, but I can't believe it's three-thirty."

They stood for a moment on the sidewalk, Rosalia's large hand enclosed between Ruth's two small ones; and then Ruth watched while Rosalia in her warm navy coat and sensible brown oxfords walked north against the traffic.

Rawlins and Swenson, Realtors
108 East 68th St.
New York, N.Y.
March 25, 1980

Mr. Alec Stafford
Stafford, Connor, Lipsky, Architects
18 Ballantyne Avenue
Glen Cove, New York

Dear Alec,

Just a further piece of information for your file. Yesterday, quite by accident, I bumped into a friend of mine who moved up to the Hudson Valley area a couple of years ago and has been doing very well in real estate up there. I mentioned your project to him and he seemed quite optimistic.

He said to tell you that he thinks it would be worth going after some of the boarding schools in that area. Many of them began on a small scale but then enlarged on the original Gothic mansion. At the moment many of them are going out of business, especially those under the auspices of the Catholic sisters. They, apparently, are running into snags of all kinds. Lee suggests that you might be able to grab something dirt cheap.

He'll be in touch with me as soon as he can track down some more specific leads.

Yours,

Steve Rawlins

2

The restaurant had been hot and stuffy, and the air that had seemed so chill before now felt refreshing. She started to walk east toward her hotel but the traffic light was against her. As she waited for it to change, a sudden impulse to walk past their old apartment made her turn and walk in the opposite direction. It was insane, she supposed, to go so far out of her way simply to walk past an apartment building. Even more insane to risk the chance of meeting someone she knew when she had been so careful to keep her trip a secret. And yet she continued to walk west and then north until she was immersed in the familiar markets and local stores of Broadway. Surrounded for so long by the unfamiliar, she found a delight in walking almost mindlessly along the street she knew so well. Children on roller skates jostled against her; middle-aged women, bent over displays of fruit, tested it with experienced fingers while the vendors looked on disapprovingly.

She turned left on 78th Street—and she was home, looking up at the small apartment building standing solid and unchanged. It was not exclusive enough for a doorman, but it had a small pleasant lobby and she stopped to look in, noticing that the same two snake plants still guarded the corner by the elevator.

Back on the street she hesitated, wondering if she should take a bus or if she could brave the chilly walk back downtown. She was caught in that moment of indecision, because crossing the street directly in front of her was Hilda Reinauer, tugging her shopping cart behind her.

Ruth wavered between happiness and chagrin. The Reinauers were dear friends; it was to them that she had been able to sublet her apartment. At any other time, a meeting with Hilda would be a delight. But how was she to explain this unexpected trip East, how especially was she to explain the fact that she had never let them know she was coming? They had been adamant in demanding that any time she came East she was to consider her old apartment her home still.

"Just remember," Hilda had repeated, "your old room is yours whenever you're in town. Peter is rarely home except for a month or so in the summer. And when he is here, he's not here, if you know what I mean." She sighed over the vagaries of the young and undisciplined.

Ruth had promised, although she knew she could never be comfortable in her old apartment once the Reinauers had moved in. Now for a moment she thought Hilda might pass her unnoticed as she struggled to pull her cart up the curb. Knowing she could not ignore so close an encounter, Ruth reached out and helped to yank the cart up the final inch.

"Well, thank you." Hilda gave a friendly nod and then caught her breath. "Ruth," she said. "Ruth Arendt!" And the cart slid backward as Hilda loosened her grasp in surprise. They both lunged to get it before it slipped out into the traffic.

"Isn't this wonderful! But I feel terrible. I suppose you were over at the apartment and couldn't get in. I must have missed your call, too. Isn't that dreadful? I'm really embarrassed."

Hilda's assumptions covered Ruth's awkwardness. "And the thing is," she continued as they walked back toward the apartment, "Harold and I are both leaving this evening for a weekend convention. I just managed to get the laundry done in time." She nodded toward the bags in the grocery cart.

"Here, hold on to the cart," she commanded as she fumbled in her bag for the keys. "Two locks, two keys. It's crazy, but there've been so many burglaries you can't afford to take a chance."

She turned the second of the locks and pushed the door open. "Here, just put the cart over here. Most of the stuff goes in the hall closet."

As Ruth turned to face the living room, she found nothing familiar in her surroundings beyond the position of doors and windows. Even the shape of the room seemed somehow changed by the dissimilar grouping of furniture. For a moment a sense of unreality overwhelmed her. Was this where she had lived? Was this the room her father had filled with people to congratulate her when she was awarded her degree? And was that the narrow hall that led to the master bedroom where her father had died? The dark polished wood was covered now by a green carpet and the walls were hung with Peter Reinauer's brilliant abstract designs.

"Don't let Peter's painting blind you." Hilda laughed. "Believe it or not, he's become quite a popular artist. I still can't take him seriously. I guess parents aren't very good at recognizing genius in the family."

Ruth stood mesmerized by a print composed of narrow green and red lines with an occasional wider stripe of bright yellow. At the bottom left was splashed in black, "Peter Reinauer, 3880 strokes." Did he count them as he went along, she wondered, or go back over the finished painting with a magnifying glass? Somehow it seemed like a futile exercise.

"Ruth, do make some tea for yourself," Hilda called from the front hall. "I simply have to get this laundry put away. You know where everything is."

She turned toward the kitchen, feeling awkward in the

midst of Hilda's bustle. The kitchen she had known had been swept away and in its place was a glory of glass and chrome, with hanging plants, green and glossy, endowing everything with the promise of spring.

"Your plants are wonderful," she said as Hilda entered with an armful of towels.

"Not mine, Harold's. He's a marvel. He's even taken courses. The light is just right, he tells me. I don't remember what you had in here."

"One mangy African violet and a spiky downtrodden begonia. Plants are not among my triumphs."

"I should think you'd be good with them. You have so much patience," Hilda observed, banging the cabinet door shut. "I'm the ultimate failure. I even killed a snake plant. Harold tells me they're indestructible, so I suppose I could consider it a kind of negative victory."

Ruth made no movement to make tea and Hilda was too preoccupied to notice.

"How's New Mexico?" she called from the bedroom, clearly expecting very little by way of answer. "Peter spent a couple of months out there," she continued, appearing momentarily at the doorway with more laundry in her hands. "He wanted to study the light, he said. I think he liked it all right. You know artists."

It needed no reply and Hilda waited for none as she went on to her next task.

Ruth stood leaning against the wall of the breakfast alcove. She had expected to feel dread or a great sadness at being "home." Instead she felt nothing but a vague sense of constriction. Although her eyes tried to reconstruct the apartment as she had known it, her mind balked, refusing to go beyond the present. Whatever life she had lived here had receded and she found herself, like an ocean castaway, out of sight of everything familiar.

"At last that's done." Hilda reappeared again. "Come, let's

sit down inside," and Ruth followed her into the living room.
"I hope you can forgive me," Hilda said, stacking some magazines in their rack. "It's just been a wild week. Student advise-
ment, plans for graduation, and a thousand committee meetings.
Wouldn't you think they'd let two old linguists beg off? Harold
and I both keep saying that we joined the University faculty to
teach, but that seems to be the least important of one's obligations
these days. It's crazy. I told Dean Cowie that pretty soon we
won't need a faculty. We'll just have administration and student
services—and maybe a few dozen token students. Like the good
Victorian he is, he was not amused."

"Cowie is in then for another year?" Ruth asked, remembering her father's tight mouth when Bernard Cowie had been
appointed dean of the undergraduate college. "He's not strong
enough," he had warned. "He'll do whatever he thinks is expedi-
ent." Apparently her father had been right.

"He's in for another two years," Hilda affirmed. "It's a
continuing disaster. He's a total marshmallow. He gets pushed
from all sides. Harold says his greatest contribution has been the
expansion of jargon."

Ruth had almost forgotten this side of the profession—the
in-fighting, the jealousies, the academic bickering. Her father had
been wise, she thought, to insist on retiring when he had. He
wanted to be only a teacher and a scholar, to foster excellence
by his influence and example. He could never have adjusted to
a university world that placed political expertise and glib popu-
larity above what he considered its true mission: the sacred seeking of truth. For years she had taken his integrity for granted;
it was only at the end that she began to understand what the
insatiable craving for truth had cost him.

"That must be Harold. He always turns the key backward."
Hilda got up to open the door as they heard a key fumble in the
lock.

"Good God, three hours!" Ruth heard Harold's crisp voice
with its slight Austrian accent. "Three hours to listen to some

idiotic appeal over non-renewal of contract. I should think he
would be too embarrassed with his wretched record to lay it out
in public."

Then in the background came a darker voice, making an
unintelligible comment, followed by a laugh.

"David! What perfect timing! You'll never guess who's
here," Hilda called.

He stood in the doorway, his hazel eyes crinkled against the
light from the windows, while Ruth struggled to rise from the
large soft pillows of the couch. She stood awkwardly, as though
caught in some illicit action. It was Harold's decisive movements
that saved her from further embarrassment. At once he was at
Ruth's side, taking her hand and kissing her warmly.

"But this is wonderful! Is this not wonderful, David?"

David nodded as he bent to kiss her, his eyes anxious and
a little hurt.

Harold, misinterpreting his silence, teased, "Ah, but this
fellow is very sly; I think he knew it all along." And when Ruth
tried to shake her head in denial, he would hear none of it. "No,
no explanations! Instead let us celebrate the unexpected. What
will you have to drink?"

Hilda looked nervously at her watch as Harold started to
remove glasses from the cabinet. "I don't want to be a killjoy,
but you know we have an eight o'clock flight."

"But it is still early." Harold was not going to be denied.
He was on his knees pulling out bottles from the lower shelf of
the cabinet. "David, I know you like brandy." He rose with an
ornate bottle in his hands. "This I can vouch for. We brought
it back from Austria last year. And you, Ruth?"

"The same, please." Ruth smiled at Hilda, caught between
hospitality and nervous concern for their departure.

"Please, sit down." Harold was clearly enjoying the reunion
of friends. "Hilda, please, sit down. Why are you fidgeting?"

"I just want to be sure we're ready when the limousine
comes."

"So, you have packed already. What else is there to do?"
"I haven't packed your notes. I don't know what you want.
I think you better look and see."

Harold shrugged. "You will excuse us a moment." And he
and Hilda went toward the master bedroom.

David's chair was too low for him and he sat awkwardly,
his knees akimbo, his hands curved around the brandy snifter.
Ruth knew he would ask no questions, and yet the need to make
some explanation was heavy on her.

"You look well. New Mexico agrees with you."

She nodded, suddenly seeing beneath the present setting the
apartment as it used to be. Where David sat was where her
father's old-fashioned morris chair used to be. There had been a
desk—a fine polished walnut—in the corner next to the window.
And in place of the couch had been two heavy armchairs, where
she and David generally sat. The narrow hall where Hilda and
Harold had gone led to her father's room. For six weeks down
that passageway, often on tiptoe so that the sound of her shoes
would not be heard on the uncarpeted floor, she had carried trays
to her father. At first she had brought him ordinary meals, but
week by week the tray had grown lighter, until toward the end
it contained only the medication he took with increasing difficulty. Down that hall too David had at first helped her father
along so that he could lie comfortably in the living room for a
few hours a day. Until one afternoon when it was time for him
to return to his room, he was too weak to stand and David had
carried him back in his arms. It was the last time he had left his
room.

The constriction that had kept these memories away was
gone and she could see them now, she and David as they had sat
the night of her father's death. The day had been surprisingly
warm for November and during the afternoon she had opened
the window on the far side of the room. David had brought her
father's morris chair into the bedroom so that she could rest her
back, and she had sat there most of the day. There had been no

movement from the bed since noon, when her father had opened his eyes and turned his head restlessly. She had put a spoonful of water to his lips and he had swallowed it without speaking. The dark came quickly and with it a little breeze that ruffled the curtains. She rose and tiptoed over to close the window. When she returned and bent over her father, she realized he was no longer breathing. She took his hand but there was no pulse beat. She continued to stand holding his hand, her sense of loss buried beneath an inexpressible weariness.

She did not remember sitting down, but when David came at seven o'clock she was sitting in the morris chair, leaning forward with one hand on the coverlet, her fingers just a breath from her father's hand.

It was David who had taken care of the funeral arrangements, David who had taken her out to supper against her will, who had offered to stay in the apartment with her during the night. But before that last suggestion she was adamant. She needed to be alone, she argued, and David had honored her decision. She supposed she slept, strange sleep, torn by emotions she would have found unacceptable in daylight. Looking back, her life seemed bitterly wasted. She had left St. Aidan's to be with her father and yet in those last weeks when he needed her most she had not been with him. She had tried to reach him but he had withdrawn from her. It was not only his weakness that separated them. It had been something far more terrifying.

The simple comforts his faith had always given him deserted him. At first Ruth had thought it was his weakness that made him restless as she tried to pray with him. But it was a far deeper struggle. She had put her mother's small silver crucifix where he could see it, but a few days later she had found it pushed out of his sight, as though even that stylized replica of a suffering god was intolerable. Helpless, she waited beside him, unable to assist him in his mysterious rite of passage.

Sometimes she felt that her presence only increased the

agonizing sense of guilt in which he lived his last days, as though he had seduced her into betraying her divine vocation.

The nightmare that she had thought she had laid to rest in the quiet months in New Mexico began to take shape again, and she moved her head abruptly in a vain effort to disconnect her imagination.

She looked up, aware that she had made no reply to David's comment, but she was saved by Hilda Reinauer's noisy entrance. She was lugging a suitcase and a garment bag with obvious annoyance. David rose to help her as she turned in exasperation.

"Harold can't find his notes. He thinks he left them in his office."

David looked at his watch. "He'd still have time to hop a cab and go down there. You could pick him up at the University."

Hilda sighed again. "I suppose so. It's just so maddening. And so embarrassing to be rushing around like this. Ruth dear, I hope you won't hold this against us. You know you're welcome to stay here. Everything's a mess but if you don't mind . . ." Her voice trailed off.

"Really, don't worry. I'm going back to New Mexico tomorrow and I'm already checked into a hotel for tonight. After all, you didn't know I was coming."

"That's true." Hilda was too preoccupied to ask any questions. "And you haven't even had any dinner. They'll feed us on the plane—if we ever make it."

"I found them!" Harold's voice was jubilant. "They were in my other briefcase. I forgot I had already packed them."

Hilda raised her eyes. "Why do I get excited? I've lived through this a dozen times."

Harold, unruffled, came into the living room with a briefcase and small suitcase. "I told you not to worry." He smiled, looking through the pockets of his coat.

"*I* have the tickets." Hilda's exasperation was clear.

"Good. I thought you would." Harold once again smiled benignly at them all.

"We really have to go. I'll just put the glasses in the dishwasher. We'll be home Sunday night."

When the Reinauers were at last safely packed off in their limousine, David and Ruth stood under the canopy of the apartment building. It had been raining lightly and the street was wet and empty.

"I'm staying at the Berwick." She could think of no other way to break the silence.

"Would you like to go there now or may we have dinner?" In his effort not to intrude he sounded curt.

"If you like." She groped for her own tone but missed it and slipped instead into his.

"What kind of food do you feel like eating?"

"It doesn't matter. I'm not very hungry. I had a big lunch." With Rosalia, she thought. Rosalia and the world of St. Aidan's. How was she to explain that to David?

"Will Greek do? There's a little family place a couple of blocks up. You probably remember it. It's never crowded and they don't rush you."

"Fine. Let's walk, David," she suggested as he started to hail a cab. "I think the rain's over. Anyway I rather enjoy it. We don't get much rain in New Mexico."

"I suppose not."

"I can't get over how much colder New York is. We were having real spring down there."

"I'm afraid we won't have that for another month or so. March has been unusually treacherous. They even predicted some snow for this week."

The strained weather report ran out at last and they walked the last block in silence.

The restaurant was empty and the patron expansively offered them their choice of tables.

"So. You have come back," David said after they had ordered.

"Just for a few days. I'm going back tomorrow morning."

"Yes. I heard you explain to Hilda."

"It's such a short visit, I didn't bother telling anyone I was coming up."

David nodded, sipping his wine attentively. Suddenly he raised his head and looked directly at her, but she could not meet his eyes. She wished she had refused his invitation to dinner and had gone straight back to the Berwick. Ultimately, of course, she would tell him about St. Aidan's, but the effort at explanation made her feel weak and defensive. Even to those who shared her faith she knew religious vocation could be a stumbling block. She could hardly expect David to understand.

As the waiter came to serve their salad, David pushed his chair closer to the table and his foot kicked against hers.

"Sorry. These tables were made for midgets."

"Not midgets, David; just people of average stature. Remember what Father used to say to you: 'David, never try to be a spy. The tall man is always captured.'"

"Especially if on top of the pillar you have this." He patted his thick red hair, wiry and unmanageable.

"And a beard too?" She was relieved at the direction their conversation had taken.

He frowned, feeling the contours of his chin. "Yes. I don't know why I did this. Well, I'm at the age where if you are married you want a divorce, and if you are an executive you chuck it up and go off to the South Seas. I don't have such opportunities for change, so I grew a beard. It is my middle-of-life independence. Maybe we all need to make some extravagant gesture when we have reached the point of no return." He laughed. "And what is your gesture going to be? What wild fancy is Professor Ruth Arendt going to follow?"

She felt hypnotized. His keen hazel eyes were filled with an ironic laughter, as though he knew her secret and mocked her for it. As concentration on a word makes it sound foreign and meaningless, she now concentrated on David until the well-known outline blurred, and the face, with the heavy unfamiliar beard, became the face of a stranger. The planes of her life slipped apart: the rich satisfying life of teaching and studying, the years of happiness with her father, the months in New Mexico—lonely but freeing, where she had been able to bury her father and discover unexpected desires in herself—and now this.

"Are you all right?" David reached over to take her hand. His hands were blunt and square, more the hands of a carpenter than a scholar.

She nodded, trying to force the diverging planes back into a single focus.

"Did I say anything . . . ?" He was awkward in his solicitude.

"Yes, you did." At last she could smile. The planes had begun to slip into place; the pieces of herself were coming under her control again. The touch of his hand had reassured her. This was no enemy to defend herself against but a compassionate and gentle friend. Of course, she would tell him about St. Aidan's.

"But I didn't . . ." He groped for what could have caused her to grow so remote.

"You asked about my wild fancy."

He looked at her intently. "You have one?"

"It's pretty wild."

"Then perhaps it should wait until we have our coffee. Coffee is very good with wild fancies. It has, as they say, a sobering effect." His voice was still bantering, but his eyes had grown speculative and the distance had again widened between them.

When she told him, he said nothing for a while. He sat, hunched forward, his plate pushed to the side, his elbows spread wide on the table. Finally he said, "I agree. That is quite a wild fancy." His eyes were fixed on his wine glass as he moved his fingers back and forth around the stem.

"I haven't come to it without a lot of thought." She had a curious need to defend herself, although no one had accused her.

"Of course. I would expect that of you." Still his eyes followed the motion of his fingers.

"You don't disapprove?"

This time he looked up, but his eyes did not quite meet hers. When he spoke, his voice had a curious formality, as though he were an adviser called in to give counsel in a disputed case.

"I think too highly of your integrity—and your intelligence—not to honor any decision you make."

The formal rhetoric unbalanced her. She had schooled herself to expect surprise, remonstrance, disapproval. Instead David had received her news with a puzzling detachment. He neither asked questions nor posed objections, yet instead of relief Ruth experienced an inexplicable anger. She felt cheated—as though she had bundled up to face a bracing wind only to discover the day disconcertingly mild. David was being respectful of her beyond her hopes, making no attempt to counter her vision with his own lack of faith; yet in place of comfort and assurance, she found only an irritating sense of disappointment.

"I thought you'd have some questions." The displeasure in her voice annoyed her further.

Again he looked up and beyond her, pushing his chair a little away from the table. "Oh, yes, some questions I suppose about when you made your decision, what you will be doing at St. Aidan's. But these are incidental questions. They do not touch the core of your decision." His voice drifted off as though he had lost interest in the conversation.

His tone disturbed her. She could not identify it. It was a curious blend of detachment and discontent. As though despite his avowals of acceptance and understanding he had found her decision disappointing.

"I know it must be hard for you to understand," she countered lamely.

But he shook his head negatively. "If one believes in a

personal god, as you do, then it seems to me that there would be great joy and satisfaction in being so wholly given to what one sees as life. No"—he pushed his chair back further, looking speculatively at the ceiling—"I have no problem in accepting such a life. I value any life lived in fidelity. What you choose, I must confess, is beyond me; but that is not to question its value for you. Your life is, after all, your own."

They sat in silence for a while and then he asked, "When will you go?"

"It's not definite yet. Rosalia—she's the nun I talked to today—said there was no reason to make a quick decision. I still need time to live with the idea."

David nodded, pouring them a little more wine.

"I thought you'd be more surprised." She did not mean to sound so accusing.

He sighed. "Yes, I'm surprised, although I wondered from your letters if something were not changing for you. And then, I must confess, your father had told me a number of years ago that you had once belonged to a convent."

She flushed, feeling awkward and betrayed, although her common sense told her that it hardly mattered now.

"So, I suppose," David was continuing, "I had a little preparation." He was again bent in concentration on the stem of his wine glass. "You know, of course, that I wish you happiness. I was about to wish you peace, but we have trivialized that word. Let me say that I hope you find the fulfillment of your vision —if that language is not too grand."

But the language was too grand, she thought angrily. She did not want David to talk so formally of vision and fulfillment. She wanted him to talk of loneliness and the separation of friends and the fear that comes with sacrifice. Looking at him hunched over in his chair, his chin in his hands, the heavy red beard showing through his fingers, she was overwhelmed by a sense of loss, a sense she needed him to share. She did not want him to give her his blessing. She wanted him to say, "I'll miss you." And for a dizzy moment there cut through her mind the thought of what might happen if he said to her, "Don't go."

Abruptly David stood as the patron hovered about their table, clearly wishing to close for the night. It had begun to rain again and they took a taxi downtown. When they reached her hotel they sat for a while in the lounge, their conversation the desultory talk of people waiting for the separation of a long journey.

"I must let you go," David said, looking at his watch. "You have an early flight."

They waited for the elevator to descend to the lobby and then he kissed her goodbye.

"You will let me know when you have come to your final decision?"

She nodded, feeling the sting of tears, and pushed the button for the twenty-fourth floor.

Her bed had been turned down but she had no desire for sleep. What she had dreaded doing was done. She had told David. Yet despite his acceptance, she felt no relief. His curious detachment had surprised and angered her. "Your life is your own," he had said, justifying her decision. She found it a chilling thought. Was it so completely her own that no one had a share in it? Would she slip off to St. Aidan's unnoticed? She had thought David, at least, would miss her; but he had seemed to accept her decision as though it hardly touched him. Her life was her own. It was a blind and comfortless thought.

Her mouth was thick and dry from the unaccustomed wine and she felt uncomfortably warm. For a while she looked down on the diminishing life of the city, seeing taxis open and close their doors but being too far away to hear the sounds. Finally, she lay on the couch, still half dressed, until, shortly after dawn, sluggish and querulous, she rose and began to pack for her return to New Mexico.

Rawlins and Swenson, Realtors
108 East 68th St.
New York, N.Y.
May 7, 1980

Mr. Alec Stafford
Stafford, Connor, Lipsky, Architects
18 Ballantyne Avenue
Glen Cove, New York

Dear Alec,

I think I might have a clue for that project of yours. I understand that there is a fine example of nineteenth-century Gothic quite close to Whitethorn, about a three-hour drive from New York.

I haven't had time to check it out beyond ascertaining that it is a sizable piece of property and that it is owned by a group of Catholic sisters. At one time they operated a boarding school but I'm not sure that is still in existence. Lee seems to feel that most of those establishments are no longer viable.

Let me know if this interests you; if it does I'll go ahead with further inquiries.

Yours,

Steve Rawlins

3

Rosalia had been right. Once Ruth made her decision, the Community had voted overwhelmingly in her favor; and on July 4, for the second time in her life, Ruth rang the bell at the massive front door, listened to the clanging within, and waited to be welcomed to the Community of St. Aidan's.

When she had called Rosalia the night before to tell her what time her train would get in to Whitethorn, Rosalia had assured her that she would have someone drive over to meet her at the station.

"Don't bother, Rosalia, I'll get a taxi." Suddenly those last minutes before she reached St. Aidan's had become very precious and she wanted to spend them alone.

"Nonsense. Why should you do that? Anyway, a taxi would cost you a fortune."

"Well, let's count it as my last luxury then," Ruth countered; but Rosalia would have none of it. There would be someone waiting for her at Whitethorn when her train arrived at four-fifteen.

The train was as dusty and unpredictable as she had remembered it. The olive green horsehair seat pricked through her light skirt and the sun shone weakly through the unwashed windows. She reached to pull down the shade but found it hopelessly stuck. She had bought a magazine in the station although she knew she would never read it. It slipped to the floor and she bent down to pick it up and put it on the seat next to her. The sun made her sluggish and heavy-eyed and she leaned back and closed her eyes. She had slept during the night despite her nervousness. From time to time she woke, confused by her surroundings and wondering what had brought her to this strange resolution; but then she had said firmly, as though to a bewildered child, "You are doing what you planned to do. Now go to sleep." And obediently she would turn over and sleep again. She was glad she had spent that last night in a hotel. There was nothing in the unfamiliar surroundings to claim her, nothing to say goodbye to. As she dressed and packed in the morning, opening drawers and closets to be sure she had left nothing behind, there was no sentimental parting. When she checked out it was clean and uncluttered, a few conventional platitudes, an exchange of bills, and she was free to go.

In the end she was glad that she had arranged to go without seeing David. She had written to him, as she had promised, telling him the date of her departure but not suggesting that they meet again. And he, when he answered, had seemed to accept her plan without argument. The apparent estrangement between them saddened her but, she reasoned, it was easier this way.

She was spared both the anguish and the exultation of that first time. Then, fresh and untried, she had given over her life with a passion that only youth could inspire. She did not know what lay ahead and, recklessly, she had thought it did not matter. She would belong to God; the thought gripped her with exultation. Her mother had shaken her head, her eyes bright with tears, as she pointed out all that she would sacrifice: a career, marriage, children of her own to love and cherish. Her father had said nothing but only held her in his arms in wordless understanding that these things were nothing compared to the vision that drew her. Her own anguish was not in the renunciation of the things her mother cherished but in the simple recognition that she would never belong to her parents in the same way again.

Then as now she had needed to make that final journey alone. When her mother had pleaded that she should let her parents accompany her, her father had dissuaded her and she had said goodbye to them in Grand Central Station amid a crowd of milling children bound for camp and boarded the train for Whitethorn alone. Even after so many years she could still remember her parents as they had stood on the platform, her mother smiling determinedly, her hand raised to wave goodbye, and her father, his arm around his wife's shoulders, protecting her from loss.

Then she had found the ride endless, but now the three hours drifted by in a kind of twilight imagery, as though she were looking at dozens of disconnected clips from old movies: there was the chapel of St. Aidan's, its three tiers of medieval stalls filled with tall black indistinguishable figures; there were her parents looking small and shy on their first visit to St. Aidan's; there was herself, surprised but happy, staring surreptitiously into a mirror the day after she received her religious habit. The white linens, pressed close around her face, had made her skin look swarthy and her heavy eyebrows startlingly dark. Except for the direct brown eyes it was a face that did not seem entirely hers. The movie ran on, turning up unexpected memories, and by the time the train stopped at Whitethorn she was submerged in the past.

She struggled down the high steps of the old-fashioned car, her suitcase bumping at her side. There was only one person on the platform: a small thin girl in a denim skirt and red-checked blouse. Her hair, long and dark, was pulled back from her face and held in place by a red clip; sunglasses obscured her eyes. She hardly seemed old enough to be from St. Aidan's, but without hesitation she waved and walked toward Ruth.

"You must be Ruth," she said. "No one else qualifies." She nodded toward the teen-aged boy and the elderly couple who

were the only other people to descend at Whitethorn. "I'm Kate
Boylan, St. Aidan's youngest," she introduced herself and reached
out a small firm hand.

They stood smiling awkwardly, their eyes narrowed against
the sun. "It was very nice of you to come for me." Ruth's voice
sounded dry and unnatural. "I told Rosalia I could easily take a
taxi."

"Oh, they'd never hear of that. All kinds of people wanted
to come to meet you, you know. You're quite a celebrity at St.
Aidan's. It's all they've talked about for weeks."

Ruth winced at the words but Kate seemed not to notice.

"Even Edwarda said you were one of the best teachers St.
Aidan's ever had and that your influence was 'quietly apostolic.'
And that's a quote!"

Ruth laughed. "She never told me that when she was my
superior."

"Maybe not. But she's saying it now and how much they
had counted on you to improve the quality of the school. And
what's more, Susannah is agreeing with her."

"How is Susannah?"

"Feisty. I think she minds growing old more than any of
them."

"And Aidan?"

"Aidan's a great lady. I wish I had known her when she was
younger. She is really your advocate. She was saying one night
that you gave the lie to all the nonsense that the best vocations
always come young. Was that what they thought when you
entered?"

"Some people did. The theory was that it was easier to form
you to religious life if you were inexperienced."

"So you were something of an exception?"

"In a way."

"Here, let me take your suitcase. The car's over there. I
parked it under the tree to keep it out of the sun. It's air-

conditioned but the seats get beastly hot." She led the way to a
maroon convertible, sleek and polished.

"Don't be scandalized," said Kate, intercepting Ruth's surprised glance. "It doesn't belong to the convent. It's our art
teacher's. She went to Europe for the summer and asked us to
mind it for her. It's safer and cheaper, she says, than garaging it.
Definitely our gain," said Kate with satisfaction as she backed out
of the station.

"How long have you been at St. Aidan's?" Ruth asked as
they headed for the highway.

"Almost five years. It seems like a lifetime to me, but I
suppose when you get older five years doesn't seem like much.
At least that's what Gregory says. 'The blink of an eye, dear,' she
keeps telling me."

"How is Gregory?"

"All right, I guess. Her rheumatism's gotten a lot worse and
she doesn't play the organ much any more. I don't know what
she used to be like, so it's hard to tell. Actually, Gregory and I
don't have much to say to each other. I play the guitar, you see,
and guitars are definitely no-nos in Gregory's concept of church
music."

Of course, they would be, thought Ruth as she remembered
the solemn pomp with which Gregory had conducted the choir.

They drove in silence for a while and then Kate said, "It
must be strange coming back, isn't it?"

Yes, Ruth acknowledged, it was strange but she refused to
enter into explanations. Kate's directness unbalanced her. It
would have been so much easier if Rosalia had agreed to her
taking a taxi. Then she would have had the silence she needed
to center herself, to focus on the reality of what she was doing.
To give her life, she thought. To give her life to God. To do it
purely and wholly with the increased wisdom the last ten years
had given her. Ahead of them was the final fork in the highway;
from then on the road was straight to St. Aidan's.

Kate had been fiddling with the dials on the radio and now a selection of golden oldies filled the car. "I saw those harbor lights," crooned an anonymous voice as they made the sharp turn onto the grounds of St. Aidan's.

After the spareness of New Mexico the woods looked wild and luxuriant. Blackberry thickets lined the road, their fruit formed but still green. Maple trees arched over them, keeping the drive cool and dark. Ruth had loved to walk here on summer afternoons, protected from the sun and solaced by a sense of privacy. As a novice she had found a little clump of rocks a few yards off the road, and during their small portions of free time she would go to sit there, healed and restored by those intervals of solitude. But when during her second year Mother Columban had discovered her refuge, she disapproved categorically. Her heavy face with its folds of flesh beneath her chin shook in annoyance. It was not, she told Ruth, "religious" to sit on a rock "in that way." The phrase was vaguely suggestive of something immoral, but Ruth made no effort to counter it. In her first months at St. Aidan's she would have pondered such a correction, trying to understand its hidden logic. But by her second year she had stopped trying, accepting instead the humiliation that she was not sufficiently "spiritual" to penetrate the arcane significance of religious custom.

Once she would have known at exactly what moment the car would swing against the last curve and the massive gray stone of St. Aidan's would rise before them; but she had forgotten the landmarks and so at each turn she held her breath and for a second closed her eyes to prepare herself. There was, she remembered, a huge holly tree to the right before the final portion of the drive, but it was gone now and without warning St. Aidan's was there before her.

In that first sight she drew in her breath and Kate glanced at her briefly. It had not changed. Ivy still covered the porte cochere, and on both sides the massive buildings rose gray and weathered as she had remembered them. They circled the round plot where the statue of St. Joseph, its base covered with passion flower vines, protected them against calamity.

"I'm going to let you off here and put the car around the other side," Kate explained as she stopped the car in front of the main door. "You don't mind, do you?" she asked. "Leave your suitcase. I'll bring it in the back way."

She did not mind. She felt instead limitless relief to struggle out of the awkward bucket seat and close the heavy maroon door. She was going to have, as she had wanted, those last moments alone. She waited until Kate drove off, watched her circle the building, and then turned to mount the smooth stone steps. Was there something she should be feeling? Or thinking? A sense of joy? of relief? of satisfaction that she had accomplished what she had set out to do? But she felt nothing, neither loss nor gain; only a vague sense of moving forward on an inevitable course of action.

Within seconds after she had rung the bell the door opened and Rosalia pushed the black iron grille wide. Beside her stood Nancy Lenihan, as tall and thin and freckled as ever. Rosalia, always awkward in moments of emotion, stood hesitantly but Nancy, spontaneous and free, had her arms around Ruth before she was across the threshold.

The front hall with its polished marble floor and high ceiling was cool and dark. As Ruth grew accustomed to the dim light, out of the shadows emerged three black-and-white figures. They came together, the three ancients, advancing noiselessly in their rubber-soled shoes, laying their cheeks against Ruth's in the solemn double kiss of welcome: Edwarda, startlingly older, her skin dry as paper and her nose sharp and long in her thin face; Susannah, round and rosy, only her mouth betraying the ill-humor she treated as her privilege; Gregory, broad-shouldered but stooped now, her eyes magnified by her thick glasses.

"Rosalia told everyone that she thought it would be easier if we didn't all gather as soon as you arrived," Nancy whispered to Ruth, "but she couldn't keep them away."

Ruth caught their appraising glances and smiled back, noticing that even among the elders there was no uniformity of dress. Gregory and Susannah were dressed in simplified versions of their original habit; Edwarda had changed nothing, the stiff linen band still framing her face, the long full veil reaching to her knees.

Their questions and comments followed the ritual of polite, reserved conversation to which they had been trained: they hoped that the train ride had not been too tiring, that it had not been too hot, that the train had not been late, that Kate had met her promptly. Would she like a cup of tea? of coffee? something cold? There was nothing said about the circumstances of her leaving or returning. Had their conversation been the only indicator, she might have felt like any aspirant entering the charmed world of St. Aidan's for the first time. But those wordless embraces had told her different; and Ruth, trained during her ten years at St. Aidan's to catch the most silent nuance, had not missed the subtle pressure of affection that had said, You have been one of us and we rejoice at your return.

Rosalia interposed at last, "We have just about an hour before supper. I'm sure Ruth would like to go to her room for a little while. Gregory, why don't you take her over."

As Ruth turned to start up the main staircase, Rosalia put her hand on her arm. "This way, Ruth," she said and started to lead her off to the left, to the passageway that led to the boarders' living quarters. Bewildered, Ruth stood, her hand still on the banister.

"We don't live upstairs in the convent?" Until she had said it she hadn't realized how much she had counted on finding her place where it had always been—not the same room, of course, but the same narrow corridors with their unexpected turns and steps, the old-fashioned bathrooms at the end of each corridor with their perpetually dripping faucets and makeshift showers. She thought she had known what her room would be like: small, bare, with whitewashed walls and just enough space for a cot, a desk and chair, a small bookcase. But apparently she had misjudged.

> Each sister will have a room of her own which she will keep in perfect order at all times. The rooms will be small and will contain nothing extraneous. The walls will be bare except for a simple crucifix and one small religious picture. No comforts of any kind will be permitted, although should health or the climate require a small rug may be used.

"Surely I told you that we had moved . . ." Rosalia's voice trailed off uncertainly.

Ruth shook her head.

"I was so sure I did." Rosalia's cheeks were turning red. "I can't imagine forgetting to tell you something as important as that."

"It's all right." Ruth's voice was barely audible. She felt the sharp sting of tears behind her eyes.

"The school's gotten so small," Rosalia explained. "We would have closed this dormitory anyway, and it seemed more sensible for us to move into it. The rooms are larger and much more convenient. We would have had to put in all new plumbing if we stayed where we were, and that seemed a foolish expense. We still use the parlor and the rotunda for special occasions."

Ruth nodded and turned to where Gregory waited to take her through the passageway and into the boarders' wing.

"Some of them are still complaining that we moved over here," Gregory confided as she pushed Ruth ahead of her down the hall. "It was strange at first, but what's the use of repining? Life's too short. Anyway I'm glad to have a bigger room. And the bathrooms are very nice. We had them all done over for the students about eight years ago."

Gregory was holding Ruth's arm in an iron grip, and Ruth

realized as she felt her waver how unsteady Gregory had become.
She should use a cane, Ruth thought as she felt Gregory bear
down on her as she negotiated the three steps that led into the
wing.

"Edwarda, for instance," Gregory was continuing. "She
says she'll never get used to it, that it was a disgrace to move out
of the convent. 'Goodness,' I said to her one day, 'don't you like
that nice hot bath in the evening and a place for a comfortable
chair in your room?'" Gregory sighed. "She said baths and
comfortable chairs don't make our life." She shook her head.
"Edwarda must be very holy by this time," she concluded skeptically.

They had turned left into a further corridor, and halfway
down Gregory paused.

"Well," she said, as though they had accomplished a singu-
lar feat, "here we are. This is going to be your room," she
announced triumphantly, opening a door and pushing Ruth
ahead of her.

Its unredeemed ugliness filled her with an immense sense of
loss. She closed her eyes instinctively to blot out the heavy vacant
space.

"They should have opened the window," Gregory was
saying, tugging at the sash.

This is all that will be mine. This dull square room with its
ugly porcelain sink in the corner and that one great creaking
window. It was not luxury that she wanted or even comfort. She
would have rejoiced at the austere purity of a whitewashed cell,
but she could not rejoice at ugliness. Again she closed her eyes,
but the gesture only brought more clearly into focus the small
cherished possessions she had left behind: a soft Wyeth landscape,
a brilliant page from a medieval Book of Hours, a scroll of
Japanese calligraphy.

"... so when we moved in—that must have been about five
years ago—Mother had them all painted. We could each choose
our own color." Gregory sighed. "Well, what excitement!"

Whoever chose this must have been mad with excitement, thought Ruth as she looked at the pale salmon walls and the dark brown wainscotting and window frames.

"Let me look at you," and Gregory took her by the shoulders, turning her toward the light. "I don't see so well as I used to," she explained, looking upward at Ruth through her bifocals.

"My, you are thin," she said, pressing her fingers into Ruth's forearm.

"I've always been thin," Ruth explained.

"That's true." Gregory nodded. "Your mother wasn't thin though, was she?"

Ruth laughed. "No, poor Mother was always on a diet."

"I guess you take after your father, don't you?" Ruth nodded, hoping somehow that the conversation would shift but unable to think of another direction. "He was a fine man." Gregory was wandering on. "Well, he's gone to his reward now, and thank God you were able to be with him right to the end."

Gregory's words were sucking her back into her father's death and she struggled to find something that would free her from her memories.

"Do you still play the organ?" she asked abruptly as Gregory paused.

"We don't have so big a choir as we used to," Gregory explained, ignoring Ruth's question with the ingenuity of the deaf. "There are only about thirty of us now. Some left; I suppose you know about that. And then the good Lord took a few: Mother John and Jerome—and then Josephine. I guess He must have wanted all the ones beginning with J." She laughed. "I don't know when he'll want the G's. I'm getting on, you know." Ruth nodded. "I still play the organ. But"—her voice had slowed—"we don't have organ so much anymore. They play a lot of guitars now."

"They," Ruth thought, not "we."

"Of course, there's nothing wrong with guitars," Gregory conceded. "That Kate Boylan . . . Do you know her?"

Ruth nodded. "She met me at the station."

"She plays very well, I suppose." And then she added, almost as though she could not help herself, "When she's here." Her annoyance was so transparent that Ruth laughed and Gregory joined her. "Well, you know how it is," she said with an all-inclusive shake of her head.

"Well, thank God you're back." She gave Ruth's arm another pat. "Aidan is tickled pink, of course. She always had such plans for you. She felt you could have done something fine for St. Aidan's if you hadn't had to leave."

"I'm not sure I could have. I'm not really a leader, you know."

"Well, maybe. Not the way some people are. But you could take hold of things, and people trusted you. Aidan always thought you had vision, that you could see beyond your nose. She had a terrible row with Josephine after you left. My, you could hear them all the way down to the front hall. Poor Josephine could never keep up with our Aidan. No vision, I suppose you could say. Just do your duty and keep the Rule. Aidan had vision. I suppose that was one reason why they never elected her superior."

"Ruth?" Nancy Lenihan was at the door carrying Ruth's suitcase. "Kate asked me to bring this up. Don't go." She reached out to restrain Gregory, who was limping toward the door.

"No, now, I'm going to leave you two together to have a little talk. I like to have some time to pray before dinner anyway. I miss not having Vespers the way we used to. We'll see you downstairs." She gave a final pressure to Ruth's arm.

"She's ecstatic that you're back, you know, although she'll probably never say it."

"I felt it." Ruth laughed, rubbing her arm where Gregory's fingers had clenched it.

Nancy grinned. "She does have a firm grasp."

"On everything," Ruth said, thinking of Gregory's courageous acceptance of change.

Nancy nodded, staring out the window. "It's been hard for them, hard for all of us. Is it a shock?" she asked, turning to Ruth. "But of course you must have known."

"I knew the facts." She wanted to say more but nothing came.

Nancy turned from the window and her light blue eyes looked directly at Ruth. "Don't try to absorb ten years of change overnight. God knows we haven't done it very gracefully, even living it day by day. The shell had to break open someday, you know." She paused. Her eyes were on Ruth, absorbing every detail. "Ruth, have you any idea, *any* idea, of what it is like to have you back? It's like a miracle that at this time, when things are so wobbly with us, you should choose St. Aidan's again."

Shaken by Nancy's affection and trust, Ruth could not meet her eyes but reached out her hands to clasp Nancy's hard, calloused fingers.

"Look"—Nancy's practical voice had returned—"I have to run down and see that everything is set up for dinner. Why don't you just stay quiet until I come up for you. As Gregory said, we don't say Vespers together on weekends."

"Don't bother coming up. I can find my way down."

"You know we don't use the nuns' refectory, don't you? That's all closed up now. When the school started to get so small we took one of the student recreation rooms and turned it into our dining room."

"O.K. I'll find it, don't worry."

"We eat at six, but it's cafeteria style so it doesn't matter if you're a little bit late." Nancy laughed. "It's a good thing Mother Josephine didn't live to see it all. She'd have a heart attack at the Sisters of St. Aidan's doing anything as plebeian as setting up a cafeteria. Remember the penances for coming late to meals?"

Ruth nodded but she couldn't match Nancy's smile. She too, like Mother Josephine, felt a clutch at her heart at the sudden change from their ritual living. It was not that she wanted the past but simply that custom and ritual had defined her life at St.

Aidan's; and although she knew it was only the rind of that life, she did not know how she would penetrate to the sweet fruit without it.

When Nancy left she stood looking out the window. The sensible thing was to unpack, but she was not quite ready to put her possessions in this alien space. She looked at her watch. Five-forty. She would go to chapel until it was time for dinner.

The sense of being an intruder shadowed her and she was grateful that the halls leading to the chapel were empty. As she reached to pull open the heavy oak door opening onto the antechoir, it was pushed outward.

"Oh, I beg your pardon." And a tall thin figure moved back against the door to hold it open for her.

For a moment they looked at each other blindly and then Ruth recognized her. "Magdalen!" she cried and reached out to embrace her. Her usual shyness was forgotten in the joy of this sudden encounter. Although she had not been close friends with Magdalen, they had both taught upper division English; and the drudgery of examinations, of preparing students for college entrance, of coaching them for oratorical contests and school plays had drawn them together.

Now as she put her arms around Magdalen she was aware of the slightest hesitation in Magdalen's response. Her hands, icy cold, rested on Ruth's shoulders as though she wanted to keep a distance between them.

"Let me see you," she said, pushing Ruth at arm's length from her. "Kate told me you had arrived, but I thought I'd give you time to catch your breath before I came up."

There was something coolly distant in Magdalen's manner that made Ruth embarrassed at her impetuous display of affection. In the shadows of the antechoir she looked as untouched and immobile as a Greek statue. Her hair, pulled back in a French knot, had turned that special shade of silver that often follows pale gold hair. Her face was less full and the cheekbones more prominent than Ruth had remembered. Years of seeking perfection had honed the youthful oval and given her face a look of passionate austerity.

Ruth found her own hands growing cold as she faced this beautiful stranger. Her moment of spontaneous joy slipped away and she turned blindly toward the chapel. I have not come for friendship, she reminded herself. Not for friendship or security or to recapture the past. I have come for something more.

"We should probably start down," Magdalen said. "Everyone will be waiting for you." And she led the way down the wide wooden staircase, carpeted now, and toward their dining room.

In the next half-hour Ruth met most of the Community in a bewildering series of embraces, exclamations, recited memories.

"Have you met everyone?" Rosalia asked, coming in late.

"I don't know." Ruth looked around, not sure if some of the missing faces were simply away for the evening or were those who had left the Community.

"Daryl Peters is away. She's at a music convention. She'll be back next week."

"Kate Boylan went back to the camp. She works with the migrant workers," Nancy Lenihan explained. "She often has to be there late at night."

"Very often," commented Rita McClellan dryly.

Rita, tall and ruddy, had always been a dominating figure; now freed from their habit she was an extraordinarily handsome woman. Her white hair was striking and she had a presence and sense of style that set her off. The dark gray eyes missed nothing, and Ruth caught her looking at her speculatively during dinner.

They stayed in the dining room long after they had finished eating, with nuns Ruth had not yet met bringing their chairs over to the table where she sat: Noreen Moriarty, slower, heavier, with the same unfocused smile; Joanne Berman, their principal now, quiet, orderly, with not a hair out of place.

For the next hour questions and answers hurtled around Ruth's head. "No, my father wasn't with me in New Mexico. I went down after his death for a few months. . . . Yes, he died

last November. . . . Yes, I heard Mother Josephine had died.
. . . Of course I remember Bridget. . . ." Of course I remember
Bridget and Josephine, George, Anthony, Ursula . . . the old
guard, doughty, formidable, alternately loving and bruising. I
remember that the halls were bare, their wooden boards polished
to perfection, that the dining room was to be called the refectory.

> Unless illness prevents them, the sisters will take all their meals
> in a common refectory. The refectory will ordinarily be a place
> of solemn silence, although on great feast-days they may express
> their joy by speaking quietly to the sister next to them. They will
> eat whatever is put before them in a spirit of humble gratitude,
> giving thanks to God for his continual care.

"Do you like the dining room? Remember, it was a student
recreation room and we painted it over a couple of summers ago.
It isn't quite finished, but don't you like the contrasting walls?
Mr. Arnold gave us the carpeting. It's really just remnants but we
patched them together. . . ."

Of course, of course she liked the new dining room and the
pretty new dishes.

"Remember those awful white plates and the big thick
cups? We gave them to the Salvation Army. We could never
have afforded these, but Regina Lewison's mother wanted to give
something to St. Aidan's when Gina graduated."

And she remembered the white walls and the huge black
crucifix behind the superior's place and the long rows of tables
where one ate silently, quickly, always the same bland nourishing
food, always with the same neighbors, until there was nothing
—not the slightest worry or craving or mannerism—that was not
mutually uncovered.

We eat so secretly, she had thought as a novice, as though
it were some unpleasant service we have to perform for our
bodies, an act we cover with ritual but of which we're secretly
ashamed.

The ritual itself was elaborate, even more elaborate than the one that surrounded the saying of the Office: the long Latin grace, with hands just so many inches out of one's sleeves; the filing into one's place and the moments of silent prayer awaiting the superior's bell; the second bell—the bell she dreaded to the point of nausea—which signaled the public penances of the day; finally, the third bell, which set them free to fold back their long black sleeves so that they could at last begin their meal. Yet with all that, the meal had never been sacramentalized for her. It established no feeling of community, no sense of real human gratitude for the food that was put before them, no joy in the fact that the Lord Himself had shared meals with his family, had indeed given Himself to his family at such a meal.

"Don't you wonder how we ever lived through all that?" Nancy sighed. "All that silence? We never had a chance to talk to anybody. We might as well have been hermits."

Yes, she did wonder how they had lived through it. The unrelieved formality, the tradition of obedience that put so many lives—body and soul—in the hands of one frail person; most of all, the unremitting sense that one had no life of one's own.

By the vows of religion they will give up not only the right to marry and to acquire or dispose of material possessions but the right to direct their own lives. Having given over their lives to God, they will reflect earnestly on the meaning of St. Paul's words: "We are Christ's and Christ is God's."

At some point the quick shifts in the conversation overwhelmed Ruth and she gave up the effort to remember, to respond, and made do with an empty nod and blank smile. It was Nancy, sensing her exhaustion as they stood outside the dining room, who pushed her toward the stairs.

"You're tired to death. Go on upstairs. They'll understand."

The late summer light had almost faded when she closed the door behind her. She reached out for the desk lamp and then hesitated, looking out onto the terraced lawn and the deeper shadows of the orchard stretching off to the left. The old convent wing was partially obscured, the dark gray stone blending into the half-light, yet even in the dusk, even after years of absence, she could make out the juttings and embrasures, the decorative towers and crannies that had been the delight of nineteenth-century architects.

When she had thought of returning to St. Aidan's it had always been the original convent building she had pictured. The circular drive with its porte cochere, the massive front door, the great wooden staircase branching into two wings, the first floor with its offices and library, the narrow halls with their unexpected steps, the small rectangular cells.

When they were novices it was as important to know the history of St. Aidan's as to be able to recite the Apostles' Creed. They had known all about the origins of the first building—how Mr. Nigel Kent had bought it, adding another wing in the dream that he could convert it into a resort hotel; how when he failed, Mother Imelda (dauntless, beautiful, and Irish) had managed to buy it "for a song." They knew when the chapel and the nuns' choir were built, how the additional wing had been converted into a school, how the novitiate and cloister walk had been completed just before the Depression. Although they rarely saw the parlors (sacred to visitors), they loved them and savored the massive wooden tables, the bronze candelabra, the crystal and gilt dinnerware locked (securely and uselessly) in their cabinets.

They had been proud of St. Aidan's as one is proud of a heritage passed on with love and with great labor. Now, looking in the darkness at the shadowy gray mass, Ruth knew it was incongruous, like a great lumbering animal that is protected only as a remnant of an extinct species. Yet its emptiness filled her with pain, with that desolation that comes of losing something one has been sure would endure. "But at my back I always hear Time's winged chariot hurrying near." But Marvell's lines were not quite to the point. In this case the winged chariot had overtaken them and then sped on, leaving St. Aidan's heavy and useless.

Once when her father had visited her in the novitiate (her

mother had not been able to come), he had looked at her appraisingly. That day for the first time in her adult life she had turned away from him, afraid of what he would read in her eyes. But he had taken her shoulders and turned her toward him.

"You remember Keats's line about Ruth: 'She stood in tears amid the alien corn.' Is that how it goes with you?"

For a moment she thought she would suffocate, so sudden and terrible was her loneliness. The exultation of the first weeks of convent living had left her and she was suffering the inevitable pain of loss. She longed for something—no matter how small—that was exclusively her own. Even more, she longed for those daily gestures of human affection that throughout her life she had enjoyed unquestioningly. Beyond all her willed resolution to keep silent, to hide her desolation, she had said, "I'm bereft."

The phrase, so archaic and precious, distanced her for a moment from her suffering and she was able to look at her father without pretense. His pain, she knew, was as keen as hers. She knew how he longed to have her with him. She knew what it cost him not to say, Come home with me. But she also knew that he would never say it. His love for her was too great for him ever to violate her freedom. He took his hands from her shoulders as though in that moment it was important that they be free of physical contact, but his eyes remained steadily on hers.

"Then," he said slowly, "perhaps you must be bereft for a while."

From the beginning her father had discerned her ideal beyond anything she had been able to articulate. He had asked few questions and none of a practical nature. It had been her mother who had pummeled her with questions: When had she decided? Who had advised her? How long would her novitiate last? What would she wear? What would she eat? What would she do? ... And over and over the perplexed question: Why? Why could she not serve God like other young women? She was intelligent, attractive. Why must she hide herself away? Why?

The questions of fact Ruth had found easy to answer. It was

the "why" she stumbled over, aware that none of her labored, rational replies reached to that center that moved her. Finally one evening her father had leaned over and put his arms around his wife. "Don't ask for so many words. Listen to Ruth's heart. She believes that there exists a God of pure love and mercy and she wishes to serve Him with all her mind and heart and body."

It had been his understanding that had quieted her mother and that later, in her own loneliness, had won her the strength to remain, to keep faith with her vision.

Youth, too, had been on her side. She had bent easily to the unexpected, even to the inexplicable, and her hope in the future was fresh and resilient. Her future was locked to that of St. Aidan's, and of that future there was no doubt. God had blessed them with what Mother Josephine proudly called "a fruitful apostolate" and "capable subjects." They had a great work to do and all the resources necessary to accomplish it. They were proud of their tradition and sure of their ability to carry it on. An aspirant had to do no more than join the line of march. What Ruth had expressed to her father had had nothing of doubt but had been a simple statement of loneliness as she felt the full wound of being cut off from everything that had once shaped her life.

In time her personal past had grown shadowy as she had been absorbed into the full life of St. Aidan's. Now the memory of that communal past reabsorbed her. Yet even as she mourned, she knew tht she did not want that past back. She had suffered under it, deeply, and even when she had bent her judgment to it a part of her mind had rebelled against its rigidity, its structure of unreality. For what then was she mourning? She hardly knew. Perhaps for the security that those forms had promised; for without qualification they had promised to lead her to God. God had in fact revealed Himself to her within the ceremonies and rituals, the regulations and customs of St. Aidan's. That He would reveal Himself to her again in this new order she had no doubt, but her faith was not enough to dispel her sense of loss.

At last she pulled down the shade and in the glare of the overhead light began to unpack her suitcase. She hung her dresses in the deep, wide closet and opened the drawers of the dresser, stiff and creaking, but neatly lined with white paper.

Before she went to sleep she had surrendered, without resentment, to a time of bereavement.

Rawlins and Swenson, Realtors
108 East 68th Street
New York, N.Y.
June 17, 1980

Mr. Alec Stafford
Stafford, Connor, Lipsky, Architects
18 Ballantyne Avenue
Glen Cove, New York

Dear Alec,

Apologies. I meant to get back to you much sooner but Julie and I decided to take a few weeks off while her sister was still free to take care of the kids. We spent most of our time in Quebec visiting old friends.

As for your project. I did some checking and discovered that the property I mentioned is still being run as a boarding school —St. Aidan's School. I admit this doesn't sound too hopeful but the sisters might be very glad to sell given the chance. I can't imagine that their school is flourishing.

I'm enclosing a newspaper clipping with a photo of the house. A friend of mine was able to get it for me. As you can see the place is a honey! What about it?

Yours,

Steve Rawlins

The heavy shade had kept out the morning light, and when Ruth woke it was seven-fifteen. I've missed everything, she thought—morning prayer, meditation, Office—and I'll miss Mass if I don't hurry. But as she reached for her robe she realized that no one had told her the Saturday schedule and she had not thought to ask. Instinctively, after all those years, her mind had veered back to their old weekend schedule.

As she walked toward the bathroom she heard no sounds. I am late, she affirmed. They're all in chapel. She was dressed in minutes and on her way downstairs by seven-twenty-five, but as she opened the door leading to the chapel wing she bumped into Noreen, still in her robe and carrying a cup of coffee.

"Goodness, you are an early bird," she said, shielding her coffee cup with her hand.

"I thought we'd be having Mass." Ruth felt unaccountably foolish.

"Oh, goodness, not at this hour, not on Saturday."

The irritation that Noreen had always brought to the surface was, after ten years of separation, as sharp as ever. She fought back a childish impulse to say, Well, how was I supposed to know? Instead she said, "We're having Mass later?"

"Yes, probably around nine or nine-thirty. The weekend schedule is always flexible. My, that's too bad." Noreen's heavy mouth turned downward. "You could have had another hour of sleep. There's coffee in the kitchen. Why don't you get a cup and take it up to your room? That's what I do." She looked longingly at the mug in her hand.

"Thanks, Noreen, you go along. Your coffee'll be getting cold." Ruth turned toward the stairs, but she didn't go to the kitchen. She felt no need for coffee to wake her up. The shock of thinking she had slept through prayers on her first day back and then the countershock of meeting Noreen had more than awakened her. She went instead, as she had planned, toward the chapel. She stood for a moment in the antechoir, where a marble statue of St. Michael, looking young and aggressive, guarded the holy-water font.

She pushed open the door and found that memory had not betrayed her. It was the way she remembered. The chapel never caught the morning sun and even in summer it was cool and dim. Down the center of the nave the heavy oak pews were as gleaming and polished as ever. On both sides rose the three tiers of choir stalls, severe and, as she recalled, demonically uncomfortable. When they were novices St. Aidan's was so crowded that they could not have places of their own and had crowded into the center pews ordinarily reserved for students. One of their dearest aspirations had been to move out of these inferior positions into a stall of one's own.

The chapel will be considered the heart of the convent. Here the sisters will assemble for both private and public prayer. They will gather for Morning Prayer daily at 5:30. They will remain in chapel for forty-five minutes of meditation, which will be followed by Mass. Each sister will have her own place, which she is expected to occupy at the prescribed hours. Should anyone be absent she must account for her absence to the superior; should anyone come late she will perform the prescribed penance.

Now both stalls and pews were empty except for a few figures scattered here and there. Edwarda, straight as a ramrod, sat in a stall close to the altar. Gregory maintained her favored place by the organ; her eyes were closed and her head nodded to one side. Two other figures were in the stalls on the far right but Ruth could not make them out. She slipped into a rear pew and closed her eyes. "Be still and see that I am God" read the plaque by the holy-water font. But there was no stillness in her. She tried to slow her breathing and adjust to the quiet, but she was overcome with restlessness.

She opened her eyes and looked at the giant crucifix in the rear of the sanctuary. "Sisters, every time you come to chapel ask Jesus on the Cross to make you faithful," Mother Columban had advised them in the novitiate. And she had done so. "Make me faithful," she had prayed, sometimes in blissful confidence, sometimes in terror. Now she prayed it again, by instinct, as one reaches out to save oneself from falling.

She sat back finally, noticing that the hard wooden kneelers had been cushioned. The sanctuary was the only thing that had changed appreciably. The old massive altar was gone and in its place was a light table with a look of impermanence about it. The heavy gold tabernacle had been replaced by a small silver box that rested unobtrusively at the side of the sanctuary.

After a while Edwarda rose and went out the side door leading into the garden. Gregory, too, shifted in her seat and started to get to her feet. This time she had a cane with her, but as she leaned forward it fell and rolled into the aisle. Ruth went and picked it up for her and Gregory nodded gratefully, keeping a tight hand on Ruth's arm.

"I hope they told you we don't have early Mass on Saturday," Gregory said as the door of the antechoir shut behind them.

"I met Noreen and she told me."

"Noreen! Don't tell me she was up early." Gregory's asperity was momentary and at once she laughed, a low amused chuckle. "It's a good thing that charity is heaven's first law and

not hard work, or I don't know what would happen to Noreen."
And she gave a shake to Ruth's arm. "Well, that's enough unkindness so early in the morning, isn't it? And how are you after
your first night at St. Aidan's?" Gregory did not wait for an
answer but plied her with questions: Was her bed comfortable?
Did she get enough hot water for a bath? Was it too noisy in
the corridor? Did she need an extra blanket during the night? And
finally, what was really on her mind: "I hope you weren't scandalized this morning, with no one in chapel, I mean."

No, she wasn't scandalized; after all it was Saturday and
school was closed.

Gregory nodded. "I know, but it still gives me a funny
feeling to sit here with just a few of us rumbling around in that
big chapel. Edwarda thinks it's terrible; but of course she would.
She always did want everything cut and dried. We'd probably
still be getting up at five o'clock if she were the superior. 'Edwarda,' I said to her the other day, 'give up grieving about the
past. It's not going to do you a bit of good. You might just as
well learn to live with what we have and get a little happiness
before you die.'" She sighed as Ruth opened the door of the
dining room for her. "Just the same it would be nice to have a
fine big choir again and one of those grand Masses we used to
have for feast days." She pushed Ruth into the dining room ahead
of her.

Nancy waved to her from a table by the window and Ruth
went to join her. "I'm almost finished," she apologized. "I have
a catechetical group over at Whitethorn at ten o'clock, but I'm
sure someone else will be over."

As Ruth was finishing her coffee, Kate Boylan came over
to join her. "May I?" she asked, pulling out a chair. "How was
your first night at St. Aidan's? I'm sure you had quite a welcome.
Did it seem like old times?"

Ruth smiled. "Not exactly. Old times were never quite so
informal. We would have thought a welcome meant lining up
in rank in the front hall, our hands in our sleeves, while Reverend

Mother delivered a few appropriate remarks in the name of the Community."

Kate shook her head in distaste. "I missed all that—the silence and all the petty obedience—and I can't say I'm sorry. I'm the only one who hasn't worn the original habit, you know, now that Marilyn and Diane have gone."

"No one else here your age?"

"Angela is about the same age, but she entered very young. She made her profession seven years ahead of me. And Peg Darcy is close to my age, but she's been here a while, too. I haven't made my final vows yet."

"That must be very hard, to be so alone."

Kate did not answer at once and then said, "I suppose, in a way, but no one else can ever really make anything easier for you."

"Sometimes companionship can soften the hard places, don't you think?" Kate's directness was making Ruth uneasy. She felt as though she were uttering comforting platitudes that were too soft for Kate's tastes.

"Perhaps. But there's not much point thinking about it, is there? I am alone, at least for now." She shrugged, pulling her hair back to the nape of her neck.

How beautiful her hair is, thought Ruth. The abundance of youth—and she probably doesn't know it. She reached instinctively to her own short curly hair.

Kate looked at her inquiringly.

Ruth laughed. "No profound thought. I was just thinking how lovely your hair is."

For a second Kate backed off and then smiled. The gray eyes widened, the firm almost stubborn lines about her mouth softened. No wonder she doesn't smile often, thought Ruth. It's too special to waste on trivia.

"Thank you." Her hands reached up caressingly. "Everyone in my family has dark thick hair. I don't know if I could have entered when you had to cut it off. Was it awful?"

"Not so awful. Part of one's expectations, I guess."

Kate nodded, the smile gone. "Yes, I can understand that. That's why it doesn't bother me to be alone. It's part of my expectation. I came by myself. It didn't occur to me that there had been another way until I got here and people kept telling me what it was like when a whole group of people entered at once." Kate frowned. "I don't think I'd like that."

"It made it easier at the beginning."

"That's what I'd be afraid of, that I'd be carried along on someone else's conviction. This way"—she groped to find a way of putting it that Ruth would not be offended by—"this way I'm sure my responses are my own."

Before Ruth could answer, Kate rose. "Your coffee must be cold. Mine is. I'll get fresh cups for both of us."

Ruth watched as she went to get her coffee. They were the same height but Kate seemed smaller. Looking at her now, standing next to Rita McClellan, her long black hair pulled back loosely, she looked hardly out of high school. But when she turned, the impression vanished; the gray eyes were cool and watchful, the head held too erectly.

"You work hard even on Saturdays," Ruth observed.

Kate shrugged. "There's a lot to do."

"They told me you work at a camp north of Whitethorn."

Kate looked up speculatively from her coffee cup. The directness was gone and she seemed unwilling to discuss her work. When finally she answered her voice was wary, with an edge of anger.

"I work with the migrant workers during the summer— and for as long as they stay in the area." She paused. "I'm the first nun who ever got permission to work full time outside the school. Some people don't like it. They say that my place is here, that I'm needed at St. Aidan's."

"Are you?" Something of Kate's directness had infected Ruth.

Her eyes met Ruth's unflinchingly. "If I thought I were, I'd be here." She pushed back her chair. "Sorry, I have to go. Saturday's a big day at the camp."

As Ruth left the dining room, Joanne was waiting for her.

"Sleep all right? I saw you talking to Kate Boylan. She's our youngest."

"She told me."

"I hope we keep her. She's a fine person but sometimes the pressure gets too much. There's no reason under the sun why she shouldn't be doing the work she's doing, but we still hang on to that old tradition that everyone should be engaged in St. Aidan's. As a matter of fact there really isn't enough work, with the school dwindling the way it is."

"A serious problem?"

"Very."

"What will you do?"

"We haven't really faced it yet. We're still playing 'let's pretend' and calling it 'hope.' Everyone is aware that the pupils aren't coming, but somehow we act as though this were just a bad period that we'll get through—like a snowstorm that the first spring rain will clear away."

"And you don't think that's going to happen, that the slump will end and things will pick up again?"

Joanne shook her head emphatically. "We'll wait a long time for the day of the boarding school to return. Everything's against it."

"It must be very difficult for you."

"Sometimes I think it should be more difficult than it is. When I listen to some of them wailing at the very possibility, I wonder what's wrong with me. I guess I'm not a sentimentalist."

And never were, Ruth thought, remembering Joanne's sangfroid even as a novice. The rest of them were by turns exalted or depressed, but Joanne's course was steady and even. Her faults were minimal: she never forgot her duties and was rarely late for

prayers. Corrections did not crumple her; and when her brother
Andrew died she came to recreation that night, her eyes swollen,
but otherwise calm and attentive.

"It's a good thing you're not a sentimentalist. I think Rosalia counts on you to get things moving."

Joanne nodded. "She's the one I feel sorry for. She can't bear
to see the older people hurt. But they will be hurt one way or
the other. Personally, I think it will be much more demoralizing
to watch the school disintegrate without doing anything con-
structive to turn the tide."

"What are the possibilities?"

"It might be possible to run a good day school here with
expanded facilities. Or we could run a series of religious education programs, which are desperately needed in this area. Everything depends on our decision to close the boarding school, and
that's what we're not ready to face."

They stood for a moment looking at the long sweep of lawn
and the pebbled drive that led to the main gates.

"I'm sorry," Joanne said, "I didn't mean to burden you with
all that on your first day back. I was really waiting to tell you
that Aidan is dying to see you. She's had a cold, so she's up in
her room—second floor, where the first-year boarders used to be.
And this afternoon we're having choir rehearsal about four. We
try to do something a little special for Sunday liturgy. Otherwise
you're free to catch your breath. Rosalia's out but I'll be in my
office. The extension is out of order, so you'll have to trot over
if you need me."

Aidan Fitzgerald was in the eightieth year of her age and
the fifty-eighth of her religious profession. Small, thin, unpre-
dictably quick, she had been from the beginning a presence in the
Community. By her own avowal she was an artist (watercolor),
a musician (the harp), and a poet of some skill in both English
and Gaelic. The Fitzgerald family's wealth was as impressive as
their cultural accomplishments, and once his daughter Cecelia

determined to give her life to St. Aidan's, Gavin Fitzgerald devoted himself to improving the school—and the nuns. Gifts of sherry and port (to enrich the blood) were sent to the convent periodically and at Christmas a dozen geese arrived by van through special arrangements with Mr. Fitzgerald.

During Cecelia's postulantship her father offered to provide the funds for building a new wing for the boarding school. When the matter was first brought up at the meeting of the convent Council, Sister Justina, the youngest member of the group and still naive in the ways of the cloister, protested faintly against the origin of the gift.

"It's whiskey money," she said, her voice trembling but determined, "and we all know what that is."

But Reverend Mother Kieran, her role as superior making her capable of distinctions of which Sister Justina was incapable, explained grandly: "Mr. Fitzgerald, Sister, does not own a *bar*. He sells liquor in *bottles*."

The vote to accept Mr. Fitzgerald's gift was unanimous.

Unanimous, too, was the vote to bestow on his daughter Cecelia the prized name of "Aidan." If some smelled a faint whiff of simony, they had learned to repress their unholy thoughts.

When Ruth and Rosalia had entered the novitiate neither of them could understand why Aidan was not the mother prioress. She seemed to them superior in every way. Small as she was, she carried herself "like an empress," as Rosalia had put it in a fit of simile. She had no brogue like her father, hardly even a lilt; but there was a kind of ripple in her voice as though her words came from a deep spring of bubbling water.

"Her hands are just like a nun's *ought* to be," rapturized Joanne, looking at her own fingers, irrevocably discolored by hours of peeling carrots and apples. How, they had wondered, could the Community have passed over Sister Aidan to elect Mother Josephine with her flat in-toed walk and her blunted New York diction?

By the time they were professed they had reached enlight-

enment. Under Mother Columban's moral discourse, the subjects
of their admiration had shifted. Quiet self-sacrifice, constancy in
one's daily tasks, and hidden fidelity were the qualities to be
valued, not charm or graciousness or the ability to enjoy life.
These were merely human qualities, qualities that had nothing to
do with—indeed, could run counter to—a life of virtue. Sister
Aidan plummeted from her pedestal and was replaced by rheu-
matic Sister Marcella, who spent her days starching their guimpes
and wimples and folding their clothes in the unheated laundry.

"For thirty-five years," Mother Columban told her novices,
"thirty-five years, Sisters, and she has never complained, never
asked to be changed to another task."

How unfair—and how ignorant—Ruth thought as she
knocked on Aidan's door, that Aidan's spontaneous joy in life had
gone so long unacknowledged. It was not until the year before
she had left—the year her mother had died—that Ruth's first
loving admiration for Aidan had returned.

"I think it's ridiculous that they aren't permitting you to
stay on with your father for a while," Aidan had said the night
Ruth had returned from her mother's funeral. "Of course he
needs you—and you need him," she had added with that decisive
nod of the head which was her only concession to anger.

For the two months that Ruth had stayed on, anguishing
between the conviction that her vows had been made forever and
the pervasive sense of her father's need of her, she had been aware
of Aidan's unobtrusive compassion. When, finally, the recognition of her father's loneliness had become so acute that she felt
his presence everywhere, her grief for her mother submerged in
her grief for him, she had made her decision.

"But your father is not actually sick." Mother Josephine
preferred statements to questions.

"He has a weak heart and he was in the hospital for a while
right after my mother died."

"But I'm sure that was simply temporary exhaustion."

From her kneeling position Ruth's eyes were level with

Mother Josephine's crucifix, which moved rhythmically in and out with her breathing.

"Sit down, Sister."

Ruth rose from her knees and took the chair at the side of the desk.

"I understand why you are concerned, of course. There is no one else that your father could live with until he's on his feet again?"

Ruth shook her head. "No, Mother."

Mother Josephine adjusted her crucifix. "How old is your father, Sister?"

"Fifty-nine."

"A young man. He could live for years—and I'm sure he will."

The comforting vision Mother Josephine held out twisted into a nightmare. She saw her father living on and on, forced to retire in five or six years, cut off from the University, which was his life. She saw him lonely, silent, his world growing smaller, more empty, until he became a caricature of the aged, shuffling in slippers too big for his feet, fearful of going out into the quick life of the streets, reduced to tea and coffee and little cans of things that could be heated effortlessly on top of the stove.

"I'm sure your father would be deeply grieved if he thought you were thinking of abandoning religious life to take care of him."

For the first time in Ruth's adult life anger so fierce that it choked her welled up in her. Unused to passion, she did not know what it was. A wave of nausea swept over her and she rose, reaching for her handkerchief, and ran from the room.

That night a little note was slipped under her door. "My dear child," Aidan had written in her tall masculine script, so at variance with her small stature, "love is our first loyalty."

It was a wildly romantic statement, but in the context of Aidan's own profound loyalties it was the message of the Gospel. When Ruth finally left St. Aidan's, silently, according to custom, she knew that Aidan alone had understood the struggle and confirmed her choice.

The voice that responded to Ruth's knock was the voice she remembered, with its subtle caressing of the final consonants. Nor had Aidan herself changed. A little smaller, perhaps, but the arched eyebrows, the white skin with its translucent glow, and the wide blue eyes were still the same. Quick as ever, she was on her feet and embracing Ruth with the customary double kiss; but Aidan could transform custom and her kiss was bright and fresh with love.

" 'Age cannot wither her nor custom stale her infinite variety.' " The words were out before Ruth thought, and she blushed at the inappropriateness of the source. But Aidan laughed with joy.

"How lovely, *Antony and Cleopatra,* isn't it? No one says that sort of thing to me anymore. And, of course, I love it. Frankly, Ruth"—and she sighed—"I don't think many of them have read *Antony and Cleopatra*. It's a good thing I'm not teaching any more. I could never go along with this new curriculum. Imagine—replacing Shakespeare with science fiction!" She sighed. "Well, I suppose I'm just an old-fashioned lady."

Ruth looked at her admiringly. "You're still like an empress."

"An empress!" Aidan's laughter rippled again.

"Of course. That's what Rosalia and I used to call you when we were postulants."

"Goodness, I hope you didn't say that in front of poor Josephine."

Ruth laughed in response. The thought of anyone calling the redoubtable Mother Josephine "poor Josephine" was extraordinary—most of all Aidan, who was so often the subject of her disapproval!

"No, we never told Mother Josephine. It was our secret."

They sat in silence for a few minutes, Aidan's hand, thin and veined, holding Ruth's.

"I don't want to bring up the past, dear. That's over and done with, but I want you to know how glad I am that you are back with us." She patted her hand. "I was glad when you went . . . but I'm even gladder now."

"I never answered your note. I thought about it but . . ."

"No need. I thought afterward that I shouldn't have interfered. But Ruth, dear, you couldn't have stayed on like that. It was terrible watching you."

"I know. The hardest part was leaving without being able to explain or say goodbye. Mother Josephine was dead set against my going." Some of the old darkness was coming over her again and she shivered.

"Poor Josephine." Aidan tapped her forefinger on Ruth's hand with a light staccato touch. The "royal touch," they had called it, for it usually preceded a command.

"Now then. What about me? What do you think of me?"

"I think you're a marvel." Ruth laughed, unready for Aidan's candid self-interest.

"Are you surprised to find me still in our old habit?"

"You look just the way I left you, and that makes me feel at home."

Aidan raised her hands to secure the two black pins that kept the veil and coif together.

"Frankly, I think those experimental habits they're making up in the sewing room are an abomination. And now it's worse. Have you seen those business suits and the little veils floating around their heads like flags? They're ugly, Ruth, ugly. There's no other word for them.

"My brother James was shocked. 'Kitten,' he said the last time he visited me. 'Kitten, you look like a queen and the rest of them look like a clutter of milkmaids.' "

"And the amount of time we spent in meetings talking about it: how many inches? what colors are appropriate? . . . Appropriate to what? I finally said one day. To our vows, they said. Blue and green and tan were all right, but we choked on maroon. What vow is maroon against, I said. I have no patience with that nonsense. People asking for our prayers and needing to be consoled, and where are we? Deciding what color the vows are!"

She took a breath. "I told Rosalia and Marian before—" She stopped. The muscle at the corner of her mouth twitched uncontrollably.

"You know about Marian?"

Ruth nodded. "Rosalia told me when I saw her in March."

The proud unlined face had suddenly crumpled. She's an old lady, Ruth realized. Old and alone. She reached instinctively to take her hands, but Aidan was not yet ready to accept comfort. Instead she slipped her hands into those long full sleeves that could hide their trembling. By contrast, Ruth's own hands, lying uneasily in her lap, looked crudely naked. They did have a place —those sleeves—she acknowledged. They gave us a little privacy in a world where we lived too close to each other.

Aidan pressed her lips together. "Marian was . . ."

Everything to you, Ruth wanted to say but knew she could not.

"Marian was our hope."

Marian Connell. St. Aidan's most gifted pupil, most promising novice. The only superior to be elected by an overwhelming majority on the first ballot. Marian Connell, who blended in herself all those disparate qualities that the Rule marked out for the role of prioress: a woman of vision, dedicated to the work of education, prayerful, prudent, courageous, compassionate, single-minded, loyal to the goals of the Community. And who left that Community in the forty-ninth year of her age and the twenty-fifth of her religious profession.

"I think it wouldn't have been so hard had she left us to . . . well, even to get married, foolish as that might have been. Love is always understandable. And sometimes one does get, even at that age, swept away, I suppose."

But Marian had not been swept away. It was precisely her combination of talents that had made her such a gift to them that had taken her away. She had watched the school diminish, watched the novitiate grow smaller. She had planned and strained —and prayed—but she had not succeeded in bringing them to her vision of life. And she could not live without that life, without scope for the leadership that was part of her bone.

"She lost hope in us," Aidan said. The simple sentence was cold and bleak, describing a fierce frost that no one could have anticipated. "I don't blame her. She was very talented."

Ruth heard Aidan strain between loyalty to the nun she had loved almost to scandal and the wound of betrayal.

"She never told me until the end, when all her plans were made. She said she couldn't bear to put me under the strain. I'm getting on, you know, and she tried to protect me." Aidan paused and turned to Ruth with a tight pursed smile. "But I would prefer to have known."

"Do you hear from her?" Ruth's throat was choked.

"Oh, yes. Things are different now. They write—the ones that leave—or visit. I had a letter." She reached to sort through the clutter of mail on the table next to her. "It's here someplace." She patted the pile. "I don't get them answered the way I used to." Aidan's correspondence had been a wonder to them when they were novices, permitted to write but a single "family" letter each month.

"She's doing very well. Of course she would with that mind of hers." Pride—and love—will win in the end even over the sense of betrayal, thought Ruth.

"She's working with a group out in California. Something about theological reflections on the nature of religious life and mission. She sent me the brochure. It sounds like an interesting group of people. They have a grant from some institution."

She turned away, her mouth trembling again. "Of course, I will always miss her."

When Ruth left, Aidan was as erect as ever, her head resting lightly against the pillow of her rocker, her hands folded, her Office book in her lap.

After lunch Ruth wandered over to the school. It was a warm sunny day and she walked out through the gardens and along the graveled walk to the side door of the school. The borders were lined with yellow and orange nasturtiums as they had always been, but there were weeds coming up through the pebbled path and the lawns were ragged. "We can't keep it up as we used to," Joanne had said. "We don't even try."

She looked in at Joanne's office but the door was closed. The classrooms were deserted, too. But as she came to the art room she could hear the sound of hammering. The door was half open, and inside Nancy was standing on a stepladder hammering at the top of a bulletin board. She had on a light blue jumper, but over it she had tied one of the long checked aprons they used to wear over their habits while working. As she reached out to steady herself, she dropped a nail and turned to reach for another.

"Ruth!" The welcome was affectionate and spontaneous as always.

She pushed the ladder aside and pulled out two chairs. "I'm sorry everything is so chaotic, but I've been trying to clean out the cabinets and get rid of some of the junk. Art supplies always seem to get in such a mess." She slid a stack of posters to the far end of the table.

"We've had a young woman in part-time for the high school art classes. She's very good with the girls, but she always leaves a disaster behind her. We haven't been doing very much with the art department since Lydia left."

So Lydia Walker had left. No one had mentioned that to Ruth. Lydia, who had arrived for the postulant's ceremony of consecration with two gold earrings dangling from beneath her black cap and who later had scandalized the novitiate by sketching her companions in the margin of her Office book. Lydia had

left. Ruth was not surprised—there were those who had predicted that Lydia would never make it through the novitiate—
but she was deeply saddened, for beyond Lydia's unconventional
behavior, her absentmindedness, her passion for her art, was her
passion to be consecrated to God. Ruth hated to believe that the
conformity demanded by St. Aidan's had vitiated that first vehe-
ment desire.

"You knew Lydia, didn't you?" Nancy asked.

"Yes, she made her final vows just before I left."

And in the week that had preceded those vows Lydia had
wandered rapt and unself-conscious, absorbed in the knowledge
of what she was about to do. Her prayer took the shape of making
beautiful things, and during her retreat they had found flowers
everywhere—dandelions and cornflowers in a battered pitcher by
the dishwasher, three yellow day lilies by the lector's stand in the
refectory, purple pansies floating in a discarded soap dish on the
ironing board. It was Lydia's translation of the maxim "Be still
and see that I am God."

"I don't think any of us realized how talented she was until
she got a scholarship to study in Chicago. The first vacation, she
got a ride back with one of the instructors. The whole back of
the van was filled with canvases."

"Was that when she left?"

"No, she came back and taught for a year, but every spare
minute she was in the studio she had fixed over in the old carriage
house. Her hands would be white with cold some nights when
she came in for dinner, but it didn't seem to bother her. The next
year she went back to Chicago and six months later she asked for
a dispensation from her vows.

"By then I think everyone expected it. Lydia simply slipped
away. There was no bitterness, no resentment. It was as though
another way of worshipping God had opened out to her and she
simply followed it. Lydia never needed all of St. Aidan's rules
and regulations. It wasn't that she rebelled against them—she
simply found them irrelevant."

"Is she still in Chicago?" Chicago somehow had the wrong ring for Lydia's impressionable spirit.

"No. She's up in Maine. Some friends have let her have a cottage rent-free. I gather it's no more than a shack, but she seems happy."

"You've seen her then?"

"Oh, yes. She drops in when she gets down to New York. She's thin as a rail but bursting with energy. Rosalia worries about her, I think. The Community always sends her a check at Christmas and Easter. She's brought us a couple of her paintings. You'll see them when you go to the Community room. We had quite a row about putting them up, as you can imagine. They're not quite St. Aidan's usual taste." Nancy laughed. "Rita condemned them as 'expressions of pagan sensuality.'"

"And Edwarda?"

"Edwarda was speechless. She's very careful to sit where she can't see them."

"Are they good?" Ruth was conscious of a keen desire for Lydia to be successful.

"I think they're very good. One of her paintings won a competition in New York. It entitled her to three months in Paris. That's where she is now."

Nancy rose and began to close the windows. "We better start over," she said, looking at the electric clock on the back wall. "We'll be late for choir practice."

Choir practice was held in a little room off the nuns' chapel. In the old days it had stored their choir mantles—long black cloaks worn for Mass and the Office of solemn feasts—and daily Office books, hymnals, the intimidating *Liber Usualis* with its dizzying black clusters of notes. Now the room seemed to be a general storeroom. Sweaters, umbrellas, and raincoats hung randomly from the rows of hooks; schoolbooks and crumpled papers were tossed where the hymnals used to be. Only one corner had escaped the disorder. Here the oldest and most precious hymnals were stacked in neat rows with a sign in fierce blue ink: SISTER GREGORY—DO NOT DISTURB.

Margaret Darcy was there ("Peg, please"). "Sorry, it's taken so long to meet you, but I work in the sisters' infirmary and sometimes there's big doings." She rolled her eyes and grinned. "No, not full-time," she replied to Ruth's question. "During school I work part-time with the boarders—sort of a house mother—but I'm an LPN, too, so I can be useful over here."

Was I ever that young and bouncy? Ruth wondered.

"What's the matter? Was I talking too fast? They all say I do."

"No. I was just marveling at all that energy."

"Oh, that." Peg laughed. "I guess it goes with the red hair and freckles. We're all like that in our family. My brothers are worse." She grabbed Ruth's arm. "There's Angela Ferrato. She must have gotten a ride home for the weekend. She's studying at the University."

For a moment Angela stood unnoticed in the doorway: oval face, dark almond-shaped eyes, long golden-red hair. Where had this pre-Raphaelite vision come from? She belonged in a heavy gold frame, not in this cluttered, bustling room.

"Angela, how great! Did you get a ride home?" Nothing slowed Peg down.

"Yes. Rosalia was in the city . . ." Her voice drifted off into a slow smile. "You must be Ruth. Everyone's been talking about your coming."

After Peg's torrent of words Angela's speech seemed artificially slow. She made no effort to shake hands, no effort to give Ruth the customary kiss. They stood awkwardly, even Peg's initial enthusiasm lost in the inviolable distance that Angela established around herself.

"Has anyone seen Kate?" Joanne's voice reached above the conversation.

"I don't think she's home yet." Peg sounded apologetic.

Joanne looked at her watch. "It's four-fifteen. She's in charge of rehearsal for tomorrow."

"I think we should get started." Edwarda's thin voice was impatient.

"Does anyone know what Kate was planning?"

The silence was accusing.

"I suppose"—Edwarda's voice had reached an even higher pitch—"she was *planning* to play her *guitar.*" The emphasis was its own condemnation.

Ruth felt her stomach muscles tighten. It was like Mother Josephine's terrifying Chapter of Faults. But now it was not a superior who sat in judgment while they found shelter in their common frailty; now the accusations were coming from that frail body. They were turning on each other.

"Perhaps we can plan something very simple for tomorrow." Joanne leafed cursorily through the hymnal. "How about number one forty-eight on page ninety-two?"

Obediently they opened their books.

"Can someone start it?"

They sat like unprepared students before a difficult text.

Joanne struggled on. "Well, I think we know it, so maybe we don't have to practice. Any other suggestions?"

The silence was that of judges at a trial.

We're not thinking of what to sing, Ruth thought. We're thinking of Kate. And two images, like a diptych, one interpreting the other, rose in her imagination: Kate, solitary and courageous, serving the poor; Kate, kneeling before them, waiting to be stoned for her infidelity to Community custom.

The sisters must never lose sight of the fact that service to the poor is their first duty. They will eagerly offer themselves for the poorest missions, remembering that in serving the destitute they serve Jesus Christ Himself.

Beneath their silent formality had they always been so harsh and so divided? Or was this a new virus for which no antibody had yet been discovered? "Circumstances do not make us, Sisters; they only uncover what we are," Mother Columban had warned. Was this what they had been? Under the veils, under the silence, under the unyielding precepts of obedience?

Ruth heard only dimly what Joanne said: that she would post a list of hymns for the following day, that Mass would be at eight o'clock, that tomorrow would be observed as a "quiet day," their monthly day of reflection.

Rawlins and Swenson, Realtors
108 East 68th St.
New York, N.Y.
July 1, 1980

Mr. Alec Stafford
Stafford, Connor, Lipsky, Architects
18 Ballantyne Avenue
Glen Cove, New York

Dear Alec,

I've been doing my homework and this is what I've discovered about your mansion.

The original house was built about 1840 on a site of approximately 350 acres. About 35 years later it was bought by a Nigel Kent, who intended to use it as a resort hotel. He added a wing and called the whole thing "Landsweep." Mr. Kent, however, seems to have been more of a gambler than a businessman and he lost the place in short order.

In 1885 an Irish lady, Mother Imelda Finney, bought the whole parcel for practically nothing. It flourished marvelously and in 1919 another large wing for the boarding school was built through the donations of Gavin Fitzgerald—a name to be reckoned with in New York City politics.

Things went fairly well until the 1960s, when both pupils and nuns went for the free life. Since then the school has been going steadily downhill. Sad for them but very nice, I should think, for you. There's no doubt but that they will be delighted to sell. The writing's on the wall for them.

Since you'll be away most of July, why don't you give me a call when you get back and we can go over whatever data I have.

Cheers,

Steve Rawlins

5

Sunday Mass seemed shadowed by the dissension of the afternoon before. Although Kate was there with her guitar, the hymns seemed subdued rather than joyful; and Ruth was glad that breakfast, in keeping with their day of reflection, was in silence.

Later in the morning she walked out through the vegetable garden and up the rise of land that led into the orchard. There was a grassy mound at the first row of trees, and she sat, her back against an apple tree, facing St. Aidan's.

From where she sat she could see the buildings clearly. The old mansion seemed to have aged the best. It stood as she remembered it, massive and gray, its towers and crenelations at odds with all the other structures. The novitiate—their newest building—boxy and practical, had stood time least well. It was closed now: the shades pulled, the screens removed for use elsewhere. Once a month or so Gregory opened it for a senior citizens' meeting, but that was not enough to sustain its vitality.

Sisters, do not drag your chairs across the floor. This floor has to last for years. Long after you have left the novitiate there will be generations of novices for whom this building will be home.

Gregory and Anna came out of the side door by the chapel, Anna, firm and sturdy in her walk despite her limp, holding Gregory by her elbow as they walked across the uneven grass.

"She really ought to use her cane more often," Nancy had said yesterday as Gregory stumbled on her way to the dining room. "Dr. Lavelle sent her a lovely one for Christmas last year —a real blackthorn stick."

"How does she manage the organ pedals?" Ruth asked.

"You know, I think that's the whole point. She's afraid that if she gets used to a cane it's going to make it more difficult for her at the organ. It's such an effort for her now. We've tried to ease up on the organ and use Kate's guitar a little more, but that's a delicate point. Anna's about the only person who can exert any influence on Gregory."

But as Ruth looked at the two figures, it seemed that it was Gregory who was exerting the influence. Anna stood, her head lowered, her arms at her sides, while Gregory waved her hand admonishingly.

Ruth could notice little physical change in Anna. Husky, broad-shouldered, masculine in her strength, she had always been a powerful figure. Anna had been the final voice in anything to do with maintenance: a new light bulb, an iron that didn't work, a flood in the laundry. Anna took care of them all with brusque efficiency. She bossed the gardeners, argued with the oil man, berated the cleaning women, who often could not understand her heavy brogue.

Sent over from Ireland shortly after she had made her vows, she had had three loves: Ireland, St. Aidan's, and Mother Mary David. In the novitiate Mother Columban had held her up as a model of simple devotion to duty and loyalty to superiors.

"Sister Anna has given up everything—her family, her own convent, even her country—because she was asked by her superior to do so. That is true obedience, Sisters."

But Rosalia, always practical, had said to Ruth later, "I don't think it's just obedience. I mean they really *like* each other.

Mother Mary David and Anna are *friends.*" And then blushed for having suggested anything so human.

In fact, Anna loved Mother Mary David. She loved her because she was Irish and because she felt loved in return. Each additional task heaped on her was another proof of how trusted and needed she was. She bent double under sacks of potatoes and flour, fixed furnaces late into the night, waxed and polished the domain belonging to Mother Mary David. She had terrified Ruth when she was a novice, not because she was unkind but because Ruth knew that Anna's unflagging devotion was beyond her. She was too young to understand that it was Anna's fierce need of love that drove her. Her world had been narrowed to Mother Mary David, who alone was free to respond to her, to reward her with that priceless gift that only superiors could give —approbation.

"That was the mar in the marble," Rosalia had said to Ruth the day they had had lunch together, "giving so much power to one person. And not only power to command but power over affections. It seems like idolatry when you look back, but that was the only model we had."

What, Ruth wondered, watching Anna walking out to the garage, what had happened to Anna Shaughnessey when the ties with Ireland were permanently broken and Mother Mary David was dead?

That night, for the first time, she had a chance to talk with Agnes Devitt.

"Don't be shocked at Agnes," Rosalia had warned her. "She's been sick and it's taken its toll." A virus that had attacked her muscles, the doctor had diagnosed; but so far none of his remedies had been able to arrest its progress. She was still able to teach part-time, although there were times when even that was too much.

"Say it out loud," Agnes said as they sat in the little garden just outside the cloister walk. "I'm an old lady."

Ruth shook her head. "You're younger than I am."

"Age doesn't matter." She kicked her cane aside. "Gregory doesn't use one much but I do."

Ruth was silent. Agnes never had room for anything but the truth.

"Rosalia had told me you'd been sick," Ruth said at last.

"Not sick, really. Just that my legs won't always do as they're told."

"How long?"

"It started about a year and a half ago. At first I thought I was just getting stiff." She laughed—that muffled laugh that had always made it seem that she had a wonderful secret. "I tried running around a little bit more—you know, limber up those muscles—but it didn't work. Then one day nothing worked. I tried to get up for Morning Prayer and I couldn't." The wrinkles around her eyes deepened. "That was the beginning. It's been awful for them." She nodded toward the convent. "I'm the last person in the world anyone expected to get sick. Maybe Daryl or Angela—they always look so fragile—but not me. The problem was always keeping me still. Remember Mother Columban?" Agnes tucked her chin in and folded her hands across her stomach. " 'A religious, Sister Agnes, *walks*. She does not run!' "

It had been Agnes who had opened the door when Ruth had come to St. Aidan's as a postulant. The gloom evoked by the marble hall with its dark paneled walls and lurid painting of martyred virgins ascending heavenward was countered by Agnes. The novice's white veil and tight linen coif had made her cheeks glow, and the wide space between her teeth gave her a mischievous look that no religious decorum could obliterate. "I think Mother Columban thinks my teeth will grow closer together if I obey the Rule," Agnes had sighed one difficult day.

Her smile was still there, but now her face was drained of color and her blue eyes were tired, and there was an unhealthy yellowish tinge around the pupils.

"Please don't look like that." She reached out and shook Ruth's arm. "I hate people being sad—you most of all, now that you've returned to us." She paused. "Have you any idea how wonderful it is to have you back? Not just me—everyone feels that way. Did Rosalia tell you they wanted to give you a party when you arrived? I think she talked them out of it. She thought you'd rather just come in quietly. Aidan and Gregory, of course, were ecstatic. Daryl, too, as you can imagine. She's away at a music convention. She should be home in a few days. And you can imagine what it was like for me and Joanne and Rosalia."

Ruth fumbled for an answer. To say, It's wonderful to be back, was a cliché to which she couldn't descend, especially with Agnes. But Agnes immediately caught her hesitation.

"Please don't feel you have to say anything. I just wanted you to know how we feel."

"And I'd like you to know how I feel, but I'm not quite sure I can make a statement about it."

"Confused?"

"Not confused about wanting to be here."

"Confused about what we've become." Agnes phrased it not as a question but as a declaration. "Is that the hardest thing for you, finding the old order gone? I would have expected you to come sailing through."

What do I find hard? Ruth wondered. Certainly she did not yearn for those narrow, silent days when all human choice was vested in the Rule, the Daily Order, or the superior, when even the simplest human communication was subject to obedience.

"I'm so glad things have changed—for your sake," Rosalia had said. "Most of us were too young when we entered to do anything except what we were told. But you were older, you had finished college. It must have been dreadful."

Had it been dreadful? After her initial loneliness, she didn't remember being unhappy except in those months following her mother's death. It was, as she had said to Kate Boylan, a question of expectation. She had freely chosen St. Aidan's, chosen it be-

cause religious life had seemed to her then the most perfect way
to dedicate herself to God. She had expected it to be difficult:
expected that the demands of obedience would run counter to her
own desires, expected that she would yearn for those things she
used to call her own, expected that she would experience that
loneliness that comes of forfeiting the right to love and be loved
with exclusive commitment.

It had been the joys rather than the difficulties that had
surprised her. She found she loved the exuberance, the candor, the
steady determination of her companions—Rosalia, Agnes,
Joanne. The older nuns, too, in a different way, by their example
and solicitude, had supported and sustained her. She had loved
the quiet hours of study, the inviolable time set aside for prayer.
That had seemed to her like a marvelous luxury, coming as she
did from a world where snatching a quiet hour demanded rare
skill and perseverance. But there was something far deeper than
any of that—a feeling of unity, a sense of purpose, aimed at so
steadily that it had sometimes made her dizzy. She had read
Kierkegaard and Camus and Sartre and rejoiced that the absurdity
and meaninglessness they pondered would never touch St.
Aidan's. Here they served an immutable God, whose will, steadily
obeyed, would sanctify them. They were safe, they were told,
with the infallible prescriptions of a Rule to protect them. They
lived with a single focus—"like the angels," her father had
commented with a quizzical smile that she had not understood.

And even when their efforts to live angelically had worn
them to depression, when their closeness had set them at odds
with each other, they had had the reaches of worship to set them
free from their own limitations and immerse them in the splendor
of adoration. Their chapel—with its aspiring arches and brilliant
stained-glass windows, its marble sanctuary and rich ornaments
—had provided them with a beauty that compensated for their
small unpainted cells and the dismal bareness of their common
rooms. Even that austerity she had loved, glorying in the fact that
all the beauty that they knew was vested in the worship of God.

"I'm sorry, I didn't mean to put you on the spot." Agnes broke the silence.

"It's all right. I'm glad you asked. No, I don't miss the 'old order'—at least not most of it. I could never have returned if we were still under Mother Josephine's iron hand."

"Or Mother Mary David's velvet glove." She smiled, remembering that gentle voice with its barely perceptible lisp and frightening power to command.

"I'm not sure *what* I miss."

"You know you've come at an awful time, don't you?"

Ruth blushed. Agnes' question made her feel like an intruder, like a guest who has wandered indiscreetly into a family quarrel.

"Ruth, I'm sorry. I didn't mean it like that. What I meant was that we've had a rocky year and it's going to take a while to get back our equilibrium."

For a while they were silent and then Ruth asked, "How long has Marian been gone?"

"Just about a year. She told us just after school closed and left almost immediately."

"No one knew ahead of time?"

"I don't think so. I suppose she told the Council before she told the Community, but I don't think she told them until she had made her decision."

Ruth tried to imagine the shock of that announcement. For any professed religious to leave was difficult for the Community, but for their superior in whom they had put all their trust to do so would have been shattering.

"It must have been awful," she said at last.

Agnes nodded. "It was. Marian was the hope of St. Aidan's, especially for the older people. We thought for a while that Aidan would never recover from the shock. Her heart's not very strong anyway, and Marian was the apple of her eye."

And what had Marian suffered? Ruth wondered. What level of hopelessness had she reached that she could find no answer except to leave? The Marian Connell Ruth had known would have found such an action inconceivable. Her devotion to St. Aidan's had been almost a phobia. What had happened in those ten years to bring her to that point where she could no longer find life at St. Aidan's?

"I can't imagine what it cost Marian," she said finally.

"I know. I think of that and I wonder how responsible we were. We see only that she left us. We're still grieving over having been betrayed, but in some way we must have betrayed her, too. Everyone says she lost faith in us. But losing faith is a two-way street."

The sun had gone down and the sky was gray, shot through with the last streaks of pink. The afterglow. From where they sat the white crosses of the nuns' cemetery rose against the darkness. I had not thought death had undone so many, Ruth recalled, knowing that in some obscure way she numbered Marian among them. Wherever she was, whatever she was doing, something had died in her.

"She never explained what had gone wrong?"

"Oh, she explained. She even had a Community meeting. Some people were upset that she did it so publicly. They said it just made it harder on everyone. I don't know. Marian was always very direct. I think she had a right to do it the way she felt best."

"What did she say?"

Agnes' smile was wry. "You know, I'm not sure anyone can tell you exactly. Once she said she had asked for a dispensation from her vows, we were too shocked to hear the rest. She tried to make it seem very positive, of course. She would never speak against St. Aidan's. She said she had felt for some time that God was calling her to a new ministry for which her years at St. Aidan's had prepared her. She said how much she had learned from the spirit of the Community—its generosity, devotion to duty, zeal for its educational works."

"But it wasn't good enough for her." Ruth was surprised by the bitterness in her own voice.

"Oh, I think that's putting it too harshly. Marian had such hopes for St. Aidan's—for how we could move forward, for changes we could make in the school. She saw potential everywhere. At the beginning everyone felt her spirit. The day she was installed as superior was like Easter for St. Aidan's. She made everything seem possible."

"And then?" But Ruth knew the answer: then the sluggish weight of age and custom had held them back. The leadership they had welcomed so eagerly in theory had frightened them in practice. They wanted new life for St. Aidan's, but within the framework they had known. They clung to the known and the secure, and no power of leadership could move them.

"I don't blame her for leaving," Agnes said. "I think it was the only thing she could do. If she had stayed she would have had to compromise. Marian could never have been happy doing that."

They sat until the last pink flush disappeared and the white crosses were blurred, lost in the darkness.

Agnes shifted in her chair.

"Are you cold? Would you like to go in?" Ruth asked.

"I'm fine. I just have to move around a little. Perhaps I shouldn't have brought all that up. We don't usually talk about it. It just makes things harder." She paused. "Sometimes I envy Marian. I almost wish I could lose hope—if that's what Marian did. But I can't. I really believe in us, in St. Aidan's, despite all the things that are going wrong.

"Is the school really in such bad shape?"

"It certainly isn't thriving. That was one of the things Marian couldn't get us to face."

"Joanne seems in favor of closing the boarding school."

"I think it may come to that. God knows there's enough other work for us to do—just ask Kate."

"Kate's a very courageous young woman."

"Courageous and overworked. I wish there was someone to help her."

"She doesn't work alone at the camp, does she?"

"Not exactly. I guess she didn't mention Diane Gannon to you, did she?"

"She did mention a Diane who had left."

"Diane hasn't really left St. Aidan's; she's on a year's leave of absence. She and Kate are about the same age and they've been great friends. I feel bad about Diane. I can't believe she doesn't have a vocation."

"What happened?"

Agnes sighed. "Diane asked permission to work full time at the camp with Kate. The Council agreed but when the Community heard about it there was such a to-do that Rosalia revoked the permission. I understand why she felt she had to do it but it was the last straw for Diane. She was raging. I think she would have left permanently then and there but Kate persuaded her to take a year's leave instead."

"So she's working with Kate at the camp anyway. That must help."

"Yes, I suppose so, but it would be so much healthier if Kate felt she had some Community support. Of course, Peg Darcy would love to go. I think if we phased out the boarding school, she'd be off with Kate like a shot. We'd have to hire someone for the infirmary."

"And Angela Ferrato?"

"Angela's studying at the University."

"In?"

"A language program. She's fluent in Italian and now she's doing a bilingual program to prepare her to work with the Latin population in Whitethorn."

Angela, silent and aloof, ministering to the needs of a Hispanic population seemed an anomaly to Ruth. She would like to have known more but felt reluctant to ask.

Agnes shifted uncomfortably. "I guess I should go in. I have all my exercises to do before I go to bed. It takes me an eternity."

Ruth leaned her folding chair against the wall and turned to find Agnes groping for her cane. "Here, I'll get it."

"You'll have to give me a hand. We have to play One, Two, Three, Up a couple of times before I can make it."

Ruth had not realized how difficult it was for Agnes to move.

"I'll be O.K. in a minute. See, I *am* an old lady." And she shuffled a few steps, getting her cane into place.

Ruth latched back the outside door leading from the cloister into the antechoir, and the light spilled in a pool on the flagstone walk. Agnes leaned her cane against the wall and put her arms around Ruth. They stood for a moment, comforted and strengthened by each other.

Agnes turned, framed in light against the dark panels of the cloister door.

" 'Ubi caritas et amor Deus ibi est.' Do you remember your Latin?"

" 'Where there is love, God is to be found,' " Ruth translated.

"That's why I don't lose hope." She gripped her cane firmly. "No, don't come." Agnes stepped cautiously across the threshold. "I like to do some things alone."

Although the period of the novitiate ordinarily lasted for two years, in Ruth's case the regulations were waived, and September 8, just two months from the time of her entrance, was set as the date of her profession. She would, it was understood, make vows of poverty, chastity, and obedience for the term of one year. At the end of that period she would either make permanent vows or—should she wish to do so—she would be free to leave St. Aidan's.

Ruth had not expected the decision to make her temporary vows to be a difficult one; she had considered it implicit in her decision to return to St. Aidan's. But Marian Connell's leaving had shaken her. Over and over she rehearsed Agnes' account of that initial promise followed by—no matter how Marian chose to explain it—disillusionment. The questions that had arisen as Ruth listened to Agnes had not been answered: To what was she vowing her life? To God, yes, but to God through the Community of St. Aidan's. And what could that Community offer her in terms of guidance and support? The vision of the old St. Aidan's was slipping away, and it was not clear what would replace it. She had told Agnes that she did not want the past, but more and more in the last month she had realized that the past still bound her.

The others had eased gradually over the years into new ways, new liberties, while she had been catapulted into them. The patterns of prayer, of austerity, of enclosure that had defined her first years at St. Aidan's were still her models. Although intellectually she was free of them, psychologically she was still bound. It was a jolt to find a group gathered around the television late in the evening, to see a car taking off for a Friday night movie, to hear laughter in the rooms and corridors that had been places designated for the Great Silence.

> Their cloister will be their home. They will not go out except for grave necessity and then only with the permission of the superior. . . . They will read only those books and periodicals necessary for their work . . . hear only those radio programs which are of world concern or of educational interest. . . . They will speak but little and never near the chapel nor in the corridors or cells of the religious.

Their lives had been regulated in every detail. The Rule was like a mariner's chart, worked out in the beginning in wisdom and experience. It indicated the sandy shoals, the hidden rocks; it detailed the shoreline, gave the mathematics of low tide and high tide, provided information on dangerous currents and sudden winds. If it was obeyed, they were told, even the frailest craft need not founder.

But with the passage of years, the earth's surface had changed and the waters with it. The shoals had shifted; water that had been deep enough to float a boat had grown shallow. Little by little the currents had changed; rocks once clearly visible now lay dangerously under water. The mariner's chart, meticulously detailed, had not been infallible. It had failed to account for the imperceptible drift of time, so that in the end they had been charting their course by that most dangerous instrument: an obsolete map.

She knew all this and honored it. Her greatest surprise was, in fact, to find how strong the pull of the old order was on her. She knew she could not force the change in herself. She needed time, and the year of temporary vows would provide that time.

A week before her profession, Kate Boylan asked if she could talk to her about the music for the ceremony.

"I'm not in charge of music," she had explained. "That's Daryl's job, but Daryl and I—"

"Don't get along," Ruth supplied.

Kate nodded. "It's too bad, but Daryl and I are plugged into opposite currents." She paused. "You're a friend of Daryl's, aren't you?"

"I think so. At least I was before I left St. Aidan's."

"Do you *understand* her? Sorry. I probably shouldn't have asked."

"It's all right. I suppose I understand her a little better than you do. I was here when she entered. I know how hard it was."

How could she explain Daryl to Kate? Like Kate, Daryl had entered alone, but that was the only similarity.

Daryl had arrived two days after Christmas in a limousine so sleek and polished that it looked as though it had just slid out of the showroom. It had been driven by a liveried chauffeur. In the back sat Daryl Peters and her mother. Ruth, opening the visitors' door, had felt that she had been suddenly cast in a play for which she had no script. Daryl was like no postulant St. Aidan's had ever seen. Her hair was platinum with the slightest curl at the ends, her eyes were blue-violet. Generations of breeding had formed the slim shoulders, the high forehead, the delicate, firm cheekbones. Her dress was navy, tailored, and severe, but the magic of design had displayed, not hidden, her grace. Her mother was dressed with equal care. Costumes for a play called *The Postulant,* Ruth had thought.

But if Ruth had no script, Mrs. Peters and Daryl had been equally deprived. They had stood frozen, waiting for a prompter who failed to give them their cues. Finally, Ruth had ushered them in, seated them in the parlor, and called Mother Edwarda, then superior.

Mother Edwarda was at no time a conversationalist. For years she had been the treasurer and seemed only at home among her figures and accounts. When she had to speak to the Community her eyes were riveted on her notes. When dignitaries came to the convent she brought someone more articulate to the parlor with her. Daryl and Mrs. Peters had taxed her to the utmost. Mrs. Peters made no effort to take the hand Mother Edwarda offered, listened in silence to Edwarda's high, thin avowals of how glad they were to welcome Daryl, her explanations of what would be expected of the postulant for the next few months, her description of the regulations for visiting and writing home. Only when Edwarda offered to show them the chapel did Mrs. Peters break her silence: "We, in our family, are not Roman Catholic." With that sentence Daryl had been cast out, "orphaned," as she would say later, "by my own choice."

When, two years later, Ruth had left St. Aidan's, Daryl still had not been reconciled with her mother.

"You know," Ruth said to Kate in an effort at explanation, "Daryl has never seen her mother since she entered."

Kate scowled. "That must be awful, but it's not all up to her mother. Daryl makes it so hard for herself. She's so uncompromising about everything."

"You don't strike me as a great compromiser yourself."

Kate laughed, and when she did her eyes brightened and

some of the tight lines softened. "Oh, I know. It's so crazy. We both just dig our heels in. I hope it won't always be this way. I admire Daryl very much. But she has such exalted ideas!"

"I know." Ruth remembered one of the rare talks they had had when Daryl was a novice.

"I wanted to take the name Lucie," she had confided, "because it means light. I want to be like that—simple and clear and transparent as light."

Ruth had been touched—and frightened—by the heights she envisioned. Daryl had been one of those who had aspired to "live like the angels." Her favorite saint had been John of the Cross, with his terrifying austerities and his passionate songs of encounter with divine love. She had found in him, she had told Ruth, the motto of her own religious life: "Descubre tu presencia"—Reveal Thy presence to me. But whatever romantic vision Daryl had of religious life, there had been nothing unreal in the way she had lived her life at St. Aidan's. She was generous, an excellent teacher, faithful to all the prescriptions of the Rule. But in the two or three conversations they had had since Ruth's return, that single-minded enthusiasm was noticeably lacking. Daryl seemed at once dispirited and frenzied.

"Daryl, dear, do take it easy," Nancy had said to her one night as they were finishing the dishes together; but Daryl continued to shove the heavy trays into the dishwasher with savage impatience.

"What's happened to Daryl?" Ruth asked Rosalia later.

"I don't know. I can't cite anything specific. She's always where she's supposed to be, but she never seems entirely present. I feel as though Daryl is straining away from us."

"Is she fed up with teaching now that the school has grown smaller?"

"If she is, she's never admitted it. If anything, she's more devoted. As a matter of fact, she and Kate had a row one day about Kate's work."

"She doesn't approve of migrant worker camps?"

"She doesn't approve of Kate's being away from St. Aidan's so much."

Ruth laughed. "I'm afraid they're doomed to tangle. Daryl's a patrician and Kate's a peasant."

"Ruth!"

"It's true. Daryl will probably always be a bit of a snob. I'm sure she doesn't want to be, but how could she help it? It's bred in the bone."

"But she's always been so meticulous about poverty and detachment. Daryl lives a very austere life even now." Rosalia was defensive.

"Of course. It's part of her mystique. She will have nothing but the best."

Rosalia sighed. "I suppose you're right. I wish Kate would be a little more understanding of her. I feel as though she baits her sometimes."

"And I'm sure Daryl more than returns the compliment."

In fact, in the months she had been back at St. Aidan's Ruth had found Daryl unexpectedly difficult and querulous, while she had grown to admire Kate's directness and generosity.

"About the music," Kate repeated, pulling Ruth back to their original topic. "You see, Daryl tries so hard to be fair with me that sometimes she goes overboard. I wanted you to know that, because she'll probably suggest that we have guitar music at your profession Mass. Of course I would enjoy playing, but I know it would mean everything to Daryl if she and Gregory could do something with organ and flute. There aren't very many opportunities for them these days, and I know they both miss it."

When Ruth approached Daryl, however, she met with little enthusiasm.

"I don't know what we could do." Daryl's frown was not encouraging.

"I wasn't thinking of anything elaborate." Ruth was annoyed that her suggestion should be turned into an imposition.

"What about one or two of the Latin hymns that used to be part of the profession ritual?"

Daryl's frown persisted; she made no concession. "I don't think we could sing any of them without practicing."

"Well, can't we practice?" Ruth could feel her own tone sharpen.

Daryl shrugged without answering.

Ruth gave up in exasperation. "I'll leave it to you then," she said and went up to her room annoyed and bewildered by a Daryl she no longer knew.

Rawlins and Swenson, Realtors
108 East 68th St.
New York, N.Y.
September 6, 1980

Mr. Alec Stafford
Stafford, Connor, Lipsky, Architects
18 Ballantyne Avenue
Glen Cove, New York

Dear Alec,

I hope you enjoyed your vacation. Nova Scotia is on our list for next year.

At last I've been up to see "Landsweep." It's well named. The land slopes upward from the road and the view from the house and especially from the gardens and orchard behind the house is very fine.

The mansion is situated about a half-mile in from the highway. The gatehouse at the entrance has been unoccupied but it's well built and could probably be renovated without too much difficulty. The entrance road is a disaster and must be even worse during the winter and the spring thaw. The mansion itself, however, is in excellent condition and the additional buildings for the boarding school are not bad. They are not, of course, built in the original style, but the design is fairly good and they would be ideal for your purpose. There is, as I mentioned earlier, about 350 acres in all. Only a small part of the gardens is still functional and the orchard is going to seed, but these are not major concerns for you.

Now, having whetted your enthusiasm, let me say that my chat with the Sister Superior (Sister Rosalia Dunne) was far from encouraging. I thought she would snatch at the possibility of selling the place. Instead, I got a very cool response. At first she thought I was interested in renting the school buildings and this seemed to interest her, but when I explained that we wanted to purchase the whole thing she cooled considerably. We had not even mentioned the subject of money, so there was no question of her simply holding out for more. Strangely enough she had apparently never thought of selling, although obviously the school is teetering.

She is a nice lady but scarcely a businesswoman. Hard to figure out why they would put someone like that in charge. At any rate, I kept pushing and she finally agreed to present the offer to the rest of the sisters. She was hardly enthusiastic and by the time I left I was practically apologizing. I can understand why selling what is, I suppose, to them the family estate would have its difficulties; but under the circumstances I should think they would jump at the chance to recoup their losses. The money they would get from the sale would be enough to fix them very comfortably in a smaller and more accessible place. I explained all this, of course, and she agreed; but something else was working there which I couldn't figure out.

So, Alec, there we are. At least the door is left open and perhaps we can count on the rest of the sisters having a little more practical sense—although if the two elderly ladies I saw walking around are any example, I doubt it. Sister Rosalia told me she would speak to the sisters before the end of September and would get in touch with me at once.

Now that I've seen the place I'm more anxious than ever to grab it up.

I'll be in touch.

Hopefully,

Steve Rawlins

6

Most first professions were occasions of triumphal celebration: the chapel crowded by parents, relatives, friends, even pupils from the school. But Ruth had begged off, pleading that she had no relatives to invite and assuring Rosalia that she would be far more comfortable with a simple ceremony at which only the Community would be present.

On the eve of her profession she started a letter to David to explain that the following day she would vow her life for a year at St. Aidan's. Except for the letter telling him when she was returning to the convent, they had not been in touch. Their easy comradeship had disappeared, as though her father's death had destroyed it. In place of the comfort she used to find in his presence she felt now a quick nervous energy that turned too easily to anger. It bewildered her and she shut her mind against it.

Now, as she tried to explain to him what her vows would mean, the old language of religious vocation came back to her. Although she knew it was no longer popular, she found a validity in it still.

"God's call," they used to say. The phrase had been orna-

mented with romantic images: child saints hearing "the call" at
their first communion and there and then consecrating their
"chastity" to God in angelic innocence; young maidens, pale and
pious, praying in a darkened chapel and hearing a divinely seduc-
tive whisper; "sinners" struck violently by a voice so impelling
that they staggered to the door of the nearest monastery. But once
the romantic imagery was cleared away, the fact of "the call"
stood clear and firm, a mystery erupting in the ordinary course
of human life. It was an inexplicable combination of the ordinary
and the mysterious. It was not simply a matter of human decision,
a choice made between butcher, baker, and candlestick maker.
The initiative was with the Other. What she was doing was, as
David had said, inconceivable on every level but that of faith in
a god of infinite mystery.

"Whoever would have thought we would have you back
with us," Gregory had said one day as Ruth helped her along the
corridor. "Dear, dear, we never know, do we?" And for a moment Ruth felt herself grow dizzy with the inexhaustible mystery hidden beneath the patter of Gregory's platitudes.

In the old order the eight days before vows had been filled
with the silence of the holy, with the translucent anticipation of
a wonderful thing, beyond comprehension, that would soon be
accomplished. "Be still and see that I am God," Mother Columban had instructed them, and she had done so with a heart
blissfully at peace. She had learned afterward that not everyone
had been so blessed, that for some the anticipation had been
opaque, dark, and frightening with the fear of what would be
exacted of them. In one of those rare moments when Mother
Columban's Celtic imagination was freed from the stern language
of duty, she had said to Ruth, "We are like pieces of amber,
rough and dull. We need God's light to transform us." Ruth had
cherished the image, rejoicing in her experience of that light.
Those days of silence, patterned by intervals of deeper silence in
which she swam in circles of light, had shaped her for years to
come. Her vow day had seemed almost an anticlimax. What was

to be done had already been done. The formula she pronounced at the public ceremony was only a pale affirmation of what had already taken place. Yet although she had dreaded the ceremony, expecting to feel stiff and shy, she found that it had thrilled her.

"It all sounds so dramatic," Peg Darcy had said, wrinkling her nose in distaste when they were planning Ruth's profession. But, Ruth reflected, religious vows *were* dramatic; and the dramatic ritual, refined through hundreds of years, had been appropriate: the solemn procession, the candles (long new ones for those to be professed—they were beyond the pinch of poverty on a vow day), the professed themselves accompanied by the full choir singing the ancient Latin hymn "Jesu Corona Virginum" —Jesus, Crown of Virgins.

When the long ceremony was completed they had risen in unison for the final hymn. "Te Deum Laudamus," they had sung, the sweep of the chant swelling in the unbroken rhythms that suggested the limitless sweep of eternity.

> You are God; we praise you.
> You are the Lord; we acclaim you.
> In you, Lord, is our hope,
> And we shall never hope in vain.

Gregory, eyes closed, black sleeves pinned high at the shoulder lest they impede the glory her fingers evoked from the organ, played in an absolute exultation of joy.

Their white veils, marking them as beginners, had been replaced by black ones, which they thought they would wear till the end of their lives. They had walked down the wide nave of the chapel, through the antechoir, still dazed by their eight days of prayer, austerity, and silence, and into the brilliant light of public congratulation.

This time she was spared the cruel transition. The ceremony was simple, straightforward, pedestrian in its outer trappings. There was no procession. She walked up the aisle with Rosalia, both looking, she thought, like reconstructed WAVES in their navy blue suits. The traditional vases of white lilies were replaced by two vases of pink and violet and purple asters from their garden, fixed by Agnes. There were new candles on the altar and the special candlesticks reserved for Christmas and Easter. Father Russell officiated, garbed in a white handwoven chasuble. It was Rosalia who posed the ritual question: "Ruth, what do you ask?" And she had answered in the simple formula she had always cherished: "The mercy of God and the grace to be received into the Community of St. Aidan's." It was Rosalia who gave her the crucifix of the Congregation and Rosalia who received her vows.

The music was, for the most part, hymns taken from their ordinary hymnals. Ruth had no quarrel with the hymns in themselves; they were tuneful, easy to learn, fine instruments for gathering a congregation together. They drew them into fellowship, but they did not make them soar. She had wanted a simple service, but she yearned for something—music, gesture, language —that would symbolize the majesty and mystery of God.

At the Offertory her yearning was acknowledged, for as she and Rosalia brought the bread and wine to the altar, Daryl, with Gregory accompanying her on the organ, played a section from a Bach flute concerto. It was, Ruth knew, their special gift to her; but Gregory, stiff with rheumatism, could no longer control the pedals. Her feet kept slipping, and too deaf to hear her errors, she played on with full volume. Daryl's clear tones were drowned by the heavy accompaniment; and finally, disconcerted by Gregory's erratic timing, she, too, lost control.

It was, Ruth thought later, the sign of their mortality: "Remember, man, that thou art dust." They would not live forever. Their bright hopes, their dreams, their human powers, would stiffen and grow old. Their own mortality they had always acknowledged; but the body of which they were a part, the form by which they lived, they had immortalized. Now that form, rigid and unwieldy with age, was dying; and Ruth mourned for it as one mourns for a parent who has brought one to life.

The incident had saddened Ruth, but it had rubbed Daryl raw. The next evening, for the first time since Ruth had returned to St. Aidan's, Daryl came to her room.

"We've lost everything," she raged. She had refused the chair Ruth offered and stood, her back straight against the door, as though, Ruth thought, she expected to be carried off to martyrdom. "Don't say we haven't, because you know we have."

Anger had made her very pale. Framed against the dark wood of the door, she looked almost insubstantial. Her skin was dull and taut, and the platinum hair, pulled tight against her ears, had lost its sheen. Of course she had aged; it was thirteen years since Ruth had ushered her into the convent parlor and watched the formal, controlled parting of mother and child. But thirteen years were not in themselves enough to extinguish so much light. She would not have been surprised had Daryl left St. Aidan's. From the beginning the price she had paid had been enormous. Ruth remembered the proud, unyielding mother who had said, "We, in our family, are not Roman Catholic." And she remembered the proud, unyielding daughter, the image of her mother in every feature, who had let that mother go. Even in her bereavement Daryl had been faithful. She had never complained. She had endured the Spartan quality of their common life: the discipline of time and energy, the poverty not simply of having nothing of one's own but of having nothing beautiful to color the empty spaces of one's life.

Suddenly Daryl left her place by the door and half sat, half knelt at the hassock near Ruth's chair.

"Please, Ruth, don't be angry with me." She reached out a hand to take one of Ruth's but Ruth did not respond to the gesture. She was too stunned by the imploring child's cry, addressed, she realized, not to her but to the mother she had lost.

"Why should I be angry?" She struggled to find the easy tone of conversation between adults, fighting against the role of mother in which Daryl had unconsciously cast her. "Daryl, what's happened? I hardly know you anymore you've changed so much."

Ruth had meant it as an invitation, but Daryl heard it only as an accusation.

"*I* haven't changed. It's St. Aidan's that's changed." The tone was contemptuous.

"In some ways," Ruth conceded, thinking of the cars, the televisions, the change in the daily schedule.

"In *all* the ways that matter. I didn't enter for *this.*" The final monosyllable was harsh with disdain.

"Why did you come?"

"I wanted to find God." All the anger was out of her voice and the words were almost inaudible.

"And He's no longer at St. Aidan's?"

"You know I can't say that. I'm sure other people find Him here."

"But you can't."

She shook her head, her hands covering her face.

To have sacrificed so much and hoped so high. No wonder the light had been extinguished.

After a few minutes Daryl looked up. Her sorrow had erased some of the harsh lines and she looked closer to the image of the novice Ruth had known.

"I think I'd better go," she said. "I can't talk about it any more tonight."

After Daryl left, Ruth took her sweater and went to walk in the enclosed garden behind the novitiate. The white blossoms of the clematis covered the stone wall and wound up the pillars at the end of the garden. The fragrance, cloying in the sun, was soft and pleasant in the evening air. It was late and the lights in some of the older nuns' rooms were already out. The heavy branches of the spruce trees obscured the path and it was colder than she had anticipated, but she was grateful for the fresh air.

She felt as though she had been sitting for a long time in a heavy, airless room, the kind of room she imagined a visiting room in a prison to be: the leaden atmosphere of confinement, the alternate panic and despair that one was locked in forever. And in Daryl's case for a crime of which she was innocent. No one had ever entered St. Aidan's with greater abandonment. The literal injunction of the Gospel had snapped the door closed behind her: "Unless one leaves father and mother for my sake, he cannot be my disciple." She had come seeking God, and in the first years at St. Aidan's she had found Him. She never spoke of what she had left; and after the first few weeks it was, for the most part, forgotten. The Community's keen eyes, experienced in judging postulants, could find few flaws in the latest aspirant. Gregory, who had been assigned to help her with her music, was charmed with her earnestness and impressed by her talent.

"She's a cut above me already," she had admitted in admiration. "She plays like the angels."

Was that the crime for which Daryl was paying so bitterly —playing like the angels? It was, Ruth reflected, precisely what she had tried to do. She had been forced to cut her ties with the past in an unnatural way, but instead of permitting herself the comfort of grief, she had fought to raise herself to a plane above the human.

> They must be dead to the world in order to live fully for Jesus Christ. Having left their families, they will not repine but will recognize in their religious communities the family provided by a loving providence.

The novitiate instructions only affirmed her uncompromising stance, for Mother Columban's spirituality centered upon an "otherworldly" god. The more they retreated from the "world" the more they belonged to God. The dichotomy was absolute.

The tragedy was that, having shaped her to its model, St. Aidan's had then taken on another form. The old dichotomy no longer held. Many of them had suspected it all along and had learned to juggle the polarities, but Daryl had never doubted. For her it was not simply a question of life-style or even philosophy. The God she worshipped, whose face she longed to see, was a god who dwelt beyond and apart and who had asked that in choosing Him she renounce everything else.

She was struggling now in the grief and anger of a double betrayal: her mother had abandoned her because she had chosen St. Aidan's, and St. Aidan's had abandoned the very ideal she had come to share.

In it all she had wanted only God, and now she did not know where He could be found.

Shortly after the opening of school, Rosalia posted a notice announcing a Community meeting on the following Sunday morning.

"I hope it's short," said Nancy Lenihan, taking a chair next to Ruth. "There's always so much to do at the beginning of school."

Joanne had come in and sat in front near the small table set aside for Rosalia.

Rosalia herself sat awkwardly, her straight skirt riding up to her knees, the blotches on her cheeks looking like the grotesque circles of a clown's make-up. The announcements she began with were merely routine: Kate would be working full-time with the migrant workers and in the Community center in Whitethorn; Ruth would be in charge of the library; Noreen would take a class of first-year Latin in order to lighten Agnes' schedule. The side door had been propped open several nights; would those coming in late be sure that it was securely locked? Dr. Lavelle had given them a donation of a hospital bed for the infirmary; would Sister Aidan like to write a note thanking him? That, said Rosalia, concluded the small business items.

Before she could continue Edwarda raised her hand. "Mother, can you tell us how the school is doing. I understand the registration is quite good." Edwarda was forever lobbying to maintain the boarding school.

Rosalia looked at Joanne to answer. "I think we'll have time to discuss it more fully another time." Joanne sounded brusque and impatient.

Rosalia looked around to see if there were other questions.

"I think we can begin then with the real business of this meeting." She reached for her glasses and began reading from a carefully prepared paper.

Joanne's hand was obvious throughout: in the careful historical résumé of the founding of St. Aidan's, its purpose, its goal; in the survey of present educational trends with their swing away from boarding schools. There was a chart showing the drop in enrollment and projecting the registration for the next five-year period.

Then in a style more her own Rosalia turned to the question of their basic purpose. "The students in our boarding school could find a comparable education in their own locality," she reiterated. This, she noted, raised the question of whether they were putting their resources to the best advantage. "Perhaps," she continued "we should think of what ministries would be available to us should the boarding school be discontinued." She pointed out the need for such work as Kate was involved in, assistance in the Hispanic community for which Angela was being trained, the need for adult education in the parishes at Whitethorn, and the needs of all kinds in the rural parishes.

"I have described our situation at some length," she concluded, "because I think it is important for us to look at it realistically in the light of what I am about to present to you.

"Several weeks ago I received a call from a Mr. Rawlins, a real estate broker in New York City, and the following week he came to see me." The rushes and lags that ordinarily characterized Rosalia's speech were gone. The words followed each other, evenly spaced, uninflected. She spoke like someone under hypnosis.

"He explained that he was representing a Mr. Alec Stafford, who had empowered him to make inquiries concerning the purchase of St. Aidan's."

The silence was neither ominous nor hostile. It was the silence with which one might, coming into a familiar room, confront a marauder armed with a deadly weapon. Surprise would for the moment delay the realization that the weapon was meant for oneself.

"I explained to Mr. Rawlins," she continued, "that I was simply the representative of the Community and could, of course, give him no answer. I told him that I would discuss the matter with you."

"Well, Mother," said Edwarda, speaking first, out of what she always presumed to be the prerogative of a former superior, "I think you should simply have told him no."

Edwarda had no patience with the democratic process. It was not only inept and inefficient; it was, as she had often told them, contrary to the basic principle of religious obedience. Had *I* been dealing with Mr. Rawlins, her tone said rebukingly, we wouldn't be sitting here now wasting our time.

"I didn't feel I had the right to do that without consulting you."

Edwarda's head shook with annoyance, but she said nothing.

"I'm sure it's something we have to consider," said Susannah, whose pattern it was to begin mildly and work to a crescendo. "I feel, however, that it would be an impossible situation. Now, these people would buy the school and we would have to live right next to them. I for one—and I think many feel the same way—need a certain amount of privacy. Goodness, it's bad enough the way the students get under foot. I don't know why they can't stay in the places provided for them."

Nancy groaned, foreseeing one of Susannah's long disquisitions on how the school had once functioned "when the students were properly disciplined." But Susannah did not pursue her usual topic; her interest was on the present situation.

"No matter how difficult things may be, I think we are far better off the way we are, and I would tell this gentleman so."

Kate had raised her hand, but Rosalia did not acknowledge

her. Instead she said, "Perhaps I have not made myself clear. Mr.
Rawlins was speaking of buying not just the school but all of St.
Aidan's."

The marauder had moved in closer and the deadly weapon,
they discovered, had been meant for them after all.

They sat lost in their isolation, groping for what these
words could mean. St. Aidan's was beyond buying or selling. It
was more than a place; it was an atmosphere, a way of life. It was
their sanctuary, holy ground. God had called them here. Even
Ruth, despite her years of absence, felt a great anger at having
such a possibility presented to her. Change, of course, but even
change must have its limits.

She saw them all caught up in sudden death: the older nuns
leaning forward, a hand grasping a crucifix, a rosary, a glass-case;
the others in more comfortable postures, an arm curved along the
frame of a chair, a leg crossed, a chin resting against a hand. She
could not look at them, nor could they look at each other. No
one could look at Rosalia. Ruth knew how irrational her fury
was, but that did not dispel it. "Kill the messenger, for he has
brought bad news."

On the other side of the room Anna Shaughnessey had
gotten to her feet. She stood breathing noisily, steadying herself
on the chair in front of her. Her lips, rarely relaxed, were drawn
downward in a grimace of anger. For the first time in her
fifty-two years at St. Aidan's she spoke aloud at a public meeting.
"May God forgive you," she said, the brogue thick on her
tongue. It was not a blessing but a cry of doom. She pushed her
chair away and walked unsteadily out of the room. They could
hear her heavy walk with its slight limp long after she had left.

Ruth saw Joanne move and thought she might be going to
end the meeting, but Rosalia shook her head and Joanne sat back.

It was Rita McClellan who broke the silence. "I think we
have to realize that Anna is upset," she began, "and rightly so.
That we should even put into words the possibility of"—she

caught herself dramatically—"of what has just been suggested seems to me to be a Great Betrayal."

Ruth had never understood Rita. She was often charming and witty, but her rhetoric could be insidious. Despite her forty years in America she still clung to a slight brogue. She thrived on dramatic situations, and lost causes had a special power over her. At the moment she had cast herself in the role of Savior of St. Aidan's.

". . . A Great Betrayal . . . the very institution which has shaped our lives . . . for almost one hundred years . . . Mother Imelda . . . that grand Irish lady . . . only one goal, one love . . . the sacrifices . . . the cold winters, the long journeys . . . all we have given . . . now our chance . . . no sacrifice too great . . . we must fight . . . we cannot give in. . . . And so," she concluded, "I feel that we must remain faithful to the ideals for which St. Aidan's was founded, and I consider it disloyalty of the most reprehensible kind to consider anything, *anything* which would run counter to the preservation of this house and school."

Almost before Rita had finished, Kate was on her feet.

"Two people have suggested that what Rosalia has done is a betrayal of St. Aidan's. I think this is very unfair. After all, she *is,* as she said, only the representative of the Community, and she does *not* have the right to make decisions of that nature by herself. I don't see what else she could have done but bring this offer before the Community."

"She could have sent that man packing, that's what she could have done." Susannah spoke in sharp staccato barks.

But Kate was not intimidated. "She had no more right to do that than to sell St. Aidan's. They are *both* decisions she's not empowered to make. She had an obligation to bring this before us, and I think we have a right to examine it." Kate's anger only sharpened her ability to speak with clarity and determination.

"And if you had a little humility, you'd know you have no right to speak here at all." Rita's tone was withering. For the first time Ruth saw why students sometimes begged not to be in Rita's class. "What have you ever done for St. Aidan's? Not a thing that I can see. You taught in the school when you had no choice, and as soon as you could you found a nice cozy job where you could go and come as you please. As far as I'm concerned none of this concerns you."

Ruth closed her eyes and leaned forward waiting for Kate's anger. But Kate did not answer, and they sat taut and silent in the circles of recrimination that Rita had generated.

It was Terezia who delivered them. Terezia Szabo had not come to St. Aidan's until 1964. She was then over forty with a remarkable life behind her. Born in Budapest, she had entered a Hungarian congregation that had been forced to disband during the war. She had subsequently worked with a refugee committee relocating families, reuniting children and parents, finding jobs and suitable housing for the destitute. Following the Hungarian revolution, she had emigrated to the United States. Free at last to live as she wished, she chose to return to religious life.

Her first connection with St. Aidan's had been through Marian Connell, whom she had met at a meeting concerned with international students. Marian, impressed by her background, had asked her to come to speak to the sisters about her work in Hungary. She had fascinated them not only by what she had experienced but by her keen spiritual sense. When, however, six months later she had asked to be accepted into the Congregation, their enthusiasm waned.

"I admire her deeply, *deeply*," Rita had reiterated, "but she will not fit in." And her opinion was seconded by a large segment of the Community.

"She will be very lonely here, poor thing," Edwarda warned, in the tone of pity she reserved for foreigners and pupils with "undesirable" backgrounds.

But Terezia was not discouraged. St. Aidan's reminded her of her convent in Budapest and she was determined to become part of it.

"They're afraid you will feel like an outsider," Marian had explained, but Terezia simply shrugged.

"I have always been an alien," she said. "I do not expect, as you say, to 'fit in.' "

And in many ways she had not. Experience and education had given her a sophistication for which the Community of St. Aidan's was no match. She was sometimes arrogant, sometimes argumentative. She had told Rosalia quite bluntly that she thought she was innocent and naive. They were qualities Terezia had shed long ago, yet there was about her an impressive wisdom and integrity.

"I think," Terezia began, "I think this morning is very sad. We are dividing into armies. You speak of the goals and history of St. Aidan's. You know that, though I am not so long here as some of you, I also love very much St. Aidan's. But it is not to St. Aidan's we have consecrated our lives. It is to the kingdom of God. So perhaps St. Aidan's will not continue. We will feel this sorrow, yes, but the kingdom of God will not end with St. Aidan's. Perhaps God has for us a new work He wishes us to do; but to do that one must sacrifice, one must compromise a little with the past, and that is very difficult. Change is not death. It is the other way around. I do not know what this Mr. Rawlins of New York City has in mind. Perhaps it will not be a good thing for St. Aidan's, but I think with Kate that we should examine it."

Rita was on her feet again. "I am appalled that we are willing to enter into these shameful negotiations."

For the first time Rosalia spoke. "There is no need to proceed any further if the Community is unanimous in rejecting Mr. Rawlins' proposal. However, if there is anyone who feels we should examine it, then I think we must leave the discussion open."

"I wish to examine this proposal." The antagonism between Rita and Terezia was palpable.

"Are there others who wish to discuss it further?"

Several hands went up.

"Then I think we must do so."

As she spoke, the chapel bell began to ring the noon An-gelus. Rosalia looked at her watch. "I'll post a notice for the time of the next meeting. Instead of going to chapel, we will say the Angelus here."

She began the familiar prayer and they echoed her, but their voices lacked substance; and when they filed out of the Commu-nity room it was in silence. On the far wall Lydia Walker's flamboyant painting looked curiously dislocated.

That afternoon Ruth, Daryl, and Rosalia walked up past the gardens and into the orchard. It was not unseasonably cold, but a sudden frost the week before had killed many of the plants. They lay now limp and dull beside the cornstalks. Ruth hated this foretaste of winter—the mountains harsh and dark, not softened even by mist. Everything shows, she thought: the mis-shapen branches, the knobbed trees, the crooked furrows in the garden, the matted, disheveled crows' nests. The green life of summer had hidden all the imperfections, but life had dropped away like an illusion and now the distortions, the imperfections were bared.

A world naked for judgment. Is this what God sees when He sees the world? And loves it? she wondered, repelled at the slime on the frozen stems of the peonies, the dark downward turn of the rhododendron leaves.

"Aren't you cold?" Rosalia asked Daryl, reaching over to feel the thin wool of her sweater.

"No." Daryl's voice was curt.

Ruth knew that tone, that ambivalent cry for help that would let no one near.

Rosalia shoved her hands deep in her sweater pockets. "I should have brought my gloves. My hands don't hold up under the cold."

"Chilblains still bother you?" Ruth asked.

"Sometimes."

"We had a bad winter in the novitiate and Rosalia got a terrible case of chilblains," Ruth explained to Daryl, trying to ease the distance between them.

"That's too bad." Her voice was flat and uninterested; but with an effort to respond, she added, "I suppose they're very painful."

"Yes, they can be. I guess there's nothing much you can do for them, is there Rosalia?"

"No, nothing much," Rosalia echoed, kicking a stone out of the path.

They walked, locked in silence, unwilling to keep up the vacuous conversation, unable to face the issue that had dulled them. The frost had caught and withered them, too. They came to the end of the orchard and stood at the wooden gate leading into the woods.

I'm sorry Daryl is here, Ruth thought. It would be so much easier if Rosalia and I could talk alone. But no, she contradicted, it's good for her to be here, to see how Rosalia agonizes over all this. And it's not simply the support of friendship Rosalia needs now; she needs the support of our common bond.

She turned. She would have liked to look directly at Rosalia to support her with something other than words, but Rosalia was hunched over staring at the ground.

"I'm sorry, Rosalia. It was a terrible meeting."

Rosalia straightened. Her nose was red with cold and her forehead and cheeks covered with blotches. Her lips trembled as she nodded.

"I can't believe," she started, then turned away, her hand rubbing the spots on her cheek. "I can't believe that they could think that . . . they would really believe that I could . . . that I would ever . . ."

"They don't. It was only that they had to find a scapegoat."

"Maybe I did it badly. I never put things very well." Her sigh was like a sob.

"You said what you had to," Ruth defended. "There wasn't

any way to cushion the shock. You couldn't save us from facing up to the issue sooner or later."

Rosalia shook her head stubbornly. "I'm not a leader. I never have been. I don't know why they elected me."

"But they *did* elect you."

Rosalia was beyond comfort. She shivered beneath her heavy sweater. "We need Marian Connell. She could pull us all together. She always did."

Ruth reached to take Rosalia's hand, but she made no response. "Rosalia." She felt as though she were talking to a child. "It isn't going to do any good to keep thinking how Marian would have managed. You'll manage in your own way. You have to count on that."

Rosalia made no answer but turned to walk back toward the convent. When they reached the back entrance she said, "I won't be at supper. I'm going out for a drive."

"Would you like me to come?" Ruth called after her. But the grating of the garage door drowned out her question. As Daryl and Ruth hung their sweaters in the back passageway they heard the car swing around the laundry and turn onto the drive leading to the highway.

Rawlins and Swenson, Realtors
108 East 68th St.
New York, N.Y.
October 2, 1980

Mr. Alec Stafford
Stafford, Connor, Lipsky, Architects
18 Ballantyne Avenue
Glen Cove, New York

Dear Alec,

I've been up to "Landsweep" again. It's absolutely glorious there in the fall. I'm convinced we have to get that place for you.

This time I had quite a long talk with Sister Rosalia. She's a very nice lady—a little shy but candid and direct. I think if I were just dealing with her the whole transaction would be relatively simple; but I have the feeling not only of a hidden agenda but a whole hidden population. This time one of the older sisters (swathed in black from stem to stern) opened the door for me —definitely a chilly encounter. She told me her name was Edwarda but she wasn't for keeping up a conversation. She looks like wax; I think they must have kept her in a closet for years.

Sister Rosalia told me she had met with the community and presented my offer. Apparently they weren't too happy but they did not reject it. The next step is a series of meetings in which they will come to some resolution. I feel sorry for the lady; she is definitely under a lot of pressure. They have an interesting background, which accounts, I think, for their determination to hold on to St. Aidan's.

I think I told you that the original nuns had come over from Ireland under a Mother Imelda Finney. In their flourishing years they started three or four other convents through the western portion of the state. Communication was, of course, difficult and little by little they grew independent of each other although still under the authority of the main convent in Ireland. Although, as I understand it, there is still some juridical bond among the houses in this country, there are no practical connections. Until the war they continued to receive Irish sisters, but after the war vocations were plentiful from this country and by that time they had grown used to being on their own. In 1947 the decision was made to break with Ireland. It was, apparently, a peaceful arrangement. Any of the Irish sisters was free to return and, I gather, many of them did. The result was that for those who stayed St. Aidan's became their world. Except for the most unusual circumstances, no one went back to Ireland, nor was there any exchange among the convents in the States. This makes their feeling about losing St. Aidan's much more understandable. I, of course, feel they would be a lot better off to sell—and we'll certainly be better off if they do.

Sister Rosalia told me she had scheduled a meeting of her council next week and that following that the issue would be reopened to the rest of the sisters. I tried to push for some target dates but she was reluctant. She's afraid, she told me, of trying to move things too fast. She agreed, however, that if they are going to sell, pupils' parents should be notified by mid-January. That at least gives us some sense of closure. This time we did talk money and I told her I would send her all the necessary information about the financial transaction so she can go over it with their lawyer.

So, there it is. I may not hear again until they make their decision. In general, Alec, I think we can be hopeful.

Best,

Steve Rawlins

7

What had happened could not be repaired. The friction they had faced over cloister or dress or the obligations of poverty had only touched the petals. This was the canker in the rose.

Years of self-control enabled them to maintain an unruffled surface. They ate together, sat next to each other in the chapel, commented on the evening news, discussed minor problems in the school. But the atmosphere was like a dry storm, dense and dark, with the sultry smell of thunder. There was no appeasing rain, only the apprehension that the lightning might come closer. Their conversation was dry and empty, a means to distance themselves and their fears.

It was, of course, each other that they feared. For their fate was no longer in the hands of one person but in the decision of the group. Fear made them harsh and they judged not out of remembered fellowship but out of anger and terror that others —fallible, weak, myopic—would shape their destiny.

Of them all, Anna Shaughnessey was caught most hopelessly in the sentence of execution. She no longer came to meals but ate whatever was left over, standing in the kitchen, her plate in her hand. At Mass she sat in the farthest pew, not answering the responses, not singing the hymns. She worked in the garden long after dusk, bringing in the last of the potatoes, carrying huge baskets of squash and pumpkin into the barn. She dismissed the boy who helped her after school and, when Joanne protested, turned without a word and left the kitchen.

"She'll kill herself," Nancy Lenihan said to Ruth as they watched Anna haul her old-fashioned lawn mower into the garage.

"Have you been able to talk to Anna at all?" Ruth asked Rosalia as they sat in her office about a week after the meeting.

"I tried."

"And?"

"She turned away. I can't force her to listen to me."

"She looks dreadful. I never thought I'd say Anna looks gaunt, but she does."

Rosalia nodded. "I know."

"Isn't there anyone she talks to?"

"Oh, Aidan occasionally. She worshipped Mr. Fitzgerald. And . . ." Rosalia hesitated.

"And?"

"She used to talk to Marian Connell. Marian was Mother Mary David's protégée, so for Anna it was a royal line of succession."

"She's lost everything, hasn't she? Has she ever said anything about Marian?"

Rosalia smiled wryly. "Not to me. I'm the usurper. Anna should have gone back to Ireland when we broke from the Mother House. It's hard for me to forgive Mother Mary David for keeping her here."

Ruth frowned. "How could she keep her? Anna had the right to make her own decision, didn't she?"

"Theoretically, but Mother Mary David didn't encourage practical freedom. I don't imagine she told Anna she couldn't go, but I suspect she played rather heavily on her loyalty to St. Aidan's."

"And to Mother Mary David."

"Of course. That was obedience. Gregory told me one day that the year before the break Mary David told Anna she would help bring her mother over."

"What happened?"

"Mrs. Shaughnessey was too sick to make the trip."

Ruth shook her head and started to get up.

"Don't go, Ruth. There are a couple of things I'd like to talk to you about. First of all, I can't tell you how relieved Joanne is that you've taken over the school library. We had hired someone part-time but it never really worked out, and then she took a pregnancy leave in January. Since then the library hasn't had any real supervision. Edwarda offered to help out but that was a disaster. She drove the girls crazy and I'm afraid they baited her. One of the weakest points on our state evaluation last year was our inadequate library facilities."

"I rather enjoy it. It's such a mess that there's real satisfaction in bringing some order to it. I don't think anything's been catalogued for the last two years."

"Probably not." Rosalia hesitated. "Do you think it will be a full-time job once you have it in order?"

Ruth was surprised. "I don't know," she said. "It could be, I suppose, depending on how much use the teachers want to make of it. Why? Is there something else you'd like me to do?"

"I was hoping that sometime this year you could do something with the archives. We've talked about getting out a little booklet on the history of the Community, especially since our centenary is not too far off. The archives are teeming with material—letters, documents, old photographs, even a few diaries —but no one has ever stopped to sort them out. Most of the stuff is in trunks and cartons in the little room behind the library. Susannah is always offering her services, but I'm terrified that zeal to keep St. Aidan's memory untarnished would make her discard anything uncomplimentary. When she finished we'd have highly laundered archives."

Ruth laughed. "I'm sure you're right. She'd feel she should canonize everyone from Mother Imelda on down. Rosalia, I'd love to help with the archives, but frankly I won't be able to take much time from the library for the next few months."

"What if there were someone to help you?"

"You don't mean hire someone?" Ruth was aware that the budget was very close to the line.

"No." Rosalia hesitated, turning her pencil slowly in her hands and then putting it determinedly on her desk. "Angela Ferrato is coming home from the University."

Ruth frowned. "But she hasn't finished her degree?"

Rosalia's eyes remained on her pencil. "No." Again she hesitated. "She's decided not to continue. She's arranged to work with Kate two or three days a week, but I thought the rest of the time she might work with you. There's no opening for her to teach languages in the school just now."

"But I thought she was going to finish her program in January."

"She was."

"But why would she . . . Sorry, I probably shouldn't ask."

"It's all right to ask, but I can't give you an answer. I thought it was strange that she came home that weekend we were having the meeting. She usually says she can't take time from her studies. She told me that evening that she would prefer not to continue the program."

"That's all?"

Rosalia nodded.

Ruth remembered her first impression of Angela as she had stood silent and withdrawn in the inviolable circle she had created around herself. Working with Angela would not be altogether easy.

"Of course," she answered, "I'll be glad to have her in the library."

"And one more thing. Would you act as secretary at our Council meetings? Joanne's been doing it, but I'd like to relieve her. And now that we'll be talking about the future of St. Aidan's I want to be sure we have accurate minutes."

It was the first time Rosalia had said anything about the proposal to sell St. Aidan's since the Sunday of the meeting.

"I suppose everyone's been talking about why I haven't done anything more. I couldn't for a while." She was playing with the paperweight on her desk, turning the clear glass over in her fingers. When she looked up she said, "I even thought of resigning."

The bruises, Ruth realized, had gone straight through to the bone. "But you didn't," she said. She had meant it to be a compliment to Rosalia's steadfast courage, but instead it came out flat and banal.

"No." The paperweight had disappeared between her large nervous hands. "I thought we'd had enough of that for a while. It wouldn't have solved anything."

"It would have untied you from the stake."

"And left it for another victim. You were right when you said they needed a scapegoat—any scapegoat. No one could talk about selling St. Aidan's without getting bruised. In a way, it's a wonderful tribute to their loyalty and devotion. We'll have a Council meeting Thursday evening here in my office," she continued.

"Is there anything I can do to help prepare for it?"

"I don't think so. Joanne has put together more information about the state of the school and has looked into other educational possibilities." She hesitated and then added, "I've seen Mr. Rawlins again."

For a moment Ruth thought she was going to say something more, but instead she smiled, a tired smile. Even the shy, hopeful smile had been bruised. When Ruth left the office, Rosalia was still turning the paperweight over and over in her hands as though out of that clear glass sphere she would find an answer.

Thursday had been rainy and toward evening the fog had swept down, hiding the hills and even the orchard behind the house. When they met in Rosalia's office it was already dark and the lamps on either side of the room had been turned on. Rosalia sat at the head of the table, flanked by Joanne and Ruth. On either side were Susannah Molloy and Peg Darcy. At the far end, her face shadowed by the light, sat Magdalen Richards. Two of the Council had been elected (Joanne and Susannah) and two appointed by the superior (Peg and Magdalen), according to the new rules for government.

Rosalia, awkward at the recent custom of spontaneous prayer, took refuge in an invocation they knew by heart:

> "Come, Holy Spirit,
> Send forth your light.
> Come, Father of the poor,
> Come, Giver of gifts,
> Lighten our burden.
> Console us in our sorrow."

Rosalia's voice, sometimes harsh and uncertain, was steady and resonant. The purity of her desire had freed her from constraint and she called them to prayer with an insistence that brought new meaning to the familiar words. They sat in silence for a few minutes, a healing silence brought to them by prayer. It was hard to pull themselves from those deeper longings to the practical business that had to be settled, for it was here, they knew, that they might founder and split.

"Although we have never actually faced the situation in the boarding school, I think we are all aware that even if Mr. Rawlins had never made his proposal we would have to make some drastic changes."

No longer absorbed in prayer, Rosalia's voice had resumed its normal tone, and the bond that prayer had established began to unravel. No one looked at her. Joanne had opened her folder of notes and was absorbed in them; Magdalen's face was lost in shadow; Susannah stared straight ahead, her small round mouth shaped into a pout. Only Peg Darcy, her eyes direct and questioning, faced the group.

"I'm going to turn the meeting over to Joanne, since as principal she's better equipped than I to discuss this." She nodded in Joanne's direction.

Joanne straightened the papers in front of her until they were aligned perfectly.

"Barring a miracle," she began, "I think we must face the fact that it is no longer feasible to continue a boarding school at St. Aidan's."

Susannah's mouth pursed but she said nothing.

"This has nothing to do with the quality of the school," she continued. "As boarding schools go, St. Aidan's is more than adequate. The fact is that the trend is away from such institutions. Most parents are not willing to spend the money to send their children away to school now that transportation is no longer a problem even in rural areas. However, Catholic schools in this area are not altogether adequate and there is the possibility of our building up a day school here that would provide an option for Catholic families in the area."

"St. Aidan's has always been a boarding school." Susannah's statement was a command for the future.

"But times change, Susannah," Peg remonstrated.

"You know nothing about it." She turned on Peg as though she had committed a breach of faith. "That was Mother Imelda's purpose in founding St. Aidan's. If you had taken the trouble to learn the history of this Community, you'd know that. It's all quite clear in the original documents."

"But that was a hundred years ago."

Ruth winced at Peg's blunt disregard of tradition. Susannah, terrified by the chasm that was opening before her, shrank into the past, the only security she had left. Her voice came sharp and uneven.

"Perhaps it was, but when Mother Mary David came here in 1932 as our last superior from Ireland, she affirmed *in writing"* —Susannah underscored the words—"to the General Council at Clonmeath that the primary mission of this Community was to maintain a boarding school that would educate its pupils to the faith and fit them for their roles as Christian wives and mothers."

> The pupils of St. Aidan's will be accepted from good Catholic families. The sisters will act as mothers to them, undertaking their training and education, instilling in them a knowledge of virtue and the practice of good works. They will have classes in suitable secular subjects, in Christian doctrine, in deportment, etiquette, and those accomplishments (vocal and instrumental music, painting, elocution) which will enable them to take their places as accomplished mistresses of households and mothers of their children.

In the novitiate, under Mother Columban's unerring supervision, they had memorized such documents, rejoicing that they were called to such an exalted mission. But to Peg, who did not share their background, they meant no more than any ancient document—a description of the first anesthesia or the original spinning jenny—an interesting and valuable achievement in its day but not a model on which to base one's life. But Susannah had based her life on it, had given her life to sustaining the dream, and now could find no life beyond that dream.

"Everybody has to suffer through change," Kate had said brusquely one evening when they had been discussing the Community meeting. "I don't understand why nuns always think they're exempt from the human condition."

Kate was right, of course. They had considered themselves exempt. It was, they had been told, part of "the hundredfold"— one of those consoling Gospel maxims that guaranteed certain inalienable benefits. You were assured of always doing God's will ("You need never wonder about God's will, Sisters. The Rule and the voice of your superior will guide you at every turn"), and in some mystical way you were also assured of a certain immutability. "Jesus Christ, yesterday, today, the same forever," St. Paul had proclaimed; and by some imperceptible distortion they had read, "St. Aidan's, yesterday, today, and the same forever."

"No one wants to sacrifice the original purpose of St. Aidan's." Rosalia's hands were clasped so tight that the nails had gone white. "But I think we have to ask ourselves if Mother Imelda herself—and Mother Mary David—would not rethink its purpose if they were alive today."

She had hoped to elicit some affirmation from Susannah, but Susannah was immovable in her refuge of silence.

Impatiently, Peg spoke up. "I'd like to ask Joanne if she really believes that starting a day school would be a successful venture."

Joanne hesitated and the hesitation was its own answer. "I don't know, Peg. I don't see how we can answer that until we try."

But Peg persisted. "I know you can't give us predictable figures, but you must have a feeling."

"I wouldn't have suggested it if I didn't think there was some chance of success."

"But you're not enthusiastic."

Again Joanne hesitated. "No, I suppose I'm not. The school board has been talking about expanding the high school and building a junior high. That will take a couple of years, but if it goes through I doubt if we would have much of a chance."

"Then what would be the point?"

But before Joanne could answer, Susannah, her color deepening, turned on Peg. "The point, young lady, would be that we would keep St. Aidan's." Susannah was used to keeping school-girls in their place.

"I guess that's really the point I'd like to get at: Is keeping a school here at St. Aidan's our first priority? Oh, I know," she said, nodding toward Susannah, "that that was our original mission. But things are different now. Mother Imelda was filling a need for her day when she set up St. Aidan's, but if we're not needed here now . . ." Peg shrugged and her voice trailed off.

Susannah's breathing was uneven and her voice came in rushes of sound. "You've never been interested in the school since the day you came here." Rosalia reached out her hand but nothing could stop her. "If St. Aidan's doesn't mean anything to you then why don't you pack your bags and go and let the rest of us who *do* care make the decisions."

Peg was scarlet but she said nothing. Throughout the discussion Magdalen had not raised her eyes, but now she looked up, nodding at Peg. In profile her regular features gave her the detached formality of a medallion.

"Perhaps it might help all of us to look for a moment at our original Rule."

The thin book, its black plastic cover cracked at the edges, its spine weakened by use, fell open to the first chapter of the Rule.

> Let the sisters live like the Israelites, sandals on their feet, staves in their hands, ready to journey wherever God shall lead, remembering that they have not here a lasting city but are to seek one that is to come.

Magdalen's voice, cool, assured, compelled them to hear every word in its full meaning. The words that for years had been read to them once each week until they had become empty sounds devoid of significance now rang like chimes, the melody hanging in the air long after the carillon had finished.

> Trusting in God, therefore, they will not hesitate to leave their convent or even their country should they be called to do so by the needs of the poor or the request of the church. Let them go

forth with firm faith, recalling that it is Truth Himself who has
assured them that not a sparrow falls without His providential
care.

Suddenly the room was stiflingly hot and for a moment
Ruth thought she was going to faint. Joanne reached behind her
and pushed the casement window open. The night air was sharp
and acrid with the smell of burning leaves. They continued to
sit motionless. The ancient Rule had caught them up in a vision
they had forgotten. Of course St. Aidan's was not their life. The
call to found it had been a call to leave home and country. That
had been Mother Imelda's call and now, perhaps, their own
moment of exile had come.

"Bearing in mind what Joanne has told us about the future
of the school and in the light of the passage Magdalen has read,
it seems to me that we have an obligation to look more closely
at Mr. Rawlins' proposal and what it might entail for us." Ruth
was not sure she had the right to speak, since she was not, strictly
speaking, a member of the Council; but she felt that someone had
to move them into the next phase of discussion.

Susannah's sharp intake of breath sounded like an aggrieved
sob but she said nothing.

"Is that agreeable with everyone?" Rosalia asked.

They nodded.

"When I spoke to Mr. Rawlins last week he explained to
me that Mr. Stafford, for whom he is acting, is a New York
architect who is an authority on nineteenth-century architecture
and decoration. For some time he has wanted to purchase a
mansion constructed in Gothic Revival style. He hopes to set up
a school, a training center for apprentices who would be trained
in preservation and restoration techniques."

Rosalia looked embarrassed. "To tell you the truth, I'm not
quite sure what that really means. He did explain, but I couldn't
follow it all. It was quite technical. At any rate, the apprentices
would live here at St. Aidan's—that's why he is so anxious to

get a place where all the staff could be in residence—and they would work under master craftsmen to restore the original mansion. Whatever changes we have made would be removed and the house returned to what it was when it was first built. This kind of restoration is very popular these days, he told me, and apparently St. Aidan's is one of the finest examples of Gothic Revival in the Hudson Valley. He has offered a very substantial sum, which, if we accept, would eliminate our financial difficulties for years to come."

"How do you know you can trust these people?"

"I don't, Susannah."

"And you're going to let some upstart swindler sweep us out of our home?" Susannah, always impatient, now leaped to the most damning conclusion.

"Of course not, Susannah. I would certainly ask the Council to meet with our lawyer, Mr. Sandler, and get his advice should we decide to pursue this proposal."

"I should think that would have been the first thing you would have done." The charge of incompetence was implicit.

"Not before consulting you." There was a firmness in Rosalia's voice that Susannah knew better than to cross.

"If we should decide to sell, then what?" Peg asked.

"First of all, anyone has the freedom to return to Clonmeath."

"The break with Clonmeath was over and done with thirty years ago."

"That's true, Susannah, but there is still a clause in our Constitution that states that in unusual circumstances any sister from St. Aidan's would be welcomed."

Susannah's cheeks were bright red. "Like a beggar. What way is that to go, telling them we don't have a place to lay our heads."

Peg started to speak, but Joanne frowned and she stopped.

"There is also the option of going to any of St. Aidan's daughter houses—St. Malachy's, St. Rose's, or St. Donald's. I know we've never exercised the option of exchanging subjects, but it is provided for."

Susannah's breath was coming in little angry puffs.

"What about the group as a whole?" Peg persisted.

Rosalia nodded toward Joanne.

"About a year ago," Joanne explained, "Father Nardecki over at Holy Rosary asked our help."

"Wasn't the school in that parish closed?"

"Yes, two years ago. The sisters who ran it were recalled the year before. The parish tried to staff it with lay people but that didn't work, especially when the parish boundaries shifted."

"He doesn't want us to start the school again?" Peg was exasperated.

"No. What he wanted were some sisters who would begin an adult education program that, if there was sufficient personnel, would expand into meeting other parish needs. At the time we had no one available."

"Are you suggesting we might move to Holy Rosary?"

"It's an option to consider."

Ruth, looking up from her notes, realized that this had become a dialogue between Joanne and Peg. Rosalia had deferred to what she considered Joanne's more competent handling; Susannah was punishing them all by her aggrieved silence; Ruth had been too busy with her notes to take part. What about Magdalen? Except for that powerful call to their original purpose, she had said nothing. The cameo profile had not moved. Her pencil, poised over her paper, kept its steady angle and wrote nothing.

Joanne turned to Ruth. "You probably don't remember Holy Rosary. It's the oldest parish in Whitethorn. Some of our nuns used to help with catechism there in the old days until they got their own school and convent. About ten years ago there was talk of several big companies moving into this area, and it seemed that Holy Rosary was in for expansion. There was a big development drive and Father Rafferty's first move was to do what he had promised twenty-five years before: build a convent for the nuns. Even before it was finished the businesses they had expected had decided to build on the other side of the river. The only change in Holy Rosary was that it grew smaller. Father Rafferty died the year after the nuns moved in—eight of them in a convent built for forty-five.

"There's been no one living there for the last two years. It's a lovely building, very well laid out. I haven't been through all of it, but I would imagine that it would be more than adequate for our needs. There's an elevator and a tribune overlooking the chapel on the second floor. There's a very comfortable solarium at both ends of the building and the rooms are individually air-conditioned."

As she pointed out the advantages, Joanne, even matter-of-fact Joanne, staggered in her recitation. Underneath the steady practical recital was the pain of understanding that nothing she described, no luxury she could promise would compensate for their loss. It was not elevators they needed or comfortable recreation rooms. They needed St. Aidan's with its dark halls and inadequate heating, its creaking floors and sporadic plumbing. They needed it for the comfort of the familiar. It had shaped them and in turn it bore the impress of their lives: the chapel steps worn thin toward the center where their processions had entered; the stone floor darkened under the holy-water font where they had stopped for a moment to make their act of faith; the dark wood of the prie-dieus faded where their hands had rested in prayer. It had absorbed in some way not only the imprint of their bodies but their identities. The fear that had shaken so many of them at the thought of selling St. Aidan's was the fear that they might cease to be. The fear of death.

Susannah's eyes were closed; her black cape moved in and out with the slow steady rhythm of her breathing. She might almost be asleep were it not for the nervous constrictions of her mouth.

"Of course"—Joanne cleared her throat unsuccessfully—"there is nothing like the grounds we have here. There's a garden and they've planted spruce trees around the convent to provide privacy. But altogether it can't be more than half an acre."

"And the work we would be doing?" Peg again, with the single-mindedness of youth, called them back to their task.

"There is more than enough of that." Joanne's voice had relaxed now that she was on home territory. "The CCD program is very inadequate at present. That needs to be overhauled. A program of adult education should be set up along with parish visiting, recreational programs, and programs for the elderly. No one would be out of work."

"And there is the additional advantage that Kate—and anyone else who wanted—could continue to work with the migrant workers and still live at Holy Rosary," Rosalia added.

"I think that sounds great." Peg's enthusiasm made her sound brash. "We'd be involved in a real ministry not just a school."

There was a sudden sharp intake of breath from Susannah and they turned toward her, startled. Her hands were against her chest and her eyes were wide open.

"Susannah, are you all right?" Rosalia rose from her seat.

She nodded, her hands pushing heavily against the glass-top table. "I think I've had enough for one evening. If I may be excused, I would like to go to my room. I usually observe the hour for retiring."

There had been no scheduled hour for retiring for years, but even so, Susannah's gibe did what she intended. It made them feel uncomfortable.

"Would you like Peg to go up with you?" It was one of Rosalia's miscalculated efforts at kindness.

Susannah stood at the door, her round cheeks abnormally pale. "I can take care of myself. Let that one"—and she jerked her head toward Peg—"stay and work out the future for all of us."

They said nothing until the door had closed behind her. Joanne shuffled her papers into order and closed her folder. "I think we've all had enough for tonight. Would you like me to set up the general Community meeting?"

Rosalia nodded. "And perhaps Peg will help." But Peg was already out the door.

Magdalen, her pen clipped neatly to her notebook, her sweater pulled over her shoulders, acknowledged them with a brief smile and followed Peg into the hall.

Joanne, Ruth, and Rosalia sat on. The room had grown cold but no one moved to close the window. Susannah's fingers had left smudges along the glass top of the table, and a forgotten notebook lay where Peg had been sitting. But at Magdalen's place there was no trace. The tabletop was clean, the chair pushed meticulously into order. It was as though she had not been there, and yet Ruth could not rid herself of that strong afterimage: the composed medallion struck from an unyielding metal.

"What's happened to Magdalen?" It was, Ruth knew, a bad moment to ask it. They were tired, anxious, distressed by the long meeting, but she could not bear the weight of one more imponderable.

"She's pretty much like that all the time." Joanne's voice was flat and closed, as though there was nothing to discuss.

"She was always quiet but now she's . . ." Ruth paused, groping for a word.

"Age changes people." There was something dry, almost hostile in Joanne's explanation.

"But Magdalen isn't old!"

"She's forty-eight."

"But that's not old; that's only four years older than I am."

Joanne didn't answer. It was Rosalia who said, "Magdalen was a very close friend of Marian Connell."

Of course. Of course she had been a friend of Marian's. Ruth remembered her first impression of them in the novitiate, overawed by all that Marian and Magdalen were able to accomplish. Their students adored them with that sentimental cult that flowered in boarding schools. Cut off from the normal affections and curiosities of adolescence, boarders satisfied their longings by fixing them on their teachers. "The M and M's" Marian and Magdalen had been called by their pupils—"sweet but not sticky," they had explained to the horrified Mother Edwarda, who had made the mistake of asking for an explanation of the nicknames.

"There is nothing those two can't do," Aidan had said complacently to Ruth the night of the school play, a production of such finish that they were asked to repeat it for a regional competition.

But it was not only as teachers that they had made their mark. Mother Columban, whose sparing praise was reserved for the sick and dying, had pointed them out to her novices as models of generous service and meticulous observance of the Rule. It seemed clear from the beginning that they had been destined to lead St. Aidan's.

"Perhaps you weren't aware that Magdalen had been principal for a number of years." Rosalia paused. "She resigned just before Marian left."

Ruth was beginning to understand the flat, uncommunicative tone of Joanne's voice.

"I admire Magdalen very much. This year must have been close to unendurable for her," Rosalia continued.

Joanne said nothing.

"Marian's leaving was hard on all of us, but I think that for Magdalen it called everything into question."

Joanne moved irritably.

"Despite all Magdalen's apparent independence, I think she was deeply influenced by Marian's ideal of religious life, more deeply than she realized probably. Then when Marian left . . ." Rosalia raised her hands hopelessly.

Yes, thought Ruth, it would be like that. There had always been something inflexible in Magdalen's unreserved loyalty. If Marian Connell had commanded that loyalty and then betrayed it, the ruin would have been devastating. At the corner of the orchard there was a maple tree that had been struck by lightning. All through the summer it had stood leafless, stripped of its bark, white and barren among the green growth of the apple trees. But it could not fall: its roots still held it upright.

Joanne tried to stifle a yawn. "Sorry, I really have to go to bed. I'm asleep on my feet. Coming, Ruth?"

She followed Joanne up the stairs and down the passageway leading to their wing, but she hardly noticed when Joanne turned into her own room. She could see nothing but that straight stark tree that had been caught in an unpredictable flash of fire.

Rawlins and Swenson, Realtors
108 East 68th St.
New York, N.Y.
October 14, 1980

Mr. Alec Stafford
Stafford, Connor, Lipsky, Architects
18 Ballantyne Avenue
Glen Cove, New York

Dear Alec,

I dropped in at "Landsweep" on Wednesday with the material you sent me. I didn't see Sister Rosalia after all; something had come up unexpectedly. It all looks so peaceful up there that it's hard to believe in "emergencies," but I suppose they have them too.

It was an interesting visit and I stayed a good bit longer than I had intended. The lady who answered the door was somebody new to me. A Sister Noreen—younger than the ancients who usually let me in. Not young, mind you; nobody I've met is young!

This one was a real chatterbox. I must confess I rather enjoyed her. I think I could have learned a lot of interesting things if Sister Rosalia's secretary (I think she must be her secretary) hadn't come along. I got the feeling there wasn't much love lost between these two. Sister Noreen left as soon as Sister Ruth came in.

Sister Ruth is nobody's fool—asked all the right questions without ever giving herself away. As it turns out, her father was Professor Joseph Arendt. He was chairman of the history department at CUNY when I was a graduate student. Small world. We parted friends and she assured me Sister Rosalia would be in touch. I think Sister Noreen would have given me a clue as to how the wind is blowing but Sister Ruth plays it close to the vest.

Keep your fingers crossed.

Cheers,

Steve Rawlins

8

She had not expected to sleep, but when the knock came she could hardly pull herself up to consciousness.

"Ruth?"

For a moment she didn't recognize the voice.

"It's Agnes. Can you help me, please."

"You're sick. What's the matter?"

"No, I'm all right. It's Susannah. She's down by the bathroom. I think she's fainted."

She felt for her slippers, couldn't find them, and followed Agnes into the hall barefoot.

"What happened?"

"I don't know. I got up to go to the bathroom and I found her. It's so hard for me to bend. I was afraid I'd fall if I tried to give her some water, so I got you."

Agnes looked small and old, almost deformed, as she bent forward, leaning heavily on her cane.

Susannah had not regained consciousness. She lay half on her side, her face buried in her outstretched arm. She had taken off her veil and cape but was still in her habit. In her fall the yoke had ridden up and was tight against her neck. Ruth knelt to turn her on her back and loosen the dress around her throat.

"Do you want me to get some water?"

"Yes, please."

But water did nothing to revive her. She lay breathing heavily but without movement.

"I think we'd better get Peg."

"Shall I go?"

"No, I'll go. It'll be quicker. You stay here with her."

Ruth rose to her feet and started for the stairs.

"Here, take my slippers, there's no carpet on the stairs." Agnes slipped carefully out of her scuffs.

"Do you think she's had a stroke?" Ruth asked as Peg knelt next to Susannah taking her pulse.

Peg shook her head. "I don't think so. I think I know what it is. Ruth, will you get Rosalia, please. Agnes, you might as well sit down. There's no point using up all your energy and this may take a while."

Rosalia looked drugged with sleep. She had forgotten her glasses and her eyes were puffy and bewildered. "What happened?"

Peg looked up. "Agnes found her."

"How long has she been here, do you know?"

Agnes sat huddled in the chair she had pulled out from an empty room. "I don't know. I thought I heard something a while ago but I was half asleep. Susannah often gets up in the night. She says she gets very thirsty."

"But she's still dressed. What time is it anyway? I forgot my watch." Rosalia looked uselessly at her wrist.

"It's a little after one." Peg got to her feet. "She may have been like this for a couple of hours. She left the meeting before ten o'clock."

"The meeting! That couldn't be"—Rosalia stumbled—"I mean that wouldn't . . . Susannah was very upset . . ."

"It's not a heart attack if that's what you're worrying about." Peg sounded brusque and annoyed.

"Then what . . . ?"

"I can't be sure, but I think it's diabetic coma. Her hands are clammy, she's pale as death, and her breath has that sweet smell. If you've smelled it once you never forget it. We should get her to the hospital right away."

Ruth turned. "Shall I call the ambulance from White-thorn?"

Peg shook her head impatiently. "It'll take a half-hour to get out here and then we still have the ride back into town. I think she has a better chance if we can get her into the station wagon."

"It's an emergency then?" Rosalia could not put the pieces together.

"Coma is always an emergency," Peg answered briefly. "I'm going to get the stretcher from the infirmary. We'll need a fourth person. I'll knock on Nancy Lenihan's door on the way up. She has a good strong back."

Rosalia knelt awkwardly at Susannah's side.

Agnes reached for her cane. "Why don't you two go and get dressed. I'll stay until Peg gets back."

Rosalia hesitated but Ruth took her arm. "Agnes is right. We'll just hold things up otherwise."

Getting the stretcher down the stairs and out into the court-yard was more of an ordeal than Ruth had anticipated.

"Cursed be all convents with narrow halls and steep stairs." Nancy sighed as they maneuvered through the back door.

"Nancy, get the station wagon out and back it over here. I think if we let down the back door and shift that seat forward we'll be O.K." Peg was all sharp decisiveness.

"Do you want me to go with you?" Nancy asked.

"I'd just as soon you stayed here with Agnes. I can't imagine that anyone will be looking for me, but just in case," Rosalia said.

Nancy nodded. "Good luck. I'll be praying."

"Diabetic coma, all right," the intern announced when he came out to them in the waiting room. "But she's pulling out of it. She'll be O.K. Lucky you found her when you did. How did she let her chemistry get so out of whack?"

No one answered and he looked from one to the other. "How old is she?"

"She'll be seventy-five in a couple of months," Rosalia answered.

"Are you the nurse?"

"No, I am. An LPN," Peg explained.

"Were you giving her her shots or was she able to manage on her own?"

Peg colored. "She wasn't getting any shots as far as I know. She was on oral medication."

"Who's her doctor?"

"Our Community doctor is Doctor Lavelle."

"When was the last time she'd seen him?"

"I don't know."

"What had he been giving her?"

There was a painful pause and then: "I don't know."

Why on earth doesn't Rosalia help her out? Ruth wondered. She must know.

The intern's patience was running short. "I thought you were the nurse," he snapped.

"Sister Susannah took care of herself." Peg was angry and defensive.

"Well, she made a fine mess of it."

"Doctor, do you think we should call Dr. Lavelle?" The intern's eyebrows rose. "I'm in charge of the sisters," Rosalia continued, "and I, we, want everything possible to be done."

He shrugged. "I don't see what good it will do to call him at three o'clock in the morning. He'll be in early tomorrow. He can see her then. Nothing's going to happen to her tonight. I can tell you this though"—and he leveled them all with his contempt —"if she doesn't get proper care you'll find her some night a little bit too late."

The fog of the evening before had turned to rain and they

drove home in silence, Rosalia gripping the steering wheel with both hands, blinking at the sudden flashes of light thrown up from the slick black road.

"I might as well leave the car out. We'll be needing it in the morning," she said as she turned into the driveway.

She put off the lights and Ruth waited to get out on Peg's side, but Peg had not moved.

"Rosalia, I'm sorry. I thought you knew."

"How could I know?"

"Susannah said she'd told you."

Rosalia fumbled with the keys. "How long has it been going on?"

"I don't know. I came across it quite by accident. Apparently Susannah managed to get her own medicine, but it came to the infirmary by mistake one day. When I confronted her with it she told me to mind my own business."

"I wish you'd told me."

"She told me to stay out of it, that you knew all about it."

"But why would she . . ." Rosalia groped for some reason why Susannah would not want her to know.

"I don't know why she wouldn't want *you* to know. She doesn't want me to know *anything*. She'd get me out of the infirmary if she could."

Ruth remembered Susannah as she had pushed herself erect at the end of their meeting. She must have known then that she was sick, but she would tolerate no help.

"Susannah is a very proud woman," Ruth said.

"But there's nothing wrong in being sick." Rosalia was puzzled.

"It's a weakness."

"But it's not like sin. It's something you have no control over."

That was precisely it, it was something Susannah could neither dominate nor placate. For all their pious considerations about God's grace and man's powerlessness, they had been trained to be creatures of will. "There is no sinful impulse that cannot be conquered, no temperament that cannot be brought into conformity to the Divine Will," Mother Columban had preached vigorously.

> They will be virile women, women of strong faith and determination, believing that they can, with God's grace, accomplish wonders far beyond their strength. They will not be cowed by obstacles or frightened by dangers, putting their trust in those consoling words of Scripture: "The weak things of the world has God chosen that He may confound the strong."

It was not enough for them to do what they could; they must also achieve what was beyond their strength. Never to complain, never to show fatigue, to fast cheerfully, to hide suffering—in short, to conquer—this had become the ideal. "The weak things has God chosen" was their daily hymn, yet implicit in their aspirations was a belief in that subtle alchemy by which their God would transform them from weak women into triumphal warriors. Somewhere along the way they had lost the vision that it is weakness itself (a God crying in Gethsemane, falling beneath His Cross), not weakness transformed, that will confound the strong.

Late the next afternoon Ruth stopped in Agnes' room to see if she could bring her some supper and save her the walk downstairs. Peg was curled up on the window seat, her head resting against a pillow.

"Come in and be the referee," she said as Ruth hesitated.

"A fight? Neither of you looks as though she has enough energy."

"I'm not fighting." Agnes smiled, but the circles under her eyes were lined and purple.

"That's just it—you're not fighting. Every day you're in more pain. Every day it's harder for you to get up. You've admitted it yourself, but you won't do anything about it."

Agnes closed her eyes. "I've done something. I've gone to

the doctor, I've rested, I've taken my medicine. What do you want me to do, ask for a miracle?" It was said half in jest but there was a cry beneath the words.

"As referee I suggest we take time out until we've all had a good night's sleep," Ruth interposed.

"That's just it. She won't have a good night's sleep. She's had a fierce headache all day and I've given her as much medicine for pain as I can without calling the doctor."

"I'll be all right if I can just be quiet."

"No you won't. You admitted last week that you can be awake all night once you get a bad headache."

Agnes said nothing.

There were times when Peg was more bulldog than nurse. "Why don't we get out and let her have some peace," Ruth suggested, opening the door.

But Agnes reached out. "Please, don't go. I asked Peg to come down and tell me about Susannah, but all she's done so far is lecture me."

"I'm sorry, I really am, but I get so upset when I see you like this."

"We're on time-out, remember? Either tell me about Susannah or let me take a nap."

"Susannah's all right. She pulled out of the coma without too much difficulty, so now it's a question of keeping her stabilized. Dr. Lavelle was furious, of course, when he found out what's been going on. Susannah had everybody fooled. She told Lavelle some story about being afraid to give herself injections and that I wasn't always home and couldn't be counted on, which is why he agreed to oral medication. She assured him that Rosalia was aware of the whole situation. It was quite a story."

"And it's all straight now?"

"All straight except that I'm not sure she's going to let me give her the injections, and under no circumstances does she want the Community to know she's diabetic."

It was the old issue again. Feisty Susannah fighting for her life—fighting against her mortal enemies, weakness and fear.

"But she has to let you give her her injections, doesn't she? What else can she do?" Agnes was bewildered.

Peg shrugged. "She was trying to talk Rosalia into getting someone else trained to do it."

"But who?" Agnes asked.

Peg's mouth was tight. "She mentioned you, as a matter of fact."

"Oh, but I . . ." Then the spontaneous reaction stopped. "I could, couldn't I?" Agnes reflected. "It doesn't take a lot of strength, and I'm around more now that my teaching schedule's been lightened."

"That's a lot of nonsense. It's my duty and I'll do it. My God, don't you have enough to worry about?" Peg's eyes were hard and angry.

But Agnes persisted. "Peg, I could do it and"—she hesitated and then went on—"Susannah and I are friends."

Peg's color rose. "Well, obviously I don't fit that role, but I am the nurse here and she jolly well better get used to taking help from people she doesn't like, because I suspect she's going to have a lot of it before she dies."

The bitterness in her voice hung in the air like blasphemy in a holy place. Peg covered her face with her hands and her shoulders shook.

"I'm sorry." Her voice was muffled and uneven. "I don't know what gets into me sometimes." She looked up and reached over to the bureau for a Kleenex. "Everything's all wrong between me and Susannah, and I've honestly tried—at least I did in the beginning. Now I just get angry every time she looks at me. Sometimes I feel she hates everyone, that it's part of her disease. And then I see her with Agnes and she's like a different person. I bring out everything bad in her and I can't seem to help it." She blew her nose. "I don't even care anymore, and that really scares me."

"You wouldn't be crying if you didn't care."

"Maybe. I don't know."

Agnes reached out and took Peg's clenched hand, but she seemed not to notice, staring past Agnes out into the cool October light. But Agnes would not let the hand go, massaging it gently until the fist opened and the fingers, freckled and stubby, lay against Agnes' knee.

"It's nothing you do, Peg, that angers Susannah. It would be the same with anyone."

"It's not with you."

"But not because of anything I do."

"Yes, it is. You're kind and gentle and patient."

Agnes shook her head. "That isn't what Susannah sees. When she looks at me she sees one thing—she sees I'm sick."

Peg turned on her abruptly, but Agnes put out her hand.

"No, I want to finish. I don't like talking like this, so I want to get it all out at once.

"When I first started having trouble I used to feel Susannah watching me, and then sometimes when I'd be resting she'd come in and talk. At first I was surprised; I never thought she was the kind of person who would want to be with the sick. She was the busy decisive type. Then I noticed that she'd always get me to talk about how I felt, about how hard it was to move when I first got up, about the fatigue in the afternoons. Even when I changed the subject she always brought me back to it. Then one day when I was helping Edwarda in the bursar's office I saw all the bills from the doctor and I knew there had to be something wrong. Then I understood. Susannah was old and sick and she'd lost power. But I'd lost power, too—and I was more than thirty years her junior. We were in it together.

"That's why I asked you if I could go to the hospital today. I knew I was the only person she could tolerate seeing. Everyone else would remind her of the strength she'd lost, but I'd just remind her of my weakness."

Let them be quick to acknowledge their weakness, both of body and soul, accepting their limitations with humility and faith. Should they be afflicted with sickness they must be patient and grateful, doing whatever they can despite their own suffering to be of assistance to their sisters in whatever way grace inspires them.

The light, even voice with its slight lisp had led them to holy ground. So this was where the little gap-toothed novice whose conduct had never satisfied Mother Columban's narrow ideal of perfection had been led. ("Sister Agnes Devitt: Your sisters have noticed the following faults in you: Sister, you walk too quickly, you are too spontaneous in your gestures, you laugh too noisily, sing too loudly, bang the door, forget the bell. Ask God, Sister, to give you a spirit of decorum and say the Litany of the Sacred Heart every night during June.") But God had been as impatient as Agnes, whirling her away past the conventual virtues of decorum and modesty and punctuality into another country where she had found a meek and humble Savior. Like the Lord she loved, she had accepted weakness that her sister might find strength.

Agnes lay back against her chair.

"Why don't we get you into bed?" Peg was already pulling down the quilt.

"That sounds good." Agnes reached toward Ruth to be helped out of the chair, but even that slight movement made her mouth tighten with pain.

"No, please, I'd rather not get undressed," she said as Ruth started to unbutton her blouse.

"Wouldn't you be more comfortable?"

"I'll do it later."

It took both of them to manipulate her the few feet from chair to bed.

"How about another pillow, would that help?" Ruth asked as she drew the quilt up over her.

"It doesn't seem to matter one way or another." It was the

first time Ruth had ever heard that voice robbed of its persistent hope.

When they had closed the door, Ruth turned to Peg. "I had no idea."

Peg shook her head and motioned her toward the stairs and up to the infirmary treatment room.

"It gets worse every day." Peg pushed a cabinet door closed with her foot.

"And there's no cure?"

"Not until they find out what's wrong."

"I thought they knew."

"First they said it was a viral infection, then when it didn't clear up they diagnosed rheumatoid arthritis. That's what Lavelle has been treating her for."

"And you don't think it is?"

"It could be, but I'm not satisfied that they've tested for other possibilities. It seems to me that the diagnosis was too easy. I want her to go to someone else."

"And she won't?"

"You heard her tonight. She digs her heels in every time I mention it."

"But why? She can't enjoy being sick. She's at the other pole from hypochondria."

Peg sighed. "I don't know why. If I did I could manage better. I wish you'd talk to her about it, Ruth. There's no point in my mentioning it again."

"And you really think it might be something that could be treated successfully?"

"It's a possibility—and what have we got to lose?"

Peg looked at her watch. "I have to get over to the school. I'm supervising dinner over there tonight. Could you bring these down to Agnes? It's only aspirin and it probably won't do much good, but I can't give her anything stronger. She's already taken as much as she's supposed to have today."

It was close to six o'clock when she left Agnes' room. She

stood for a while looking out the window. She could hear the clatter of dishes from the dining room, but she had no appetite for either food or companionship. There would be a glorious sunset at Overlook Point if she could find a car free. But just as she started the motor in the one remaining car Kate Boylan waved from the back door.

"Could you possibly do me a favor? I'm in a mess. I'm supposed to pick up Angela Ferrato at the station in Whitethorn and I forgot to reserve a car. I was late at the camp. We had to get one of the children to the hospital." She sighed in exasperation. "It's been a terrible week."

"No problem. I was only going over to Overlook to watch the sunset." Ruth handed the keys to Kate.

"Sure?"

"Absolutely."

"Why don't you come, too? It's a nice ride and we could talk on the way. I hardly ever see anyone to talk to." Kate handed the keys back and slid into the passenger seat. "You don't mind, do you? It would be so luxurious to sit back and be chauffeured."

"I'd be delighted." Ruth had never thought, she realized, of Kate having needs or wanting comforts. She seemed so dauntless, so preoccupied (almost to the point of rudeness at times) with her clients that she discouraged concern for herself.

As they turned onto the main road, Kate laughed. "I think my subconscious must have been working when I asked you to come along."

Ruth looked quizzical.

"I really don't want to ride back with Angela alone."

"But I thought you two were going to work together?"

"We're supposed to, although I've never been quite sure why. Frankly, I can't imagine Angela doing the kind of work I do."

"It was her choice, wasn't it?"

"All the way. It wouldn't have been my choice, I can tell you that. I'm afraid Angela will be more concerned with herself than with the people she'll be working with—and I told her so.

It seems to me that she's just making stopgap decisions without facing what she really wants."

"What does she want?"

Kate shrugged. "You've never had a chance to know Angela, have you?"

"No. She entered a few months after I left and I've only seen her two or three times since I've been back. Are you close to Angela?"

"No one is, that's what makes me sad. She has this crazy feeling about being the only Italian in an Irish community. She says no one will ever really understand her. That's why she wants to work with minority groups—because she understands how they feel." Kate's disbelief was patent.

"Well, she is a minority at St. Aidan's, isn't she?"

"In a way." Her concession was grudging.

"Wouldn't you find it difficult to be the only Irish nun in a community where most of the members were second-generation Italian?"

"I suppose so," Kate conceded grudgingly. "But you're not Irish and it doesn't seem to bother you."

"My mother was though, and it does make a difference, I assure you."

"OK, I'll accept that, but with Angela I feel as though she's exploiting the ethnic thing—as though she wants to feel alien. I don't know. It's all too complicated." And she curled up on the seat. "By the way, how was your Council meeting?"

"Painful but good, I think."

"I know it's secret and all that, but did they really face the problems or was it just more compromise?"

"Anything but. It would have been easier if it had been," she added, remembering those charged moments between Peg and Susannah.

"But not easier in the long run."

"No," said Ruth slowly, "sooner or later we'll have to face the issues and decide what it is we want."

Ruth took her eyes from the road for a second to catch Kate

looking at her speculatively. They drove for almost another mile before Kate said, "I keep trying to figure out how all this seems to you. Two weeks after you make your vows you find out that maybe St. Aidan's might go out of existence. How do you deal with that?"

That fact was, of course, that she had not dealt with it. She had pushed it aside, telling herself that there was no point worrying about an unpredictable future. Now she tried to make light of Kate's question. "We're both in the same boat, aren't we? The only two who haven't made final vows."

But Kate would not be turned aside. "Not really. I'm not wedded to St. Aidan's, not the way the older nuns are. I want religious life and I want to serve the Church, but I could do it in a lot of places. I haven't been here long enough to get my roots down. You had ten years at St. Aidan's before, when it was flourishing; but then you've had ten years away, too. I understand how the rest of them feel. St. Aidan's has been their life. But you" —Kate paused—"you're caught right in the middle, aren't you?"

Ruth nodded and said nothing. All the fears and uncertainties that she had been trying to suppress had surfaced with Kate's keen observation.

They had driven off the highway onto the main street of Whitethorn. Kate moved uneasily. "I'm sorry. I guess I pushed too hard. I'm always getting my knuckles rapped for being too direct."

"No apologies, please. I don't have anything to hide. If I could tell you how I feel, I would. When I listen to you and Peg I sense new life if we were to sell St. Aidan's. Then I look at people like Gregory and Edwarda and I feel only pain."

"And for yourself?"

"For myself . . . You've already said it, Kate. I'm caught right in the middle."

The conversation on the return trip to St. Aidan's was strained and stilted. Angela sat between them quiet and lovely, her red-gold hair caught up and back in a silver clasp, her smile, attentive, assuring, promising her full interst in whatever they said. It was, however, a promise that lacked substance.

It was Kate who assumed the burden of the conversation. Susannah was in the hospital at Whitethorn, she recited. Agnes seemed to be having more trouble walking. There were two new boarders in the school—from Peru, she believed. They would be in Nancy's class. Community meetings about the future of St. Aidan's would begin next week. Each subject was received with the same half-smile, the same slow appropriate response. But nothing generated conversation. It was as though Kate dropped pebbles in a bottomless lake. The rings of water widened and then disappeared, leaving the surface as unruffled as before.

"Listen, I think I have something lined up for you at the camp."

Ruth heard the tension in Kate's voice, the fierce effort to bring Angela closer to them.

"Rebecca, the woman who's been running the nursery school, is finding it a bit much. I think she'd like to settle for three days a week. I don't think there'd be any problem in getting you the job for the other two days. As a matter of fact, I think they'd be delighted. Rebecca's Spanish is terrible, and the Mexican children would benefit from someone who knows their language."

The quiet half-smile never changed. Angela was like someone deaf who had cultivated a single expression to protect herself from the need to understand and respond.

Kate plunged on, driven by Angela's silence. Usually blunt, almost abrupt, Kate now lost herself in a spate of words, describing her work, Angela's possibilities, the state of the camp, the political tangles, the need for more education, more money, more social awareness. Although it had been Angela who had asked to work in the camp and Kate who had reservations, all the interst, all the effort was on Kate's part. One might think that Angela had been coerced into a distasteful task.

It was, of course, the mystery of Angela's return to St.

Aidan's that lay at the core of the difficulty. It stood in their path
like a huge boulder that they had to use all their ingenuity to
avoid. Had Angela once referred to the University, to her studies,
to any part of the life she had been living, it would have eased
the tension. Yet not once did she allude to the past or to her plans
for the future. She managed to create an atmosphere in which the
simplest questions became incursions on her privacy.

Only once did she initiate a comment. As they turned into
the drive of St. Aidan's, she leaned forward looking at the over-
arching maples, the yellow and gold of their leaves still touched
with the last of the day's sunlight. "It's very beautiful, isn't it?"
she said.

It was a curiously detached observation, an observation a
traveler might make in coming unexpectedly on something
lovely that captured her for a moment but with which she had
no lasting connection.

As they drove up under the porte cochere, Rosalia, an old
white sweater thrown over her shoulders, was standing at the
front door.

"Welcome, home," she said, as Angela came up the steps,
and kissed her.

Rawlins and Swenson, Realtors
108 East 68th St.
New York, N.Y.
October 21, 1980

Mr. Alec Stafford
Stafford, Connor, Lipsky, Architects
18 Ballantyne Avenue
Glen Cove, New York

Dear Alec,

I've been trying to make arrangements for us to get up to "Landsweep" next week. It's at its peak right now. In another week or so the leaves will be pretty much gone.

So far I haven't been able to get in touch with Sister Rosalia but I'm sure we can make an appointment for next week. When I called I was told she was at the hospital. Apparently one of the old nuns was taken sick quite suddenly. When I said I was sorry to hear it, whoever was speaking said, "Well, Mr. Rawlins, it's nice to know that you are." She sounded as though she thought I'd put the evil eye on the poor old lady. So don't be surprised, Alec, if you don't get the red carpet treatment.

The whole setup is beyond me. Anybody with a brain in her head would grab at the offer we're making. They have no pension plan, no Social Security—and over fifty percent of the sisters are over sixty! I always thought the Catholic Church took care of any of their organizations that got into financial difficulty, but when I said this to Sister Rosalia she laughed. Apparently they're entirely on their own.

Well, enough of that. I'll try Sister Rosalia again toward the end of the week and let you know as soon as I have something definite.

Cheers,

Steve Rawlins

9

Susannah came home from the hospital the following Wednesday and immediately resumed her place in the Community. She was in her seat for early Mass, came to the dining room for meals, took up her ordinary duties, and offered no explanation of her illness. When Kate asked her directly, she answered curtly that it was a "false alarm." The implication was that Peg was incompetent. Yet something had changed in Susannah; something of her independence was gone. She had loved long walks up through the orchard and into the woods. Even in the snow she would pull on her boots and trudge off, her shawl pulled tight around her shoulders, her short legs taking disproportionately long steps. Now, despite the sunny October days, she never wandered far from the school, walking along the covered cloister or out past the novitiate, always close enough to be observed from the convent.

"She's frightened, isn't she?" Ruth asked Peg as they watched her one afternoon from the infirmary windows.

"More than she wants to admit. I think she's more afraid of unconsciousness than she is of dying. She remembers almost nothing of what happened the other night. She doesn't even remember falling."

Yes, death would be preferable for Susannah, who could not brook the humiliation of being out of control. Even her rare bouts of absentmindedness had always been covered by some transparent excuse. The possibility of hours when she would be blindly, helplessly in the hands of others would, of course, be intolerable to her.

"What about her shots?"

Peg smiled. "I gave in on that. Agnes will take care of them. Maybe it will be good for both of them. God knows, Susannah is facing enough without having to face me too."

It was Angela, who had seen Susannah only infrequently, who noticed the difference in her most.

"She's so thin and her color's gone," she said to Ruth as Susannah left the library one morning. "She used to look like an apple—all red and frosty."

"You know what the girls used to say—'Looks like an apple and acts like a lemon.' " Ruth laughed.

"She doesn't anymore. She looks little and wrinkled, like an apple that's been lying on the ground too long." Angela's half-smile was gone, her eyelids lowered. "It must be awful."

"To be sick?"

"To be old. And have nothing to look back on."

Ruth's first reaction was laughter. It was such an adolescent interpretation of religious life—the sort of thing the boarders might say. But as she looked at Angela she realized that for once the careful script had been laid aside and that she had said what she was thinking.

Before Ruth could find a response, Rita McClellan pushed the library door open. "Good. I was hoping someone would be here. Library hours have been so erratic this term."

Ruth found Rita's imperious manner difficult to deal with. "Someone is generally here in the mornings," she answered curtly.

Rita looked startled. She was used to cowing people into apology. "I don't usually have time to come in the mornings."

"Now that you're here, what can we do for you?" Ruth could not soften the edge in her voice.

Rita looked around the room appraisingly. "I have a class of fifteen students I'd like to bring in this afternoon." Before Ruth could answer, she added, "I suppose you won't be here this afternoon."

Ruth had instinctively risen to her feet at Rita's entrance but even so she felt small and colorless next to that imperious presence. "She thinks she was born to rule," Gregory had said with a wink at Ruth one day when Rita had held forth at a meeting.

"I'll be working in the archives, but Angela will be here. She'll be here three days a week taking care of student services. I'm trying to get the archives in order."

Angela, bent over a drawer from the card catalogue, looked up slowly, pushing a stray piece of hair behind her ear, her smile widening to welcome Rita. But Rita met it with the same appraising look she had given the furniture.

"I didn't know you were a librarian," she said.

"I'm not. I'm just filling in." Angela's speech became even slower when she was nervous.

"I thought perhaps you took courses in that too at the University." Rita's brogue sharpened with her sarcasm.

The baiting was palapable, but Angela's smile never wavered. It was as though she were being addressed in a language she didn't understand.

"I hope the work will be more to your taste than your studies seem to have been," Rita continued as she walked down the aisle examining the history collection. "I'll bring the girls in at one-fifteen. They'll have a list of what they will need." The swinging door shut behind her.

Angela bent over her work, her hair shadowing her face. The silence was unnatural. Rita's sharp presence hung over them like a reprimand.

Angela, usually so careful, turned awkwardly as she replaced the catalogue tray, knocking it against a vase of asters on the corner of the desk. The metal drawer slipped from her hands and crashed to the ground, the vase shattering around it. Loose cards, scattered on the floor, were caught in the stream of water from the broken vase. The asters, their fragile stems damaged, lay heaped against the blue-gray fragments of porcelain. Ruth knelt to mop up the water with a handful of tissues, but Angela did not move. She stood with her arms by her side, her eyes fixed on the floor.

Ruth rose, throwing the sodden tissues into the wastebasket. "I think we need some paper towels," she said.

Angela brought them from the supply closet without a word. They worked on their knees, drying off the cards, wrapping the asters in an old piece of newspaper, sweeping up the small ceramic splinters. When they finished, Angela sat back on her heels, her hands cupped around the fragments of the vase.

"Rita was very cruel," Ruth said finally.

Angela's eyes were still on her lap. "She always is." Then she looked up, her eyes dark with anger, her hands still cherishing the broken vase. "It's her substitute for power."

Although she had never thought of it that way, Angela was probably right, Ruth thought. The barbed wit and the instinctive tendency to put others in their place were very likely Rita's substitute for power. For the first time Ruth realized something of Rita's struggle—the struggle to live a life of powerlessness when the most fundamental need of her being was for control.

"Rita is a very complex person," she said finally.

"Of course. She's Irish."

Ruth, remembering Kate's comments about Angela, observed wryly, "I didn't know that was an exclusive ethnic trait."

"It's their privilege." Angela's quiet voice had not changed but there was venom in the undertone.

"Their privilege for what?"

"To be anything they want and expect people to accept them."

"Isn't that what we all do more or less?"

"The rest of us don't get away with it. At St. Aidan's you have to be Irish to have the right to do as you please."

"That's rather unfair, isn't it?"

Angela looked at her speculatively. "I don't think so." She paused and then added, "I rather expected you to understand with a name like Arendt, but I forgot your mother was Irish."

Ruth ignored the bait. "I'm not sure what I'm supposed to understand." She was dizzy with her effort to be patient.

"That the Irish are privileged: 'You mustn't mind Sister Susannah; the Irish are very quick-tempered.' 'Don't laugh at Noreen; the Irish are very sentimental.' 'Be patient with Anna; she's homesick for Ireland.' I wonder if they'd make excuses like that for me."

Ruth fought back the impulse to say, I think they make a great many excuses for you. Instead she said, "How would you like to be treated?"

For the first time Angela's composure was shaken. Her eyes were startled and her grasp on the fragments of vase tightened. Kate with her sharp, direct vision was right, Ruth thought. Angela did not want to fit, did not want to feel accepted. She wanted to be an alien but could not assume the responsibility. Instead she would place the responsibility at the door of St. Aidan's.

"I'm not loved here." She turned her head away and stared out the window. It was a line and gesture from a melodrama.

"How would you be treated if you were loved?" Ruth tried to keep the annoyance out of her voice.

Angela's slow, quiet voice had recovered itself. "I don't want to blame them. They don't mean to be so cold. It's the way they are."

Angela circumvented every question, shifting positions, turning the conversation round and round in her effort not to implicate herself.

The childish judgment angered Ruth as she thought of

Agnes, affectionate and peace-giving; of Peg and her unobtrusive vigils with the sick; of Kate and her fierce concern for the migrant workers. Most of all of Rosalia in her bewildered efforts to help Angela herself.

"I'm afraid we have different concepts of love," she said at last. "I've never felt unloved here."

"Perhaps you don't need very much love."

The thoughtless blow penetrated to some mysterious depth and Ruth caught her breath at the keen and unexpected pain. Her impulse was to leave the library and let Angela come to grips with the things she had broken. Instead she walked to the far end of the room and slanted the Venetian blinds against the sun. Gregory was walking in the courtyard, using her blackthorn stick at last.

"I hope Angela is going to be all right," Gregory had said to Ruth after Mass on Sunday. "She must have had a hard time at the University, although they say she's very bright." Her tongue made a little clicking sound against her teeth. "It's hard to be away from home. I was in the hospital for two weeks just before my Silver Jubilee. My, that was hard." Gregory had shaken her head at the thought of those lonely days.

The memory of Gregory's compassion increased her anger, and although she heard Angela behind her, she did not turn.

"Ruth?"

She took a perverse pleasure in her momentary hesitation. When she turned it was to face an Angela whose inner disorder had erupted. She stood frightened and shaken, her arms tight across her breast as though they could hold her in place.

"I never meant . . . it was just that I had hoped . . . that I had counted on you. I thought you would understand. That was why I asked Rosalia to work in the library." She had cut her finger on a piece of the vase and the blood ran unheeded across her hand. "Then when you acted as though you were on their side . . ." The words were uneven and groping, the artificial control abandoned.

"I didn't know we were choosing sides." Ruth's harshness was deliberate.

"Not sides, but it seemed that you understood them and I needed you to understand me."

She paused, sucking the blood from her finger.

"It's been so awful coming back and knowing everyone is talking behind my back."

"I don't think that's true."

"But they must be."

"You need to think they are."

Angela looked puzzled. "Why would I . . . ?"

"To justify yourself."

For a moment Ruth thought she would face the issue, but then, characteristically, she turned aside.

"It's so hard and I've been so lonely." There was something pathetically immature in the way her mouth pouted. "I don't belong here. I never will."

"Didn't you ever belong?"

"Not really. I thought I did. I was too young to understand."

"She was only seventeen when she entered," Kate had told Ruth on the way over to pick up Angela. "She's only twenty-eight—two years older than I am—and she's been at St. Aidan's eleven years."

"Too young to understand what?" It was another effort to push Angela into her own reality; but like the last effort, it failed.

"I was only seventeen and everybody thought it was a good idea for me to enter. It was a great thing in my family."

"And you didn't think it was a good idea?"

"Well you know . . ." She rubbed her wounded finger in absorption.

"And all those years you were never happy?"

Angela raised her hands to her eyes. "I didn't know what happiness was."

Ruth winced at the platitude but recognized that the tears

at least were genuine. She pulled out a chair from a table in the corner where they would be shielded should anyone come in to the library.

"Then when I went to the University I began to realize all I had missed. People really liked me there. I wasn't just another nun."

The script was tattered with use, all the lines hopelessly predictable. How far back would one have to travel to find the real Angela. Ruth wondered, aware that St. Aidan's was not without complicity in shaping this illusory self. In many ways Angela had been the compliant victim of other people's ideals.

"But you came home," Ruth pursued.

"I had to."

"You wanted to," Ruth emended.

"I had no choice."

If once, just once, Angela could acknowledge that she had some element of free will, that she was a determining factor in her own life.

"I was going to ask for a dispensation from my vows, but I wasn't sure how to do it. I didn't want to come back to St. Aidan's. I thought I could do it from the University, but when I went to the chaplain there he thought I should come home for a while. He didn't think I'd given it a fair chance."

She had stopped crying and the resentment was back in her voice. "I told him I'd given it eleven years. All that time wasted!"

Don't, Ruth wanted to plead. Don't talk about wasted years and being understood at last. Don't talk about being alien and unaccepted in an Irish community. Don't blame your family's domination. Say the one thing that's driving you now: you're in love.

But it took another fifteen minutes of wandering explanations before Angela brought out the final piece of the pattern.

"There's a man I met at the University. He was in one of my classes. He's supervisor of a bilingual program in Connecticut."

Her hesitation begged Ruth to take the initiative, to make the obvious connections.

"He used to be a brother, but he's been out six years." She probed the cut on her finger, pressing the lips of the wound together.

"He wants to marry me." Even now, in such a crucial issue, she refused the fence, slipping aside, placing someone else in the role of initiator.

"And what do you intend to do?" The question was so direct that evasion seemed impossible.

"He says I could probably get a job in the same program he's in. I could finish my degree next semester."

"You could do that without leaving St. Aidan's." It was more brutal than she had intended, but pity and exasperation had confused her.

Anger pushed Angela beyond her defenses and she took her life in her hands. "I'm in love. Don't you understand that? I want to marry him."

The cry broke the deadlock between them, but instead of the emotions she expected Ruth felt envy circle her like a steel belt. She breathed heavily trying to ease its pressure, but it was too strong for her. There had been something rapturous in Angela's admission and, beyond all expectation, she envied her that rapture.

"Isn't there anything you love?" Angela sobbed.

The weapon that earlier had probed Ruth's weakness now plunged into her heart. Without warning she was lost in the memory of her last dinner with David. She heard again her controlled, rational explanation about returning to St. Aidan's. She heard his answer, gentle and understanding. He had not questioned her or countered her. "I think too highly of your integrity not to honor any decision you make," he had said. It was all she had hoped for, yet instead of relief she had felt only a disconcerting anger.

Now as she looked at Angela, flushed and determined to

keep the love she had found, she understood that anger. She had wanted David to oppose her; she had wanted him to beg her to stay. She had wanted him to love her. How simple it was. It explained everything: the unexpected anger, the movement toward tears, the stinging sense of disappointment that had kept her sleepless during that last night in New York. She had wanted him to love her. She wanted it still.

"Angela told me last night that she wanted a dispensation from her vows," Rosalia said as she walked back with Ruth from examining the old barns and stable.

Ruth knew that Rosalia would bring up the issue sooner or later but she felt no courage to face it. Any mention of Angela sent her plunging back into her bewildering and shameful revelation: she who was vowed to celibacy wanted someone to love her. Not God in His spiritual mercy and compassion; not Agnes with her sisterly embrace or Aidan with her steady wisdom. She wanted someone who would love her with a passionate and exclusive commitment.

"I'm glad you were able to talk with her," Rosalia continued. "I wouldn't have been any good. She needed someone who could help her get a sense of direction."

The irony made Ruth burrow further into her confusion and she made no effort to respond.

"I hope this marriage is going to work. Angela seems like such a child sometimes." Rosalia sighed. "I suggested that she wait for a year or so, but she looked at me as though I'd lost my mind."

"She's in love." Ruth's voice sounded dry and distant, as though she spoke to Rosalia from across a great arid space.

"I know, but—" Rosalia was awkward in the presence of such an uncompromising statement. "Well, there are other considerations."

"I doubt if Angela is aware of them."

"That's what worries me. I wonder if Angela knows what

she's doing. It's such a serious step. Especially at her age. I would hate to see her hurt."

"You can't save her." Or me, Ruth thought, feeling a limitless distance from Rosalia.

"I know." Rosalia was hurt by Ruth's curtness. "But she has been a member of the Community for eleven years, and I do feel responsible."

"Angela has to make her own decisions."

"I know that. It's just that I can't help being concerned."

The word grated on Ruth. To be concerned. It was part of their religious vocabulary and, especially in the old days, of their religious mystique. Having given their lives to follow the Lord, they imperceptibly slipped into the role of savior. Their passion was to make things right, and in their zeal they were unable to absorb the reality that the passion of the Savior they followed had been to leave men free.

"For the first time Angela is taking charge of her life. Don't let your concern undermine that," Ruth cautioned.

"I don't mean to *undermine* it." Rosalia was aggrieved. "It's just that you never know what will happen with someone as emotional as Angela. I tried to make some suggestions, but she seemed to have the whole thing worked out when she came to see me." They had turned off the service road and into the school drive. "I suppose I should get in touch with the Bishop right away."

"You might as well. And I think it might be good to let Angela wait for the dispensation someplace else instead of staying at St. Aidan's."

"But I wouldn't want her to think—"

"She won't."

"But I'd like her to know she's welcome to stay as long as she likes."

"She's gone already." Ruth could not control the coldness in her voice.

Rosalia looked puzzled.

"She's been gone a long time, I think. That was the problem: she had left us without being able to admit it to herself."

Ruth held the door open when they reached the convent and Rosalia preceded her, stopping to hang her sweater on a hook against the wall. The narrow hall was dark and heavy with the boarding-school smell of cooking, musty clothing, and wax.

"That light's been out all week. I keep forgetting to remind Anna about it. Someone could have an accident."

In the dim light Rosalia looked pale, her wide cheekbones giving her face a hollow look. "You know," she said, "sometimes when I come in this door or when I walk up the back stairs I think of what it will be like never to see this building again. And I wonder if we have any right to ask that sacrifice."

"You won't ask it. They'll decide for themselves."

"I could have said no to Mr. Rawlins when he first called. No one would ever have known."

"Could you?"

Rosalia shook her head. "No, I couldn't. But I almost wish I had."

"These are the worst months for you. It won't be so bad once the decision is made. They'll rally round." Ruth tried to pull herself out of her desolation, but her words were empty, without depth or conviction. She watched them slip away, too insubstantial to meet Rosalia's need.

"Oh, it doesn't matter about me. I was thinking of people like Susannah and Edwarda. And the nuns in the infirmary." Rosalia was lost in the vision of that final exile. But Ruth could not sustain the vision. She was tired of Rosalia's unwearying concern for others, tired of a way of life in which the happiness of others was always to take precedence over one's own. She wanted something for herself. She remembered the night when she and Agnes had stood in the darkness comforted and strengthened by their embrace. "Where there is love God is to be found,"

Agnes had said. But Ruth felt no love now, only a fierce need to grasp at anything that would solace her, no matter who paid the price.

"They're ringing my bell," Rosalia said, but she did not move until the shrill buzzer sounded a second time.

Ruth knew that she should look up, that she should give at least that simple comfort; but she did not. The silence between them was opaque. Rosalia turned finally toward the stairs, her feet hard and slow against the wooden steps.

Ruth stood in the dim passageway. Rosalia's sweater had slipped from the hook and she stooped to pick it up. She held it for a moment, its bulk warm and comforting.

She had lost something.

She wondered if this was how a woman might feel after a miscarriage, empty and angry—and guilty, too, as though she should have been able to keep the life within her pure and strong. The life she carried within her was tainted now, its single-hearted focus distorted and blurred.

> By their vow of chastity the religious will consecrate their bodies and hearts solely to Jesus Christ. They will repulse with all their strength any thought or desire that could impair the total dedication of themselves to God.

The smell of cooking was nauseating her and she groped her way along the passage, past the sweaters and raincoats and umbrellas and into the main corridor, where Gregory, without her cane, was limping resolutely toward the chapel.

Rawlins and Swenson, Realtors
108 East 68th St.
New York, N.Y.
November 2, 1980

Mr. Alec Stafford
Stafford, Connor, Lipsky, Architects
18 Ballantyne Avenue
Glen Cove, New York

Dear Alec,

Thanks for the materials for Sister Rosalia. I'll get them delivered within the week.

I'm delighted you've seen the place at last. I knew it would whet your appetite. As you saw, the mansion itself is in amazingly good shape—and the school is made for our purposes. It was interesting to see how the whole thing struck you. Yes, it is a mysterious place. You picked up a lot more of the nuances than I did. Ah well, that's what comes of being an artist instead of a businessman!

What did you think of that Sister Angela who opened the door for us? Hard to believe she's a real nun—she looks so young. What do you suppose she does in a place like that? Do you know that Sister Rosalia told me that until 1966 they never went out except for medical reasons!

Well, Alec, you've seen it at last. All we have to do now is persuade them to sell.

Luck,

Steve Rawlins

10

Angela left St. Aidan's the second week of November. She would stay with her brother in New Jersey until her dispensation from her vows came through, she explained to Ruth. She thought it might be possible to make some arrangement with the University so that she wouldn't lose her whole semester's work. She hoped to be married in the spring.

"What do you intend to tell the Community?"

"I thought Rosalia could put up a note, after I've gone."

"I thought you hated secrecy and coldness?"

"I do, but I can't tell them—"

"Why not?"

"Tell Susannah and Rita . . . ?" She was aghast.

"Why not? You say they have a right to know."

"But they'd ask me questions!"

"And . . . ?"

"But they don't like me."

"Do you think they'll like you any better if you avoid them?"

"But what will they think of me?"

"Is that so important?"

It was a foolish question, shaped out of her own irritation. Of course it was important. All her life Angela had, unconsciously perhaps, acted to win approbation; the pity was that the structure of their lives had endorsed such motivation. Mother Josephine's dry voice issuing judgment ("I am displeased with you, Sister") had been a condemnation received in terror, for the mystique of their lives had confused the judgment of superiors with the judgment of God.

> They will strive with all the powers of their soul to see God in the person of their superiors, recognizing in their commands the Will of God and accepting them, therefore, with joy and alacrity.

In the end, Angela told only the people she knew would neither coerce nor condemn her. For the rest there was a note on the bulletin board saying she was going to take a vacation for a few weeks. The evasion was, of course, transparent.

"She'll never come back," said Rita triumphantly. "I could have predicted years ago that she had no vocation—if anyone had asked me."

"She had a very *strong* vocation until she was *influenced.*" Edwarda's thin voice was strained. Ruth was surprised by this championing of Angela until she remembered that Edwarda had been the superior who had admitted Angela as a postulant.

There seemed no doubt in anyone's mind that Angela's "vacation" was the first step in her permanent separation from St. Aidan's.

"Poor child," said Gregory. "She had a lovely little voice. She sang second. She used to help me with the children's choir. My, they adored her. She looked just like a madonna when she wore the old habit." She reached to push her glasses up on her nose. "But there was something . . . I don't know what. I just felt she never really felt at home."

"She didn't."

Gregory nodded slowly. "You could tell. My, all those years. Now that took courage. The first week I was a postulant, goodness, I was homesick even though I'd gone to school right here. I marched right in to Mother Kieran—she was the superior then, the first one after Mother Imelda herself—and I stood next to her desk—I didn't know you were supposed to kneel down —and I said, 'Reverend Mother, if I still feel this bad by Friday I'm going to ask Papa to come and get me.' Goodness, when I think now of saying that!"

"What did Mother Kieran say?" It was not that Ruth wanted to hear the end of the story but that she found an unexpected comfort in being with Gregory.

"Oh, Mother Kieran. Well, she said didn't I want to love and serve the Lord and that she was disappointed in me for letting such a little thing upset me. I suppose it was very bold (she told me afterward that no one had ever spoken to her like that), but I just said that I didn't see how I could love and serve the Lord very well if I was going to cry all the time. And I was sorry she was disappointed but I didn't think the Lord was disappointed because He made us to be happy."

"How old were you?" Gregory's simplicity was reaching through her bleakness, and she didn't want the quiet voice to stop.

"I was just eighteen. They took me after I graduated from high school. Mother Kieran was always strong on young vocations. She said it was easier to mold the young. Of course, nowadays, things are different. I always thought Angela was too young, but . . ."

As Ruth turned to help her down the corridor, Gregory's powerful fingers curved around her wrist. "Things are not quite right with you, are they?" she asked with unexpected directness.

Ruth shook her head, unable to meet Gregory's eyes.

"Well, now, that happens. I don't know what the dear Lord is after sometimes." She sighed. "Maybe it's November. A lot of people have trouble in November, they say. It's something about the stars, I think. But just the same I'll say a little prayer for you every day."

When Ruth looked up, Gregory's gray eyes were looking

straight at her. Trained never to show affection by any physical means, she stood awkwardly, shaking Ruth's hand up and down in the only permissible token of affection she could think of.

"I've asked Noreen to help you in the library," Rosalia said the day after Angela had left.

"That's not necessary." Ruth caught her peremptory tone and tried to soften it. "There's not so much to do just now. I'm sure I can manage."

"I've already asked her." Rosalia was apologetic. "I thought she could take care of the students so that you could get on with the cataloguing."

"Yes, that would be a help." But the fact was that she did not want Noreen with her slow, irritating mannerisms and endless patter. She did not want anyone, preferring her own brooding darkness to the effort companionship demanded.

"I suppose this was Angela's desk?" Noreen asked as she opened and closed the drawers.

"Yes, although you don't have to keep it there. Angela liked it close to the catalogue."

Noreen looked around speculatively. "Maybe I'll move it near the window. I like to get the morning sun."

Without thinking Ruth looked at her watch.

"I didn't think you'd expect me before ten-thirty."

Ruth thought Rosalia had said nine-thirty, but she didn't want to make an issue of it. "It would be a help if you could be here by ten. A lot of the girls come in during their first study hall."

Ruth's brittle tone was lost on Noreen, who was absorbed in angling the desk into the sunlight. "Well, I'll try. You know how it is. Now this morning the dryer wasn't working. I called Romanelli's but they didn't have anyone they could send out. Then I tried Compton's but they only service their own machines. We never had any trouble when Mr. Morgan was alive.

'You just call me any hour of the day or night, Sister,' he always said. And he sent us a lovely basket of fruit for Christmas, too. He—"

But before Noreen could plunge into further detail, Ruth interrupted. "I'll be back in the archives. If the phone is for me just push the second button."

The archives were small and dark. Usually she left the door open into the main library, but today she closed it resolutely. She sat at her desk with her eyes closed wondering how to endure Noreen's endless chatter. As she reached for the folder of clippings she was going to work on, the door opened a crack.

"May I come in?"

She thought it was Noreen and without looking up started to say, I'm busy.

But it was Nancy Lenihan. "Sorry to bother you but I wanted to check something for the files. Goodness, it's stuffy in here, don't you want the door open?"

"I'd prefer it closed."

"Aren't you hot?"

Ruth didn't answer. How could she say she preferred to be hot, preferred any inconvenience to Noreen's meaningless chatter. But Nancy caught her mood.

She nodded toward the door. "She does go on, doesn't she?" But there was no derision, only amusement in the wide smile. "She's a good soul, you know. She picks up all the little odds and ends the rest of us don't want to be bothered with."

Nancy's tolerance only set Ruth's teeth on edge. "That's easy enough to do with all the time she has on her hands." She should have been ashamed at her unkindness, but she felt only a malicious pleasure in saying something sharp and wounding.

Nancy's broad tolerance remained unshaken. "Noreen's not an achiever. She's satisfied with less than most of us."

Perversely, Ruth chose to interpret the comment as a reproach for her own industry.

"If she didn't talk so much she'd get more done." It was the sort of petty remark she deplored and knew she would never make about anyone else. From the beginning of her religious life Noreen had aroused in her a spirit of self-righteousness.

"I have disdainful thoughts about one of my sisters," she had once whispered in the confessional, hoping for a remedy against her persistent fault. But Father Dowling, old, arthritic, and weary of nuns' confessions, only whispered back, "Now, now, we mustn't be like that. Think of our blessed Lord."

She had thought of Him but He had provided no cure for her sin. Everything about Noreen grated on her: the halfhearted preparation for her classes, the slow, exaggerated movements of her mouth when she ate, the aimless hours poring over catalogues and magazines, the listless genuflections in chapel.

Nancy's pale blue eyes with their thin lashes looked at her thoughtfully. "You've always been hard on Noreen, haven't you? You expect too much of her. She can't put as much heart—or mind—into things as you do."

The unmerited compliment made Ruth flush with irritation and guilt. After Nancy left with the information she needed, Ruth sat for a while doing nothing, indifferent to the work piled on her desk. The door was ajar and she could hear Noreen humming a commercial in a voice slightly off key. Shortly after, she heard the telephone and then Noreen's phlegmatic steps coming toward the inner office.

"It's Joanne, for you. I thought you said the second button but I wasn't sure so I thought it would be just as quick if I—"

Ruth nodded, picking up the phone. None of Nancy's tolerant reflections were strong enough to stem her impatience.

"Ruth? Joanne. Would you be free to take Daryl's class for the rest of the morning? Yes, right away if you can. I'll explain when you get over here. It's Room 108. I'll meet you here."

When Ruth arrived Joanne was standing outside the door of Daryl's classroom.

"Sorry," she apologized, "but I couldn't find anyone else free."

"What happened?"

"Daryl fainted. One of the girls came running over to the office. They were scared to death, of course."

"Is she all right?"

"I guess so. We couldn't bring her to for a while. Peg came over with a wheelchair and brought her back to the convent. I wouldn't have bothered you, but they're in the middle of a standardized test and it will be invalid unless someone is here to supervise. It's just a question of timing them on the different sections." Joanne looked at her watch. "They have about an hour and fifteen minutes to go. The time will be up on this section in ten minutes."

Ruth nodded, looking in through the glass partition of the door. Most of the children were still bent over their papers but a few had already finished, sitting correctly, their pencils on their desks, their hands in their laps. Daryl was a strict disciplinarian.

"The instructions are on the desk and the electric timer is set."

"Fine, I'll manage."

"Leave the papers in my office when you're finished. If I'm not there you can put them in the top drawer of the file. Just close it tight and it will lock automatically."

It was after one o'clock when she was free to go up to the infirmary and find out about Daryl.

Peg was cleaning up lunch trays. "She's back in her room. I wanted to keep her here for the rest of the day but she had her own ideas." Peg was obviously irked by Daryl's obstinacy.

"What happened, do you know?"

"The girls say she was standing over by the window and the first thing they knew she had crumpled up on the floor. Daryl says the room was very hot and she had been standing too long." Peg sounded skeptical.

"That's possible, isn't it?"

"Of course." She paused. "Except that it didn't seem like a normal faint."

"What does that mean?"

"That there was no change in respiration, no change in her color. Ordinarily a stimulant—spirits of ammonia, for instance —starts the blood pumping and the person comes out of the faint. None of those things happened with Daryl. I don't know if Joanne told you but she was unconscious for a long time. She didn't really pull out of it until we got her back here in bed."

"Did you call the doctor?"

"He's coming this afternoon anyway to see Michael. He can take a look at her then—if she'll let him."

"But she has to let him."

"That wasn't what she was saying when I left her. She assured me that she was fine. The most I could get her to agree to was staying in her room for the rest of the day." Peg banged the trays back in the cupboard. "I'd rather have six bed patients than one Susannah or Daryl."

"May I go up to see her?"

"Please do. Maybe you can talk some sense into her. I can't, God knows."

Daryl was still in bed when Ruth went up. When she hadn't answered her knock Ruth had opened the door quietly and tiptoed over to the bed. She thought at first that Daryl was asleep but a narrow movement of her eyelids betrayed her.

"Daryl?"

She opened her eyes and her face brightened. "Ruth! I'm sorry, I thought it was Peg." She looked embarrassed at her admission. "I don't want to argue anymore about seeing the doctor and all that."

Ruth sidestepped the issue. "How are you?"

"Fine. I should get up." She reached for her bathrobe.

"Stay there," Ruth said, pulling a chair over to the bed. "What happened?"

"Oh, it was just hot in the classroom. Anna always turns the heat way up. I should have remembered to open a window."

"Peg says you were unconscious for a long time."

Daryl didn't answer.

"She feels it wasn't a normal fainting spell."

"I didn't know fainting was normal."

"Don't you think it would be sensible to see the doctor when he comes this afternoon?"

"What for?"

"Just to be sure there's nothing wrong."

"There's *nothing wrong.*"

Ruth rose and pushed the chair back against the wall. Daryl was a master of provocation. In less than five minutes she had transformed Ruth's sympathy into annoyance. As she turned to go, she asked, "Would you like something from the library?"

"No, thank you."

Ruth knew the tone. It was the cool veneer Daryl used to conceal her loneliness. There had been a time when Ruth would have found it impossible to ignore that cry for help but now she resisted it angrily. She wanted no part of Daryl's struggle; she wanted only the strength to face her own. Yet the ingrained habit of compassion held her as she turned to go, and in that moment of hesitation Daryl called her.

"Ruth, please don't go." She had lifted herself up against the pillows, her robe thrown across her shoulders. "I have to talk to you."

Ruth's hand was on the doorknob, her back against the door. I can leave, she thought. I can say I'm busy, that I have to be in the library, that I'll come back later. Her terror was out of all proportion to what was being asked of her. Was it so hard to listen to Daryl, to help her untangle her bewilderment, to solace her in her desolation? She had done it before; and while it had drained her to watch Daryl's angelic aspirations clash with the life St. Aidan's offered her, her own life had not been shaken. Then she had listened out of sureness and strength. Now she had neither.

It was at such times, they had been taught, that God is closest, most ready to supply His divine strength for their human weakness.

Let prayer be their first recourse in all their difficulties. Especially in times of desolation, they must renew their efforts to seek God in prayer. Let them believe with unwavering faith that God is present to all who call upon him in loving humility.

But she had no "loving humility," that quality that would make God bend toward her needs. She was arrogant and without mercy. She had closed the door against Noreen, had deliberately withdrawn from Rosalia. Those narrow shafts of light that the loving kindness of her sisters brought into her darkness lasted for only a moment, and then she was left cold and dark again.

"Please don't be angry, Ruth."

Even that timid child's plea aroused no love. It was only remembered love that caused Ruth to move the chair back again to Daryl's bed. She grasped at one last evasion.

"Don't you think it might be better if you waited to talk until you feel stronger?" Last exit before the bridge, she thought.

But Daryl, oblivious of the signal, plunged straight over the water. "I don't think I'm going to feel better until I get some things sorted out."

"Have you been sleeping?" She veered toward the spur, directing the conversation toward anything that would keep them from the dangerous route Daryl was following.

"Not much. Being awake is better than the dreams." She twisted her narrow gold profession ring around her finger.

"What kind of dreams?" Another attempt to sidetrack.

"Oh, variations on a theme. I'm always out swimming. It's very beautiful and there's a float way out. It seems too far to swim, but then there's a figure in the water and it keeps beckoning to me and I know it will be all right, because if I can't make it he'll help me. So I keep swimming and he keeps smiling and waving. And then when I've run out of strength, when I need him, his smile goes all wrong—and he turns on me."

In the silence Daryl was drawing little patterns on the white sheet. "It's not very nice, is it?" Her consonants were hard and clipped as though they would protect her from her nightmare.

"It's a betrayal dream." In her effort to fight free of her emotion, she sounded, Ruth realized, like a psychology text.

"Of course." There was a hint of mockery in Daryl's controlled tone. She had taken off her ring, turning it to see the motto inscribed on the inside. " 'Reveal Thy presence to me.' " She looked up suddenly at Ruth and smiled.

"For God's sake, don't, Daryl." They were directly over the water now at a height greater than she had imagined.

"Don't worry, I'm not blaspheming." The cool voice was steady and ordered by years of discipline. "It isn't God who has betrayed me. I've never once thought that."

For Daryl the betraying figure was St. Aidan's. Two months ago Ruth would have argued with her, cogently, steadily, that since God had led her to St. Aidan's, then it was at St. Aidan's that He was to be found. But those strong, healthy arguments on which she had staked her life had been caught in an unexpected blight and she had nothing to offer in their place.

"I don't think I can find God here anymore, Ruth." It was both a statement and a plea for help. But every plea for strength only probed deeper into Ruth's weakness. "Seek the Lord where he is to be found / Cry to Him and He will answer," they sang at Mass. But was there a place where He was to be found? "Do not seek God abroad in the world, for it is in your own heart that He is to be found, closer to you than you are to yourself." She had always believed that, not by investigation or analysis but by that simple in-breathing by which one affirms life. She had sought Him in her own heart and for years she had found Him. But now she found nothing and she had no will to continue the effort. Like Daryl, she too had dreams. She was crawling along a narrow, rocky cave, the ceiling only inches above her head. In the dark, spidery things crawled over her but she was too tired to fear them. Unable to go on, she lay huddled in the darkness, shunted between despair and the wavering hope that just a few feet beyond her lay food and drink.

"I know you believe in St. Aidan's—and I do, too, in a way

—but it isn't right for me anymore. I've been thinking and praying for over a year and I think I'm ready to do something."

"What?"

"I'm going to leave."

It was the moment Ruth had dreaded. She was shaken with anger, an anger more terrible because she knew it was unjustified. Then leave, she wanted to cry. Do whatever you have to do but don't drag me into it. I'm tired of being concerned about other people. I want something for myself. Her reaction shamed her, but no shame could bring warmth to her voice.

"Where will you go?"

"There's a small solitude community about a hundred miles northwest of here. I've been in touch with them and they've offered me a place for a trial period."

"What do you want me to say?"

Daryl was bewildered by her coldness. "I guess I'd like to know what you think."

"What difference would it make?"

"Well, it would help to know . . . to feel that someone understands."

"And if I don't, would it make any difference?"

Daryl's cool veneer had worn off, and it was a wistful child who spoke, but a child of invincible determination. "I think"— the words were slow and evenly spaced—"I think I'd have to go anyway."

Her ring was back on her finger and she turned it absently. "I know it won't be easy. This has been my home for so long. And it's especially hard now when things are so unsettled. But I don't think I can hold out much longer. God has to be some-where."

The yearning in Daryl's voice was so pure that for the first time she evoked a responsive love in Ruth. "Then go wherever you think He's to be found."

"Will you pray for me, please?" Daryl asked as Ruth turned toward the door.

She knew that if she said anything it would be a cry of impotence: I can't pray. God is gone. Instead she smiled and nodded and Daryl smiled back.

The chapel was dark and empty. Someone had opened a front window, and a triangle of light settled on the altar steps. Tense and straight, Ruth knelt on the side, back near the old confessional. She fixed her eyes on the large wooden crucifix behind the altar. "Look at our Lord on the cross and you will see that your own troubles are very small," Mother Columban had instructed them piously. "Only a very selfish person can look at a crucifix and still be wrapped up in her own sufferings." The sentence that had shamed so many novices once again carried its condemnation. She was selfish, Ruth knew it, yet while it shamed her she clung to it as her only possession.

She needed to be strengthened and comforted, and she found no comfort in the crucifix, only another image of suffering, another inexorable demand that she could not meet. She needed sweetness (she could find no other word)—the sweetness of compassion, of a hand placed over hers, of a look that asked nothing in return. The emptiness inside her was like a great tumor that swelled against her lungs and constricted her breathing. She thought she had given up everything when she returned to St. Aidan's, and she had done it gladly. "To give up all things in order to possess their Single Treasure," the Rule had read. But the Rule mocked her. She had found no treasure; she had found only confusion and fear and a dozen different motives tearing them apart. What had this to do with the God of love? Daryl had come close to the bone when she had talked of her sense of betrayal. Unbidden, the words of the thief who was crucified with Jesus rose in Ruth's mind: If Thou art the Son of God, come down from the Cross and save yourself and us.

Her bitterness and anger frightened her and she closed her eyes in an involuntary gesture against despair. But the darkness brought her no peace. Desperately she summoned up a psalm to fill the blank reaches of her mind:

> As a deer longs
>   for running streams
> so longs my soul
>   for you, my God,
> My soul thirsts for God,
>   the God of life.

But the words she had always loved could not penetrate the darkness. After a while she let them drift away and knelt on without thoughts or words.

She stayed on past the hour, kneeling until her back was numb, hardly aware of what she did beyond the obscure memory that Daryl had asked her to pray for her.

Rawlins and Swenson, Realtors
108 East 68th St.
New York, N.Y.
November 5, 1980

Mr. Alec Stafford
Stafford, Connor, Lipsky, Architects
18 Ballantyne Avenue
Glen Cove, New York

Dear Alec,

Sister Rosalia just telephoned to apologize for not having been available when I called last week. A number of unexpected things had come up and she had had to put off the discussion with the sisters.

Meanwhile she sent our material to her lawyer for his opinion. The meeting with all the nuns is scheduled for this Sunday. I asked her how that worked—whether it was just a consultative process or whether the group had deliberative powers. Nowadays everybody has a vote, she told me. That surprised me; I had always thought of those church institutions as controlled pretty much from the top. It used to be that way, she said, but now the process is much more democratic. I said I bet she wished she could make the decision herself and get it over with. "Oh, no," she said, "I would never want to make a decision like that." She certainly is not a power-hungry lady. Interesting to know how they ever put someone like that at the top. She was elected, I found that out.

I asked when the result of the meeting would be available to us. That seemed to throw her. She said this was just the first of a series and that no effort to reach closure would be made just now. I can't quite figure out why everything is taking so long. We've made our proposal; they know their options. They must realize it's a marvelous deal for them. I asked if she didn't have an executive committee to deal with major issues like this, but that bothered her, too. All the sisters must have a chance to express their opinions in the hopes that they will reach a consensus. It's not enough for a decision to be made, apparently. It must be made in harmony! Try that in your committees!

She did say she'd let me know how the Sunday meeting goes.

Best,

Steve Rawlins

11

Rosalia had originally scheduled the first of the Community meetings for Sunday morning, but Peg begged to have it put off until after dinner.

"You know they'll want to come down from the infirmary, and I just can't cope with all the morning work plus getting people dressed and in wheelchairs by ten o'clock."

"Can't some of us help you?" Ruth asked.

"That would be great. They'll have an early dinner, so if you come up when you've finished dinner we should be able to get things settled by one-thirty. If that isn't too late for Rosalia?"

Rosalia shook her head. "What about the school, Joanne?"

"No problem. It's a long weekend, so almost everyone is away, and Mrs. Adams will cover the desk until six."

When Ruth went up to the infirmary floor after dinner, Rita was already in Bridget McGuire's room helping her to get dressed.

"You have to wear your hearing aid," she was shouting at Bridget. "This is a very important meeting. You have to hear what they're saying. Is that all right now?" And then louder, "Is that all right now? Can you hear me?"

"I can hear you."

"Well, keep it on like that and don't turn it off. No, *don't* touch it. You should have a new one anyway."

"I like this one. I've had it a long time."

"That's the trouble. They have better ones now."

"It's good enough."

"Well, *don't* touch it. Leave it the way it is. It's very important that you listen to everything they say. They're trying to take St. Aidan's away from us."

"Who? The communists?"

"No, the sisters right here."

There was silence.

"Did you hear what I said?"

"I heard."

"So you see why it's ve-ry im-por-tant that you listen to every word. Otherwise they're going to sell St. Aidan's." The last three words rose in a crescendo.

"Nonsense. This is our home. Who'd want to sell it?"

"Oh, there are people who want to, you mark my words. Some of those young people right in this house."

"What about us?"

"They don't care about you. All they think about is themselves. You stay there. I'll be back in a minute to help you downstairs." And Rita came out of Bridget's room, a basin and facecloth in her hands. The smell of battle invigorated Rita. Her eyes were bright, her complexion in ruddy contrast to her pale gray dress. She was on top of Ruth before she noticed her.

Ruth was taut with anger. "That was the most insidious thing I've ever heard."

Rita's arched eyebrows rose higher. "Somebody has to protect them."

"You're not protecting them. You're deliberately setting us against each other."

"I told the truth, that's all. Sometimes the truth is very divisive. Even our blessed Lord said His truth would be like a two-edged sword."

Nothing angered Ruth so much as this rhetorical trick of

covering issues with pious platitudes. She started to snap, Leave "our blessed Lord" out of it, but caught herself in time. There was, she knew, no point in argument. In a fight she was no match for Rita.

"We must have very different conceptions of the truth," she said evenly. "Will you excuse me, please?" and she walked around Rita and down the hall to Timothy Higgins' room.

When she knocked on Timothy's door she could barely hear the voice that answered her. Timothy Higgins looked no older than when Ruth had left St. Aidan's. Tall and thin with swarthy skin and dark gentle eyes, her looks were at variance with her name.

"Is her name really Timothy Higgins?" Ruth had asked as a postulant as she tried in bewilderment to yoke the Latin face with the Irish name.

"Her mother's name was Castellanos," Magdalen had explained. "Her parents met while her father was working in Mexico."

Timothy had taught Spanish, written poetry that was published occasionally in small religious magazines, and turned St. Aidan's into a greenhouse. Her first twelve years had been spent in Mexico, and she had brought to the dark, heavy halls of St. Aidan's a flair for color and living things. Two years after Ruth had left, Timothy had been stricken blind. It had happened so suddenly that there was no period of preparation. For three months she sat in a darkness so profound that nothing reached her. They came and sat with her, read to her, offered to take her for walks in the garden, but she had turned to stone. Peg dressed her in the morning, undressed her at night. She made no resistance, but she offered no help. For the rest of the day she sat wherever they put her, her hands hidden in the long black sleeves, her eyes closed as though this voluntary privation could keep her from that other uncontrollable darkness. In the evening they took turns feeding her, giving her only liquids or baby foods because she made no effort to chew anything solid. They talked while they fed her—of the school, of events in the Community, of alumnae they had heard from—but it was like speaking to the dead.

Gregory was among the most faithful visitors. Timothy had loved music as she had loved color, and it had been their custom to spend Sunday afternoons together in the music rooms, Gregory lost in the joy of playing and Timothy providing a rapt audience. As Gregory grew older, the clear notes blurred and her heavy foot on the pedals made the music sound frenzied and uncontrolled, but Timothy's admiring attention never diminished. It was a friendship that had lasted through the years.

One night as Gregory was feeding Timothy her hand shook and a spoonful of food slipped down Timothy's chin and onto her habit. Timothy, unaware, made no effort to wipe it off but let it drip down uncaring. Gregory reached for a facecloth but the sight of that still beautiful face smeared and mindless was more than she could endure. Without warning she began to cry, not quietly but with the long wrenching sobs she had repressed for weeks.

"Timothy, help me," she had cried. "Help me." She had closed her own eyes against a sight she could not sustain; but as the storm subsided she looked up and saw Timothy's hands creep, slow and tenuous, from her sleeves and reach out to take Gregory's own large hands. Timothy made no other gesture. Her eyes were still closed, the expression on her face unchanged. But Gregory asked for no more. That silent moment of life had given her hope enough.

"Don't count on it too much," Peg had said when Gregory told her. But the next morning Timothy opened her mouth voluntarily when Peg fed her and in three weeks she had pushed aside the darkness in which she had wrapped herself and began to confront that other darkness.

Those months of death were never mentioned. Timothy spoke matter-of-factly of her blindness but never of what it cost her. Her eyes had not lost their beauty; if anything they looked larger and more yearning.

She didn't want to be a burden and insisted on doing things for herself. Now as Ruth opened the door, Timothy's room looked like a scene in a fun house. Nothing was in disorder but everything was slightly askew. The bed was made but the spread hung down at an awkward angle. Her slippers, neatly placed at the head of her bed, went backward—from right to left. The crucifix on the wall had slipped sideways, so that it looked like a surrealistic sculpture, one arm groping vainly toward heaven. Timothy herself was dressed and ready to go.

"I'm sure I could make it by myself," she said as she took Ruth's arm, "but Peg gets nervous if I wander too far. She's always afraid I'll miss the steps."

"Well, they do come at strange places."

"Oh, but I'm so used to them, you know, after all these years. Maybe we won't have to worry about it much longer." She gave Ruth's arm a little nudge as though losing St. Aidan's was their private joke.

"That must be very difficult to face after fifty years."

"Sixty years. I'll be here sixty years on July sixth."

"It will be a terrible sacrifice."

"Yes." They were standing on the landing leading down to the Community room. "There used to be a statue of St. Francis here. Do you remember that?"

Ruth nodded, remembering too late that Timothy couldn't see the gesture.

"Marian Connell had it removed. It was bad art, she said. I don't think anyone misses it anymore. We've outgrown it." She paused. "Perhaps we'll outgrow St. Aidan's." The sightless eyes were fixed on the stained wall where the statue of St. Francis had been. "I'll remind them of that if they ask me," she said as Ruth led her into the assembly room.

This time there were no surprises. They knew what they were about.

The Council had made its preparations with scrupulous care. Rosalia would chair the meeting, providing the details of

Mr. Rawlins' offer; Joanne would explain the possible ministries available to them if they were to leave St. Aidan's.

To listen, not to coerce. Ruth reminded herself of Rosalia's final counsel as she looked around, taking the measure of the groups. Rosalia's group consisted of Daryl, Rita, and Gregory. Rita's power of persuasion would have only limited scope in such an environment. Magdalen's group included Anna Shaughnessey and Terezia. Ruth did not envy her. Anna and Terezia were at opposite ends of the spectrum. Even ethnically they were at war: Terezia the Hungarian aristocrat, Anna the Irish peasant. It would take a strong and diplomatic hand to keep the fires banked. Susannah and Edwarda were in Joanne's group. Not easy, but she'll manage, thought Ruth. She can keep an even keel in any weather.

Her own group, with Peg as its leader, consisted of Nancy and Kate, and Michael Nolan and Timothy Higgins from the infirmary. As Peg, justifiably nervous, cleared her throat to begin the opening prayer, Michael pushed her wheelchair forward and asked, "Well, are we selling St. Aidan's?"

Michael had always had a strong deep voice, and age and the effort of communicating with Bridget McGuire had made it deeper. Now it resounded through the room. Peg, prepared to lead diplomatically into the discussion, sat agog, her notes in her lap. Nancy started to laugh, and Michael lifted herself sideways in her chair and winked.

"Stole your thunder, didn't I?" she asked, nodding at Peg, her own laugh ending in a cough. "I'm too old to fool around. If things are going to change we might as well get them going. I tried to say that to Bridget, but she can't hear a thing, poor soul. I'd rather have rheumatism. At least I don't miss anything!" And she laughed again.

It was Michael, earthy and practical, who set the tone for their discussion. Peg was unexpectedly cast in the role of temporizer, assuring Michael that nothing was settled yet, that there were many considerations to be discussed, other options to be

brought forward, time reserved for personal reflection. "No decision has been reached yet," she assured her.

"Well, it should be," Michael interrupted. "I've no patience
with fiddle-faddle. 'Does the Lord want this, does the Lord want
that!' 'Try it and see,' I said to Josephine one day when she was
mooning around, Lord rest her. 'What do you expect, a crown
of roses to tell you when you're right?' All this talk!" Her thick
eyebrows came together. "That one knows what I mean," she
said, nodding toward Kate. "Don't you, young lady?"

Kate's smile was one of pure joy and affection. They're
friends, Ruth realized. Sixty years between them but it doesn't
matter.

"Oh, we've talked some things over. When Kathleen first
wanted to go to the camp, I said to her, 'If that's where you're
needed, then you go—and let them talk. You can't stop them.
They've been doing it for years—some of them.' "

Peg started to interrupt, but Michael went on, caught up in
her own apologia.

"I've never been afraid of movement. I've always kind of
liked it. Maybe it was because my father was a railroad man.
'Mark my words, Nonnie,' he used to say to my mother, 'this
country will go where the railroads go. There's no keeping it
back.' And he was right. Some things you just can't hold back."

The lap robe that Peg had put over Michael's knees had
slipped down and Kate bent over to fix it for her. She said
nothing but held Kate's hand for a moment, nodding gratefully.

Peg's careful introduction was brushed aside as Michael
pushed them full tilt into their discussion. The group had few
doubts about selling St. Aidan's and most of their discussion
centered on the direction life might take if they went to Holy
Rosary.

By the time Peg announced that they had just time to break
for coffee before the general session, they had carried the discussion as far as they could.

Ruth was the last to leave the room and she found Kate
waiting for her at the door.

"Are you going to get coffee or could we talk for a few minutes," she asked.

"We could do both, couldn't we?" Ruth suggested.

Kate scowled. "I'd like to talk to you alone without all these people milling about."

Ruth nodded, unable to catch Kate's mood. She tried to smile, but Kate did not meet her eyes.

She seemed both angry and embarrassed as she said, "This isn't easy to say, but I think we have to be honest with each other and I suspect you agree with me."

Again Ruth nodded, unsure where the conversation was going.

"You know when you came back to St. Aidan's I was impressed," Kate began. "Someone choosing religious life for the second time, someone who knew what being a nun was like and doing it all the same. That really impressed me. I felt as though having you here was going to be a support for a lot of us. You weren't caught up in the old rituals and the old loyalties. You seemed free and honest, and people respected you—even some of the old ones."

Ruth could feel her spine grow tight. It was clear that Kate's compliments were only a prelude to something less pleasant.

"And then . . ."

And then what? Ruth wondered. And then you noticed that I was not so free or so wise. You noticed that I could be prickly and sharp, that I sometimes avoided people who might burden me. What else did you notice? she thought bitterly. Did you notice that almost everything I had associated with St. Aidan's had been sloughed off? Did you notice that I still grieved for my father? Did you notice that God left me alone?

"It seemed to me that you started withdrawing," Kate continued, "that I couldn't count on you to say what you were really thinking. For instance, at the meeting just now, you hardly said anything."

"There wasn't any need, was there? Everyone seemed pretty much agreed."

"That's not the point. It's true we didn't need you to argue or explain. But if you really cared what happened to St. Aidan's, wouldn't you want to say something? It seemed to me that you didn't much care which direction we went in, as though your life didn't touch St. Aidan's, like someone observing from the sidelines. . . . It's none of my business, I know, but it made me wonder if you had decided not to stay."

As soon as she had said it, Kate realized her error. She reached out to touch Ruth's arm. "I'm sorry, really. That was out of line. I don't know what made me say it."

"Because you were thinking it." Ruth's voice was rasping and unsteady. "You find it easy to make judgments about people's lives, don't you?" She felt as though she had turned to ice except for the two spots flaming in her cheeks. "It's easy when you're young to expect perfection from everyone except yourself. Maybe when life chews you up a bit you'll be a little more understanding."

Kate's mouth was pulled thin like a child who was trying not to cry, but when she looked up her eyes were as direct as ever. "Yes, I suppose I am too harsh sometimes, but I'm not asking for perfection. I'm asking for commitment. I thought that's what religious life was supposed to be. Is that too much to ask?"

She turned abruptly and followed the others who were filing back into the Community room.

"Coming, Ruth?" Nancy called and Ruth nodded dumbly, pretending to rearrange the plants on the windowsill. She stood after they had passed, frightened and dizzy at the implications of Kate's question: Is that too much? Tell me that, Ruth Arendt. Is commitment too much to ask of you?

Rawlins and Swenson, Realtors
108 East 68th St.
New York, N.Y.
November 6, 1980

Mr. Alec Stafford
Stafford, Connor, Lipsky, Architects
18 Ballantyne Avenue
Glen Cove, New York

Dear Alec,

Here are some papers that Hal Sandler, St. Aidan's lawyer, sent on to me. I forgot to enclose them in my last letter.

Well, Alec, by the time this reaches you their first big meeting will be over. The last time I talked to Sister Rosalia she sounded as though she were going on trial for murder. Too bad we can't videotape the proceedings!!

I'll be in touch soon.

Steve Rawlins

12

The accord within Peg's group had lulled their anxieties, and they were unprepared for the divisions that became obvious in the general session.

Edwarda gave the report of the first group, her stiff white band pulled tight across her forehead, her long black veil scrupulously following the prescriptions of their former Rule. Her dry, precise voice made it very clear that, except for Joanne, no one in their group was in favor of moving from St. Aidan's. Rita's report was equally negative, weighted, of course, with her own implications of dark things being plotted against them. She had won not only Bridget McGuire but Gregory as well to her side. Rosalia was flushed and angry at the obvious manipulation, but she was powerless to stop Rita.

"Damn free speech!" muttered Peg under her breath.

Nancy's report was succinct and positive. All six of them favored the proposal to sell St. Aidan's and begin a new ministry at Holy Rosary. She had hardly finished when Susannah's hand shot up.

"May I ask a question?" She waited for no recognition but plunged ahead. "I would like to know the members of Sister Anne Elizabeth's group."

Nancy hardly recognized the formality of her own name.

"Our Council member was Peg. The other members of the group were Timothy, Michael, Ruth, and Kate."

"Would you repeat that, please. I'm not sure we all heard."

It was Susannah's means of underscoring her disapproval, but Nancy maintained her equanimity.

"Timothy, Michael, Ruth, and Kate," she repeated.

"What was the last name?"

"Kate Boylan."

"And the group leader?" Susannah persisted.

"Peg Darcy."

"I see," said Susannah. "Thank you very much, Anne Elizabeth."

She had made her point. Peg and Kate were dangerous infiltrators who had coerced or tricked the remaining membership. Susannah's implicit observation was clear: this group should not be trusted. It did not represent the true membership of St. Aidan's.

Peg shifted angrily in her chair but said nothing.

It was Magdalen who spoke for the final group. "I'm afraid our report is not so clear-cut as the others. We have very strong and divided opinions on the proposal to sell St. Aidan's."

"I bet," whispered Peg. "Anna and Terezia!"

"When we moved on to consider the opportunities available at Holy Rosary, one of our group pointed out that we had not given ourselves sufficient space to examine other options. This led to a discussion that others found irrelevant but that, I think, we must take into consideration. I really don't feel competent to summarize this part of our discussion; and so, with your permission, I would like to ask for a little extra time for Terezia to speak on the plan she presented."

"I knew it," whispered Peg. "I knew they could never agree."

Terezia did not speak from her place but went to the podium at the front of the room. No matter what the occasion, Terezia's manner carried an air of authority. It was not that she was deliberately imposing. Her manner was often apologetic, acknowledging that her English was imperfect, that she did not know St. Aidan's as they did. Yet with it all there was a sense of leadership. She carried herself with freedom and fearlessness: her shoulders back, her long legs striding purposefully. Her dark hair, only partially gray, gave the effect of white wings above her temples. She made no effort to placate or coerce, yet despite the frequent opposition to her ideas, she was always listened to intently.

"It is not a plan I have." She smiled apologetically. "It is a little question only. I wonder if it is good to jump so quickly to a conclusion. We have thought only to go to Holy Rosary should we close St. Aidan's; but are there not also other places, perhaps not so close in miles but closer to the heart?"

The attention was all hers now.

"St. Aidan's was not the only convent begun by your Mother Imelda Finney." Her accent gave an exotic flavor to the familiar Irish name. "There are also three other convents: Donald's, Rose's, and Malachy." Hesitant over the unfamiliar name, she put the accent on the second syllable.

Anna clicked her tongue in disgust and Michael's deep voice roared, "Má-la-ky."

"Yes, thank you. Má-la-ky." She was unperturbed by the correction. "It is of Má-la-ky I would like to speak."

"*Saint* Má-la-ky." Michael, pleased with the success of her first correction, offered a second.

"So, *Saint* Malachy. This, I understand, was also a boarding school as we are here; but then when boarders were not coming they began another work. They are now, I think, a center for retreats—and this work goes for them very well. Is this not so?"

Terezia had undoubtedly meant it as a rhetorical question, but Edwarda was immediately on her feet.

"That was a very different situation. Very different. Perhaps they did have to close the school. I don't want to make judgments about that. But as for the retreat center, that would never have flourished, never, except for the Benedictine Fathers. I had the opportunity of visiting there once with Sister Marian, and the superior explained the whole situation to us."

Terezia was smiling encouragingly. "Yes. This is very good. You would tell us about this situation?"

Edwarda found herself trapped by her own precipitancy. She had spoken to dismiss St. Malachy's and now she was presented as a commentator on its success. Her thin lips pressed together in disapproval.

"Well, there's very little to say. There is a small Benedictine monastery about a mile from St. Malachy's and the fathers there wished to broaden their work to include retreats, conferences on theology, and so forth, but their own monastery was not big enough. Of course, in this day and age they could not afford to build, and so it was providential that St. Malachy's was available. I believe they are using the school buildings and, of course, the chapel for this work. Sister Assumpta told us when we were there that they could do a great deal more work but they do not have the sisters. They are not getting vocations," she concluded triumphantly, happy to be able to end on a note of failure for St. Malachy's.

Terezia, however, had heard no note of failure. She had heard what pleased her immensely and she nodded and smiled happily at Edwarda. "This is very interesting, what you have told us."

But there was no answering smile from Edwarda. She stood stiff and fearful, like an animal that senses danger but cannot discover the direction from which it will come. She had set herself resolutely against Terezia, but her very efforts to discredit her opponent had only plunged her further into danger.

"So," continued Terezia, "there is now a flourishing work at St. Malachy's."

Again she smiled encouragingly at Edwarda, but Edwarda's mouth was a thin line. Frightened and bewildered by this unexpected turn, she was unable to counter Terezia.

It was Rita who interrupted the unequal dialogue, her strong voice deep with discontent. "I quite understand what Magdalen meant when she said that a member of her group had introduced an irrelevant topic." Her r's trilled in annoyance. "The direction St. Malachy's has taken is very interesting, I'm sure, but it is no concern of ours. Perhaps Terezia does not have sufficient knowledge of the history of St. Aidan's and the locale in which we are working to know that it would be an impossibility, a total impossibility"—Rita's rhetoric was heavily dependent on repetition—"for such a program as is now in operation at St. Malachy's to be successful here at St. Aidan's. I am sure that anyone—anyone—who knows and understands the background of St. Aidan's will bear me out."

Her color had risen as she spoke, and when she finished she stood flushed and triumphant at having so easily cast Terezia in the role of alien. They stood for a moment in silence, like two fencers, Rita's thick white hair and fair skin in dramatic contrast to Terezia's swarthy coloring. With her black turtleneck sweater and heavy wooden crucifix suspended from a leather thong, Terezia looked more gypsy than nun.

She nodded toward Rita in acknowledgment, but her smile was gone. "Perhaps I have not yet made myself clear." It was not an apology for incoherence but an implicit accusation that Rita had deliberately misinterpreted her. "I, too, understand that the work of Malachy's cannot be the work for us here. It is something else I am suggesting. I am suggesting that we consider to join the Community of St. Malachy."

Even Terezia, dauntless though she was, was touched by the enormity of what she was proposing, and her hand reached up toward her crucifix as though that could save them from the pain she was inflicting.

They had assembled to discuss the possible loss of their ministry and their home. For all of them, no matter how they saw the future, leaving St. Aidan's would be a kind of death. For those who had not yet come to see the need, it would be a death unredeemed by hope. But at least their identity would not suffer; they would remain together as a body. Their work would change, their home would change, but their identity as a community would be unimpaired.

Now Terezia threatened even that. "I am suggesting that we consider to join the Community of St. Malachy," she had said in her alien syntax. She was suggesting that they disappear, that they die not only in the externals of what they did but in the very blood and bone of their religious existence.

As in October, when Rosalia had first placed before them the proposal to sell St. Aidan's, now they sat silent and motionless, caught again in unexpected death. Michael strained forward in her wheelchair, her mouth working nervously. Bridget McGuire, having missed Terezia's statement but sensing the sudden tension, pushed and jabbed at her hearing aid. As always in moments of crisis, they took refuge in that age-old regulation of keeping their eyes cast down. Even Timothy in an instinctive and gratuitous gesture inclined her head and lowered her lids over her sightless eyes. How deeply they had been penetrated by those years of discipline, so deeply, thought Ruth, that there will never be the sound of tears or mourning even in the face of death; and when finally, released from immobility, we lift our heads there will be nothing in our faces to give away the depth of our anguish.

> Believing that all the circumstances of their lives are regulated by the hand of a loving God, they will never permit themselves to be moved by unregulated emotions. Both joys and sorrows alike will be received as precious gifts of God. Consequently, their faces will always reflect harmony and peace rather than sorrow or any other purely human emotion.

"I am appalled by this manipulation." In unison they raised their heads at Rita's sharp voice. "Surely it is testing our credulity to ask us to believe that Terezia just happened to think of this plan at the last minute. It is clear to me that this must have been discussed at the Council; and while, of course, we have no control over the Council, I certainly would have considered it more honorable had they presented the idea themselves rather than getting it on the floor in this underhanded way."

Peg and Joanne were on their feet in an instant; but Rosalia raised her hand for silence. Her navy dress, a size too large, hung awkwardly from her shoulders, yet despite her appearance there was integrity and authority in her manner.

"I wish to state in behalf of the Council and in my own behalf that the idea that Terezia has brought forward has been neither discussed nor mentioned in Council. It comes as as much of a surprise to me as to anyone here."

But Rita was mounted and spurred. "I can scarcely believe—" she began again, but Rosalia stopped her.

"If you cannot believe my word then I don't think there is any place for you in this discussion." She sat down suddenly, as though someone had pricked her and let out all her life.

Again there was silence, but the timbre had changed. Their first bewildered terror was wearing off, and now they were carefully circling Terezia's proposal. Terezia herself had not moved from the podium. Her hand had dropped from her crucifix, and she reached toward them, half beseeching, half commanding.

"Please, if I could say a little more. There is something fine here at St. Aidan's, something fine and strong that should not be lost. It comes, I think, first from your Mother Imelda. And so also it must have been her gift to those other convents she founded. And while I understand you have been independent of each other for many years, yet in spirit there must be a"—she hesitated—"a bound."

No one corrected her and she continued. "It is, perhaps, time to find again this bound. Then, too, the work they are doing at Malachy's is for the Church such a need. It speaks to me of the spirit that is here at St. Aidan's. This other place, Holy Rosary" —her eyes narrowed and she hesitated—"of course, this work is also good . . . but to be the sisters of this small parish only

. . . this could be very narrow. I wonder if in the years to come this will satisfy."

As she paused, Edwarda, her eyelids red and puffy as though she was fighting against tears, protested: "But we know Holy Rosary. It's so close to St. Aidan's." The hostility was out of her voice, and in its place was a wistful, childlike pleading not to be sent away from what had so long been her home.

"I understand perfectly how Edwarda feels," Joanne interposed. "It was also my first reaction. But then I began to see the wisdom of what Terezia was saying: that in a sense St. Malachy's is our spiritual home much more than Holy Rosary. And once we've left St. Aidan's—should that come about—it won't matter very much whether we are fifteen miles away or five hundred."

Anna shuffled her feet impatiently and said something under her breath; but Joanne caught it and blushed. "I'm sorry if what I've said seems like a betrayal. It would be a deeper betrayal not to speak the truth as I see it."

Susannah's sigh whistled through her teeth. "I think it would be the height of presumption to expect them to take us in."

"But it is not to charity that we would come." Terezia shook her head vehemently.

"I don't know what else you'd call it." Susannah's voice was sharp and shrill.

Nancy had raised her hand. "Before we start wrangling, could we get a little more clarity on exactly what Terezia has in mind."

"Yes." Terezia needed very little encouragement to regain her enthusiasm. "I suggest only that these two convents, both founded by the same woman, now in their time of need, be joined together. I believe there is in our Constitution provision for such a move. Is this not so?"

"Maybe so." Susannah's breathing was quick and heavy. "But to subject us to the humiliation of begging for a place to live from sisters we hardly know!"

"No, Susannah, no!" Terezia raised her arms in exasperation. "Not to beg but to suggest that we join them in their work. Edwarda has told us that they could extend this work but they lack sisters. So, you see, we are here ready to help them."

Rosalia rose to join Terezia at the podium. "Terezia has brought up a major consideration," she said, vainly trying to clear her throat, "one that none of us had foreseen. It seems to me that before we can continue any fruitful discussion about the future of St. Aidan's we need to explore Terezia's proposal."

Joanne raised her hand. "I think before we do anything else it is important to know if this is a viable option from St. Malachy's point of view. I would like to suggest that you get in touch with them at once, Rosalia, and that two or three sisters visit St. Malachy's to discuss the situation."

The meeting had gone on far longer than they had intended, and by the time Joanne suggested that they adjourn the room had grown dark. In the heat of their discussion they had not noticed the fading of the light, but now, as they rose, they found themselves in twilight. They shifted their chairs out of their formal arrangement and back into their ordinary positions. No one spoke, and the carpeting absorbed the noise of the furniture as they moved dim and silent toward the door. At the other side of the room Noreen turned on a lamp, and the sudden glare came like an explosion into their muted world.

Ruth had taken Timothy's arm and was leading her back up the stairs to the infirmary. At the elevator Kate waited with Michael's wheelchair.

From the stairs they could hear Rita explaining to Bridget, "We didn't vote. No. We *did not* vote. Of course you can't hear. You turned it in the wrong direction. Don't touch it. Did you hear what I said: don't touch it." All Rita's anger and frustration was heaped upon Bridget.

"Would you like me to get you a cup of tea?" Ruth asked Timothy as she guided her into her chair.

"No, dear. Never mind. They'll be bringing supper soon, I guess. What time is it?"

"Almost six."

"That late! You run along and get your supper."

In the corridor Kate was wheeling Michael's chair to the utility room at the end of the hall. Unwilling to face more confrontation, Ruth tried to slip past to the stairway, but Kate turned just as she reached the stairs.

"Ruth?"

For a moment Ruth pretended not to hear, but it was clear that Kate intended to pursue her.

"Ruth, I was going to see if I could find you as soon as I finished here. I don't quite know how to apologize for what I said this afternoon." Despite her embarrassment, she looked squarely at Ruth. "It's an old fault—speaking out of turn. I've been warned about it enough, but I guess I still haven't learned."

Suddenly Ruth felt lassitude creep through her like an anesthetic. She leaned against the door wondering if she might be going to faint.

"Of course, I can't take back everything I said," Kate went on. "Some of it I still believe. I do feel sometimes that you've withdrawn, that you don't really trust us with what you're thinking. But I forget that it must be hard for you in ways I don't even understand. You've given up a whole life to come back to St. Aidan's—and then to walk into this mess!" She sighed in exasperation. "You will forgive me, won't you? I know all about 'words spoken can never be unspoken,' but just the same I'm hoping you can forget this afternoon."

Ruth nodded. It didn't seem worth the effort to speak. Forgiveness was, after all, not the issue. The issue was this new perception of herself—a new self, in fact, who frightened and confused her.

"It's really because I've admired you so much that I said what I did. You understand that, don't you?"

Ruth nodded again, wearily. Kate's voice came to her muffled and indistinct, drowned by the clamor of that other penetrating question: Is commitment too much, too much to ask?

"I know you don't feel like talking about it now, but could we someday? I don't mean about you personally, but about the whole question of commitment. It seems to me that that's central to anything we decide about St. Aidan's, don't you think?"

This time Ruth was able to smile in agreement. How young Kate was with her resilient optimism, presuming that a few words of apology and a smile of acknowledgment made everything all right between them.

"Are you coming down to supper?" Kate asked as she pushed the door of the utility room closed.

"Not tonight. I think I need a little walk. It was so stuffy during the meeting."

"O.K. I'm going down to see what I can find. See you tomorrow."

Ruth hadn't actually intended to go out, but at the end of the corridor she felt a draft; and, looking down, she saw the fire door slightly ajar. She went to close it and then on impulse took a sweater from the coatrack and walked out onto the narrow gravel path that ran along the side of the dormitory.

The moon was full and bright, and the fog that would envelop the mountains later in the night had not yet formed. The students were back from their long weekend, and the lights from the classrooms and dormitories fell in wide patches across the lawn. A little way beyond stood the vacant novitiate, looking small and geometric under the shadows of the giant spruce trees surrounding it. It was warm for early November, and she walked slowly up through the gardens and onto the dirt path that led to the orchard. The windows of the school social room were open and she could hear the steady beat of music behind her. In her need for silence she walked on, trying to outdistance the insistent blare of the phonograph. There was no path through the orchard, and she veered off to the right; following the narrow road that led to the nuns' cemetery.

The light and noise from the school had faded, and as she pushed against it the metal gate rasped in the silence. In the moonlight the crosses stood out in sharp relief. A short distance inside the gate was a massive iron cross, and ringed around it in concentric circles were the graves of the dead. The earliest of the nuns were buried in the inside circle, but beyond that there was no distinction. The crosses were identical, with only the script of name, date of profession, and date of death to identify them. There was nothing to distinguish those redoubtable superiors— Imelda, Mary David, Kieran, Josephine. They were leveled now with those they had ruled, their power as insubstantial as their flesh and blood.

> The glories of our blood and state
> Are shadows, not substantial things.

Yes, death was the leveler. "Scepter and crown/Must tumble down." She leaned back against the iron cross, finding the cold hard metal somehow comforting. Mother Mary David had been the first nun she had ever seen die. She had been a novice-assistant to the infirmarian and had watched day by day the steady diminution of power. Mother Mary David had been their aristocrat. Confident and imperious, she had ruled them with the steady power of a medieval abbess. Some of the older nuns, restive under her unflagging authority, called her "Milady" behind her back. But when Mary David came to die, she died without her title. Little by little her powers were stripped away from her—her elegance, her precision, her dominance. The agony for them all as they watched her was that she could not let her power go. The half-paralyzed body fought angrily against their help; the distorted mouth still tried to command.

But the scandal to Ruth had been the final fear. Mary David fought death with a terror that kept her living long after the doctor's predictions. In the last twenty-four hours she struggled like a soul doomed to hell. Her body jerked and twitched and her eyes, wide-open and depthless in terror, beseeched them not to leave her. From time to time her mouth rounded grotesquely and her teeth dug into her lower lip as she tried to form again the last word she had spoken, " 'Fraid, 'fraid."

She could take no oral medication; and when the infirmarian came to give her an injection to relieve her pain, she countered with a spasm of fear, lest unconsciousness be a threshold to death.

Her dying had plunged Ruth into a crisis of faith. What had Mother Mary David to fear? Whatever her sins, they were not unforgivable. Jesus would be her judge and Jesus was the merciful God to whom she had vowed her life. Bewildered, she had gone to Mother Columban. Usually impatient with novices' fears, Mother Columban was surprisingly gentle.

"Don't think too much about it," she had said. "It's not usual for nuns to die in such torment. Even when there is a period of difficulty, at the end there is usually great peace."

"But," Ruth persisted, "why would Mother Mary David be so afraid?"

"We can never know how God deals with a soul. Especially at the moment of death."

"But she knew what heaven would be," Ruth struggled on.

Mother Columban shook her head. "None of us knows that."

"But she knew what God was. All her life she knew that He loved her. Otherwise she wouldn't have been a nun."

For the only time in their relationship Mother Columban reached out and took Ruth's hands. The heavy lines at the side of her mouth had deepened and her cheeks were flushed.

"Sometimes," she said, "the image we have had of God fails us. Sometimes because it is too narrow, too incomplete. He wants us to expand our image of Him. And when that happens"—Ruth felt a sudden involuntary pressure of Mother Columban's fingers —"when that happens we must sometimes live for a while with no image at all. Our old ideas slip away and we cannot be sure what will appear in their place. This can be very frightening, especially should it happen when our bodies and minds are very weak."

She had let Ruth's hands go and was sitting in her usual position, her fingers interlaced against her stomach. "Do you understand?"

Ruth nodded. "A little, I think."

"Since you were so moved by her death, you should pray for Mother Mary David, and I'm sure when she reaches heaven she will intercede for you."

Ruth smiled and nodded at the pious injunction, but she never prayed for Mother Mary David. She wanted to distance herself as far as she could from that small emaciated body, racked not only with physical suffering but with a terrible fear of what lay beyond.

She had struggled to understand Mother Columban's explanation. She knew that her knowledge and love of God was not a static thing, that like any relationship it would expand and deepen in ways she could not foresee. But she had not been able to understand how it could bring her to the brink of terror. Whatever else might change, she was unwavering in her belief that her faith in God's love and mercy and tenderness could not be assailed.

But now the image of the merciful savior on which she had built her life had slipped into darkness. Jesus blessing the children, Jesus seeking the lost sheep, Jesus forgiving the woman taken in adultery—all those comforting and familiar images that had promised divine compassion had wavered and disappeared. Instead she had only the image of her father's last hours of guilt and fear and the unrelieved darkness in which God had let him die.

She moved away from the supporting iron of the cross and toward the first circle of graves. There in the stiff November grass she knelt beside Mother Mary David's small weatherbeaten cross.

She bowed her head and rested her hands against the transverse beam. She did not pray to her or for her but asked her pardon, as one sister to another, for having taken scandal before her witness of humanity.

Rawlins and Swenson, Realtors
108 East 68th St.
New York, N.Y.
November 22, 1980

Mr. Alec Stafford
Stafford, Connor, Lipsky, Architects
18 Ballantyne Avenue
Glen Cove, New York

Dear Alec,

Thanks for calling; sorry I wasn't in the office. I should have gotten in touch with you but I was waiting to hear from Sister Rosalia. After I got your message I called St. Aidan's but the venerable lady who answered told me that Sister Rosalia was "away." When I explained who I was and asked if Sister Rosalia would return my call when she came in, I was told that she would be "away" on "very important business" for several days. I tried a few more questions but all I could get was: "Sister Rosalia will be in touch with you, Mr. Rawlins." Very high-level security there!

I should have a call from Sister Rosalia by the end of the week or at least by Monday. I'll be in touch.

Steve Rawlins

13

Two weeks later, at the beginning of the Thanksgiving vacation, Rosalia and Joanne left for St. Malachy's. It was still dark when they left and most of the nuns were still in bed; but Ruth, hearing Joanne moving about in the next room, had gotten up to fix coffee and toast for them. Edwarda, too, was fluttering around, still faithful to her days as superior when no nun left the convent without being embraced and blessed for the journey by the superior.

> When obliged to go outside their convent, they will first present themselves to the superior who must apprise herself of the reason for their going before giving them the customary blessing. Should the superior not be available they will then go to chapel asking the blessing of God on their journey.

Joanne had pulled the station wagon under the porte cochere, and they stood for a moment in the front hall putting on their coats and checking last-minute arrangements.

"Do you have the directions?" asked Edwarda. "I remember it was very difficult to get to."

Joanne waved a map.

"It won't be marked on the map. It's a very small road. I can't remember just where you turn off from the highway."

"Don't worry, Edwarda, we can ask directions."

This was clearly not sufficient assurance for Edwarda. "What about your lunch? Did Noreen pack you a lunch?"

"We can stop along the way," Rosalia assured her.

"But suppose you can't find a place, a fitting place, I mean. Some of those restaurants, I am told, have bars that are open all during the day." Edwarda blinked nervously at the possibility of religious women in such an inappropriate atmosphere.

"We'll stop someplace where we can get some junk food." Joanne's effort at reassurance failed.

"Junk food?" Edwarda found the term offensive.

"You know, hamburgers or hot dogs, something like that."

"I see." But very clearly she did not see, nor did she wish to. A religious was first of all a lady. It was implicit in her commitment, and no lady would be guilty of the conduct Joanne's answer suggested—sitting in a car eating with her fingers from a paper plate. It was conduct that could only be described as "common."

"Goodbye, Edwarda. Thanks for coming down to see us off." Rosalia bent down to kiss her.

Ruth and Edwarda stood at the top of the steps as the travelers put their suitcases in the back of the station wagon. As always before dawn, the fog was thick and the headlights illumined only a few yards as the car headed down the drive. They stood watching until the red taillights grew dim and finally disappeared around the curve.

"Why don't you go back to bed for a little while," Ruth suggested. "We're having an evening Mass today."

But Edwarda shook her head. "I'm going to chapel." She sniffed twice in rapid succession, and for a moment Ruth thought she might cry. "We have very much to pray for. I can't believe our dear Lord . . ." She turned suddenly, pushing open the door leading to the chapel corridor.

By noon Ruth had finished correcting a set of papers for
Joanne, repotted a limp begonia in Rosalia's office, and typed the
Community diary. The afternoon stretched before her. She had
intended to work in the library; but when she went over to the
classroom wing, she found the chairs piled on the table and Mr.
Finley's cumbersome waxer leaning against the wall.

On her way back to her room she stopped in the chapel.
Someone had left the window open near the statue of St. Joseph
and a few dry leaves had blown in. She leaned down to pick them
up and discovered that the floor and window sill were wet. She
pulled the window closed with a bang. Why couldn't anyone
remember to close the windows when it was raining? She rummaged in the sacristy to find a cloth to dry the sill, but she could
find nothing. In annoyance, she used her handkerchief, taking a
perverse pleasure in seeing how dirty she was getting it.

As she left the chapel wing, she met Noreen going upstairs
carrying a mug of cocoa and an armload of magazines. She smiled
smugly. "Enjoy your free afternoon. I'm going to have a good
read." A good sleep, more likely, Ruth thought sharply as she
nodded and continued down the corridor.

Her annoyance was out of all proportion. She knew it and
was ashamed of it, and yet she clung to it. The feeling of
emptiness was not a new one, nor was it uniquely hers. From their
novitiate days they had been warned against the desolation that
might descend upon them during holidays. But, Ruth thought
angrily, at least then we had each other. We worked together;
we decorated the refectory and cleaned the chapel; we helped
with the vegetables and polished the silver. They had grown
weary with work, but it had united them. Now, it seemed to her,
there was nothing. The school dormitory was closed, its shades
pulled down in even rows. Peg and Kate were both working over
at the camp. Daryl, as so often these days, had gone to her room,
making it clear that she wanted to be alone. Anna was in the
kitchen cleaning their turkey and enjoying a cup of tea with old
Mrs. Daly, who used to work for them.

Was this what she had come back to? An empty life to be filled up with magazines and television like Noreen's or with unending work and resentment like Anna's? Of course there were the Joannes and Terezias and Rosalias, but they could not bring back the spirit of St. Aidan's. "Like St. Paul, the religious will surrender all things, with deep interior joy, in order to gain the inestimable riches of Jesus Christ," the Rule had read. Yes, she thought ironically, that would be a fair exchange. But she had given up all things and found nothing. How long, she mused, since she had truly prayed? How long since she had been totally present before God? Prayer had become like a picture show, full of memories and longings.

Hardly acknowledging what she did, she walked down the corridor, opened the door to Rosalia's office, and turned the button on the phone that would open up the long-distance line. She had no need to check the number; she knew it by heart. For a moment, when she heard his voice, she almost hung up; but fear and anger were stronger than prudence.

"David, it's Ruth."

"Ruth!" It was an unequivocal cry of joy, and she found herself smiling in response. "Where are you?"

"I'm at St. Aidan's."

There was a silence as though he had expected something else.

"David?"

"Yes, yes. I can hear you. I thought perhaps you were in the city."

"No, but I'd like to come in."

Again a pause and then cautiously, "Does that mean . . ." He stopped to let her finish the sentence.

"I was going to suggest that we have lunch tomorrow. It's Father's anniversary."

He sighed and for a moment said nothing. "Of course. Of course I remember. And, of course, we must have lunch. Will you take the train in?"

No, she explained, she would drive. It was much quicker; and since they had had no snow, the roads were still good. No, she'd prefer not to meet at the University Club; there'd be too many people they both knew. Pommey's over near the UN Plaza? Fine. Yes, she could make it by one. Yes, she, too, looked forward.

The next day the drive into New York took longer than she expected, and she was more than a half-hour late arriving at the restaurant.

"I was afraid something had happened. They were predicting sleet further north," David said anxiously as he rose to greet her.

"No, the weather was fine. I just got a late start."

She did not tell him that she had almost not come at all, that she had called his home to tell him that she would not be able to make it and then hung up as his phone began to ring.

"We still have time for a drink before lunch."

"I don't think so. Thanks anyway." Her voice was thin and dry.

"You are in a hurry?"

"No, it's just that . . ." Just that what? she wondered. That I am afraid of being here? Afraid of what I might say, what I might do?

"Then why?" He looked puzzled. "Ah, it is against some rule, is that it?"

"Not so far as I know. I'm just afraid it will go to my head."

He looked at her inquiringly. "I think it would be excellent for something to go to your head. You look very tired."

Yes, she was tired. She realized it as she sipped her wine as they waited for their lunch. They were seated in a circular booth where there was plenty of room for David to stretch his long legs. At first she groped for something to say and then accepted the silence as a necessary transition.

"So, you are a nun still," he said as the waiter brought their salad.

"Does that surprise you?" Ruth fought unsuccessfully against a sudden truculence in her question.

He shrugged. "I have often wanted to call, to find out how things were with you. But I was not sure if there were regulations about such things."

"There used to be. Now the problem is purely practical—how forty people manage with only three extensions."

He raised his eyebrows. "And how is it with you in this public arena?"

She hesitated, and he raised his hand. "Please. That was stupid. I criticize the lack of privacy in such a life and then I demand that you talk about it. Forgive me."

As they ate their lunch Ruth's silence became progressively more self-conscious. David spoke of a new man hired to teach nineteenth-century intellectual history, of the reception of Raoul Clay's recent book on the Falangists, of his own discovery of some interesting sources for the early Tolstoy. They were subjects that would normally have led her to a dozen questions and a dozen comments, but today she could find nothing to say beyond an appreciative cliché. Nothing had the power to interest her except her own emptiness. Her mind no longer followed David's, but stopped along the way, preoccupied with its own confusion. She doubled back on it again and again, lost in the tangle of loneliness and guilt.

She looked up as David refilled her wineglass, and the compassion in his eyes swept her back to the day in the garden when, cold and awkward in her unaccustomed veil and habit, she had said to her father, "I am bereft." She looked down again, but David had not missed the lost moment.

"Is it so hard?" he asked.

The answer was beyond words; and even if she could have found them, she heard out of the past Mother Josephine's shocked condemnation: "I cannot believe, Sister, that you would have spoken of your difficulties to your father." Never again, during all the years she had remained at St. Aidan's, had she confided to her father the slightest struggle. Even now, twenty years later, she could still feel the strong pull of obedience as she circled David's question. Yet now it was something other than obedience that kept her silent, something other than loyalty to St. Aidan's that kept her from answering his question. She hardly knew what it was that held her back, what strong instinct turned her from a confession of her personal struggle to the more objective recital of the decision facing St. Aidan's.

"We've been going through a very difficult period. We're considering a proposal to sell St. Aidan's."

David was puzzled. "To sell? What does that mean?"

"Just that. There's an architect interested in restoration who wants to buy St. Aidan's. He's offering us a very substantial sum."

"And you would consider this?"

"We *are* considering it."

"This money is so important to you?" David was clearly perplexed.

"It's a major consideration, although it's not the only one. Our boarding school is going downhill. This year we have less than half our former enrollment, and it isn't going to get better. The day of boarding schools is over for a while. Even if we turned St. Aidan's into a day school I don't think we'd make it. There are too many factors against us. Sooner or later we'd have to give up." She was on firm ground again and her voice was cool and competent.

David was hunched forward rubbing his hands slowly over his cheeks. "But after all these years there must be money so you could continue to live. You say that for many years this was a first-rate school."

"It was, and it did very well financially."

"So?"

"So whatever money came in was used to make it a better school—to build another building, buy more equipment, redecorate the dormitories. The convent kept nothing except what was necessary for daily needs."

"Insurance?" David looked baffled.

Ruth shook her head. "No insurance, no pension, no Social Security. Just a daily invocation to God, the Father of the poor, and to St. Joseph, who was official patron of material needs."

"So now there is nothing?"

Ruth nodded. "And every year there will be a little less."

"In fact, then, you have no choice?"

"No, I suppose we don't. That, I think, is what makes it so difficult, especially for the older nuns. They feel themselves prodded and pushed, squeezed from the outside. Nothing in their experience has prepared them for anything like this. Everything was always supposed to stay the same."

"Eternal and immutable." David smiled, looking over her head. "Beyond mere humanity."

"That's not quite true." She came to their defense.

"An exaggeration, I know. But to feel immune from change, does this not strike you as living beyond humanity?"

"We tried to live a little bit above ordinary humanity, I suppose," she conceded.

"Yes, 'above humanity.' And that is a dangerous course. If you come to shipwreck in such deep waters, there is not much hope of being saved."

Shipwreck, she thought. Was that what she was heading for? The waters had once looked smooth and free, she recalled as she remembered the lines she had wanted printed on her first profession invitation:

> And I have asked to be
> Where no storms come,
> Where the green swell is in the havens dumb,
> And out of the swing of the sea.

"Where no storms come." The phrase came to her with bitter irony as she felt herself pushed and tumbled about in a tumultuous ocean. She struggled to free herself, finding her napkin crushed between her hands, and David's bright hazel eyes looking at her quizzically.

"The old order was easier, you know." She plunged on, knowing she had lost her direction but unable to stop. "We didn't worry much about shipwreck. We kept the deep waters under our control—or thought we did. There was a maxim we were encouraged to live by: If you keep the Rule, the Rule will keep you. The Rule ordered everything: when you got up, when you prayed, when and how and what you ate, when you spoke, what classes you taught. And at the end of the day you checked off all the good things done and subtracted the bad things and the things left undone; and every night you gave an account to God and every week to your superior."

"And inside the shell of this perfection, what went on?"

"The same thing that goes on now, I suppose. Some people became generous and loving and compassionate, and others took care of themselves and left the stale cake for their neighbor."

"So what was the advantage?"

"Arithmetic is an exact science. It can be very comforting."

"And this infinite and mysterious God who, you tell me, rules all this—He favors arithmetic?"

"We used to think so."

He nodded reflectively. "And now that you have abandoned the exact science of arithmetic, what is this God for you now?"

David's question hung over her, huge and unanswerable. What had happened to her, she wondered in terror, that she could not answer, that she could not identify the God to whom she had dedicated her life? David, sensing her confusion, reached out to take her hand. The casual gesture of affection aroused her like a kiss, and she felt light-headed with the warmth that swept through her. Frightened and embarrassed, she drew her hand away abruptly. Slowly David, too, withdrew his hand, the compassion in his eyes changing to something bleak and bewildered.

When he spoke, his tone was formal. "Please forgive me. I've asked an impertinent question. There is no reason why you should share such things with me. After all, your life is your own. I have no right to intrude."

It was the same thing he had said to her the night she had told him about St. Aidan's. Then it had shaken her into unexpected anger; now it shattered her final reserves. Her life was her own. She knew it and it terrified her. She did not want a life that was an inviolable possession. She wanted it to be given and received. She had thought it would be enough to give it to God, that most spiritual of lovers. But God, if indeed He had accepted it, had done so without palpable affection or tenderness. A promise of future glory was not enough. She wanted to be loved, now, without mediation. It was what Angela Ferrato had wanted, too, and what, finally, she had had the courage to pursue.

Heedless of the instincts that warmed her of her danger, she began to tell David the story of Angela Ferrato. "Last month one of our sisters asked for a dispensation from her vows and left St. Aidan's."

But having begun, she did not know which direction to take. David waited, but when she said nothing further, he asked, "A good friend of yours?"

"No. Someone I hardly knew. I had only lived with her for a couple of weeks." She was bewildered by what she had begun.

"But her leaving has upset you. You feel she has made a foolish decision?" His voice was cautious.

"Quite the opposite. I think she's made a perfect decision for her." Each sentence plunged her further into the current.

"And yet it does not make you happy to think of her." He spoke tentatively, trying to take his lead from her.

"Not because of her, because of me." She was speaking very slowly, intent on balancing her butter knife between thumb and forefinger and placing it carefully at right angles to her fork. "Angela was in love. Love made her courageous. She wasn't a very courageous person by nature, but suddenly there was a sense of rapture that turned her into someone quite dauntless. I envied her that." She was caught full in the current now, and it was carrying her beyond her depth.

David hesitated and then shook his head impatiently. "For her this is a sudden flash, like a Roman candle that is very brilliant. But you have always been courageous. Why would you envy such a thing?"

"I envy the Roman candle," she said simply. "Watching Angela made me see my life in a different light." She was appalled by what she was saying, but she could not stop. "Love made her world expand. There was nothing she couldn't risk or hope." Her plea for love sounded like a timpani in her ears, a clamor that almost deafened her.

"And your world?" David put the question so quietly that it seemed almost as though he spoke to himself.

Her world. It seemed ironic to call that small airless space she inhabited a "world." "My world seems very small, as though my life is closing in on me instead of expanding." Her voice sounded light and unreal against the heavy timpani.

Again he nodded, but he did not look at her. "Perhaps every life must go through such a narrow passage. Perhaps it's the only way we can be forced to go deeper, to achieve new depth and new values."

The sententious reply humiliated her. He had not heard the crash of cymbals. She had pleaded for love and he taught her philosophy. Anger and fear and a driving hunger gave an edge to her voice. "And suppose instead of going deeper one goes dead?"

David's strong, blunt fingers were pressed against the table, the nails showing white from the pressure. When he spoke he still did not look at her. "Is it St. Aidan's that has taken life away from you?"

For a breathless instant she was balanced on the crest of the wave. Yes, she wanted to say, oh, yes. But before she could speak she slid shakily into less dangerous waters. She did not answer but raised her hands in a gesture of unknowing. She hardly realized she was crying until she felt the tears on her chin. She brushed them away and reached for her pocketbook. She was too shaken to understand what was happening; she knew only that she must escape before another wave would take her and pull her out beyond her depth again.

Her hand was trembling as she looked at her watch, but her voice sounded surprisingly calm. "I think I ought to be going. It's a long ride back and I may run into some snow."

He stood at once, helping her on with her coat but saying nothing. At the door he turned. "Wait here. I'll get a cab."

"Thank you. I'd rather walk. I left the car further uptown."

"I'm afraid you'll be caught in the rain," he warned, but she didn't answer. They stood awkwardly looking into the street.

"Ruth," he said, but when she turned to look up at him he hesitated. "I'm sorry it hasn't been a happier lunch."

"It isn't a very happy day."

"But I would like to have lifted the clouds a little."

"We can't dictate the weather." She couldn't keep the bleakness out of her voice.

David nodded gravely, pushing the door open for her. He made no effort to kiss her goodbye or even to take her hand until she reached out to him. She held his hand for a moment and then began walking north.

The rain held off until she crossed the bridge out of the city and began the long drive back to St. Aidan's.

Rawlins and Swenson, Realtors
108 East 68th St.
New York, N.Y.
November 25, 1980

Mr. Alec Stafford
Stafford, Connor, Lipsky, Architects
18 Ballantyne Avenue
Glen Cove, New York

Dear Alec,

Just a note before I close for the day. Sister Rosalia called
me about an hour ago. The lady is definitely not a telephone
personality.
Here's the script:

She was sorry she had not been able to return my call
sooner. She had been away.
Yes, I had been told that. I hoped that it had not been
anything unpleasant.
No, not unpleasant.
It was a pity she had other responsibilities when she
would probably like to concentrate on the future of St.
Aidan's. (My futile attempt to probe!)
It was really about the future of St. Aidan's that she'd
gone.
I see. Well, I hoped it had been a profitable trip.
Yes, she thinks so.
We can feel encouraged then?
Yes, we can feel encouraged.

And there we are, Alec. Your guess is as good as mine

as to what a trip to Batavia has to do with the selling of St. Aidan's. You don't need a realtor; you need someone trained in interrogation!

Steve Rawlins

14

It was close to 8 P.M. when she pulled into the driveway at St. Aidan's. The drive from New York had taken much longer than she had anticipated. She pulled down the garage door from the inside and let herself into the convent through the laundry. She headed for the utility room to put the car keys away and pick up her mail; but when she realized she'd have to go through the TV room, she turned. She could hear the croaking of the Muppets followed by Nancy's laugh, then a shift to the earnest sincerity of a commercial and the indistinguishable hum of several voices. No one would need the car keys tonight; time enough if she put them back in the morning before Mass.

She walked back through the corridor and up the stairs to the pantry. She wasn't really hungry but she wanted something. She opened the door of the walk-in fridge and looked around aimlessly. The milk pitchers were already filled for breakfast and the individual butter patties arranged on their circular tray. Of course. Edwarda was in charge of breakfast this week, so nothing would be left to chance. The plate of cold cuts did not tempt her, nor did the leftover chicken with its cold shriveled skin. Maybe just a cup of tea, she thought as she closed the door and felt a delayed chill. She put the kettle on the hotplate they generally used when they were fixing things for one person. She hated tea bags, but she could find nothing else, although Joanne, knowing her penchant, had told her she had put a tin of English breakfast tea in the pantry cupboard.

She stood for a moment looking out the side window that faced the parking lot and then turned impatiently toward the kettle. She was reaching up to find a mug when the swinging door was pushed open and Noreen said, "I saw the light and just couldn't imagine who it was."

"I thought I'd get a cup of tea before I went to bed." Ruth wished she had never stopped in the pantry, but there was no way out of it now.

"Is the kettle full?" asked Noreen, going over to lift it.

"I just put in enough for one cup. I'm sorry."

But Noreen missed the point. "Oh, that's all right, I'll just add some more."

Mine is almost boiling, Ruth wanted to scream, but instead she turned back to the window.

"I think it makes better tea when you start with it cold," Noreen said, putting her finger under the faucet. "Might as well fill it up. Somebody else might come in. You never know."

They were words of execution, but Ruth could not stay them.

"That's going to take a while," Noreen continued. "I filled it right to the top. Well, after all, there's no rush. To look at the way some people rush around you'd think they were responsible for running the world." Noreen moved a stool out and sat down heavily.

Ruth turned and did her best to smile, remembering Nancy's accusation that she expected too much of Noreen, demanded levels of her that she couldn't reach.

"You might as well sit down. That burner takes forever. Gas is so much quicker. I said once to Mother Josephine that we made a terrible mistake not putting in gas for cooking. But some man

down in town advised her and promised he'd always be on hand
to service the equipment if anything went wrong. And what
happened? He closed up the store and took off for Albany without a word to anyone."

Noreen was rummaging around in the small fridge. "I
thought maybe there'd be some of that pecan pie we had for
supper. My, wasn't that good?"

"I wasn't here for supper. I didn't get back from New York
until a little while ago."

"But you ate, didn't you?"

"I had a late lunch."

"But that was hours ago." Noreen's shocked tone made it
seem that she was verging on starvation. She started toward the
walk-in fridge and Ruth could see the machinery of a three-
course dinner go into operation.

"Please, Noreen. I'm not hungry."

"But you have to have more than tea. That will never keep
you going."

"I'm not going any place except bed." Ruth meant it to be
humorous, but Noreen continued on oblivious.

"That's just the point. I read an article the other day. It
wasn't a whole article. It was just a summary from the *Reader's
Digest*. It's probably around someplace. I'll see if I can find it for
you. Anyhow, this doctor—I think he called himself a nutrition-
ist—said that a lot of broken sleeping patterns are brought about
by improper diet. Now isn't that interesting?"

"Like cheese dreams?" Ruth was doing her best to contrib-
ute.

"Not at all. He says—I hope I can find that article. You'd
find it very interesting—there's nothing in cheese to cause
dreams. His point is that an *empty* stomach can cause insomnia.
I said to Edwarda after I read it, 'Now if you'd just take some
milk and crackers before you went to bed, you wouldn't be
complaining about being awake half the night.' But you know

Edwarda. She still thinks it's a sin to eat between meals. My, she's scrupulous!" Noreen shook her head sadly as she turned back to the refrigerator.

"Now. What are we going to get for you?"

"Nothing. Truly."

"Well, you have to have something."

"Some toast, then. Just one, Noreen," Ruth cautioned as Noreen started to fill both sides of the toaster.

"Did you have a nice lunch?" Noreen asked as she took the butter from the refrigerator.

"Very nice." Easy, Ruth thought, just go easy. Don't go back over it. Sit down and answer her questions. Let her cut the path. You just follow.

"One of your New York friends?"

"Yes. The head of the history department at the university where I taught. He was a very good friend of my father's."

Noreen looked suddenly and unaccountably stricken. Everything in her face drooped—the mouth turned down, the corners of her eyes slanted, the lines at the side of her nose became more prominent. Yet even so, she did not achieve a look of sadness. It was as though she had learned to mold her features into a conventional mask of grief.

"Ruth, we just felt dreadful when we realized it was your father's anniversary. Of course, there was no way we could have known. And with Rosalia and Joanne away—" She stopped to reset her face in the image of sadness. "Daryl was the only one who remembered. We should have had an anniversary Mass this morning. Susannah said it was your responsibility to have reminded us. Of course, if Rosalia had been home, she would have taken care of it."

Noreen's voice trailed off, and Ruth flushed at the thought of all this talk about her father's anniversary behind her back. In fact, she had been relieved when no sign had appeared on the bulletin board and no announcement had been made at the beginning of Mass. She had dreaded sharing her grief, even though she knew it would be responded to with kindness and love. It wasn't their lack; it was her own, but that made it no easier.

Noreen had put her tea bag on a paper napkin in front of her, and Ruth watched the dark brown stain radiating outward.

"Of course Edwarda called Father immediately, and the Mass tomorrow will be for your father. You probably saw the sign on the bulletin board when you came in."

"I came in through the laundry."

"Well, you wouldn't have seen it then."

Ruth shook her head, positioning her tea bag next to Noreen's.

"It wasn't a very nice day to be in New York. I suppose it rained there, too. Well, it must have been a consolation to be with someone who had known your father. I always think that must be the hardest part for only children. Goodness, when my father died all eight of us were there. To tell you the truth, we had a grand time."

The mask of sorrow had been relaxed, and Noreen's face had resumed its flaccid good humor.

This path Ruth knew she could not follow, and she picked up her dishes and took them over to the sink. Noreen followed behind her.

"Now you just leave those. You must be dead tired. I'll take care of them. Some of them are watching TV. They say there's a good movie on. It's about a girl who is left all alone when her parents die and she meets a boy who's been deaf from birth and they both help each other find happiness. My, it's an example to us the way people help each other, isn't it? Last week I saw a beautiful movie. It was about a man whose wife divorced him because he was drinking and lost his job and he met this young girl, a woman of the streets I guess you'd call her."

Ruth was tempted to turn the water on full force to drown out Noreen's sentimental wanderings, but instead she let it trickle over her dishes.

"Anyway, this girl took him in and was so kind to him he stopped drinking and got a job. I told Magdalen she should have watched it. It was just like our blessed Lord and Mary Magdalen. Of course, our Lord didn't drink or anything, but it was kind of the same. Just full of love." Noreen was drying the dishes and putting them back in the cabinet. "You don't watch much TV, do you?" she asked.

"Well not tonight anyway. I think I'll go right upstairs. Good night, Noreen. Thanks for tidying up."

She made her way carefully through the darkened dining room and up the stairs to her room. She turned on her desk lamp, bending the gooseneck away from her eyes. It made the wall look steep and mountainous and the rest of the room ominously dark. She had left her window open a crack and the room had grown cold. She cranked the window closed and set herself to the complex task of adjusting the shade, which, large and cumbersome, had to be pulled upward by an intricate system of pulleys.

She longed for a hot bath, but her conversation with Noreen made her wary of further encounters. The Community bathroom with its multiple showers and sinks had been her greatest penance as a novice when her need for privacy was a far sharper pain than that caused by their fast or vigils. She heard the shower running now and knew she could not face any further conversation. She lay down half dressed, pulling her afghan over her, deciding to wait until the others had gone to bed before taking her shower.

When she woke it was close to one o'clock. She might well have slept all night were it not for the cold. The heat had gone off at eleven, and the lacy afghan had little real warmth. She sat on the edge of the bed fumbling for her slippers, stiff and disgruntled. She didn't dare take a shower now; it was sure to wake up someone. But there was, she remembered, a guest bathroom on the first floor where no one would be able to hear her.

She stayed under the shower for a long time, her eyes closed, the muscles in her back responding to the warmth of the water.

As she came back upstairs, she felt she was ready to sleep again; but as she reached the second-floor landing she saw Aidan's door open a crack and the light on. She could hear nothing and, worried that Aidan might be sick, she opened the door further and looked in. The bed, heaped high with pillows, was empty, the blankets pushed to one side. Startled, she looked toward the floor, frightened of finding Aidan as they had once found Susannah. But Aidan was tucked comfortably in her rocker, a quilt pulled over her and a book in her hand. She put her finger to her lips as Ruth started to speak and motioned her to close the door.

"Edwarda's a very light sleeper," she explained in a whisper.

"I was afraid you were sick when I saw your light on."

"No. I get a little restless at night. My bones just won't lie right. I suppose I can't expect much better at eighty." She smiled, the small triangular face looking ageless under the white ruffled nightcap. "I feel every draft, right here," she explained putting her hand over the top of her head. "And what about you?" She looked quizzically at Ruth. "What are you wandering about for at this time of night?"

"I fell asleep and came downstairs to the guest room to get a shower. I didn't want to wake anyone up."

But Aidan passed over this practical explanation and reached to the bone. "It was your father's anniversary today. We should have had a Mass for him this morning. I hope you'll forgive us."

"No one realized. I should have said something."

"I asked about you at noon, but they said you'd gone in to New York."

"I went to have lunch with a friend of my father's."

"Thank God. That must have been a comfort for you."

Ruth nodded, not trusting herself to speak. I ought to go, she thought, but she could not force herself beyond the circle of light.

"Won't you sit down?" Aidan asked, motioning toward the hassock next to her chair.

"Oh, I shouldn't. It's almost a quarter to two."

"I think it's rather exciting to be talking in the middle of the night. It's rare enough, goodness knows."

The sisters will regard the rule of silence as their greatest safeguard to a life of prayer and contemplation. During the day they will talk only when their work demands it, learning to speak concisely and directly in order to avoid useless words. Only during the period set aside for recreation will the rule of silence be relaxed. The Great Silence will be observed in all its solemnity from night prayer until the end of Mass the following morning. No one will speak during this time without the gravest necessity and without rendering an account to the superior as soon as possible the following day.

This was the only spot of light in all of St. Aidan's. Everyone else would be asleep, shut off from each other by the sturdy walls between their rooms and far more by their unshared dreams. Night was their inescapable solitude. It was not only a time for sleep but a time when, having surrendered the burdens of the day, they carried the full weight of their aloneness. If you were fortunate you slept; but if you were not, you waited through the hours, knowing with a clarity that daylight obscured that you were a solitary not by some accident that time might correct but by both choice and promise. Your dreams and your nightmares would always be your own. There would never be the affectionate comfort of an encircling arm or the tenderness of watching a familiar sleeping face. You knew then the cost of being vowed in celibacy to an invisible god. It was your secret witness to a love that reached you only in faith.

She sat on the hassock that Aidan had offered, her hands clasped around her knees, her eyes fixed on a pieta hanging just above Aidan's head. But the composed grief of the madonna was too much and she turned away. She felt like a child taxed beyond her strength. She wanted to be comforted, she wanted Aidan to reach out and stroke her hair and tell her that there was nothing to worry about.

Aidan's eyes, keen and inquiring despite the blue-veined lids, caught Ruth's mood.

"Gregory is worried about you," she said. "She says you don't seem quite yourself these days. Of course, none of us are. How could we be, the way things are going!"

When Ruth said nothing, she continued. "We talked a little bit about you this morning. Gregory felt so bad that we had missed your father's anniversary."

Ruth blushed, filled with guilt, as she acknowledged how little thought she had given to her father. Aidan's concern embarrassed her and she tried to turn it away. "Please don't worry. Actually it was easier that way. I don't think I would have coped very well with sympathy."

Aidan reached over and patted Ruth's hands. "Yes, I can see that. The first anniversary is always hard. I said that to Gregory, that it was probably easier for you to get away for the day, especially to be with someone who knew and loved your father."

David. And with Aidan's innocent comment the flood of images she had resolutely blocked came tumbling toward her. She felt herself drowning in them, losing track of Aidan's conversation, the soft, thin voice coming to her in wispy patches like fog.

"He was an extraordinarily sensitive man," Aidan was saying, "and so deeply read. I remember saying to Marian that for me he represented the purest type of true Christian humanist."

The Christian humanist who had lost his god, Ruth thought bitterly as those terrible hours before her father's death opened up before her. She saw again her father's gaunt face with its stubble of beard, those deep gray eyes, wide and restless in his last elusive quest. "God was very important to my father, more important than to anyone I've ever known," she said.

Again Aidan took her hand out of the protection of the quilt and, reaching over, laid it on Ruth's knee. "My dear child, that is an extraordinary tribute. I'm afraid I could never say that about my father, despite all the money he gave to charity."

"It didn't make it any easier for him in the end." Ruth heard the bitterness creeping into her voice. "He died in great . . . great . . ." She could not find a word that described that tortured unknowing.

"But in the end he entrusted himself to God; that is all that matters," Aidan consoled her. She had withdrawn her hand and hidden it under the quilt again.

Ruth nodded, remembering those hours when she had knelt next to him, saying over and over, "Into Thy hands I commend my spirit, into Thy hands. . . ." He had been beyond speech but from time to time his eyes had opened and he had looked at her beseechingly. "Into Thy hands," she would repeat, and the words had seemed to comfort him.

"Yes," Ruth said at least. "In the end he entrusted himself to God."

Aidan didn't answer. Her head was resting back against her chair and her eyes were closed. She had withdrawn as though she were contemplating an inner world of her own. When, finally, she turned and looked at Ruth, the lilt had gone out of her voice.

"That's the final testing, isn't it, for all of us?"

The comment took Ruth unaware but Aidan didn't notice.

"St. Aidan's is going now," she continued. "We all know that. I've been here almost sixty years, and some of the others even longer than that. St. Aidan's has been our life. The life hasn't always been easy, but we've had certain securities—more than most people, I suppose: our convent, our school, our work, certain values and ideals, and a way of life that was unalterable." Her voice drifted off and she closed her eyes again. Without opening them she said, "Now we are facing death."

Ruth reached out instinctively to comfort her, but pain made Aidan more solitary. She sat straighter than before, her hands folded on the quilt, her lips tight, only the tic at the corner of her mouth betraying her.

"When we first came to St. Aidan's we were very young, most of us, young and full of high hopes." Her voice was almost a whisper. "The Rule said we had come to 'die to self in order to live to Jesus Christ.' But, in fact, we had come to live. We had come to do great things, we thought: to live lives of great sacrifice, great endeavor, even great humility." She nodded and smiled wryly. "We had chosen God and we were very pleased with our choice. But what were we then? Only silly girls playing at holiness, decked out in our habits and veils and aping the manners we saw around us. Our first choice was really ourselves, not God. Then God asks us to choose a second time. That's the time that counts, it seems to me."

She reached out gently and took Ruth's hand, wet with tears. "Is God asking you to choose Him again? Is that what is happening to you?"

Ruth's head was bent on her knees and she made no effort to answer. When finally she looked up, Aidan was smiling at her. "I never saw you cry before. I used to wonder when you were a novice what happened to the tears you never shed. Tears won't stop the pain, but sometimes they ease it for a bit."

Neither of them spoke for a while and then Aidan said, "The Second Choosing can be a terrible thing, you know. Perhaps it has to be that way. So often God is absent and the lovely things of the world so temptingly present. Is that how it is with you?"

Ruth nodded, wiping the tears from the corners of her eyes. Aidan sighed. "Yes, that's what Gregory thought. She prays for you, you know. And when Gregory prays, they're real prayers."

Ruth smiled and started to her feet. How tired Aidan looked, and frail. "I must go and let you get some sleep." But when Ruth moved to help her back to bed, she would have none of it.

"I can manage quite well by myself," she said.

Impulsively, Ruth bent over and kissed her. "Thank you," she said. She could think of nothing else.

"Just hold on a bit until the storm passes," Aidan said, pressing her hand. "It will, you know. It always does. He comes to save us in the end."

Ruth closed the door quietly behind her and went upstairs to her room. Her clock said two-thirty. Although she knew she would not sleep, she got into bed and pulled up the blankets. The effect of her bath had worn off and she was cold again. Although it was not yet twelve hours since she had left David, already some of her fierce, hot terror had abated. The long drive up the Hudson had given her time—not, God knows, to think—that was still beyond her—but at least to breathe more quietly. She was still bewildered, not only by her own emotions but by David's re-sponse. David, usually so sensitive, so quick to catch her mood, had apparently caught nothing. She should, she realized, be feel-ing the embarrassment of rejection; instead, she felt relief. She felt like someone waking from a dream, a dream in which in an effort to escape from something unpleasant one runs headlong down a dark alley into further danger. It was anger and the fear of loneliness that had driven her to him. Perhaps it was true, as she sometimes thought, that she didn't belong at St. Aidan's. Yet even so, she knew she could never abandon it so impetuously.

David was part of the storm. David and her father's death and the plight of St. Aidan's. The clouds had converged upon her until she could hardly distinguish one from the other. "Hold on a bit until the storm passes," Aidan had pleaded. She would try. Her own faith seemed too weak to hold her, but perhaps the faith of her sisters would keep her steady.

The following afternoon they returned from St. Malachy's, and Rosalia called a Council meeting that same night. They were tired from the trip, but there was a sense of vitality as they took their places around the table. The visit to St. Malachy's, they said, had confirmed all of Terezia's hopes.

"I think it could be a real home for us," said Joanne, "not just a refuge. I must confess I had never thought of Holy Rosary as anything but an interim measure. It didn't fit our spirit some-how. Although, I suppose, if that was our only option we would have had to adjust."

"And this does fit our spirit?" Magdalen's questions, no matter how direct, always seemed to have a hidden meaning.

"I felt it did." Joanne looked at Rosalia for confirmation. "After all, that shouldn't surprise us. Mother Imelda was the foundress of both convents, and St. Malachy's remained a daughter house of Clonmeath even after we had become autonomous."

"Even the buildings are very much like St. Aidan's," she continued. "They look sort of like this." She ripped a piece of paper from her notebook and started to sketch an outline of St. Malachy's. "You see, you have here the main building—it even has a porte cochere like ours—and then over here are the original school buildings. The chapel is very different from ours. It was a question, they told us, of getting a design that would enable them to build within the contour of the land. You see, over here there is quite a rise." And she sketched the land behind the main buildings. "Their novitiate is not a separate building but just an extension on the main building, like this."

Peg and Magdalen had left their places and were leaning over Joanne's shoulder. "Well, that gives you some idea, anyway," she concluded.

"We took some pictures," Rosalia said, "and we'll have them developed in time for the Community meeting."

"What about their work?" It was Magdalen's cool question again.

"I found it very exciting," Rosalia said and outlined the kinds of work the nuns were involved in. The emphasis was on retreat work and adult education. "They have a highly successful program for training catechists, which was worked out by one of the monks from St. Bede's. He studied at Louvain for a number of years and is very well known in the field."

"Is all the work centered in the convent, or do they go out to any of the rural parishes?" Peg asked.

"A few of the younger ones do. They'd like to do a lot more work in that area, but until now they haven't had the personnel," Joanne explained.

"Then there is a need that we could fill?" Peg continued.

"No question." Rosalia's normal hesitancy was gone. "One of the projects they've just started—and I thought of you, Magdalen, and Ruth—is an edition of early Christian texts on spirituality. Brother Anselm is in charge and he told me there's a great deal of translating and editing to be done."

Magdalen smiled across the table at Ruth, her self-conscious composure replaced by a look of anticipation. Ruth tried to mirror her smile, but their words had no reality for her. They drifted about her like comfort at a deathbed. The storm will pass, she made herself think. The storm will pass. But she could find no substance in Aidan's promise.

"Of course the thing that has made all these works possible," Rosalia was continuing, "is the proximity of St. Bede's. It's a perfect reciprocal arrangement. Both groups are very candid in admitting that they probably wouldn't be in existence if they had not entered into this cooperative ministry."

"So far I haven't heard a single negative comment. Aren't there any minuses?" asked Peg skeptically.

Joanne laughed. "I suppose the most obvious minus is that they're a strongly German community. That area was settled mostly by German farmers, and when Mother Imelda established her convent they drew their vocations from the local population."

Peg rolled her eyes. "Mother Imelda's daughters German?"

They laughed, but Joanne said soberly, "I think it would be a shock for some of the older people. We've become unhealthily inbred. I think we ought to try to minimize the differences as much as possible."

"I shudder to ask," said Peg, "but I suppose they all have the names of German saints?"

"Sister Nicholas is Rosalia's opposite number," said Joanne.

"And Sister Ermentrude is in charge of retreats," contributed Rosalia with a grin.

Magdalen, with small tolerance for teasing, brought them

back to the issue of the merger. "So far we've talked mostly about the advantages to St. Aidan's and how we would feel about such a merger. How did they respond to our situation?" The question was addressed to Rosalia.

"We were very frank when we talked to Sister Nicholas about the situation here, and I think she understood perfectly. They had faced a similar problem some ten years ago but without the possibility of selling. In a sense their situation was worse, if not so dramatic. They were left with a failing school and no resources to take care of their debts."

"As a matter of fact," interrupted Joanne, "she thought it was miraculous that we had had such an advantageous offer."

"Although she in no way minimized the difficulties of getting everyone here to agree to the move," Rosalia continued. "She said she could imagine some of the nuns at St. Malachy's chaining themselves to their beds if they'd ever been asked to leave."

"But then she said"—Joanne laughed—"that maybe the Irish weren't so stubborn as the Germans."

Peg groaned. "Give us time and we'll enlighten her."

"In effect," persisted Magdalen, "there's no serious practical reason against our considering a merger?"

"None," said Rosalia. "We met with their Council twice and we felt nothing but affirmation. Of course, the Community will have to meet in the Chapter to make the decision, but Sister Clara did not foresee any difficulties. She said the fact that such a merger would provide additional personnel and so enable them to expand their ministries would be a major consideration. They are extraordinarily enthusiastic about what they're doing."

"And not just personnel either," Peg reminded them. "We'd be bringing a sizable sum of money."

"We also met with the abbot of St. Bede's," added Joanne. "He's only in his early forties—very young for an abbot, but very impressive. They say he's the creative mind behind all that's going on. At any rate, he thought the possibility of the communities joining together was a stroke of providence."

"Rosalia"—Magdalen was frowning—"exactly how does such a merger work? There must be all kinds of legal procedures. I can't imagine that we can just sell St. Aidan's and take off with the money to another diocese."

"It has to be done through the two bishops involved," Joanne interposed. "I know for a fact that Bishop Lonergan would not raise any opposition. He's been concerned about our future here for some time."

Rosalia nodded. "I had spoken to Bishop Lonergan last month about the offer we'd received. I felt he should know even if we decided to turn it down."

"And?" asked Peg.

"He thought it was an offer that demanded very serious consideration. His only hesitation was about our moving into Whitethorn."

"But I thought Father Nardecki was very anxious to get nuns for that parish." Peg was always annoyed at clerical interference.

"He is, but I'm not sure the Bishop is behind him. I think he feels that Father Nardecki's view is rather shortsighted. Although he didn't say so, I got the impression that he feels Holy Rosary is a dying parish," Rosalia explained.

"But how would Bishop Lonergan feel about our leaving the diocese with a sizable cash settlement?" Magdalen asked.

"I don't know," Rosalia answered. "I'm going to see him this week."

"Presuming he agrees and presuming our decision is in favor of a merger, what is the legal procedure for carrying it out?" Magdalen persisted.

Ruth looked up from her notes in time to intercept a look between Joanne and Rosalia and a nod from Joanne that said, O.K., go ahead.

In the space of that exchange Rosalia's confidence diminished noticeably. A red patch began to appear on her forehead and she cleared her throat unnecessarily.

"Sister Nicholas and I had an appointment with Bishop Roscoe while we were at St. Malachy's," she began. "He's very much in favor of uniting our two houses. As a matter of fact, he feels that mergers like this should take place much more frequently, even between communities with no common heritage. However"—Rosalia was meticulously folding a piece of paper into smaller and smaller quarters—"he pointed out that strictly speaking this would not be a merger."

Magdalen's attention was concentrated like a gymnast's.

"The easiest way to facilitate this process, since we are selling our entire property, is to nullify our corporation. Following the sale, St. Aidan's would be suppressed by an act of Bishop Lonergan and the members of the Community absorbed into St. Malachy's without retaining their corporate identity."

They reeled before the word "suppressed." They had known, of course, that if they moved to St. Malachy's they would no longer exist in the old way; but they had skirted the fact that they would be, in the juridical language of the Church, "suppressed."

Peg had put her hands over her face, and when she took them away there were two white patches where her fingers had pressed against her cheekbones. Fear made her seem very young as she looked around the table like a child waiting for the grown-ups to tell her she had misunderstood. But there was no solacing explanation, and finally she said, "That sounds so awful, Rosalia—suppression."

The word hung over them like a lethal cloud. It was one of the harshest words in the Church's vocabulary. A convent could be suppressed for heresy, for teaching doctrine that would taint the pure orthodoxy of the Church, for persistent laxity in observance of the Rule. Or one could be suppressed for flagrant immorality. There were less dramatic, more subtle reasons, of course—such reasons as they were now caught up in. But in its historical context the word itself carried the weight of shame and death. It was the Church's ultimate judgment of failure on a religious community.

"We've talked about it, of course," Joanne said, breaking the silence. "I suggested to Rosalia that it might not be necessary to explain the full process to the entire Community. It seems to me that it would be sufficient for them to vote on joining the St. Malachy Community and to leave the legal forms in the hands of the Council."

But Rosalia shook her head. She had given up the ragged piece of paper, and her fingers were interlocked in her lap. "They have a right to know."

"But they won't understand," Joanne argued. "It's hard for us to accept it, but can you imagine what Bridget and Michael, and even Gregory and Edwarda, will make of this?"

"I know that." Rosalia had dug her heels in. Ruth recognized the signals and knew that nothing could move her.

Magdalen said nothing. The expression on her face had not altered. She was absorbed in waiting, as though the slightest pressure would bring her into action.

"As a matter of fact," Joanne reminded them, "there is no practical difference involved in the process Bishop Roscoe has outlined. We will still sell St. Aidan's; we will still—provided Bishop Lonergan agrees—bring the money from the sale with us; we will still join the St. Malachy Community and participate in their ministry. In any case, the result will be the same."

The color had returned to Peg's cheeks, but her voice was weary and defeated. "I know, but I think talking about suppressing St. Aidan's will make people vote against it. Even people who would not be opposed to our joining St. Malachy's. It sounds so humiliating."

It was Peg's last word that exerted that delicate pressure that Magdalen had been anticipating. From where Ruth sat, the cameo profile was perfect: the gracefully arched eyebrows, the perfect nose, the mouth, usually too thin, slightly parted as she prepared to speak. Except for a slight turning of her shoulders and an upward movement of her head, she barely moved. That imperceptible quality of leadership that she could never wholly repress had drawn them into her orbit. Whatever she says, Ruth thought, will be of immense significance.

What she said was not an opinion or an argument, not even a suggestion for a course of action. Instead, Magdalen repeated a text from the Scriptures, a text that had been put before them since their novitiate days, a text that they had been told was the very core of the life and teachings of Jesus Christ and that must form the basis of their own lives.

"Unless the seed fall into the ground and die," Magdalen quoted, her hands resting quietly one on top of the other, her eyes looking beyond them, "it will remain alone. But if it die, it will bring forth fruit in abundance."

Had they never heard that text before because until now nothing in their experience had called forth its full meaning? Perhaps. But now it enveloped them like a cloud and they were caught up and made radiant in God's shining revelation. Whatever else they were called to, they were called to this first: to follow Jesus Christ, to live His message, to insert themselves into the life-giving mystery of His death. The only real death was to refuse the gift of His life.

For a second, in a sudden intake of breath, Ruth felt a shock like lightning. Her darkness was riven, and for an instant she was able to affirm the presence of light—not only for herself but for all of them struggling out of darkness. When she looked up, the moment of transparency had passed. They looked no different from before. Yet the very heart of their dedication had been touched. For a moment what had worn the mask of death had been transfigured with life. The vision, like all visions, was transitory, but like Elijah, they might be able to walk in its strength until they reached their home.

"What if"—Peg's voice was almost a whisper—"what if

they—we—aren't able to accept this"—she hesitated and then brought the word out, hard and cold—"this death?"

Magdalen's eyes were down and the softness had gone out of her mouth. "Then," she said in her clear voice edged with frost, "then I think we deserve to be suppressed."

Rawlins and Swenson, Realtors
108 East 68th St.
New York, N.Y.
November 30, 1980

Mr. Alec Stafford
Stafford, Connor, Lipsky, Architects
18 Ballantyne Avenue
Glen Cove, New York

Dear Alec,

I had a long talk with Hal Sandler, St. Aidan's lawyer, last
week and went over our proposal point by point. He obviously
recognizes that it is a generous offer but keeps cautioning me not
to be too optimistic. I asked if there were any changes we could
make that would facilitate matters but he kept repeating that the
issues were "of a different nature." So I guess all we can do is
wait. (And pray?????)

I called St. Aidan's to see if there was any further news. I
got my buddy Noreen, who told me that December 6 has been
scheduled as the date of their big community meeting, and the
final voting will take place around the first of the year. "Oh, my,
Mr. Rawlins," she said, "it's going to be a very sad Christmas here
at St. Aidan's."

I'll be away from December 15 until the 28th. I'll call you
when I get back.

Steve Rawlins

15

When the Community met on the first Saturday of December, Peg's anxiety was realized. Rosalia, fearful of the response and knowing that she was acting contrary to the advice of some of her Council, was ill at ease from the beginning. Even when she outlined those facets of life at St. Malachy's for which she had shown such enthusiasm at the Council meeting, there was something nervous and foreboding in her manner. She was anticipating trouble, and the Community, sensitive now to the slightest nuance, picked up her fear.

It was Rita, of course, whose keen ears first heard the word "suppression." She was on her feet in an instant warning them against this "treacherous act," labeling suppression "the most terrible stigma ever to touch a religious community." As she spoke she gained power, for the words she used were those which evoked an aura of virtue: loyalty, faithfulness, preservation of their heritage, gratitude for the past, constancy in their vocation. She recalled them to what she called their "original purpose" with a force it was difficult to counter. Her words poured over them, inundated them, swept them away in the passion of her rhetoric.

Ruth watched the confusion, then the distaste, and finally the horror on the faces of Gregory, Michael, Timothy, and Edwarda as Rita played on the hidden significances of the word "suppression."

"It is the official proclamation of Holy Church that St. Aidan's has failed," she proclaimed, the lilt in her voice thickening into a brogue. "It is the same decree by which convents and monasteries were suppressed in the past—convents guilty of the most shameful abuses of all kinds." She paused, giving her audience time for their imaginations to gather together a procession of those shameful abuses. "It is the decree that closed convents that had become places of moral and spiritual laxity. It is the same decree that finally closed a convent of nuns where diabolic possession had replaced the worship of Jesus Christ." Timothy's pure face was raised in horror and disbelief, as though she had suddenly been condemned for some crime so terrible that she could not name it.

For God's sake, wondered Ruth, why doesn't Rosalia stop her? But Rosalia, who had deliberately taken the risk of stirring the waters, sat with her head bowed as though she had no course but to wait until the storm abated.

But Terezia had no such scruples. She rose to her feet, her dark skin swarthy with anger. With a gesture of supreme authority she raised her hand, her palm facing Rita. "Please," she said. The petition was a command. The miracle was that Rita obeyed it. They stood for a moment in silence, Rita with her arms folded across her chest, Terezia motionless with one hand still raised. Against Terezia's smoldering control, Rita's verbal torrent seemed shallow and artificial.

"You make of history a mockery," Terezia said, and her voice was dark with contempt. "Yes, there have been terrible cases where the decree of suppression was necessary in order to end a scandal, but there are many other cases also that have no mark of shame. To be suppressed is not to fail. It is to acknowledge that we have finished the work God gave us to do. I think also you will read in the Gospel of St. John the words of our Lord before His death: 'Father, I have glorified you on earth by completing the work which you gave me to do.' And then in a little while He died. Perhaps also the people around Him thought they were suppressing Him, and by a death that had great shame. But out of this death comes life.

"These words we use, they are not important. What difference what they call this thing if in the end it brings life? I think the name does not matter. May-be"—she pronounced it always as two words—"like Jesus Christ we have finished here. So we shall go somewhere else. And may-be, also like Jesus Christ, we shall bring life." She had lowered her hand and now it was in a typical gesture covering her crucifix.

While Terezia was speaking, Rita had slowly taken her seat. Without her leadership some of the opposition subsided, and the meeting moved into a more temperate atmosphere. Joanne provided them with all the specifications of the grounds, the convent, the work space, the chapel of St. Malachy's. Some of the photographs they had brought back had been enlarged and these, in addition to brochures describing their work, were displayed in front of the room.

"Everyone always likes pictures," Joanne had said as she tacked up her display. She had been right, of course. Even those who had listened with intolerance to Rosalia's explanations were caught up in the visual images.

"Goodness," said Gregory, pushing her heavy glasses up on her nose, "that front with the porte cochère looks just like St. Aidan's."

Susannah sniffed in disapproval, but Joanne smiled and nodded at Gregory, using her pointer to show other parts of the building similar in style to their own. "Mother Imelda used the same basic designs for both convents, so the main buildings are very much alike. Of course, the later additions changed things, just as they did here at St. Aidan's.

"Here," said Joanne, her pointer moving off to the left, "we have what used to be the novitiate rooms. Some of the walls have been knocked down and they have created several large areas that are used mainly for retreat conferences."

Susannah, in spite of herself, was peering nearsightedly in the direction of Joanne's pointer.

Another hand went up, but Joanne, having pulled them into an orbit of interest, now led them back to the main issues of the meeting. "Why don't we get on with things and then afterward I'll be glad to show you more about the house and grounds."

When, however, she began to describe the ministries in which the nuns were engaged, the temperate atmosphere began to change.

Edwarda indicated disagreement from the start. Her nose looked longer and sharper than ever and her head shook just enough to register extreme disapproval. The motions were familiar; they were Edwarda's final, and most infuriating, means of denunciation.

When Joanne had finished her presentation, Kate, who had been facing Edwarda, raised her hand.

"Edwarda obviously doesn't approve of what you've described, Joanne, and I'd like to hear some of her hesitations."

But Edwarda simply shook her head more vigorously. "I'm sure no one will share my sentiments, so there is no point in airing them. You just go on with your meeting."

Kate's jaw was set and it was clear she wouldn't accept Edwarda's answer. "I think that's very unfair. You're making a judgment on what we think without any evidence."

Edwarda's lips grew thinner but she said nothing.

"It would help all of us to hear your reactions, Edwarda," Rosalia encouraged her.

Edwarda gave a final sniff. "Well, since it's Sister Rosalia who is asking," she began, with her customary deference to authority. "My hesitation is very clear: I do not approve of this *union* with *men*." The words were unequivocally underlined.

Ruth felt Peg begin to giggle and glared her into silence.

"And," Edwarda continued, "I would expect anyone who takes her consecration to our blessed Lord seriously to feel the same way."

The sisters will at all times observe in their speech and behavior that modesty that is appropriate to those vowed to Jesus Christ. When it is necessary for them to be with members of the opposite sex they will speak only of necessary issues and without prolonging the conversation. They will at all times keep their hands covered by their sleeves. They will not offer to shake hands but will acknowledge an introduction or a departure by a simple bow. No men, including clerics, will enter the cloister without specific permission from the superior. When workmen, such as carpenters or plumbers, are needed they will always be accompanied by two religious who will remain with them for the duration of their work.

For a moment no one said anything; then Joanne interposed, "There is really no question, Edwarda, of anything more than mutual assistance in apostolic work that neither group could carry on alone."

But Edwarda, having begun, now warmed to her task. "Yes, and these monks traipsing in and out—Oh, I know it's all for a good cause, but just the same, coming in and out of the convent at all hours of the day and night."

Rosalia struggled to bring peace. "There's no question of anything like that, Edwarda. Of course there are evening meetings when—"

"Precisely," interrupted Edwarda. "Precisely, and what next? I might ask."

"I think," said Joanne, "that you must have some confidence in the honor and integrity of the people involved."

"Honor and integrity. That's all very well, but if you look at the Rule Mother Imelda left us you'll see very clearly all the safeguards women religious must take in situations where they must deal with the opposite sex."

It was Aidan, who rarely spoke at meetings, who raised her

hand. "I prefer to live in the present rather than the past," she began, her voice light and lilting after Edwarda's persistent sibilants. "But as long as we're invoking history, I'd like to point out some letters in the archives—and anyone who would like is free to read them. They're from Mother Imelda herself, and I find them very instructive. They were written to St. Aidan's while she was journeying about looking for property. There are many interesting details, but I'll just refer to one episode. When she was looking for a place to establish St. Malachy's she traveled for ten days in a carriage—a closed carriage, I might add—with Bishop Donaghy without so much as a companion. So if we want to build our life on the past," she concluded, nodding at Edwarda, "I think we shouldn't be so simple-minded about what that past included."

For a moment their eyes locked and the years of friction between them ignited, years when Aidan—charming and free and graced with admiring friends—had to defer to the narrow constraints that Edwarda's authority had imposed. Ruth looked toward Rita, expecting her to champion Edwarda's cause, but she was sitting, arms crossed, eyes fixed on her lap, her silence as intense as her controversy.

When finally the meeting was adjourned, January 2 had been set as the date for the formal convocation at which they would vote on the future of St. Aidan's.

That evening they began the season of Advent, that period of expectant hope in which the Church prepares for the birth of Jesus Christ. It was a season characterized by yearning, by silent waiting, by joyful anticipation. They prayed for a savior, pleaded that he would come to them, in full confidence that he would come indeed and would not delay. At Vespers they recited the ancient verses, "Drop down dew, you heavens . . . and let the earth be opened and bud forth a Savior." Before supper they gathered around the table in the Community room to light the first candle of the Advent wreath. The smell of the pine boughs was pungent and living, and the four purple candles with their virgin wicks waiting for light signified the four weeks of their expectation. Each week an additional candle would be lit, and each week they would pray, "Rouse up your power, Lord, and come," until by Christmas Eve the candles would be burned down with their yearning and they would sing with the intensity of the final hours, "The days have been accomplished. . . . This day you shall know that the Lord is coming."

For Ruth there had been no other period in the Church's year in which she felt more at home. Her first Advent at St. Aidan's had been a turning point in her religious life. During the drab weeks of November everything had tempted her to return to the life she had loved. "November is the month in which we especially remember the dead," Mother Columban had instructed them. Surely that was not hard to do, Ruth reflected as she watched the cornstalks grow pale and withered, the shrubs around the novitiate glaze and turn black in the freezing rains. She had come to St. Aidan's with the single-minded desire to live entirely for Jesus Christ, but the endless days of November almost worsted her. For consolation she had tried to remember the music she loved, playing it over and over in her mind in invitation to the Lord to come and save her. She had found a little book of poems one day in the nuns' library, but Mother Columban had taken it from her with the admonition "We do not read poetry here, Sister, not even religious poetry. We go to God by faith and through the Scriptures."

Then into that bleak world had come Advent. It came bringing joy beyond the most sensitive poem or the finest symphony. It came bringing the presence of the Lord, lifting her, as the Scriptures had promised, "out of darkness into His wonderful light."

"Here at St. Aidan's, Sisters," Mother Columban had instructed them during that first year, "you will find that we do not prepare for Christmas in the same way as people in the world. We do not look for gifts. We are not interested in the fancy trappings but in preparing our hearts for the coming of the

Savior." During that time of preparation, she warned them, there would be no Christmas decorations or Christmas music; they would neither write nor receive letters; should presents come from their families they would go directly to the superior's office to be opened only on Christmas Day.

Although it was not strictly a time of fast, they were encouraged to discipline their bodies in order that their spirits be freed from all human preoccupations. "Don't you think we could pray better if we weren't so hungry?" an innocent postulant had asked during the novices' instruction period. Mother Columban's abstract explanation of the dichotomy of flesh and spirit failed to satisfy her, and she left shortly before Christmas. The rest of them persevered to their first Christmas but not without difficulty. As they came to the fourth week of Advent, Rosalia cried every night at Compline—cried for her brothers and their huge Christmas tree, cried for the presents she could not give, for all the delicious secrets she had once been a part of, for the sheer exuberance of those last days of Christmas preparation.

The more the others fought against their memories of past Christmases, the more Ruth was drawn into the life of the Spirit. She fasted and prayed, kneeling motionless long after the other novices had gone to bed. Her body obeyed her like an instrument sensitive to her slightest touch. Hunger and fatigue were simply forces that moved her on and she was filled with a spiritual energy that nothing diminished. It was not compulsion that drove her but a yearning for God so powerful that it pervaded everything she did. Sometimes in bed as she lay blissful in the surrounding sense of God's presence, she wondered what He might ask in return for such gentle love. Yet no worry could shake her happiness, and she met the disquieting thought with a further act of trust. "Into Thy hands," she said, feeling no reluctance at surrendering the future into hands at once so powerful and so tender.

There had never been another Advent quite like that first one, yet even in the darker ones that followed she had found strength and beauty in those weeks of silent waiting. During that time there was recreated an atmosphere of a world that begged to be delivered from its darkness, that begged for the healing power of a savior. And when, finally, they gathered on Christmas Eve, fasting and silent, to hear the stirring promise of Isaiah sung in the soft haunting melody that had come down to them unchanged through the centuries, they responded like a people newly freed from prison:

> Comfort, comfort my people;
> —it is the voice of your God;
> speak tenderly to Jerusalem and
>   tell her this,
> that she has fulfilled her term of bondage
>   that her penalty is paid
> . . . .
> Awake, awake, put on your strength, O Zion,
> put on your loveliest garments, holy· city
> of Jerusalem!

Their "loveliest garments" had nothing exotic about them; but the linens that framed their faces were starched white and stiff, their habits pressed, their veils folded and creased according to the prescriptions of the Rule. Even with so small a scope, their vanity found room and there were subtle distinctions between the "well-dressed" (a matter of pleating a habit or folding a veil) and the merely ordinary. But beyond vanity was that more profound desire to give to the Lord the best of oneself, not only in spirit but in body—those bodies that, they proclaimed by vow, belonged to Him alone.

For the ten minutes before midnight the convent bell proclaimed the good news to the barns and woods and the few neighbors within hearing distance, and precisely at midnight they began the splendid ceremony of the Lord's birth in Bethlehem. Gregory, restive under the regulation that no organ be played during Advent, was now freed at last and overwhelmed them with music. Although the Gregorian accompaniment to the Mass restricted her exuberance, when the service was over she pulled out the organ stops until her listeners grew breathless in the unaccustomed explosion of sound. She played until the air itself was dense with music, until they could feel it within them pulsing like the motion of their blood. Long after they had left the chapel and had their Christmas cocoa taken in silence in the refectory, Gregory played on. Timothy had not yet lost her sight, and she sat on the edge of the organ bench tapping her fingers against the side of the organ and singing under her breath all the verses Gregory played.

But that had been in the days when they could anticipate Christmas with unalloyed joy. This year their Advent expectation was blighted. When they lit the first Advent candle they knew that when the last one was lit they would be within days of their ultimate decision for St. Aidan's. Christmas was a feast of life, yet now it was inextricably bound with death.

"To think that your first Christmas back has to be like this," Nancy commiserated as they were cleaning out the sacristy closets one Saturday morning.

Ruth was kneeling on the floor sorting candles, and she didn't look up. "It's not easy for anyone." She turned Nancy's sympathy aside. "I'm sure it's even harder for those of you who have been here all along."

"Perhaps. I don't know." Nancy took two old sets of vestments out of the closet, looked at them critically, and put them aside. "There's no point holding on to things like that." She paused. "Especially if we're going to be leaving."

Ruth said nothing and in a few minutes Nancy went on. "I hate the thought of Christmas this year. God forgive me, but I do." There was an undertone of vehemence in Nancy's mild voice. She yanked another vestment off its hanger and folded it on the table. "Every time I say, 'Come, Lord, and do not delay,' it isn't Bethlehem and the crib I see, it's the Chapter meeting with the chairs in their straight rows and that ballot box on the table and Michael and Bridget miserable and confused, in their wheelchairs."

When Ruth looked up, Nancy was standing by the window, her head bowed, her hands over her face.

Ruth rose and went over to her. "Do you remember what it said on the holy card Mother Columban gave every novice on her vow day?" Nancy asked.

Ruth frowned. "I don't think so."

" 'Who knows what days I answer for today / Giving the bud I give the flower.' "

They stood looking through the small geometric panes at the lawn behind the convent.

Nancy turned back to the worktable, but Ruth stood looking blankly out on the frozen ground, rehearsing the question she could neither answer nor forget: Is commitment too much to ask?

Christmas passed quietly, itself only an advent, a prelude, to their day of decision. On the afternoon of January 2 their waiting was at an end. At one o'clock they assembled in the chapel to recite the prescribed prayers that would open their formal Chapter. From the chapel they filed in silence to the oratory, where, it had been decided, the convocation itself would be held. The room was smaller than their Community room and without any of its comforts. It had at one time been a large storeroom and sewing room where the serge for habits, the black veiling, and heavy white cloth for bandeaus and wimples had been kept. Two years before, at Daryl's suggestion, it had been made into an oratory, a room where a sister could come to read or pray, or where a group might meet for shared reflection.

Ordinarily the room contained a dozen chairs of various kinds, a few scattered prayer rugs, and some banners proclaiming "Jesus is Lord." But today it had been especially arranged for the Chapter. Straight-back chairs, the original furniture of the Community room, had been brought down from the attic and ar-

ranged in six straight rows. In front of the room was a long
narrow table on which had been placed a ballot box, two heavy
candles in solid brass candlesticks (squat and ugly but prized as
Clonmeath's gift to their first daughter house), and a copy of the
Rule open to the section regulating the extraordinary Chapter.
The banners had been removed from the walls and in their place
hung the photographs of the former superiors of St. Aidan's and
the dates of their office: Mother Imelda Finney (1885–1922),
Mother Kieran Dougherty (1923–1931), Mother Mary David
Sweeney (1932–1938, 1950–1956), Mother Gerard Regan
(1938–1944), Mother Josephine Ryan (1944–1950, 1957–1963,
1969–1972), Mother Edwarda Ruff (1963–1969), Mother
Marian Connell (1972–1979).

Bordered by identical frames, the faces had a disconcerting
similarity. Each faced the camera unflinchingly, without art or
artifice. The protective bands of linen that framed their faces left
little to be seen: a small section of cheek, eyebrows, nose, eyes,
mouth, a bit of chin.

"How can you tell them all apart?" her father had asked in
bewilderment one visiting Sunday when she had introduced him
to three sisters at once. He could not credit it when she told him
that at a hundred feet, even from the back, it was quite easy to
distinguish any of the eighty-three nuns then at St. Aidan's. He
sighed, shaking his head. "It must be a work of grace," he said,
smiling at her.

But the work of grace was not the recognition but the
sinewy power of individuation that had enabled them—despite
the regulation habits and veils and shoes, despite the prescriptions
controlling their walk, their tone of voice, their posture—to
protect their identities and reveal them in a dozen subtle ways.

Marian Connell's portrait stood out, of course, from all the
rest. She was the only one not wearing a religious habit. She had
on instead a white blouse, tightly buttoned at the neck. Her wiry
hair was pulled back uncompromisingly from her face. Even in
such unprepossessing dress it was a face that commanded atten-

tion. Her eyebrows were straight and heavy, strikingly darker than her hair. The straight mouth, the resolute gray eyes, promised integrity and directness. It was a face that approached life with great purpose and expected the same seriousness from others.

Ruth had been surprised to find Marian's picture placed with all the others, but Joanne had shrugged.

"The regulation says we should have pictures of all our former superiors, and Marian was that. Nobody thought of establishing protocol for a former superior who leaves the congregation."

They sat now under her shadow, grieving or angry or bewildered by their memories, but acknowledging that under God she had been their legitimately elected leader for over six tumultuous years and that in some mysterious way she had had a part in bringing them to this difficult turning.

The election of tellers had already taken place; and Susannah and Nancy in that official role stood on opposite sides of the table waiting for Rosalia to announce that the Chapter had begun. It would be their duty to take the roll, to pass out the prepared ballots, to see that they were inserted one by one in the ballot box, and finally to count the votes, making sure the number tallied with the roll call.

Nothing was left to chance; every contingency was provided for in those solemn rubrics formulated by the Church for the protection of its religious members. But the machinery, once splendid with solemnity, now seemed topheavy. When Ruth had first come to St. Aidan's, there had been eighty-seven members in the congregation. Her first solemn Chapter, at which Edwarda had been elected superior, had filled her with pride and awe. It was, she thought, like a papal conclave in which every individual was—for the time at least—of equal worth and dignity. The voting had taken place in chapel and they had sat in their choir stalls, their hands in their sleeves, their eyes cast down while the tellers counted and recounted as though the talley was of immense significance.

Now something smaller and poorer had replaced that solemn pageantry. She looked up again at the portraits of their superiors, startled to find Marian looking small and insignificant compared to the imposing stature and formidable presence of St. Aidan's other spiritual leaders. The triumphalism of the old order was gone, the triumphalism that had filled churches and convents, that had sent processions chanting through the streets, that prescribed morality for a listening world. It was over. The vastness and splendor of their buildings were relics of a past. Instead there was now the remnant, the Biblical "anawim," that poor remainder of God's people who kept the faith without trumpet or fanfare. Quiet, unpretentious, reduced to one-third their original number, they sat in their dark blue suits, their skirts and blouses, their tailored dresses, veiled or unveiled, bonded together by no external sign: their unity their invisible but enduring faith in Jesus Christ.

Rosalia had taken her place at the table, and Nancy and Susannah began the roll call. As each name was called, beginning with the youngest, the sister stood, bowed to the teller, and resumed her seat while the second teller checked her name on the official list.

When the roll call was finished the tellers took up the ballots and Rosalia read the statement she had prepared: "We are now ready to vote on the first question: to sell the entire property of St. Aidan's according to the stipulations which we have already discussed. On your ballot there are two statements: the first, to sell St. Aidan's; the second, to retain St. Aidan's. Please check in the space provided whichever option you favor. A simple majority—that is, one more than half of the votes counted—will determine the decision. Although you have the right to abstain, I caution you that an abstention in effect neutralizes your vote. Please be sure that your check is made so that it is easily visible to the tellers. Should there be any further questions, please raise your hand. Should anyone need a pencil, please indicate this and the tellers will bring you one."

But no one needed a pencil, nor were there any further questions. There was no time left for hesitation. Within a minute the ballots were in their hands, and in another thirty seconds they had made the single check that had threatened and divided them for four months.

They did not look at each other; even those who were in agreement did not permit themselves the comfort of their solidarity. They sat straight and motionless. They might as well have been back in their veils and habits and ceremonial cloaks, for they had reverted to their ancient cloistered ritual. Most of them had folded their ballots as soon as they had made their mark, as though they could not bear to look at what they had done. And now they held them self-consciously, waiting for the tellers to call the roll again. This time they would rise and walk to the ballot box, slip in the folded ballot, and return to their seats. This time it was Nancy who called the roll and Susannah who scrutinized them as they came forward to cast their votes.

"Kathleen Mary Boylan." And Kate, looking very small and young in her corduroy jumper, rose and dropped her ballot in the box. When finally the last and the oldest had cast her vote the box was opened and the number of votes tallied with the voting membership. The actual counting of the votes was done silently, and as they watched they could see the two piles grow apace. When the tellers had finished, they counted again and only after this second tabulation did they jot down the result and pass it to Rosalia. The votes were torn into small pieces to be burned at the conclusion of the Chapter, and the tellers resumed their places at Rosalia's side. Rosalia did not rise to read the result. She did not need to, for every eye was fixed on her.

"The decision has been reached by a majority of two to sell the property of St. Aidan's."

Into the silence came a long-drawn intake of breath, as though each of them in perfect synchronization had breathed inward in mingled sorrow and relief. That was their solidarity: not in how they voted but in how they anguished. For them there would be no lamentation. They would remain as they were: their backs straight, their heads slightly bowed, their hands laced in their laps or cupped, palm up, to receive what was still to come. Nothing betrayed their sorrow but that single imperceptible fluttering of breath.

"Now," said Rosalia, reading tonelessly from her prepared instructions, "we shall proceed to the second step of the Chapter in which we must decide whether in leaving St. Aidan's we shall go to Holy Rosary or to St. Malachy's."

The question was of immeasurable importance, yet Ruth could not exert herself to meet it. She was listless and inert, drugged with desolation. "Sadness, Sisters, can be an addiction," Mother Columban had constantly warned her novices as she noted their moodiness, their inability to accept correction with resilience. "The soul generously dedicated to the Lord has no room for sadness." Even at the time, some instinct told Ruth the words were too facile. Now they seemed part of that cruel myth that implied that all good religious lived in quiet happiness, that anxiety and desolation were the mark of the worldly, the vain, the self-seeking.

"The storm will pass," Aidan had assured her, and she had tried to live in that comfort. She was faithful to her time of contemplation, she was present for Community prayer, she attended daily Mass. "I believe," she repeated each morning as Father Ritacco held the host aloft in his dark, heavy hands. "I believe. Help Thou my unbelief." But even these two simple sentences slipped away from her before she could center herself in their meaning.

"The storm will pass." She no longer dared ask herself if she believed it.

The procedure for the second voting seemed much longer, although in fact the method was the same. The ballots were distributed, the votes cast and counted, then counted again.

"The decision has been reached by a majority of three to suppress the Congregation of St. Aidan and to ask to be received into the Congregation of St. Malachy."

This time there was not even that single intake of breath. Ruth's eyes were riveted on her hands. Will we ever look at each other again? she wondered. Will we speak to each other? And about what? Will the wounds be healed and the dissensions mended? And in the meantime, how will we live?

"According to the ceremonial," Rosalia was continuing, "the Chapter will end with the singing of the 'Te Deum.'" We shall, therefore, proceed to the chapel, where this Chapter will be officially concluded."

Automatically they filed into chapel, taking up their office books and turning to the prosaic English translation of the Church's great hymn of praise. They recited it simply, without music; but in memory Ruth heard the great swell of the Latin phrases as Gregory—her hands flexible and strong—had played them at her first profession. Now they limped raggedly through the invocations, striving in their desolation to pray those words that they knew—no, not by heart, she thought ironically—by rote:

> May your mercy, Lord, your loving kindness always remain
> with us;
> For we have placed our confidence in You.

Rawlins and Swenson, Realtors
108 East 68th St.
New York, N.Y.
January 21, 1981

Mr. Alec Stafford
Stafford, Connor, Lipsky, Architects
18 Ballantyne Avenue
Glen Cove, New York

Dear Alec,

Thanks for dinner the other night. Julie and I both enjoyed it. Acquiring St. Aidan's certainly deserves a bottle of champagne.

I had an appointment with their lawyer last Monday. Now that they've voted in favor of selling, he seems quite pleased. He told me something that really surprised me. The sisters aren't staying in that area; they're joining a group near Binghamton. This, of course, explains the mysterious trip in November. Apparently there is some connection between the groups; I'm not sure what.

Since I was up there I dropped in at St. Aidan's. I hadn't seen Sister Rosalia since they'd made their decision and I thought we should shake hands. She was away, however, driving one of the sisters someplace. My old buddy, Sister Noreen, opened the door.

This one always tells me more in ten minutes than the rest of them would in a month. When I congratulated her on the decision and wished her happiness in her new home, I got an earful of who's for and who's against. Sister Rosalia's plan for consensus obviously didn't come off.

So much for my convent journal for today,

Steve Rawlins

16

On January 17, just two weeks after the Chapter, Daryl left St. Aidan's. She told the Community that she was going for a long retreat. No one openly questioned her, but her explanation was received skeptically.

"What's this place she's going off to?" Edwarda had little patience with disrupted school schedules.

"It's a small solitude community, which accepts people who wish to make a retreat or live for a few months in a spirit of prayer and reflection," Nancy explained.

"And I suppose there's no spirit of prayer at St. Aidan's!"

"Of course there is, Edwarda. But Daryl feels she needs something more just now."

"When I was a young sister we didn't go off in the middle of the school year, let me tell you. When we made a retreat we made it right here with everyone else in the middle of the summer when there was time set aside for that sort of thing."

"But things have changed since then and—"

But Edwarda gave Nancy no chance to finish. "Oh, don't tell me about change. That's all we hear about these days: if it's change then it must be good. Thank God poor Josephine died when she did." And Edwarda, with a final sniff, sailed out of the Community room.

Nancy looked over at Ruth regretfully. "It's none of my business, but I wish you could convince Daryl not to go."

"I'm afraid her mind's made up."

"But she looks dreadful. She's as thin as . . ." Nancy looked around for something to compare Daryl to.

"She thinks some time away from St. Aidan's will help."

"But going out in the country in the middle of the winter? And don't forget that Nordwyck is a couple of hours north of us."

Ruth said nothing and Nancy sighed. "I know. It's her decision. What bothers me is that I don't think she'll ever come back if she leaves. You don't have to say anything," she assured Ruth, who looked uncomfortable. "I don't want you to violate a confidence. If she has to go she has to go, but I hope she's spared some of the criticism."

But Daryl was not spared. Kate had it out with her directly.

"I can't believe she's going up there in the middle of winter to live by herself in a hermitage with all the turmoil that's going on down here," Kate had argued with Ruth.

"Maybe we need someone who's fasting and praying to get us through all this," Ruth countered.

But Kate shook her head impatiently. "It's an escape and I told her so."

"Don't you think some people think the camp is an escape for you?"

Kate half-smiled. "All right. I'll concede that one. But," she added stubbornly, "I still wish she weren't going. It isn't just that she's leaving at a bad time. It's"—she hesitated, her gray eyes narrowing—"it's as though she's trying to crawl back into something instead of being willing to move forward."

When Ruth didn't answer, Kate went on. "You'll help her, won't you, Ruth?"

"I don't think I can."

"Yes, you can. She trusts you."

It was, she knew, Kate's highest compliment; but she flinched from it like a blow.

"I trust you, too." Kate bestowed her accolade, jealously guarded, rarely given. Ruth doubled under the weight of the honor. She wanted no trust; the burden bruised her.

"Daryl has a mind of her own," she said, evading Kate's comment.

"I know. But maybe you can save her."

The phrasing was so absolute that Ruth was startled. "From what?"

"I don't know," Kate said slowly, bewildered at the discovery of her own incomprehension.

"They think I'm deserting them, don't they?" Daryl asked as she sat on the window seat in Ruth's room the Saturday before she was to leave.

"Is that what they've said to you?"

"Oh, they don't say much. That's the clue," she said bitterly. "One thing I'm sure of. They don't believe—most of them at least—that I'm going for a long retreat."

"Did you expect them to?"

"It seemed like a logical explanation."

"People who love you aren't generally content with logic."

"There's no one here I'm close to anymore."

"I often wonder," Aidan had said to Ruth after she had heard of Daryl's decision, "how much her estrangement from her mother is responsible for what has happened to Daryl. I can't believe that things can be right with God when such a fundamental human relationship is so distorted."

"Daryl," Ruth said impulsively, "have you ever—"

But Daryl, preternaturally quick to sense danger, reached over to take Ruth's hand. "Please, let's not argue. I want to go in peace."

The moment had gone. And, thought Ruth, what good

would it have done to have brought it up? Daryl would find a means of evading it. And she was right, she should at least have the freedom to go in peace.

"How long will you be gone?"

"They've agreed to a period of three months. Then if that works, I'll come back to make arrangements to stay permanently."

"If it doesn't work . . .?"

"It will work."

"I hope it does, but in case it shouldn't—"

"It's going to work." The purple circles under Daryl's eyes made her skin look sallow and unhealthy. It was useless to try to counter her resolution. She was like someone in the grip of an obsession.

"How are you getting to Nordwyck?" Ruth asked, changing the subject.

"Rosalia and Nancy are going to drive me up. I tried to find a bus, but nothing goes close. We'll leave early Monday morning. They should be back by evening." They stood awkwardly at the door.

"Would you like me to write to you?" Ruth asked.

"You'll be too busy."

"That's not the point."

Daryl hesitated, then she said, "No, I'd rather you didn't. I think it's important to be absolutely cut off."

From what? Ruth wanted to ask but felt sure that if she did Daryl would not be able to answer.

In fact Rosalia and Nancy did not make the trip to Nordwyck in one day. It was Wednesday afternoon before they were able to return to St. Aidan's.

"We tried to call," Rosalia explained, "but the wires were all down. I'm sorry you had to worry like that."

"When we heard the weather reports we knew what had happened," Joanne assured them, taking their coats and putting them in the closet. "Don't worry about those things," she said as

Nancy stood looking for someplace to put her boots. "I'll take care of them. Why don't you go on into the dining room. Anna's fixing you some lunch."

"How about an omelet?" Ruth asked as she poured the tea.

"Wonderful, I'm starved," Nancy said, cupping her frozen hands around the teacup. "Something happened to the heater for the last fifty miles or so."

"Where did you run into the snow, at Nordwyck?" Joanne asked.

"No, it wasn't snowing when we left, although they were predicting it any minute. I thought the Community might ask us to stay over, but they didn't."

"They really don't have any room," Rosalia exonerated them. "And anyway we didn't realize how bad it would be. We drove for about an hour and then we were lucky to find a motel. We tried to call, but by that time the lines were down. Even this morning the driving was still bad. I'd probably still be there if it weren't for Nancy. She did all the hard driving."

"Daryl's the one I feel sorry for. They got the full blast of the blizzard at Nordwyck."

"What's it like?" Joanne asked.

Rosalia and Nancy looked at each other. Ruth found nothing reassuring in their look.

Rosalia shrugged. Her hands looked ugly and raw from the cold. "It's very isolated, as you can imagine. It's about five miles in from the highway on a dirt road. Right now the snow is packed so hard that the road is fairly manageable, but it must be awful in the spring thaw. There's a beautiful grove of blue spruce as you drive in. They'd had some light snow the day before we got there. The whole thing looked like a Christmas card. It must be lovely in the summer with all those pine needles on the ground."

She's hedging, thought Ruth, plying us with details to avoid what she's feeling.

"And Daryl?" prodded Joanne.

Again that exchange of looks. This time it was Nancy who spoke. "Daryl seems very happy with what she saw. There are twelve small hermitages on the grounds. They're about fifty yards from each other and situated in such a way that you can't see one from the other. So Daryl will have maximum solitude."

Joanne shivered. "How do they keep warm?"

"I'm not sure they do. But each house does have a wood-burning stove."

"Not enough," said Joanne, shivering again.

Rosalia said nothing. She was staring into her teacup as though she expected to find there the design of her fortune—or Daryl's.

"It's very primitive," Nancy agreed. "I'm not sure I could stand it. There's no electricity. They use oil lamps. And as far as I could see the water situation is rather primitive too."

They were silent, thinking of Daryl, fastidious and delicate, coping with the rigors of Nordwyck.

The swinging door from the kitchen pushed open and Anna put a large platter of omelet next to Rosalia. Rosalia, lost in her dreams, hardly noticed; and Nancy, quick to cover the lapse, smiled at Anna. "It looks delicious, Anna. We're sorry you had all this extra trouble."

But Anna looked straight ahead, her hands clasped under her white apron, a curt nod her only acknowledgment of Nancy's compliment. "Is there something else?"

"No, this is fine, isn't it, Rosalia?"

Rosalia looked up from her dream. "It's just right, Anna. Thanks so much."

Anna ignored Rosalia's effort to thank her. Her mouth was clamped hard over her yellowing teeth, and the downward slant of her eyes made her face obdurate and almost cruel. "If there's nothing else, I'll go back to my work," she said flatly and limped heavily from the room.

The sun, which had been partially visible, had gone behind

a cloud; and the corner of the dining room where they sat was darkened by a yellowish glow.

"We've never made peace, Anna and I," Rosalia said. She had forgotten to pass the omelet and played absently with the serving spoon in front of her.

"You can't make peace until she wants it," Joanne counseled her.

"There must be a way," Rosalia said stubbornly.

"There are a lot of ways." Joanne had reached over and passed the omelet to Nancy. "But they won't work until Anna lets them work. Right now I think she needs her anger."

Rosalia looked up in disbelief.

"I mean that, Rosalia. Anna's lost everything—or feels she has. The only dignity she has left is her anger. Don't take it away from her before she's found something else."

"But she's so miserably unhappy."

"Maybe this isn't her time for happiness."

"But I feel so responsible." Rosalia was pleating her napkin into little pieces.

"No, Rosalia"—Nancy's voice was sure and firm—"you're not responsible. Anna is a strong woman. She can stand a time of unhappiness. Some of us have to divert ourselves because we don't have the courage to admit unhappiness, but Anna can face things alone. Don't force her to capitulate until she's ready."

I wonder, Ruth thought as she listened to that wise, direct voice, if Nancy will be our next superior? And then she remembered. St. Aidan's would never have another superior; Rosalia was the last of the line.

Two weeks later the Community had a long letter from Daryl. It described Nordwyck in detail and explained with Daryl's scrupulous precision the orientation and style of life. Nordwyck was, she explained, an effort to re-establish the early Christian eremitic tradition. They gathered together for morning and evening prayer—rising and retiring according to the rhythm of the sun—but the rest of the time was spent in their individual hermitages. They fixed their own meals from a common store. So much bread, cheese, tea, and other staples were given to them at the beginning of each week. They never ate meat, and while fish was permitted it was generally too difficult to get. In the summer each hermitage had a small garden and each hermit was encouraged to grow her own vegetables and also to practice some useful craft. In winter, however, most of the day was spent reading and praying, although a good part of it, Daryl admitted, was taken up by the simple tasks of keeping a sufficient supply of wood and water available. On Sunday, following Mass, they had dinner together in the main house. Aside from this, they lived alone.

She was well and happy, she assured them. It had been unusually cold, but she was sure she would adjust. She prayed for them each day and hoped that the season of Lent would bring them renewed joy in the Cross of the Lord. She would write to them again at Easter. Until then she trusted in their prayers for her.

"What kind of a letter is that?" said Peg in disgust as she flipped it across the table to Kate.

"What's wrong with it?"

"It sounds like something out of those books of inspirational letters from the seventeenth century."

Kate was frowning. "She says she's well and happy," she said as she perused the letter.

Peg snorted. "That doesn't tell me anything."

"Did she tell you any more when you lived with her?" Kate countered.

"No. But I guess I thought that if this was a happy time for Daryl she'd be able to loosen up a little. Have you heard from her?" She turned to Ruth.

"I had a note she'd sent along with the Community letter."

"And?"

"Nothing she doesn't say in the general letter." Kate was watching her keenly, anticipating something more, but Ruth pushed back her chair and said good night.

Daryl's note had not reassured her. It affirmed that Nordwyck was all that she had hoped, that she welcomed the days of solitude and the spareness of her life. Yet Ruth could find no spontaneity in her avowals. The words seemed cold and studied. She feared that instead of freeing Daryl Nordwyck was only binding her further.

When at the beginning of March St. Aidan's entered the season of Lent, it came to them as a relief. They were ready for psalms of sorrow and intercession, for purple vestments and fasting. "Remember, you are dust," the priest intoned on Ash Wednesday as he signed their foreheads with ashes. It was not hard to believe. The bitter signs of their mortality were all around them.

Letters had gone out to the parents as soon as the decision to sell St. Aidan's had been made, and Joanne was besieged by irate replies protesting their action. Mothers called reminding them that St. Aidan's had educated three generations in their families, parents from Latin America wrote offering to pay whatever raise in tuition was necessary to keep St. Aidan's open. Susannah, who helped Joanne in her office, was a party to it all and triumphantly spread stories of the injuries they were doing by forcing children into public schools.

"Of course the education is inferior," she proclaimed, and then added in a more ominous tone, "and that is not the worst of it." Her small mouth was pursed in disapproval.

Rita jubilantly tacked up a letter she had received from a parent, "a man of high professional standards and an excellent Catholic, excellent." He was shocked, the writer said, that they would so easily give up not only a school but a convent which had flourished for almost a hundred years. But, he reflected, he should not be surprised, since they had already given up everything else of value in their lives.

"Doesn't that make you *sick!*" asked Nancy in disgust as she stood reading the letter which Rita had placed in a strategic spot.

"Poor Joanne!" Peg said. But Joanne had become stoical in the face of criticism. Her ordinary composure had hardened to flint. She never raised her voice or lost her temper, but something warm and responsive in her had retreated. She had ceased to direct and had begun to rule.

"My, Joanne certainly wants everything very perfect these days," said Noreen, her bewilderment her only criticism, as she emerged from Joanne's office with all her class records to retype in proper order.

In the days following the Chapter, the tension of decision-making was succeeded by something darker. Although they had outwardly accepted their decision, they were not reconciled. They lived in sullen endurance, alienated from each other and without other comfort. Even that sustaining moment of vision that Magdalen had called forth during the Council's discussion of the suppression of St. Aidan's had lost its power.

Ruth remembered it, but vaguely, like a comforting dream that slips away at day's light. Sometimes as she walked through the halls or sorted books in the library, she repeated the text: "Unless the seed falls into the ground and dies, it will remain alone." But the words, heavy and hard as stones, resisted all her efforts to cement them into meaning. Sometimes she felt light-headed from the strain, as though she floated beside her body, all the experiences of her senses just a centimeter beyond her fingertips. At other times it seemed she had turned to lead and could hardly free herself from lethargy to do her ordinary work.

How do they pray? Ruth wondered, as she sat in chapel reciting with the others the psalms of the day. Were they, like her, aloof and insensible to the familiar words? Or, restless and mistrustful, did they count the days left to them and wonder what use this holy place would be put to?

The sisters will make a meditation of at least forty-five minutes each morning; they will spend the same amount of time in adoration each evening. They will attend Mass daily and recite morning and evening prayer according to the formula of the Church. They will never permit anything to violate this sacred trust, neither the demands of their work nor a spirit of disaffection for the things of the spirit. Let them apply their minds and hearts to prayer with diligence and trust, believing that even in times of darkness and distraction they have a duty of faithful obedience.

One day as she returned to her place after receiving communion, she looked up and saw Gregory walking back from the altar. One hand was clenched around her cane, the other resting over her heart, and the strong, almost masculine, face was crumpled in bewilderment. Ruth never looked up again.

The strain was taking a toll on them all. Agnes had grown more crippled in the last two months; and although Ruth often went to spend time with her in the evening, they had never regained their intimacy. Something stood between them; it was something other than the loss of St. Aidan's, something more personal. Ruth lacked the heart to confront it directly; and Agnes, with a bland opacity, countered all her oblique efforts. Susannah's eyes had grown worse, Peg had told her. "It's almost inevitable with diabetes, but I can't get her to admit it." Gregory rarely went without her cane now, and the effort to get on and off the organ bench was more than she could manage. Fortunately they needed no music during Lent.

Only Timothy retained her serenity. She's like Lazarus, Ruth thought as she helped her with her supper tray one night. She had gone down to death, but Gregory's love had called her back. Death can never touch her in the same way again.

"What do you hear from Daryl?" Timothy asked as she put her teacup hesitantly back on its saucer.

"Not very much. She says she's happy." Ruth couldn't keep the skepticism out of her voice.

"Gregory is very worried about her, you know. She thinks she won't come back, that she's gone to that place—what do they call it?"

"Nordwyck."

"Yes, well, that she's gone there for good."

"Daryl's had a very hard time the last few years."

"That's what Gregory says. But off in a hermitage like that! And they say she's very delicate. Do you think it's right for her?"

"I suppose there's no way to tell unless she tries it."

"Gregory says she'll never give in. She says she's stubborn as sin. That's not a nice way to put it, is it? But you know what I mean."

"I hope you pray for Daryl." Ruth could think of nothing else to say.

"Indeed I do. I said to Gregory the other day, 'The Lord has His own ways, and if Daryl isn't supposed to be there He'll find a way to bring her back.'"

Timothy's prediction came true far sooner than she could have expected. Two weeks later Rosalia knocked on Ruth's door as she was making her bed after breakfast.

"I just had a call from Nordwyck. Daryl's sick."

"She wants to come home?" Ruth's first reaction was relief.

Rosalia shook her head. "She's too sick to come home." She was rubbing her raw, swollen hands nervously.

"Are you going up?"

"I can't." She looked at her watch. "Joanne and I have an appointment with the lawyer at eleven and then a meeting with the Bishop early this afternoon."

"Can you go tomorrow? Or later this afternoon?"

"I don't want to wait. They're predicting more snow this afternoon."

"Do you want me to go?" She was deliberately channeling her mind to the practical issues, unwilling to face her fears for Daryl.

"Could you? And you'll have to take someone with you. It's a hard drive."

"Nancy?"

Rosalia shook her head. "She's too busy in the school. I don't want to ask her to do anything else."

They stood thinking of who might be free to go.

"I could take Noreen. I'm sure she's free."

But Rosalia was impatient. "I'd rather have someone more reliable. Ask Magdalen. She can let her school work go for once."

"Do you have the directions for Nordwyck?" Ruth asked.

"Daryl's not at Nordwyck. They moved her to Cliffhoven. That's the nearest hospital."

"What happened?" Ruth faced her fears at last.

"She has pneumonia. They're not sure she'll pull through."

They stood, avoiding each other's eyes, Ruth remembering the set pale look with which Daryl had vowed, "It will work."

Rosalia looked at her watch again. "I have to go. Call me as soon as you get there."

Ruth nodded dumbly, and then as Rosalia was closing the door she called, "Rosalia, what about Daryl's mother?"

Her hands went to her cheeks in dismay. "I never thought."

"You go ahead. I'll take care of it. Can I get into your files to get her address?"

"The key's in a little box in the middle drawer of the desk. The records are in the first drawer of the file."

While Magdalen went to pack a suitcase Ruth looked through Rosalia's file, but when she called the number listed on Daryl's record she got a woman who had never heard of Mrs. Peters.

"You must have an old number," she said. "We've been living here about five years now."

"You don't remember the name of the woman who had the apartment before?"

"No, I don't. We got it through a real estate broker. We

did sublease it at first. He did say something about a lady who lived alone and wanted a smaller apartment. Sorry I can't help. Is this an emergency?"

And when Ruth said it was she offered to give her the name of the broker. But the man involved had changed his job and the receptionist informed Ruth curtly that such information could not be given over the phone.

It was already ten-thirty and clouds had begun to form in the west.

"I don't think we should waste any more time," Magdalen said. "We can get the number from Daryl when we get there."

"Maybe she doesn't know it," said Ruth.

"We'll have to take that chance," Magdalen answered grimly.

The snow caught them on the way. It was heavy and wet and blowing straight out of the north. They passed cars stopped along the way but they pushed on, not speaking, alternating driving from time to time in silent agreement. It was after dark when they reached Cliffhoven. It was a small town and there was no difficulty finding the hospital.

As they came into the lobby a tall man in ski boots and corduroy jeans came to meet them. "Sister Rosalia?"

"No, but we're from St. Aidan's," Magdalen answered. "I'm Sister Magdalen and this is Sister Ruth."

He nodded. "I'm Brother Jeffrey. I guess you know that Daryl is very sick."

They nodded. "What happened?" In her anxiety Magdalen sounded peremptory.

Brother Jeffrey raised his hands helplessly. "I noticed she had a cold on Friday when she was at Morning Prayer. I stopped afterward to ask her if she needed anything but she said she was fine. That was on Friday. On Saturday we have no common prayer. We observe Saturday as a day of vigil before the Sunday celebration. So of course we didn't miss Daryl. Had we known, we would have gone to see her. As it was, we didn't miss her until Sunday Mass. One of the sisters went over then."

He looked embarrassed. "Daryl had had no fire for almost two days. She hadn't been strong enough to make one." Again he raised his hands with the same helpless gesture. "I hope you understand"—his eyelids blinked nervously—"that we are not indifferent to each other's needs. If any one of us had realized . . ." His voice trailed away and Ruth nodded impatiently. His emphasis on exculpating the Community irritated her.

"When did you bring Daryl to Cliffhoven?"

He pushed his hand uncertainly through his hair as though making an extraordinary effort to recall a distant past. "Today is Tuesday, isn't it?" he said at last. "Well, Sunday, when Ramona found her we didn't realize how sick she was, and Daryl said she'd be fine once they got a fire going. But that afternoon she"—his hand was wandering through his hair again—"seemed a little worse. We tried to get a doctor, but the roads out near Nordwyck are very bad, so—"

"When did she come to the hospital?" Magdalen had reached the end of her patience.

"We brought her in our truck yesterday afternoon."

Magdalen turned away abruptly and walked toward the desk.

Jeffrey continued apologetically. "You see, Father Clement is away and there isn't really anyone in charge. We've never had an emergency like this." He waved vaguely toward a couch. "I'll just wait over here. I know Dr. Sievers has been waiting to see you."

Dr. Sievers was as small and efficient as Jeffrey was vague. He nodded peremptorily. "She's been critical all day. I can't tell how things will go. Is her health generally good?"

Magdalen and Ruth looked at each other. "Yes," Ruth said hesitantly, "although she's lost a lot of weight in the past year."

"Well, she's lost more now, I can tell you that. How long

has she been at Nordwyck? A month? That's enough. They don't eat enough. They don't sleep enough. And how they keep from freezing to death in weather like this, I don't know. That's my medical opinion. I'm not a Catholic, and I don't pretend to understand the other values involved."

He turned quickly and led them down the corridor. "As you can see, this is a very small hospital—only thirty beds. We don't have all the fancy equipment you'd get in a place like New York, but I think we can guarantee good care."

But even with so much warning, they were not prepared for Daryl.

"Is she asleep?" Ruth asked at last.

"She's been delirious or unconscious since they brought her in. It's a wonder she didn't die in the truck."

"How long will she be like this?"

"Hard to say. We've been able to get her fever down. We're running an IV with antibiotics." He turned to Ruth. "You've notified her family?"

Magdalen stepped in. "We've had difficulty locating her mother, but we'll get right to it now."

Dr. Sievers was at the door. "Where does she live?"

"New York," they said simultaneously.

He nodded. "They've made arrangements for you to stay at the hospital. There's room enough and there's no hotel in town. Tell Miss Dowling to let you use my phone. Those pay phones will drive you crazy." And he left.

They sat in a small office with a New York directory on the table between them. No Harriet Peters was listed.

"Would it be under her husband's name?" Ruth suggested.

Magdalen ran her index finger down the page and shook her head.

"We should have admitted to the doctor that we don't know how to reach her mother," Ruth said hopelessly.

But Magdalen was flipping through the phone book. "There's just a chance." Her finger caught a name and she looked up. It was not sorrow in her face or fear; it was resolution of an awesome kind, as though for a moment she had steeled herself to a daunting task and could not bear to be deflected by even a second's hesitation. "Would you mind waiting at the desk?" she asked Ruth. "I'd rather do this alone."

Twenty minutes later she emerged. "Mrs. Peters will get the earliest possible train in the morning. There's nothing out tonight. I told her we'd be waiting at the station."

Magdalen's voice did not encourage questions and Ruth nodded silently.

"There's a snack bar in the basement. Why don't we go down and get something to eat." Magdalen led the way.

When they were drinking their coffee, she explained, "There's a law firm in New York that my father used to use. I remember someone mentioning that Mrs. Peters was a client of theirs, too. The office was closed, of course, but fortunately I was able to catch the senior partner at home. Mrs. Peters has an unlisted number and he didn't feel he could give it to me. He called her and she called back here."

"It must have been a terrible shock."

Magdalen smiled wryly. "A shock that Daryl's ill or a shock that we called?"

Ruth didn't answer for a minute. "She wanted to come, didn't she?"

"She's coming."

"Suppose"—Ruth hesitated, alarmed that it hadn't occurred to her before—"suppose Daryl doesn't—"

"Doesn't want to see her mother?"

Ruth nodded.

"Daryl may die without ever regaining consciousness."

"But if she's conscious . . ."

"In any case, they have to have their chance."

"But it could be so painful, more painful than if—"

But Magdalen cut her short with unaccountable vehemence. "Nothing is more painful than not having a chance."

Before Ruth could get to her feet, Magdalen had picked up her tray and left the cafeteria.

Dr. Sievers smiled encouragingly when they met him in the hall the next morning. The snow had stopped during the night, and Daryl's room was filled with a gray winter light. Ruth could see no change in her. She lay as she had the night before. Her eyes were still closed and her hair, close-cropped now, made her face look smaller than ever.

"She's got a pretty good chance." Dr. Sievers was carefully scrutinizing her chart. "What about her mother?" he asked, looking up. "Were you able to get hold of her?"

Ruth looked toward Magdalen.

"She's coming in on a train that gets into Evansville around noon," Magdalen answered.

"The twelve-seventeen. Are you going to meet her? I doubt if she'll be able to get a taxi. It's about a twenty-five-minute drive from here. Have them page me when she gets here." He paused at the door. "Meanwhile, don't alarm her, but don't make it sound all clear either. She's got a rocky road ahead of her yet." He jerked his head toward Daryl.

They stayed after the doctor had left, sitting in two plastic chairs close to the window. At first they watched Daryl intently, but the heat of the room made them drowsy. Once there was a slight movement from the bed and when Ruth looked up Daryl's eyes were open; but before Ruth could move into her line of vision she had closed them again and drifted off.

"Do you think I should tell the nurse?" Ruth asked.

Magdalen nodded. "I'll go."

The nurse came in and felt Daryl's forehead and took her pulse. "She's a little stronger. She'll probably keep waking up for a few seconds at a time. Don't try to talk to her. It will be too much of a strain."

Two or three more times Daryl opened her eyes, but she did not see them. Toward eleven-thirty Magdalen rose. "I'm going to start over to Evansville," she said. "I want to leave myself plenty of time. I imagine the roads will be pretty bad."

Ruth sat on, ashamed of herself for dozing but unable to fix her attention on anything, even on Daryl. One of the humiliating side effects of sorrow, she thought. Although it had not been that way when her father was dying. Then she thought she would never sleep again. Her whole body had been pitched to an unendurable consciousness.

It was close to two o'clock when Magdalen brought Mrs. Peters into Daryl's room. She acknowledged Magdalen's introduction, but her eyes were fixed hypnotically on Daryl's bed. They stood for a while, the three of them, saying nothing, absorbed in watching. Mrs. Peters had changed less than her daughter. The pale gold hair had grown more yellow, but her face, despite the cluster of wrinkles about her eyes, was still beautiful and her figure straight and thin.

As they watched, Daryl's eyes opened; but her head was turned away from them, and before her mother could reach her, she had drifted again into unconsciousness.

Ruth started to say that the nurse had assured them that Daryl was stronger and that these moments of consciousness would increase, but the look on Mrs. Peters' face stopped her. For a moment her composure was gone, and in its place was fear and anger, sorrow and self-accusation. So might a suicide look at the edge of death, regretting too late his irretrievable loss.

Ruth and Magdalen withdrew to the side of the room, but Mrs. Peters waited on, refusing the chair that Magdalen offered. Her composure had returned and there was nothing in her posture to betray her anguish. That is how Aidan would look, Ruth realized—the same aristocratic control that concealed such passionate affection. How Aidan would have looked if she had lost a child. And for a moment the image of Marian Connell replaced Daryl in her consciousness. For the first time she cried and did nothing to stop the tears. She cried for them all, grieving and bereft. For Daryl and Harriet Peters, for Aidan and Marian. For her father and Mother Mary David, who had died deprived of the only image of God they had known. As she turned she caught Magdalen's face, half hidden in shadow, and knew with unerring clarity that Magdalen, too, had endured a loss to which she had never been reconciled. Blindly she moved to take Mrs. Peters' hand, then stopped, knowing that, like Aidan, Mrs. Peters would suffer her pain in solitude.

The winter light had darkened, and as Magdalen rose to light the floor lamp in the corner of the room there was a slight movement in the bed. Daryl had turned her head and opened her eyes. Her hand slid over the sheet and Mrs. Peters grasped it in both her own. Daryl's dry lips tried to smile. "Mummy," she said, the word hardly formed before she slipped off again. But in that moment of consciousness there had been no surprise, no confusion. It was as though, awakening in the nursery after a long troubled sleep, she had found her mother bending over to comfort her as she would have expected.

The following morning Dr. Sievers pronounced Daryl on the road to recovery, and the next day Ruth and Magdalen started back to St. Aidan's. Mrs. Peters would remain in the hospital until Daryl was strong enough to travel.

"Just call us and we'll come up to get you," Magdalen had offered.

But reconciliation had not made Mrs. Peters any less independent. "That's very kind, but I'll hire a chauffeured car."

The roads were clear and the driving much easier as they headed south. Even so, they said little.

"I'll be glad to drive when you're tired," Ruth offered twice.

But Magdalen rejected the offer. "I'd just as soon, if it's all right with you."

They made no stops, and Magdalen drove with an insistent speed that made Ruth wonder what she was trying to outdistance. It was just three o'clock when they arrived at St. Aidan's.

Rawlins and Swenson, Realtors
108 East 68th St.
New York, N.Y.
March 24, 1981

Mr. Alec Stafford
Stafford, Connor, Lipsky, Architects
18 Ballantyne Avenue
Glen Cove, New York

Dear Alec,

Thanks for filling me in on those figures; I shouldn't have to bother you again. Everything is moving ahead on schedule. We haven't set the date for the closing yet, but that's the only thing left to settle.

This is for your "Small World" file. I was having lunch at the club the other day and I was introduced to a lawyer who used to live in Whitethorn. I asked him if he knew St. Aidan's. He did indeed. His mother-in-law, his wife, and his two daughters all had gone there to school. He is enraged over the closing of the school. He thinks the whole thing is a disgrace—not just the sale of St. Aidan's but everything that's happened in the last fifteen years. He assured me I was not to blame (gracious of him!). The nuns are entirely at fault. Once they'd given up their habits and their cloisters and started walking about "like normal women" it was all over.

I foolishly asked if he didn't think the nuns were happier with a little more independence; he assured me that happiness had nothing to do with it. He said he had written several letters to St. Aidan's exhorting the sisters to return to a "proper way of life."

Poor ladies! I'm sure they don't need that. Here I am, getting to be a champion of nuns. What next!

Steve Rawlins

17

The day before Daryl was to be released from the hospital she called Rosalia.

"Mother would like to take me for a little vacation," she explained apologetically. "There's a ski lodge up here that she knows about."

But before Daryl could finish, Rosalia assured her. "By all means. Stay as long as you like."

"It'll only be for a week," Daryl explained. "I want to be back at St. Aidan's before Holy Week."

"Don't worry about Holy Week. Stay until you feel stronger. I'm afraid St. Aidan's wouldn't be very restful these days. Do you need anything, Daryl?" she asked.

"Oh, no. Mother's taken care of everything." There was amusement rather than resentment in her voice.

"Daryl's going to Castlecraig with her mother for a week or so," Rosalia said to Ruth, who had stopped in at the office. "I hope it's for recuperation and not another gesture of self-sacrifice."

"I don't think you have to worry. If you'd seen them together in the hospital, you'd recognize that Daryl's need is just as keen as Mrs. Peters'."

She sighed. "I sometimes wonder if Daryl is going to spend her life making extravagant gestures."

"Very possibly. After all, she comes from a long line of extravagant people."

Rosalia sighed again. It had become a habit with her. "Ruth, would you tell Gregory that Daryl won't be home for another week. She's been upstairs getting her room ready all morning. If she mops the floor once more she'll take the wax off."

Ruth, however, had not been able to find Gregory. She was not in Daryl's room or in her own. She knocked finally on Timothy's door in the hope of finding her there, but Timothy was alone.

"No, dear, I haven't seen her all morning. She said last night she was going to be fixing Daryl's room for her this morning."

"That's why I'm looking for her. Daryl won't be home for a while."

"She's not sick again?"

"No. She's fine." Ruth came and sat on the hassock near Timothy's chair. "She's taking a little vacation with her mother."

"Well, thank God for that." Timothy reached gropingly to turn off her radio. "I can't imagine what Gregory would do if anything happened to that child now. It's like a miracle, isn't it? Going off to that place and getting so sick and then finding her mother again after all those years. Gregory didn't think they'd ever be reconciled. She told me she tried to talk to Daryl about it once but she wouldn't hear a word."

"The real miracle was finding Mrs. Peters. Rosalia had only an old address and her telephone was unlisted. I don't know how we would have found her if it hadn't been for Magdalen." As soon as she said it Ruth felt as though she had betrayed a confidence. There had been something inexplicably private in the phone call that had located Mrs. Peters.

But Timothy betrayed no curiosity. She sat nodding quietly, a pucker at the corner of her wide mouth, as though she were putting together the pieces of a puzzle. "Of course," she said finally, "as soon as Aidan heard about Magdalen getting in touch

with Mrs. Peters she figured it out right away. I never knew all
the ins and outs of that trouble with Magdalen and her father,
but Aidan was on the Council at the time and, of course, her own
father was involved, too, you might say."

It was clear that Timothy thought Ruth knew the story, but
the oblique references meant nothing to her. "Are the families
connected?" she asked.

Timothy turned toward her, the dark eyes fixed just above
her head. "You don't know about Magdalen?"

"I guess not." Ruth hesitated, not sure what it was she was
supposed to know.

"There's no reason why you would. I keep forgetting that
you didn't come to St. Aidan's until . . . let me see. What year
did you come?"

"Nineteen fifty-nine."

"Well, of course, it was all over by then. Although I
suppose it's never been over for Magdalen." She paused and then
went on. "I don't think I'm betraying any confidence by telling
you. Anybody who was at St. Aidan's knew something about it."
She smiled. "It's funny how much you can learn even with a rule
of silence. Of course we never talked about it, although Aidan
did come and discuss it with me one day. She and Josephine were
always at loggerheads and I think she would like to have blamed
it all on poor Josephine, although, as I said to her, Josephine just
inherited the trouble.

"You see, Magdalen came from a very prominent family.
I hate to admit it but that used to mean a lot, especially to
superiors. Aidan suffered all her life because of it. I know there
are some who say that she was spoiled inside the convent and out,
but I don't know." Timothy's long face was filled with compassion. "I think life would have been much easier if her father
hadn't been the wealthy Gavin Fitzgerald.

"Well, I suppose that's neither here nor there. Mr. Richards
was a very important lawyer for the government. He was in
Washington a lot, especially after his wife died. Poor man, I

suppose he was lonely. When Magdalen came to St. Aidan's he was very disappointed. Of course he was a very good Catholic and wouldn't oppose her openly, but he wanted something better for her. She was very bright and, well, I suppose he had his plans. He was very difficult at first, but Mother Mary David got around him. Gregory used to say she could change the mind of the devil himself. She told Mr. Richards that we were going to have a college at St. Aidan's and that Magdalen would be sent on for all sorts of degrees so that she could be in charge."

"Did Magdalen know all this?"

"You know"—Timothy's mouth puckered again—"I don't think she did, unless her father told her. Mary David talked a lot more outside than in. She never told her nuns very much. It was always the lawyers and the bankers who seemed to know what was happening at St. Aidan's."

It was one of the few times Ruth had ever heard the gentle Timothy veer toward criticism.

"Then, of course," she continued, "when the whole thing blew up there was a terrible fuss."

"Mother Mary David changed her mind about the college?"

"Goodness, dear"—Timothy reached out to pat Ruth's hand—"she never changed her mind. Not that one. She was pure granite through and through. But when her term as superior was up she was replaced by Josephine and, of course, there was no love between them. If one said black the other said white. You must have noticed that."

"I never really knew Mother Mary David. She was already retired when I was a novice."

"Well then, you were spared something." The asperity in Timothy's voice was startling.

"The thing was, you see, that Mr. Fitzgerald had promised money to get the college started, and then when he died so suddenly there was very little provision in his will. I suppose he meant to change it and like so many people just put it off. Actually, I think Josephine was relieved. Mary David would have thrived on it—the architects, the builders, the contractors—but Josephine wasn't that sort. I think in her heart of hearts she thought higher education was a dangerous thing, that it made people proud.

"It seems that Mr. Richards had given quite a large sum toward the college, and when he heard there was to be no college he wanted his money back. I think he'd only given it because he'd been assured that Magdalen would be at the head of it. But the money was gone. Mary David had already used it to spruce up the boarding school."

"How could she when it was marked for another purpose?"

"Oh, she could. She was a charmer, but she didn't bother much with the rules. She always expected to be plucked out of danger by an angel from heaven. Some people called it a great spirit of faith." The irony in Timothy's voice was unmistakable.

"What happened?"

"Poor Josephine was left picking up the pieces. Mr. Richards accused St. Aidan's of swindling him and seducing his daughter."

"And how did Magdalen take it?"

Timothy shook her head. "That was a funny thing. I never saw a girl so crazy about her father and yet she was like a rock. She refused to listen to a single bit of criticism against St. Aidan's, although it was justified, God knows. Aidan told me that Magdalen's father begged her to leave, told her it was no house of God where such dishonesty could take place. Finally he threatened that if she didn't leave he would disinherit her and never speak to her again. I'm sure he never thought it would come to that, but Magdalen wouldn't move. The next month he sent his lawyer up with some papers for her to sign. It must have been the same gentleman Magdalen called the other night—a Mr. Linder or Lindler. I can't rightly remember. Aidan would know."

"And she never saw her father again?"

Timothy shook her head. "About two years ago, or maybe

it was three—I lose track sometimes—right around Christmas, Judge Richards was on his way home and some young hoodlum mugged him. He died right there on the street of a heart attack. It was all on television. That's how Magdalen found out." Timothy closed her eyes. "Aidan begged her to go to the funeral. Of course, by then we had permission to go home and all. But she didn't go. She told Aidan she had no right. That she had never been a daughter to him while he lived."

Ruth saw again Magdalen's bitter, desolate face and heard the hard, set voice as she had said in the cafeteria, "Nothing is more painful than not having a chance."

"I've often thought"—Timothy was continuing—"that she might have left years before when her father had pleaded with her, but Marian was a great influence on her in those days—she was right up till she left—and Marian maintained that nothing could justify being unfaithful to one's vows. Marian was always a very strong personality. And, of course"—Timothy stopped as though she had second thoughts about what she had started to say and then continued—"Marian was very close to Mary David. She always took her side. She was Mary David's protégée, you might say. I don't want to speak against Marian. She did a great deal for us, God knows, but I always felt Mary David encouraged her to want power. I suppose she meant well. We aren't supposed to judge. But all the same . . ." The peace had gone out of her face and the wide mouth had narrowed. "All the same, Mary David did a lot of harm."

Timothy turned her head away from Ruth and toward her bed until her blind gaze rested by habit on the crucifix hanging above it. It was, as always, slightly askew, tilted so that one arm reached gropingly upward.

"What did Mother Mary David do to you, Timothy?" The question was out before Ruth realized the intrusiveness of it.

There was no hesitation in Timothy's answer. "She told me" —and the timbre of her voice had subtly changed—"that my friendship with Gregory was unhealthy and unreligious, that it was vicious and corrosive, corrosive of my vows and of the spirit of community."

The words were not Timothy's but Mother Mary David's, remembered in their phrasing and their intonation all those years.

"She forbade us to speak to each other during her term of office. That was for three years. During the second year, my mother died."

> The sisters will love each member of the Community equally. They will show no favoritism or in any way, by word or deed, betray an affection for one rather than another. They will shun such particular friendships as an infidelity to the Lord and as dangerous to the spirit of the Community. Should any sister notice the signs of such a friendship, she will be obliged to report it at once to the superior, who will take whatever means she deems best to put an end to the abuse.

"Poor Gregory." Timothy was absently smoothing the heavy black serge of her habit over her knees. "Gregory would have stood up to her. Gregory was always outspoken, you know. But she couldn't. She knew it would just have hurt me more.

"Mary David said my mother's blood and those years growing up in Mexico had infected me with Latin ways. She made it sound"—her dark liquid eyes turned from the crucifix as though the word she grappled with could not be said while she looked at the image of the crucified Lord—"she made it sound *impure.*"

The word came like the accusation of a shameful disease. Ruth felt again, welling up inside of her, that terrible nausea, her response to anger too great to be stomached, which had once sent her running from Mother Josephine's office when she had belittled her father's loneliness.

"I've never told anyone that," Timothy said at last. "Although if you'd been here you would have known." The gentle mouth came together harshly. "She announced it to the whole

Community. She was like that. That was the worst of it, of course —not just missing Gregory but being afraid to speak to anyone. I thought they must all be thinking terrible things of me.

"Of course, it was right in the Rule. But Mary David wasn't always so particular about the Rule. She knew how to bend it when it pleased her. I used to watch her spending hours talking to Anna and letting her wait on her as though she were her servant."

Neither of them heard the knock on the door, and Peg pushed it open with Timothy's lunch tray in her hands. "Sorry, I didn't realize anyone was here. I didn't hear any talking." Peg bustled about pushing the small tray table over where Timothy could reach it.

"Ruth came in looking for Gregory," Timothy said at last.

"I just saw her downstairs. I think she was fixing Daryl's room."

"You'd better run along and find her," Timothy said, patting Ruth's knee, "before she starts worrying about Daryl."

Ruth found Gregory tidying up the broom closet but as she explained about Daryl, she hardly heard Gregory's answer. She was conscious only of that strong furrowed face, the eyes distorted behind the heavy glasses, and thought of all the unjust suffering to which she had been condemned. She knew that she should be able to see beyond it, to see that Gregory and Timothy had been freed at last, and that whatever blight had been laid upon them had not destroyed them. But she was locked into Timothy's anguish, feeling what it must have been to have had that young innocence tainted by what she was so arbitrarily accused of. For it was clear that Timothy had not only endured an unjust accusation but had suffered the shame of uncertainty, wondering if in some dark place she had not yet plumbed she was, in fact, impure.

Ruth avoided the dining room and walked out into the garden. There was still a remnant of snow along the borders; and beyond in the pine grove, hidden from the sun, the ground was still white. But patches of crocuses were already blooming along the side of the convent, and on the path near the garage a clump of daffodils edged their way through the moist soil. It was their last spring at St. Aidan's, but they were incapable of sharing its promise. Not once had she seen Susannah rummaging among the flowerbeds; and Anna, too, had remained indoors, her muddy boots thrown carelessly at the top of the cellar stairs. They had imprisoned themselves in winter, unwilling to risk the hope of new life.

At the beginning of Holy Week they received a letter from Marian Connell in response to Rosalia's letter informing her of the decision to sell St. Aidan's and merge with St. Malachy's. She expressed her sympathy for all the sorrow and loss they must be experiencing and assured them of her hope for a bright future at St. Malachy's. The conventional phrases of condolence only underscored her distance from them. No matter how deeply she had shared their life, it was clear that she was no longer one of them.

She had asked that someone dispose of the few things she had left behind in her trunk, and Ruth had gone up to the attic with Nancy to see to it. Marian had left little: some folders of notes that could be thrown out, a number of theology books to be given to the library, a shapeless black shawl heavy with the smell of camphor, a half-knit sweater, and some tangled balls of black yarn. In a long box at the bottom of the trunk they found her habit, neatly pressed, with a veil and starched linens beside it, as though she had expected to be asked suddenly to resume it. Ruth lifted it out of the box and a photograph fluttered to the floor. It was obviously a profession day photograph. Marian and Magdalen stood in their full-length black habits, the traditional crown of white roses on their heads. On each side of them stood their fathers. Marian was looking straight into the camera with that direct, resolute look that she had in every photograph. But Magdalen was looking toward her father, half smiling, her regular profile matching his; and if one looked closer, one could see that their hands were clasped, half hidden in the folds of her habit.

At the bottom of the box was Marian's Rule book. The binding was loose and the pages yellowed; the margins were full of penciled notes and the text itself underlined and queried. Marian, it was clear, had begun to question the old order long before a revision of the Rule had been undertaken. As Nancy thumbed through the book a holy card slipped out. It was a small reproduction of the Good Shepherd from the cathedral at Chartres. On the back, in Mother Mary David's unmistakable Irish script, was written, "Feed my sheep," and under this the date of Marian's profession, June 12, 1951. From the beginning Mary David had determined that Marian would one day be St. Aidan's shepherd—and had told Marian of her choice in order that she might prepare herself for it.

"I don't think it was necessarily a bad thing," Nancy mused. "Marian had leadership—anyone could see that right from the beginning—and Mary David wanted to be sure she recognized it and used it for the best purpose. I don't think either of them ever thought of their goals as ambition."

"You don't think that Mother Mary David misused her power?" Ruth was still too close to Timothy to keep the resentment out of her voice.

"Oh, I grant you that. Lord Acton was right. It's not easy to keep power from corrupting."

"And Marian?"

"No," Nancy said slowly. "I don't think Marian was ever corrupted, not like that."

"Then what was it?"

"She never said, so I suppose we'll never know. But I think she was infected by Mary David's dream for St. Aidan's. She wanted to make it into something wonderful." Nancy smiled wryly. "And then when she came to office it all seemed so small. The school had already begun to dwindle and vocations had dropped off. She kept striking away with her flint, but we never caught fire. All those years she had prepared herself for some great task, and instead she had a small school and a group of insignifi-

cant nuns. I think she never realized how small and weak we were
until she tried to lead us up the mountain."

They were sitting on two trunks, facing each other. Nancy
sighed, looking at the confusion around them. "When I come up
here and see all that has to be cleared out and thrown away I
wonder how we're ever going to move."

Ruth looked over the rows of trunks—some of them belonging to sisters who had been dead for years—the piles of
books and yellowing magazines, the useless chairs and broken
lamps heaped together in a corner, remembering that this was
only one of their three attics. "Have we made any arrangements
for cleaning out all this stuff?" she asked.

Before Nancy could answer there were steps on the stairs
and Terezia turned on the overhead light. "I am looking for
Nancy," she said, nodding toward them and pushing aside the
sticky strands of a cobweb clinging to her hair. "If you would
please go down to Joanne's office, there is a man there about art
supplies."

Nancy looked at her watch in chagrin. "Mr. Bredin! Good
heavens, I'd forgotten all about him. Thanks, Terezia." And she
started down the steps.

"So," said Terezia, looking about her. "You have found
here a little hermitage like the good saint in Hungary who spent
her life spinning under the eaves of her father's house."

"Not quite. We came up to take care of Marian's trunk, and
then we started talking."

Terezia looked at her keenly. "But not of happy things."

"St. Aidan's isn't a very happy place."

"God asks much of St. Aidan's. To be asked to die, this is
not a little thing."

"But we're not doing it very graciously, are we?"

Terezia shrugged. "Perhaps it is not possible to be gracious
in such suffering. For that we need a little something beyond—
what the French call the *pourboire*."

God's *pourboire*. That little extra tip of grace. Nothing they could demand or merit but something that a God rich and lavish in mercy could in His liberality bestow.

"For me"—Terezia's arms were crossed tight against her breast, her head lifted, her black eyes narrowed—"I think this is our *notte oscura*. How do you say—'the black night'?"

"Dark night."

"Yes. Dark night." She nodded. "You remember, St. John of the Cross says this must happen to the soul who seeks God. Perhaps this black night is not for the individual only."

"St. Aidan's dark night of the soul."

"Yes, a period of darkness for all of us. And because of the darkness we are separated from each other, unable to help each other, even though very deep in our hearts we would wish to do so." She paused, but Ruth said nothing. "Does this make for you some sense?"

Ruth nodded. St. Aidan's had always dwelt apart on its mountaintop, living in rarefied light. But now they had been humbled, swept from their pinnacle into the valley. Once privileged to see meaning everywhere, now they could find it in nothing. Only God's compassion, that divine gratuity, could deliver them out of "darkness and the shadow of death."

It was Daryl who opened the channel of God's compassion for them. She had returned the week before Palm Sunday, thin as ever but with good color and a brightness in her eyes that Ruth had never seen before. Even as a postulant there had been a tautness in Daryl's face, as though she were forcing herself just a fraction beyond her endurance. But the reconciliation with her mother had freed something in her, as though an organ that had grown hard and distended with pain had relaxed and softened into healthy tissue. She was beautifully dressed in a dark green suit and suede shoes, obviously of Mrs. Peters' choosing. "Mother keeps buying me things," she had said apologetically to the nuns' scrutiny, but she obviously enjoyed both the luxury and the affection that offered it.

That night Daryl curled up on the window seat in Ruth's room. "Do you remember the last time I sat here?"

"All too well."

"You never thought I'd come back, did you?"

"I hoped you would, but it seemed as though it would take a miracle, you'd wandered so far away."

"I know. Gregory said when she saw me, 'It's like having someone come back from the dead.' And it is for me, too. And not just from pneumonia but from that other terrible weight. It was like seeing God's mercy incarnate to wake up out of that fever and see Mother bending over me."

"I wondered if you'd remember that first moment. You drifted off again so quickly."

"I remember. And it all seemed so right. No shock. All just as it should be. I remember wanting to take her hand."

"You did. It was the first time you'd moved."

"If I hadn't been so sick it might not have been so easy. But I had no strength to resist."

Daryl said nothing for a few minutes and then she looked at Ruth directly. "Ruth, what's going to happen to St. Aidan's?"

Ruth shrugged. "We're going to move to St. Malachy's," she said, deliberately misinterpreting the question.

Daryl shook her head impatiently. "You know that's not what I mean. I mean what's going to happen here, between us, among us?"

Ruth said nothing.

"We can't go on like this. Don't you feel how wrong it is?"

"We all feel it, Daryl. We've been living with it ever since you went away." Her tone was sharper than she had intended.

Daryl blushed at the implication. "I know. It's not fair to come back at the eleventh hour and be so critical. But I don't mean it as criticism. I feel as though for the first time in years

I'm at peace, that I truly understand reconciliation. I can't bear to think of us at enmity with each other."

"Perhaps it's a stage we have to go through." Ruth felt cold and unyielding beside Daryl's new hope.

"Maybe. But perhaps there's something we can do."

Ruth was silent and Daryl continued. What they needed, she said, was some visible means of expressing their sinfulness and their faith in God's mercy.

"Don't we have that every evening at Night Prayer?" Ruth objected.

But Daryl was not satisfied with their evening contrition. "That's a formula. I don't think it says anything anymore. We can say those prayers without even thinking what the words mean."

"Then what are you suggesting," Ruth asked irritably, "an old-fashioned Chapter of Faults in which we each say how we have offended?" The thought was distasteful.

Again Daryl shook her head. "That's a formula, too. That's why it never worked even when we had it. People just rattled off a few little things every week. It never touched the core of things."

Ruth could not conceal her skepticism. "Surely you don't expect us at this stage to make public confessions."

"No," Daryl persisted. "I don't mean confession. I just mean a sign, but a personally chosen sign, that says we—each of us—are sinful and weak. A sign that calls on God's mercy."

Ruth frowned, she could not share Daryl's optimism.

"I was thinking of a time of quiet prayer," Daryl explained, "all of us together before the Lord. And then anyone who felt moved could just, well . . ." She faltered. "I haven't thought it all through. But we could have a bowl of holy water on the altar, and maybe a large crucifix, and the Scriptures. And people could kiss the crucifix or wash their hands or read a passage from the Bible as a sign of purification. No one would be forced to do anything," she assured Ruth. "But it would be a sign that acknowledges our guilt and our belief that we can be reconciled only by God's mercy."

Ruth said nothing, and after a while Daryl said, "You don't believe it would work, do you?" Still she could not answer and Daryl said so gently that the accusation was blunted, "When did you lose faith, Ruth?"

She was filled with a terrible guilt that she had revealed to Daryl—who had depended so often on her strength—how weak her faith had become. But when she looked up she realized that her doubt had done nothing to shake Daryl. She was still radiant with God's mercy and the joy of reconciliation. The mastery had passed to Daryl, and Ruth put herself in her hands.

"I want to believe," she said. "Go ahead, Daryl, ask Rosalia and see what she says."

Rosalia suggested that Daryl present her plan at the end of their monthly Council meeting. The Council at first responded with the same slow skepticism that Ruth had shown.

"Suppose nothing happens?" Joanne's hopelessness betrayed itself.

"Don't you believe that God will answer us if we open ourselves to Him in faith?"

Ruth turned away. It was hard to counter Daryl's resolute eyes with their fearless plea for faith.

"All those years," Daryl persisted, "I had hardened my heart against my mother, without even knowing it, and yet even when I didn't ask, God opened His compassion to me."

Terezia's *pourboire*. The divine gratuity of grace.

"But you were very sick, Daryl, near death," Rosalia objected. As soon as she said it she blushed, sensing the accuracy of the parallel.

No one spoke. They sat quietly, avoiding each other's gaze, resting their eyes on their still hands.

"How do you suggest we go about it, Daryl?" Peg asked, as though in the silence they had come to resolution.

The service of reconciliation took place on the Saturday preceding Palm Sunday. The statues were no longer veiled as they had been in the past, but a purple drape covered the front of the altar and on either side two silver vases had been filled with palm. In front of the altar stood the triangular candlestick used only during Holy Week. The fifteen candles, darker than the ordinary Mass candles, were tall and new. On the altar table was a cut-glass bowl filled with holy water, with a linen towel beside it. On one side lay the crucifix reserved for use in the liturgy of Good Friday.

Daryl had prepared everything, and as they gathered in the chapel she spoke movingly of the meaning of healing and reconciliation. Her own experience of death and new life gave her words a special power and poignancy. When she finished they knelt on in silence, absorbed in their need for mercy and forgiveness. Only grace, that touch of God, could heal them. Only grace could bring them to reconciliation with each other and to the loss of St. Aidan's, a loss not only of a place but of a way of life they had come to think of as immutable.

Ruth knelt upright in her place, the muscles in her shoulders already beginning to ache as she strained toward prayer. She had chosen a seat in the back of the chapel, but despite her efforts to block out everything but her own need for healing she was distracted by those who sat in front of her: Susannah, Nancy, Joanne, Anna, Edwarda . . . all with their private burdens, their secret infidelities that slowed and confused them on their way to God.

As for herself . . . For four months she had lived in Aidan's promise—holding tight, waiting for the storm to pass. And at last, even though the waters were still turbulent, she knew she had slipped imperceptibly beyond the eye of the storm. The tempest that Angela had unleashed and that had almost brought her to wrack had spent itself. It was clear to her now that her hunger for affection had been only that. The inevitable loneliness following her father's death and her own dramatic change of life had erupted in a need to be comforted and cherished—singly, uniquely. She had mistaken the hungry craving for love. David had unwittingly identified it: a Roman candle. A powerful and brilliant display of color, it had darkened everything else in her world. Looking back, she was appalled by how close she had come to losing her way.

For her way, it was becoming increasingly clear, was to be the way of St. Aidan's. Yet the illumination had not transformed her desolation. Although she tried to cling to the faith that God was her strength, her rock, her salvation, her faith did not warm her or dispel her doubts. Only the touch of God's presence could do that. "He comes to save us in the end," Aidan had promised. But although she had waited, He had not come.

> The sisters will live lives of solid faith, based on the Gospels and the teachings of the Church and not upon the graces and consolations which God may deign to bestow on them from time to time.

She waited, still clinging to the belief that this was where God wanted her, trusting that in time she would feel the touch of His transforming love.

Now she continued to kneel, her eyes closed, her hands gripped tightly together, begging against hope for the grace that would touch them and heal them. Their silence was palpable. Then into that silence came the sound of Daryl's flute. She was playing "Jesu, Joy of Man's Desiring." Although she had practiced very little in the last few years, the notes were clear and true. Gregory was accompanying her, but instead of the unsure tumultuous chords they had grown to expect from her, her accompaniment was slow and measured. The steady, powerful chords were like level ground below Daryl's soaring flight. The familiar melody drew them together, drawing them from their solitude, and there was a sudden shifting of tension in the chapel. With only a brief pause Daryl and Gregory played the melody through again, as though Daryl, like Orpheus, would charm them from their underworld. The yearning in that sweet flute entered Ruth like light, and for the first time in months her empty silence was filled with the stillness of God. She knelt on unmoving, blind to time, alive to the faint stirring of hope.

It was Nancy who began the acts of reconciliation by opening the Scriptures and reading a passage from Ezekiel:

"The hand of the Lord came upon me, and he carried me out by his spirit and put me down in a plain full of bones; he said to me, 'Man, can these bones live?' I answered, 'Only thou knowest that, Lord God' . . . 'Prophesy, therefore, and say to them, these are the words of the Lord God: O my people, I will open your graves and bring you up from them, and restore you to the land of Israel. . . . Then I will put my spirit into you and you shall live and I will settle you on your own soil, and you shall know that I the Lord have spoken and will act.' "

The melody of Bach's "Jesu" still lingered, a counterpoint to Ezekiel's measured words. For the first time hope was alive in Ruth, and she began to pray that God's promise be made true in them, praying that He would at last open their graves and bring them to life.

One by one, in their own time, they began to leave their places and go to the sanctuary. Some—Rita, Edwarda, Terezia among them—simply went to the altar, kissed the crucifix, and returned. Susannah, too, had bent to kiss the crucifix, but as she turned to come down from the altar, her failing sight made her almost miss the step and she stood frightened and unsure. Peg started up and then hesitated, not wanting to be rebuffed at such a time; but when no one else moved Peg went up and reached out her hand. For a moment Susannah stood irresolutely and then grasped the hand Peg extended. For a moment they stood there, Peg's hand held tight in both of Susannah's small round hands. It was her silent act of contrition.

The sound of Anna's heavy limp preceded her as she made her way from the back of chapel. Laboriously she climbed the altar steps, hesitated for a minute, and then plunged both hands up to the wrists in the bowl of holy water. "For all the world as though she were working in the laundry," Nancy said later. When finally Anna removed her hands, it was not to dry them on the towel provided. Instead she turned to face the congregation and, lifting her hands high above her head, sprinkled them all as far as she could with holy water. The downward thrust of her mouth was gone and her lips were puckered at the sides. It was as close to a smile as they had seen in a long time. In the tension Peg started to giggle and soon a ripple went through the chapel. Anna nodded to them abruptly as she descended the altar steps. She had made her point: Yes, she had acknowledged, I have sinned. So have we all. I forgive and beg to be forgiven.

As Ruth watched Anna she knew what she would do. She needed to be cleansed. She waited until Anna had returned to her place and then walked up the long nave, genuflected as she reached the altar, and immersed her hands in the bowl of holy water. Into this water Rosalia and Anna, Peg and Noreen had also plunged their hands begging to be washed clean. The water felt cool and healing as she rested her hands at the bottom of the bowl. She felt strengthened and assured not only by the purifying ritual but also by the sharing of their common sins. To share life, she realized, also means to share guilt. She closed her eyes for a moment and begged to be cleansed—of her selfishness, her lack of hope, her hunger for a love that lay outside her consecration.

The ritual cleansed her of months of indecision. Kate's question—so long unanswerable—could be faced at last. When her temporary vows expired in September, she would make them permanent, consecrating herself forever to God through the Community of St. Aidan's wherever that Community would take her.

The towel on which she dried her hands was damp and wrinkled by others' use. She folded it and placed it beside the bowl of holy water. As she raised her hand to make the sign of the cross an instant of fear constrained her. Suppose the darkness should seize her again? It was not, she knew, a groundless fear. The light in which she now moved so surely would not last. The darkness would come again. The only constant was their faith—a faith that would hold to God's word even when that word was silent, a faith that could say with Job, "Even though he kill me yet will I trust him."

Once again the image of her father's last days rose before her to erode her trust as it had done so often. But now, as she relived that final bitter struggle, she found her vision subtly changed. Her own dark passage had given her eyes new depth. Her father had been tested to the end of endurance but not beyond it. True, the God of Consolation had not visited him; but the limitless, sustaining God of Life had never left him. At the end, when all the familiar images and rituals had lost the power to touch him, the simple words "Into Thy hands I commend my spirit" had penetrated his darkness and quieted his confusion.

With that realization, Ruth felt herself delivered, as though she were spiraling up out of nightmare waters into the clear air of truth. "Into Thy hands . . ." The words came unbidden, initiated by a spirit deeper than her spirit. And with them she offered to God her father's death—and her own life—in deeper faith than she had ever known.

Timothy was among the last to leave her place. Peg led her up the steps and toward the altar where the holy water and crucifix lay, but she shook her head and gestured in the direction of the lectern. She rested her hands lightly on the closed Scriptures and began to recite from memory those solemn "Reproaches" of the Lord to his erring people that form part of the Good Friday service. Timothy was not a public speaker. Her voice was ordinarily soft and almost monotonous. Now her very weakness was her strength. There was little intonation in her voice. She recited the words like someone in a trance and by so doing they became incantatory.

"My people, what have I done to you?
How have I offended you? Answer me.

I led you out of Egypt from slavery to freedom
but you led your Savior to the cross.

For forty years I led you safely through the desert.
I fed you with manna from heaven,
And brought you to a land of plenty
but you led your Savior to a cross.

I planted you as my fairest vine,
But you yielded only bitterness.

I led you from slavery to freedom
I opened the sea before you
I led you on your way in a pillar of cloud.
But you have led your Savior to a cross.

My people, what have I done to you?
How have I offended you?
Answer me."

For a long time after Timothy returned to her place no one moved, and then came Agnes. She was in a wheelchair, and Peg pushed her toward the steps of the sanctuary. Peg leaned over to speak to her, but Agnes shook her head vehemently. Peg shrugged, obviously disapproving, and bent to put the brake on the wheelchair. Her arm around Agnes, she helped her to her feet. Agnes reached for her cane and turned slowly to face them.

The afternoon sun sent a ray of light slantwise, leaving her face in shadow but forming a pool of light at her feet. It gave her a strange look, as though she inhabited two worlds—a world of darkness and a world of light. Agnes was their saint. They loved her without exception. They loved her patience, her humility, her kindness; and since she had been sick they praised and reverenced her uncomplaining acceptance of suffering. She looked so small and helpless with the lines of pain etched around her mouth that instinctively they leaned forward fearful of missing a single word. But Agnes' voice was surprisingly strong.

"Something happened to me here this afternoon," she began. Yes, their saint. "I thought I knew when I came to chapel what I had to be reconciled to. I thought it was to suffering and the humiliation of being useless"—she paused and added—"increasingly useless." The wave of their sympathy was palpable. She took a firmer grasp on her cane and Peg reached over to help her, but Agnes shook her head. "I know now that I was deceived by my pride and my fear. It isn't suffering that I have to be reconciled with." She raised her head and looked at them, calling them to a new vision. "It's with hope."

It was as though Daryl had begun to play her flute again but in a higher key.

"All these months when I have been so accepting, I have been accepting only what I wanted to accept. Giving up St. Aidan's was so terrible to me that it was easier to hide. If I were sick, with no hope of getting better, then I had no responsibility. I need do nothing but be resigned. I convinced myself that it was abandonment to God's will. I know now that it was despair." Their disbelief was fading before her compelling witness.

"When Timothy read—recited—the Reproaches I knew in an instant what I was guilty of."

In her stall on the other side of the chapel Timothy raised her head and turned slowly toward the sound of Agnes's voice.

"It has been easier for me to accept darkness than light," Agnes continued. She paused for a moment as though she herself was confused by the mystery of what she was saying. "I don't understand why this should be, except that there is a darkness in all of us, something we cling to even when it makes us suffer. It's the thing in us that we've never quite given to God. When we hope, it means that we have given everything away, that we are entirely in the hands of someone else."

She started to say something else, then faltered and reached toward Peg to help her back to her wheelchair. The western sun had moved into the sanctuary, forming little geometric patterns on the translucent marble of the altar. After a while Rosalia rose from her place and, reaching up, lit the highest candle on the great triangular candlestick.

That night they said the First Vespers of Palm Sunday and so entered into the liturgy of the Lord's Passion and Death. God's sinful people—weak, perverse, unfaithful—they took up their staves, cleansed now and reconciled, and prepared to walk with Him to Jerusalem and beyond. They had touched the wood of the Cross and kissed it, knowing that for those washed in His mercy it had already blossomed into the tree of life. "The Hebrew children," they sang, "cast their garments before Him, shouting in exultation, 'Hosannah to the Son of David.' "

Rawlins and Swenson, Realtors
108 East 68th St.
New York, N.Y.
June 14, 1981

Mr. Alec Stafford
Stafford, Connor, Lipsky, Architects
18 Ballantyne Avenue
Glen Cove, New York

Dear Alec,

I'm running into more difficulty than I had anticipated in setting a date for the closing. I had expected the nuns to be out of there by the end of August at the latest, but when I was talking to Sister Rosalia yesterday, she told me that they would very much like to use the chapel for one last ceremony on September 8. It seems that Sister Ruth will be "pronouncing her final vows" (quote!) on that date. I would have thought she had done that years ago. I guess I showed my surprise, because Sister Rosalia conceded that "the circumstances were unusual." Whatever that means. Anyway no one can say she's too young to know what she's doing.

By the way, I received an invitation to St. Aidan's graduation; I suppose you did, too. It was nice of them to think of us, but I'm sure they don't expect us to attend. It would be a little like the Lord High Executioner sharing the condemned's last meal.

How do you feel about postponing the closing. I hate to push the ladies, and I wouldn't imagine a week or two would make much difference to you. Let me know what you think.

Cheers,

Steve Rawlins

18

The weeks between Easter and the end of the school year left no time for anything but work. Nothing could be left undone. All the records had to be up to date; every student had to be sent on to another school with all her forms complete. "Get them to clean out everything or else we'll have to do it after they go," warned Joanne, who set up work shifts so that every cabinet and closet in the school would be emptied and put in order. Even Noreen, notoriously untidy in her management of the home-ec rooms, began to organize and dispose of the debris of the years. Susannah and Edwarda stalked the storage rooms like secret police, determined that every suitcase and trunk, every clutter of notes and books, every discarded stuffed animal, be traced to its owner and sent packing with her.

Parents who would not concede the closing of St. Aidan's continued to call and write, invoking the help of the local clergy to badger and besiege Joanne and Rosalia. Those more sympathetic were equally vexing. They were determined to do something elaborate and time-consuming as a gala display of gratitude and affection.

"If Lucy McNamara's grandmother calls," Joanne said to

Ruth, who was covering her office one afternoon shortly before graduation, "please tell her we can't have a garden party for alumnae and friends of St. Aidan's."

"But Mother Josephine *always* had a garden party," mimicked Ruth.

"I know. And Mother Gerard always gave the graduates a spray of white roses with their diplomas, and Mother Edwarda encouraged the alumnae to run an annual bazaar that kept the school solvent, and Mother Mary David would never have let the school get so run down in the first place."

"Anything else?"

"Yes. If Monsignor Wiley calls, tell him I'm not sure how many extra tickets for graduation I can get for him. Tell him I'm doing everything to arrange for an outdoor graduation, but I won't know for certain until the end of the week."

"Joanne, you're not? How will you manage it?"

"How will I manage it if I don't? Everybody in the county wants to be at St. Aidan's last graduation."

"But suppose it rains?"

"Then we'll just put the Bishop under an umbrella and hope he doesn't run—his vestments, I mean."

"Bishop Lonergan is coming?"

"Maybe two bishops—top brass and an auxiliary."

"Whatever for?"

Joanne shrugged. "Duty, good will, nostalgia."

"But two?"

"The auxiliary is Alice Markham's great-uncle. He wants to see her graduate. You must admit it's an event."

"How come we never knew about him before?"

"Alice considers him a terrible humiliation. At her age all bishops are terrible, but a family bishop is too shameful to be acknowledged. She explained very solemnly last week that he was only an uncle by marriage. That seemed to reduce the embarrassment. A graft, you see, nothing produced directly by the family."

But the real work of closing St. Aidan's began after graduation. Joanne had hired people to help with the cleaning and packing, but the initial organization had to be done by the nuns themselves. July and the beginning of August passed in a haze of work.

"Why did we keep all this stuff?" Nancy sighed, crawling out from behind a sagging sofa in the corner of the main attic.

"It was always going to come in handy, remember?" Peg volunteered.

"And now what?"

"The men from the St. Vincent de Paul Society are coming over with two trucks. They'll take care of it."

"But some of it isn't even good enough to give away," Nancy protested. "What can anyone do with that?" She prodded a chair with one rocker broken off.

"They said they were used to getting stuff like this," Peg affirmed. "I told them they weren't getting any prizes, and they said that was O.K."

The furniture was the easiest part. It was the small objects, colored by personal association, that were the stumbling blocks.

Edwarda had offered to clean out the old trunks left in the attic. "It requires very little energy," she had answered when Rosalia had protested. "I can just bring a chair right over to the trunk and just make a few neat piles that someone younger can dispose of when they're ready."

But the simple task grew unending. One afternoon when Ruth had gone up to see if she could help, she found Edwarda, her glasses off, a music book in her lap. "It's very hot up here," she said defensively as she wiped her eyes and put her glasses back on.

"I don't know how this got mixed up here," she said, turning the pages. "It belonged to Sister Catherine, Sister Josephine's younger sister. I never saw two sisters so different. Sister Catherine was only fifteen when she entered. They said she shot up so that first year that they had to make her habits over. They were halfway up to her knees."

Ruth knew the story of Sister Catherine by heart. She was the saintly young sister—"our own Little Flower"—whom Mother Columban had eulogized for their edification during their novitiate. But she listened again to Edwarda's version.

"She died the year after I entered. She was just twenty-seven. I'll never forget it. You just knew she was holy, she was so pale and thin," Edwarda explained, invoking the criteria of a past generation.

"Maybe you'd like to keep her music book," Ruth suggested, hoping to terminate the history of the pious Sister Catherine.

"Perhaps." Edwarda turned ruminatively to another page. "They said she played beautifully. Chopin and Stephen Foster and all those musicians. You can see this page is all marked up. That must have been a very hard one."

"Why don't you take it with you," Ruth suggested again.

Edwarda sighed. "I don't know. I thought maybe I should give it to Gregory. She's the real musician and she was here with me the year Catherine died."

"That sounds like a good idea. Why don't you do that?"

Edwarda gave another sigh. "I'd like to think about it." And she put the book down in front of her on top of the large pile that needed "a bit more thought."

Joanne, their most efficient organizer, was too caught up in the business transactions to help with domestic affairs. She and Rosalia had made several trips—to St. Malachy's, to see the Bishop, and to settle the practical aspects of the merger.

"I think we're all settled," Rosalia said one day when she came back from the Chancery Office. "All the papers are in order —or almost in order."

"When will it happen?" Ruth asked, pouring Rosalia a cup of tea.

"The dates still aren't quite settled." Rosalia frowned. "Mr. Rawlins would like us out by the end of the month, but I think he'll agree to September fifteenth. I'm not even sure that's going to be enough time." She looked around anxiously at the shelves of books lining her office and the untidy piles of papers spilling off her desk onto the chair next to it. "I suppose we'll get it done somehow, but there are still so many things to be settled."

Over their heads they could hear the scraping of furniture as the men from the St. Vincent de Paul Society began removing the discarded chairs and couches from the attics.

"They wanted to take some of the pews from the chapel," Rosalia said, looking toward the ceiling. "They're trying to find furniture for a little oratory over in Whitethorn, but I thought we should leave the chapel the way it is until the last minute. I didn't want it to look makeshift for your profession."

"Rosie, would it make it easier if I waited and made my vows at St. Malachy's?" She dreaded the possibility, but she had to make the offer.

Rosalia looked at her, startled. "That never occurred to me. I thought . . . I just took it for granted . . . Would you prefer to have the ceremony at St. Malachy's?"

"Of course not. I'd prefer it here. But there's so much to be done. I don't want to make things any harder."

Rosalia shook her head impatiently. "Then we'll have it here. God knows we have the right to enjoy a last profession, although I'm afraid it will be a weepy ceremony. Gregory and Aidan will be weeping for sorrow over our leaving and for joy that you're staying." Rosalia rubbed her hands self-consciously. "I don't have to tell you how happy I am, do I?" She looked up, meeting Ruth's eyes. "I've never said anything, because I didn't want to intrude, but I know it hasn't been easy for you. There were times this winter when I was sure we'd lost you."

"I'd almost lost myself. I've wondered sometimes what would have happened to us without the reconciliation service."

Rosalia shivered. "I don't want to think. I must confess that

I had very little faith when Daryl proposed it. And even afterward I wondered if it was only wishful thinking. I kept waiting for the effects to wear off."

"But they've lasted, haven't they?"

Rosalia nodded. "It didn't turn us into saints, but it brought us together."

"And washed us clean of some of our bitterness."

"Even Anna smiles at me sometimes," Rosalia observed ruefully.

The noise overhead had stopped. "They've finished taking the furniture, I guess. I better go down and see the driver and find out if they have to make another trip. Ruth, if we settle your profession for September eighth, that will still give us a week before the closing and give you time to get away for a few days of retreat."

"I couldn't go away," Ruth protested, "when there's so much to be done here."

"We'll see. Things may move along faster than we expect."

In fact, Rosalia's prediction turned out to be correct. By the last week in August work at St. Aidan's lagged. Most of the big things had been done, and the others would have to wait until closer to their actual moving date.

On August 24, Kate drove Ruth over to Whitethorn to get a train for Cold Spring and the Franciscan Retreat House.

"When will you be coming back?" Kate asked.

"September first, probably on the afternoon train."

"Let me know for sure and I'll meet you."

But Kate, as usual, was better than her word and on the final day of Ruth's retreat she found a message slipped under her door. "Sister Kathleen called. She says not to take the train. She will pick you up here tomorrow around 4 P.M."

The next afternoon Ruth brought her suitcase down to the front hall and was standing looking out the window when she saw the St. Aidan's station wagon coming up the drive.

"I brought someone with me who wants to meet you," Kate said as she took Ruth's suitcase and led her over to the car.

"Diane," Kate called, and the girl in the driver's seat shoved away the magazine she'd been looking at and opened the door. She was no more than an inch or two taller than Kate, but she was stocky and solidly built.

"Ruth," Kate said, "this is Diane." For a moment Ruth hesitated, unable to make the connection that was obviously expected of her. Diane caught the hesitation and for a moment looked embarrassed. "Diane Gannon," Kate explained; "she's been working with me at the camp."

"Of course." Ruth put out her hand. Like Kate, Diane was slow to smile, but she met Ruth's smile directly. "You were very good to come down to pick me up."

"We enjoyed it. I wanted to meet you, and then it gave Kate and me a chance to talk." She reached for Ruth's suitcase. "We can put this in the trunk. Unless you don't mind sitting three in front. In that case, we can just stick it in the back seat."

"That's fine with me," Ruth assured her. "We're three little people. We shouldn't have any trouble fitting in front."

Diane wrinkled her nose. "Don't underestimate me," she said. "My brothers used to call me 'little brick house.' Not very flattering when all the ads warned you that you'd never make it unless you were willowy and curvy."

They were quiet as Diane maneuvered them through the summer traffic and up the thruway.

"Do you mind if we go a longer way?" Diane asked as she cut over to a road bordering the Hudson. "I know thruways are practical but . . ." She shook her head and squinted against the sun as she braked on a curve. They drove in silence for a while, and then Kate, after turning to look at Diane, said, "We came especially to meet you, Ruth, because we have something to tell you. We wanted to tell you ourselves before you got to St. Aidan's."

Ruth felt a tightening around her heart. She tried to look

at Kate and smile, but her lips didn't move. She's going to tell me she's leaving, she thought. She's going to tell me that she's made up her mind that she can't go to St. Malachy's. She and Diane are going to stay together and work at the camp. And in that downward plunge she felt an affection for Kate so deep that nothing could express it except the physical release of taking Kate in her arms. But she said nothing, did nothing, except to hold her hands tightly in her lap.

It was Kate who reached out to her, putting her own hand, still without the gold circle of her profession ring, on Ruth's unadorned hand.

"I know what you're thinking but it's not that, Ruth. It's that Diane is coming back. She's terminated her leave of absence. We're both going to make our perpetual vows at Christmas."

In her moment of relief Ruth closed her eyes and felt Diane's hand move out to rest lightly on Kate's. They sat without speaking, sharing the communion of that triple bond.

"That's a wonderful coming-home present," Ruth said finally. "I know how much your decision must mean to Kate," she said, turning to Diane.

Diane nodded and then said, "Kate hasn't told you all of it yet."

"Diane is afraid you won't think the rest is such good news," Kate said. "Some people don't, but I told her you'd understand. The Council has given us permission to stay on at the camp and form our own Community. When Peg has all the infirmary sisters settled down and feeling at home at St. Malachy's, she'll come to join us. There'll be three of us."

It was, Ruth knew, the perfect solution. A new beginning springing out of the death of St. Aidan's. Kate, Diane, Peg. Young, determined, with a vision beyond anything St. Aidan's had offered them. She understood and she rejoiced; yet she could not share their freedom. A part of her was bound by ties and memories that could never affect them. They had never journeyed through the landscape that had shaped and molded her. She could not expect their allegiance to St. Aidan's to match her own, because they had never experienced the life she had once found there.

"Of course we'll be part of St. Malachy's," Kate was explaining. "Their Council had to vote on this, too, but they didn't have any problem with it. We'll form a kind of branch house."

"And Joyce Eberhardt, who's been working with us at the camp this summer, is going to live with us." The enthusiasm in Diane's voice was compelling. "Joyce was a novice with the Sisters of Holy Compassion over in Glenmont, but that didn't work out. They're pretty stuffy, I guess. Anyway Joyce didn't want to spend the rest of her life running a Montessori school for rich kids, so she left. She's got lots of ideas about what we can do for the children at the camp."

As Diane paused, Kate turned to Ruth. "You are glad, aren't you? I told Diane you would be."

Yes, she assured them, she was glad. It would have been unfortunate for them to have to leave the camp when they were able to do so much there.

"You won't believe all that's happened at St. Aidan's in the last week," Kate went on. "Peg has been over at St. Malachy's all week getting the infirmary set up, and she's moved a lot of the infirmary furniture."

"We've been able to clear out the whole second floor," Diane added with satisfaction. "Let's see," Kate mused, "what else do we have to tell you."

"You never told her about Agnes," Diane reminded her.

Ruth turned abruptly to Kate. "What's happened to Agnes?"

"Nothing bad. Actually I wasn't going to tell you. I was going to let you see for yourself."

"See what?" Ruth knew it must be good news, but Kate's hesitation irritated her.

"See Agnes. You won't believe the change in her. Remember just before you left Peg was taking her to a new doctor in New York?"

Ruth nodded.

"Well, Peg was right. Agnes didn't have rheumatoid arthritis. This specialist diagnosed her right away. It's called poly-something rheumatica." Kate sighed. "Sorry I can't remember the whole name. Do you remember, Diane?"

But Diane could do no better than Kate.

"Anyway, it's not a common disease and generally it only attacks people over sixty, so we can't be too hard on Dr. Lavelle. The great thing is that once it's diagnosed it can be treated by medication. The doctor in New York told Agnes that she would respond 'dramatically' and she really did. At the end of the first week she was out of her wheelchair and able to get around her room by herself. Yesterday she was out in the garden with just a cane."

"Is this just a remission?" Ruth asked skeptically.

"No. That's what's so wonderful. She may have to keep taking the medication for a while, but as long as she does she'll be fine. So much for poly-o-whatever."

They had turned into the grounds of St. Aidan's and Diane stopped the car at the back door. "You don't mind if Kate and I don't go in with you, do you? We have a meeting at the camp this evening and we'll just make it."

Kate helped her pull her suitcase from the back seat, and Ruth waved them off down the drive. She opened the back door and stood for a moment at the foot of the stairs. The sweaters and raincoats and shawls had all been removed, and the hooks along the wall were empty. There was a new light fixture at the side of the door, and the banisters had been freshly waxed. From the laundry she could hear the whirr and thump of their old dryer. There was no one in the first corridor although she could hear the clatter of plates in the pantry. She looked at her watch. Five-thirty. Almost time for supper.

The door of her room was slightly ajar, letting a triangle of light into the dark corridor. She put her suitcase down at the threshold and pushed open the door. Standing at the table by the window, one hand holding a spray of white and lavender phlox, the other steadying her against a chair, was Agnes. Thrown across the bed at the other side of the room was her cane. Frowning in concentration at the bowl of flowers she was fixing, she did not hear Ruth. Although her shoulders were still hunched, she was standing without difficulty, and her arm moved easily to the vase she was fixing and back again. The lines around her mouth had relaxed, and delivered from pain, she was free to immerse herself in the pleasure of her task.

So this was hope. Fragile, tenuous, but absorbed in life and no longer indentured to the past. "When we hope, it means that we have given everything away, that we are entirely in the hands of someone else," Agnes had said at their ceremony of reconciliation.

"I wanted to surprise you," Agnes said after their long, extravagant embrace.

"You did. I haven't been hugged like that since I told Fiona McLaren that she passed her geometry Regents exam."

"Poor Fiona. I wonder whatever happened to her."

They stood, absorbed in each other, sensing the new life in each of them. Their intuition spiraled down to where that life was rooted, leaving them indifferent to questions of detail and circumstances. The depth of their communion made them suddenly shy, and they turned toward the flowers Agnes had been fixing.

"This is the last of the phlox," Agnes said as she pushed a pink spray forward in the vase. "I thought I could find a few asters, but I guess they'll take another week or so."

"We had them on the altar for my vows last year. You fixed them, remember?"

Agnes nodded. "I was still able to get around then."

They were both intent on the design of the flowers.

"I can do an even better job this year," she offered. "In another week I'll be able to stand on my head."

"It's quite wonderful enough to see you on your feet."

"Were you surprised or did Kate tell you?"

"Actually Diane gave it away."

"And did they tell you about their plans?"

"That they're going to form a community near the camp?"

"Yes. It hasn't been easy for them, but they seem up to it."

"Do you think it will work?" Ruth asked.

"Oh, it will work. Maybe not quite the way the Council meant when they gave the permission. We still think in terms of patching things up," Agnes continued, "like reshingling a house, protecting it from the outside. But Kate and Diane are building from the inside, growing the way plants grow, upward and outward with no way of knowing the final shape they will take."

They had left Ruth's room and had started to walk down the stairs to the dining room. Ruth reached out to help, but Agnes shook her head. "I love to do it myself. It may sound crazy, but walking downstairs by myself is a heady experience for me."

There were only a few people in the dining room. Joanne and Rosalia were both out on business, and some of the older nuns, tired from a day of sorting and packing, had had a late tea and gone up to their rooms. Nancy Lenihan had almost finished her supper when Ruth and Agnes joined her.

"I don't mean to rush so," she apologized. "I guess I've gotten used to eating on the run these days. There's always so much to be done."

The dishwasher was being overhauled and they washed their dishes by hand in the small pantry off the kitchen. When Ruth reached up to put things away she found that the cabinet where the cups and saucers had been kept was empty.

"Just leave them," Nancy directed. "We're trying to clear everything out. Mr. Stafford, thank God, is buying most of the kitchen equipment along with the pupils' dishes. Our good set is all packed for St. Malachy's. Most of these"—and she waved toward the stack of heavy white plates and bowls—"we can ask the St. Vincent de Paul Society to pick up."

Rosalia and Joanne came in just as they were finishing, and later Ruth followed Rosalia to her office. The bookcases were empty, and the wall where the file cabinets had been was marked and discolored. The rest of the furniture, too, had been removed except for Rosalia's desk and two straight chairs.

"I'm sorry I wasn't here when you got home," Rosalia said, putting a set of keys into an envelope in her desk. "It seems as though there's always a little more business to do. We had to have some of the locks changed and some more keys made. Edwarda broke a key over in Joanne's office. You'd think she'd broken all ten commandments, poor soul." Rosalia sighed and pushed the desk drawer closed. "There was a phone call for you while you were away. Did Kate tell you?"

Ruth shook her head.

"A man." She rummaged distractedly through the papers on her desk. "I wrote it down but . . ." She shrugged helplessly.

"David Abramoff?" Ruth felt self-conscious as she said his name.

Rosalia sighed in relief. "Yes, that was it. I asked him if he wanted you to get in touch with him when you got back but he said he'd be traveling. He said he'd call you the first week of September."

"He didn't say why he was calling?"

"No. Just that he wanted to get in touch and that he'd get back to you when he got home."

In fact it was September 6 before David called. Ruth had been over in the chapel wing helping Daryl clean out the sacristy. The worktable was covered with candles of various sizes, two heavy chalices, and the ornate gold monstrance they had used at Benediction. Propped against the wall was a huge plaster crucifix with lurid wounds and a crown of thorns. Absently Ruth fingered the design of the old silver censer she was cleaning.

Grains of incense were still encrusted around the inside and the heavy smell filled the room.

This was how they had once worshipped God: the marble altar covered with handwoven Irish linen and the tortured body of the Crucified suspended above it; the massive bronze candelabra with their pure beeswax tapers; and everywhere—in their hymnals, in their clothes, in their skin—the sweet triumphal smell of incense.

She was lost in those memories when Peg, out of breath, appeared at the door. "Ruth, there's a phone call for you. We've been ringing your bell, but I guess you can't hear it over here. It's long-distance. Rosalia says to take it in her office."

Ruth, too, was out of breath by the time she picked up the phone. David's voice was muffled and the first few sentences were lost in a bad connection. "I called before I went on vacation," David said. "But they told me you were away. I wanted to see if I could arrange to see you."

The request startled her. "When would you be coming? We'll be leaving St. Aidan's on the fourteenth." She realized how ungracious she sounded but David's request had put her off balance.

"Yes, I know. The sister I talked to earlier explained that to me. I could come up tomorrow afternoon if that would be convenient. I checked the train schedule and I could arrive at Whitethorn about two-fifteen."

"That would be fine." She wondered if her voice sounded as distorted as David's did to her. "I wish I could say I'll meet you at the station, but our car is tied up these days."

"Please, no. I understand. I will take a taxi. I should arrive by three at least."

"Fine. I'll be waiting."

She waited the next day in the front hall, and when she heard the taxi stop she opened the massive front door before

David could ring the bell. He looked around appraisingly at the high ceilings, the huge brass chandelier, and the marble entrance hall lined with cartons and crates.

"So," he said, "this is a convent."

"Not anymore. We're almost out."

"I'm sorry to come at such a bad time, but I didn't have much choice."

"I'm glad you came. In another week I'll be at St. Malachy's." She steered him out the side door and into the garden.

"Could we walk for a bit?" he asked. "I need to stretch my legs. The train ride was very long."

They walked up past the novitiate and through the orchard and then into the woods. He had gone to California with the Reinauers, he explained. Peter was having a one-man show in San Francisco. They had come back through Canada, stopping at Vancouver and Lake Louise. "And you," he said, "you have been away, too, I understand."

"Only for a few days to make a retreat."

"Yes, the sister told me."

"I'm going to make my perpetual vows tomorrow." They had come back into the garden and were sitting on two stone benches just off the path.

"Yes, the sister told me that, too, and also I received your letter." He brushed his hand across his face and then sat staring at the ground. "That was why it seemed important to see you, although I realize it is an inconvenient time."

She said nothing, feeling the touch of fear.

"I have no diplomatic way to say what I am going to say to you, so I shall plunge in. The day we had lunch together in November it was clear that something was wrong. If I had followed my instinct I would have called you after that—or even come to St. Aidan's to find you. But I hesitated, first, because I kept expecting to hear from you, but even more because I felt I had no right to interfere. After that day I could no longer honor your decision. Something had happened to you. You know that, don't you?"

Fear had moved in and she could only nod.

"All the brightness had gone out of you. And all the sureness. I listened to you tell me about the struggles of St. Aidan's, but nothing you said accounted for the change in you."

She started to say something, to ward him off, but he stopped her.

"Please let me finish. When you first told me, the night we had dinner in New York, that you were returning to the convent, I tried to understand or at least to accept. I told you then that I honored your decision and, in spite of how I felt about it, I did. I had learned from your father, you see, to trust your insight, your spiritual sense.

"But that day in November . . ." He hunched his shoulders as though he suffered a chill. "I could not trust you then. I tried to hear beyond your words, but I could hear only confusion. I wondered that day if I had asked you what you were doing with your life, what you hoped for, if you would have been able to tell me."

In place of the hunger she had once felt for his love, Ruth felt an immense tenderness, a desire that they love each other not as lovers but with an affection that would free them from misunderstanding and embarrassment.

"I waited, you see, because I was so sure that one day you would come to see what you were doing to yourself, and you would write to me to tell me you were coming home."

She had crossed her arms against her chest, holding on to herself as though the sun had turned cold.

"The day your father told me that you had once before been a nun, he told me also that he thought you would never marry, that you felt a different vocation. But I cannot believe . . ."

She reached out, desperate to stop him. "David, listen. Everything you've said is true. That day in November I hardly knew what I wanted or who I was. It seemed that everything I had counted on had betrayed me."

She paused, leaving herself open, she knew, to a thousand questions, but David asked only one: "And now?"

And now, she thought? To her sisters she could say, "I have been lifted free, my bonds broken, my eyes uncovered. I have felt the touch of God and I have been healed." To David she said, "I'm myself again. I know what I want. I know I want to make my vows tomorrow."

He looked at her and nodded. He looked very crumpled and awkward, sitting hunched over on the low, narrow bench. She wanted to take his hands and hold them and tell him that, perhaps, in time there would be a new understanding between them.

Finally he stood up, looking at his watch. "I told the taxi to pick me up about four-thirty."

They walked around to the front of the house and stood by the steps waiting. "I want you to know," he said as they heard the taxi make its way up the long drive, "that I promised your father always to look out for you a little. That's a promise that lasts forever. You understand?"

She nodded and he put his arms around her. "Let me know how it goes with you," he called as he waved goodbye.

When the taxi was out of sight she went back to the garden and sat on the bench, still warm from her body. The bees were clustering on the clematis in the late afternoon sun. She watched them as they sucked out the sweetness, going from blossom to blossom without pause, oblivious to everything except their single-minded quest for the substance they would transform into honey. It was comforting to see them, intent and sure of their task. They burrowed into each blossom without hesitation, their instincts guiding them flawlessly to what they were seeking.

Watching them quieted her. What, she wondered, might David have said had she not reached out to stop him? For a moment she had been sure he was going to tell her that he loved her. The temptation to hear him say it, to know beyond doubt

had been very strong. To know that he had loved her would have
been a treasure, a secret jewel she could carry with her wherever
she went. It would console her and warm her against loneliness,
providing her with hidden riches in which she could feel secure.
But she had no right to secret treasure, not even, she knew, to
the treasures of the spirit.

Tomorrow she would make her vows in the chapel of St.
Aidan's. There would be very little resemblance to her first
profession, when the chapel had been filled with nuns, imposing
in their heavy ceremonial dress, the altar aglow with burnished
gold vases of calla lilies, and the air heavy with incense and organ
music. Tomorrow the ceremony would lack those rich adorn-
ments. Despite Rosalia's efforts to keep the chapel intact, many
of its ornaments had already been removed: the statues of the
Blessed Virgin and St. Joseph, the massive ceremonial candles, the
wall plaques commemorating the passion of Christ—all were
gone. There was only the tabernacle housing the Eucharistic
presence and the altar of sacrifice with its simple white cloth.
There would be no bishop in his pontifical vestments to celebrate
the liturgy but only little Father Kanisky with his heavy Polish
accent.

Yet in what mattered nothing was changed. She would
make her vows to God forever. She would promise to have no
other lover, no other treasure, and to follow Him wherever He
led. Before their first profession, Mother Columban had gathered
them together for her final spiritual conference. Joyful, fearful,
anxious, Ruth had been too excited to hear all she had said, but
one thing had struck her.

"It is an ancient tradition, Sisters," Mother Columban had
said in her measured voice, "that when you make your vows you
enter into a special relationship with our Lord and that as token
of that relationship He gives you a special name, a name that only
He knows. This is the secret name by which He will call you and
that He will reveal to you only at that glorious moment of your
death when you will see Him face to face."

They had sat in awe, imagining that mysterious name that would give God a special communion with each of them.

"And it is also an ancient custom," Mother Columban continued, "that at the moment of your vows you give God some special treasure, a secret gift that is meant only for His eyes and that will confirm your loving bond with Him."

Then Ruth had been at a loss, hard put to find such a gift. Now as she walked back through the garden to the convent, it was very clear to her. Her special gift would be the secret treasure she had relinquished, the rich, comforting knowledge that David might have been in love with her.

Rawlins and Swenson, Realtors
108 East 68th St.
New York, N.Y.
September 8, 1981

Mr. Alec Stafford
Stafford, Connor, Lipsky, Architects
18 Ballantyne Avenue
Glen Cove, New York

Dear Alec,

We're all set at last. The sisters will be out of St. Aidan's
by September 14. Sister Rosalia and Sister Joanne will stay over
and we will have the closing on September 15.

Why don't you come into the office that morning? We'll
drive up and have lunch on the way. I suppose it seems like a
long time to you but it's not bad to have completed such a major
transaction in just over a year. Actually the whole thing went
through with no complications. You will be able to start some
of your renovations before the cold weather sets in. The timing
is perfect!

See you a week from today.

Best,

Steve Rawlins

19

On the Sunday afternoon following her profession, Ruth and Daryl offered to help Gregory pack and cart her precious music supplies.

"I know they won't need these at St. Malachy's," Daryl said as they packed a collection of old hymnals, "but it would break Gregory's heart if we told her so."

By five o'clock the cartons were packed and carried out to the front door. "I'm going back to chapel," Daryl said, rising from her knees. "Gregory says there's just one more load of sheet music she wants packed separately."

Ruth nodded and stayed to mark the cartons and check off the lists Gregory had printed in her large, determined script. When she finished she stood looking out the door to the untended flower beds where the pink and purple asters had just begun to bloom. After a while she looked at her watch and started back toward chapel wondering what had kept Daryl so long.

As she opened the door to the chapel corridor, the heavy door at the other end opened and Gregory, her arms full of music, carefully made her way down the three shallow steps. Suddenly she stopped and looked straight at Ruth but with no sign of recognition. Her mouth opened slowly as though she were yawning; then in a spasmodic movement her hands went to her chest and the music, carried so carefully, slipped in pieces to the floor. Gregory stood for a moment, her head thrown back, her mouth still open, and then fell heavily forward on top of her music.

Ruth ran toward her and, kneeling, tried to turn the inert body so that Gregory could breathe. At the same time Daryl came out of the antechoir, her arms loaded with books. Between them they turned Gregory on her back and Daryl, lifting her head, was able to remove the cumbersome veil and wimple.

"I'll get some water," she whispered, starting to get to her feet; but Ruth shook her head. For a moment they knelt on either side of the body, Gregory's uncovered head with its wiry gray hair cradled on Ruth's arm. Daryl had removed the thick glasses, and the eyes, still open, looked small and light without their heavy protective lenses.

As they knelt there, the outer door opened and Nancy started down the hall. Even then Daryl did not take her eyes from Gregory, but Ruth turned. "It's Gregory," she said.

There was no question that Gregory would be buried at St. Aidan's.

"It was her home from the time she was eighteen," Edwarda reminded them, her nose looking longer and thinner than ever in her pale face. "Thank God she doesn't have to leave it."

The funeral Mass was very simple. Rosalia had asked Kate about singing, but Kate had shaken her head.

"She didn't really like my kind of music. If she can't have what she loved then I think at least we can let her have silence."

At the end the "In Paradisum," which Gregory had played for so many funerals, was said quietly in English. "May the angels lead you into paradise; may the martyrs receive you at your coming, and lead you into the holy city Jerusalem. May the choir of angels receive you, and with Lazarus, who once was poor, may you have everlasting rest."

The procession, with Kate and Diane leading the way,

passed down the nave of the chapel, out through the main doors of St. Aidan's, up through the gardens, and out into the cemetery beyond the house. There, gathered around the central iron cross, they waited while the casket was lowered into the ground and the final rite was read by a visiting priest from Holy Rosary.

Had Gregory given them time, they would have prayed with her in her last moments with those solemn petitions of the Church: that she might be freed from her sins, that God would remember the firm faith in which she had lived. "Remember, Lord," they would have petitioned, "she is Your creature, not made by strange gods, but by You, the only living and true God. For there is no other but You." But she had not given them time, slipping beyond them, her arms filled with music to the last.

Unconsciously they had formed little groups as they entered the cemetery: Edwarda and Susannah and Aidan at a little distance; Anna and Rita, looking harsh in their sorrow; Agnes and Joanne; Kate and Peg on the outer limits with Diane just behind them. Noreen, Magdalen, and Nancy standing next to Ruth; and close to the grave Timothy, tall and straight, her sightless eyes fixed far beyond the cemetery and her fingers tightly locked around Daryl's hand.

The cemetery, like the gardens, had been neglected and vines had grown across some of the graves and had begun to climb up the white wooden crosses. Ruth looked toward Mother Mary David's cross, remembering the night she had knelt before it, penetrating a little more deeply into the mystery of unknowing. Again she asked her pardon and the pardon of God whose spacious mercy she had so often mistrusted. Without anguish, she let herself remember her father's face, even in its last hours of hopelessness. She saw again the dark eyes with their imponderable question: God? God? remembering that no image or symbol that she could offer could satisfy that plea. Now she knew that in his last hours he had been drawn beyond their categories, closer to the immense harmony of God Himself.

As she looked up she saw Timothy's gaze shift until it rested unknowingly on Mother Mary David's grave; and at the same time she saw her move her arm across Daryl's shaking shoulders. We hurt each other, Ruth thought. We misjudge, ignore, resent, and yet we give each other life. We lead each other into mystery not because of what we are but because of what we believe.

Gregory's death had strengthened them; she could feel it. Beyond their sense of sorrow was that mysterious sense of life, the life that pushed through triumphant, the life that is itself prayer. She heard again the prayer from the Mass: "O Lord, for your faithful, life is changed not taken away."

From the chapel the bell began to toll, proclaiming their mortality and Gregory's eternal life. They turned from their groups to reform their procession, following the youngest down the hill, back through the gardens, to the convent.